Ebook ISBN: 978-1-963134-23-0

Paperback ISBNs: 978-1-963134-21-6, 978-1-963134-22-3

Hardcover ISBN: 978-1-963134-20-9

Book Cover by Jax Hnat

Editing by Kenna Kettrick, Alisha Nygaard

Sensitivity read by Sarah Mesh

Interior Illustrations by Charlie Arpie

First edition 2025

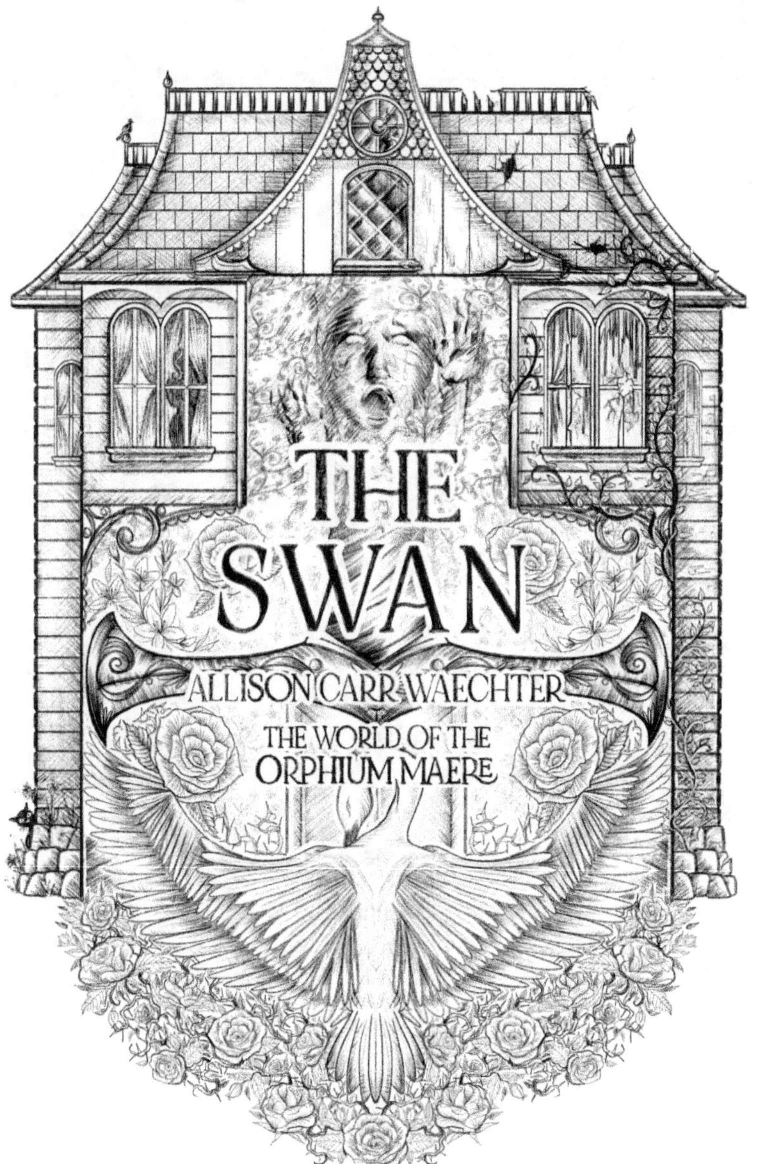

THE
SWAN
ALLISON CARR WAECHTER
THE WORLD OF THE
ORPHIUM MAERE

For every babe who's been betrayed one time too many.

May you make friends with your darkness,
and wield it like a sword.

CONTENT GUIDELINES

For Content Guidelines please go here:

THE
WORLD OF
THE ORPHIUM MAERE

THE AUTHORITY

The human-led government that has ruled Kraitos for the past two thousand years.

THE CONSULATE

The shadow organization on Kraitos that mediates between parapsychs (those with paranormal abilities) and humans. Formed to protect parapsychs as the Authority came to power.

THE TRINITY

The three main groups of parapsychs, ruled by three dynastic "families" across the Three Cities.

THE NECROLINE DYNASTY

Those who interact with the dead.

THE COGNOSCENTI DYNASTY

Those who see outside the parameters of reality.

THE THAUMAS DYNASTY

Those who perform miracles.

THE MAERE

Fifteen immortal warriors who stand between the Consulate, the Trinity and the Authority.

THE THREE CITIES

Three huge city-states that make up the known population of Kraitos, as much of the world, is covered in monster-inhabited oceans. Between each of the Three Cities sits the "Wastelands," vast, dangerous areas of wild land that is best avoided.

Orphium *(City of the Dead)*
Aradios *(City of Miracles)*
Palladiere *(City of Foresight)*

THE SAINTS

St. Amarante *(immortality)*
St. Paloma *(miracles)*
St. Tanith *(death)*
St. Cassandra *(foresight)*
St. Ekate *(magic/the underworld/Hel)*
St. Irys *(tricksters/Fate)*

CHAPTER 1

RHIANNON

OLEANDER COTTAGE. SIX WEEKS AFTER THE HEIST TO REGAIN THE ORPHIUM MAERE'S SWORDS.

OLEANDER COTTAGE WAS ravenous for new blood. It would devour us whole, and we would feed ourselves willingly to its gaping maw. The rose print of the wallpaper in the kitchen was a hedge maze of hunger and rage.

And I was lost in its depths. These days, there was nothing I wanted more than to stay in bed and never get out, but here I was, staring at angry vintage wallpaper in the middle of the night. Again.

A deep voice distracted me from trying to work out if the floral pattern went somewhere, or if it simply repeated endlessly. "I don't..." he paused. I glanced sidelong at Eryx Necroline, whose arms were tucked tightly around his bulky chest. He flicked his fingers at the wall. "...like the wallpaper."

"No?" I asked, trying not to gawk at his chest.

His Pizza Queen t-shirt fit snugly, showing off hard-earned muscles. Eryx had a body that did things. I knew he went to the gym. But those muscles were from years of enacting violence as much as workouts—just like mine.

He shook his head, and his messy dark waves shifted into his pale green eyes. "It reminds me of that story about the fiends. Did you know that one as a child?"

I shook my head, rocking back on my heels. It would be easy to claim I didn't remember. It had been centuries since I was a child, in either of my lifetimes. But I did remember, all too well.

No one told me stories as a child.

My biological mother never had time for that—she'd been too busy being the ruler of our island nation to perform such mundane tasks. And when I was reborn… well, I'd done my best to forget my human family.

It helped that they'd been dead for thousands of years. I barely remembered *their* faces now. The bruises they'd left on me, the fear that remained when someone I trusted showed even the slightest sign that they might betray me were a different story altogether. It turned out that having two fucked up families of origin left a mark whether I remembered the finer details or not.

Eryx stared at the wallpaper. "The fiends come out of the walls at night, rising up from the depths of the under-world to eat naughty children. You can smell them coming, according to the story. This wallpaper looks like a monster might crawl out of it."

I grimaced a bit. "That's an awful story to tell a child."

He shrugged. "Necromancer mothers are a different sort, I guess."

My phone buzzed. When we'd ended up here before, my phone hadn't worked. The whispers would begin and the EMF, I presumed, was too strong to get service. Tonight, for some reason, it was different. It buzzed again. I slid it out of my pocket and glanced down at the text message, smiling as my fingers flew over the keyboard in response.

"Who are you texting?" Eryx asked, an eyebrow arched with incredulity.

"Sera," I responded. "She wants to know the mystery pen name of her favorite romance author."

Eryx's arms tightened across his chest, as his frown deepened. "A simple internet search would yield that information. It's the middle of the night."

Irritation flashed through me, and surprisingly, it wasn't with him, but with the fact that he was right. Why *couldn't* she just ask the internet like everyone else?

I slid my phone back in my pocket, not liking how easily he'd changed my feelings about the text. The fact that Sera was texting me was proof that she wasn't angry at me. It was proof that the horrible things I said to myself weren't true. It was a competing narrative with the one that said that I had ruined the Maere's lives.

I *needed* those texts.

Eryx didn't understand. He was so well liked—he and his best friend, Avaline Reyes. They were the necromancers the entire city was terrified of and fascinated with. Ares, the leader of the Necroline Dynasty, was simply feared. But they were adored. Of course, he couldn't comprehend the things someone like me had to do to be liked.

To be loved was another level altogether. One I certainly couldn't achieve these days. He wouldn't understand that. Heat rose in my chest, and a distinct feeling of flailing that made me want to scream into the wallpaper. Everything was too hard, too sad, too complicated.

As he uncrossed his arms, moonlight caught the waves of his dark hair, and I drew another sharp breath in. There was no use in getting flustered by Eryx Necroline. He'd made himself painfully clear about where we stood. Or at least I thought he had. I frowned. The night of the heist was hazy in my memory, all of a sudden. What had he said that made me so sure he wasn't interested in me?

I couldn't remember. Things were blurry now, here in the cottage. My head felt fuzzy, but I knew he'd rejected me—hadn't he? I was still embarrassed that he'd turned down my suggestion to share a bed in celebration of reclaiming our swords. That much I knew.

What I'd really needed was someone to prove to me that I was still worthy of attention, still worthy of even the basest form of love. After learning of my mother's betrayal, her complete lack of confidence in me, all I'd wanted was some scrap of proof that—well, it wasn't worth pondering.

He'd said no, and from what I could remember through this infernal haze, I'd continued to want him. A deeper irritation bloomed under the surface of my thoughts. It didn't matter that I was thousands of years old, couldn't die for shit, and should have known better. I was as weak as any of the other moths the necromancer drew to his flame. Especially with the odd reverence he had for me, combined with the fact that I was currently sure he would never sleep with me.

At first, I thought it was just professional respect. I was the Maere's assassin, and he was the Necroline Dynasty's primary enforcer. It made sense that he'd admire my prowess in our trade. Not everyone dealt death with the efficacy we did. I had assumed that once the Maere regained our stolen swords, we'd both move on with our lives, and the silent infatuation I'd let fester while we'd planned the heist would fade.

But the two of us kept ending up in this eldritch hovel.

I glanced at Eryx again. He was still staring at the hypnotic maze of flowers in the wallpaper. I got why *he* kept ending up here. He was a necromancer, and Oleander Cottage was one of the most haunted places in Orphium.

But why was I pulled here nearly every night alongside him?

"Your phone goes off at all times of the day—and you always answer right away. Why?" Even at a whisper, his voice was deep, resonating through me with the most pleasurable of vibrations.

I opened my mouth to answer, but no words came out. Nothing I thought made any sense.

He leaned towards me, his eyes hooded and serious. "It seems like it wears you out."

That was why *I* ended up here every night. That *look*. The way he noticed everything about me. The way he saw me. *I liked it.*

I liked the way his eyes skimmed over me, with just enough desire to push the boundaries of being respectful, without actually going past them. It didn't really matter, though. Whatever spark might have flickered between us was snuffed out already.

I was certain he'd already told me everything I needed to know about him—and suddenly the fuzziness in my head cleared. Whatever it was the cottage did to me when it drew me in like this was either giving me a reprieve or torturing me further. My mind flickered back to the night we got the swords back. The first night we'd ended up here, in this very kitchen.

The night *he* didn't seem to remember.

The night he'd rejected me *twice*.

I'm not the kind of man people should have relationships with, he'd said, that handsome face so grim. *I'm not good for anyone.*

Not that I'd asked him to have one. I'd only asked him if he was seeing anyone because he'd acted so damn interested in me and then didn't understand that I'd been suggesting we sleep together. I shoved down the humiliation I still felt about his declaration. About the obvious rejection.

"How do we keep ending up here?" I breathed, not expecting him to answer.

"Fairly certain we both walk across the garden and come inside," he replied, his tone so dry I couldn't gauge its meaning. His blithe tone was warranted. I asked every time we came here. He shook his head as he turned, bending a little to peer out the window above the deep farmhouse sink. "It's the middle of the night. I was asleep, I think."

I followed his gaze. The night was clear, the moon a sliver. I frowned at the sky. Had it been clear when I walked across the garden? I still couldn't remember. In my peripheral vision, Eryx shifted his weight, crossing his heavy arms over his chest again. He hadn't answered my question, not really. But he was right.

It *was* the middle of the night and I was exhausted, so I went with the easiest answer. "I suppose."

I moved to leave, but Eryx moved with me—graceful as a dancer—blocking the back door to the kitchen. "Don't you want to know *why* we keep ending up here?"

His voice was low, sultry in a way that heated my skin almost instantaneously. A trick. It was always tricks with men like Eryx Necroline. Too handsome for their own good. So many lovers that no one was special. Always someone eager to get on their knees. What must that be like?

"I think I just asked you that," I snapped.

"No," he snapped back. "You asked *how* we keep ending up here, and I told you."

Pedantic. In my limited experience with him, that was

unusual. We were both on edge. I looked away from him, moving slowly towards the little alcove with a table surrounded by a banquette upholstered with a fabric that nearly matched the kitchen's rose wallpaper. The cottage was called "Oleander" and I had to wonder why roses were the primary floral theme. They were everywhere in the tiny cottage.

"I don't care about *why* we keep ending up here," I muttered, bitterness clouding my voice. My eyes followed the maze within the roses once more. "I just want it to stop. Ember can't ward this place off fast enough, in my opinion."

He stared at me for a long moment, as though something about what I'd said bothered him. Finally, he sighed, moving out of the doorway. "Then go back to bed."

Eryx made a sweeping motion with his arm, stalking back to stand at the sink. He closed his eyes, and took a deep breath, as though there were a thousand things he might say, but I wasn't worth saying them to.

I wasn't sure why he was so annoyed with me, but I was annoyed with him too. He turned as I passed him, our fingers brushing, electricity crackling between us. It was nothing more than static, but time seemed to slow, our eyes meeting as we both attempted to snatch our hands back from touching.

"I thought you were going to bed," he snapped.

"I am," I shot back, but I didn't move.

I couldn't move. I was trying, but it was as though my mind and body wouldn't connect. And then my feet were moving. I was out the door, in the garden. Running for the house.

Running *away* from Eryx Necroline.

CHAPTER 2

RHIANNON

OLEANDER COTTAGE. THREE DAYS LATER.

THIS PLACE WAS CURSED, but I knew that. Panic nearly overtook rational thought. *I haven't been sleeping*, I reminded myself. *That's all this is.*

The explanation was threadbare at this point. Oleander Cottage was a menace. It had been affecting all of us, since the night we'd arrived on the property, but it seemed to be hitting Eryx and I the worst, because here we were again. Maybe this was punishment for the fact that I'd been foolish enough to suggest that Ember buy Oleander Cottage and Hemlock House.

Back when Orphium was still ruled by the Necroline Dynasty, this little compound had been their seat of power in the city, but eventually Roman Necroline had sold it. After that, the cottage had become unlivable, the spirit activity here so intense, so violent that even the city's best necromancers couldn't remedy the problem. Though, aside from the strange way Eryx and I kept ending up here, I hadn't seen much evidence of the haunting.

But Eryx was a clairsentient. Spirits could speak through him, and I assumed he sensed them differently than the rest of us. Necromancers could see ghosts all the time, but the ways they interacted with them varied. I knew from the heist that Eryx could channel difficult spirits, that they trusted him more than other necromancers, but not much else about his power.

We were back in the kitchen, seemingly unable to leave or to go into any other room in the cottage. In the real world, the daytime world, I barely remembered being here. It was almost like a dream. But then night fell and the house drew us in.

"Do you see them?" I asked. "The ghosts?"

"Not right now." He shook his head, frowning as if there were something wrong with that. As if he expected something horrible to happen. The mere thought of that sent a chill down my spine. Necromancers rarely feared the dead. They were used to them. When he spoke again, his eyelids drooped with worry, as though the burden of what he knew and I did not was too much to bear. "I hear them, though. The whispers."

I had been trying, only somewhat successfully, to ignore the whispers. Come to think of it, they were quieter when we were *inside* the cottage. In my room in Hemlock House, they kept me from sleeping or even resting, and I needed to rest. Badly. "Do you know what they're saying?"

Eryx's eyes darkened. "Some."

I let out a huff of frustration. Everything about this man was irritating. Why couldn't he just be straightforward with me? "Are you going to tell me?"

He was in front of me in an instant, so close I could feel the heat from his body. I turned, backing up against the kitchen sink, the cold porcelain leaching through my thin silk robe. His arms caged my body. For a moment, I felt small. Delicate. Nothing more than a rush of blood and a fluttering heart, as heat pooled between my legs. *How had things gotten so intense, so fast?*

Eryx's head bent towards mine. "No."

"No… what?" I asked, all thoughts having disappeared with his proximity.

"No, I'm not going to tell you what they're saying." His eyes blazed with an intensity that stirred something deep within me. "It doesn't make any sense, and…"

Eryx trailed off, his breath catching as our eyes met in the moonlight. He had that same look on his face he'd had the night of the heist. He looked at me like I'd hung the stars, like I was something special, not the reason for all my loved ones' unhappiness. That look was a balm I didn't deserve, in a world that only ever hurt, but it was also confusing.

How could he look at me like that, but not want me?

Emotion clawed at my throat. I didn't have relationships either. I didn't do one-night stands. For years, I'd refused affection so sternly that I wasn't sure how to even begin a bid for it now. And Eryx was a poor choice of partner. There were so many reasons we shouldn't be here alone together. That we shouldn't be standing so close.

Maybe he was right to reject me.

Despite that thought, my back arched away from the sink, as my mind swept all those reasons aside. Some terrifying part of me was done with the iron grip I'd kept on my control. My body hungered to press against his, to wind myself around him and forget the chaos in my mind. It would feel so good to let him drive deep within me, to push out everything but the pleasure and pain of the moment. To let him use me the way he used all his other playthings.

To use him right back might feel good too.

Something so ill-conceived wasn't like me, but visions of us in bed together—upstairs, our damp skin sliding against one another in the summer heat—filled my mind. *Yes.* That was what I wanted. The bedroom. The heat. The rough feeling of him covering me with that impressive bulk, making me forget.

His fingers gripped my chin. I arched into him, sliding my thigh between his legs as I wound my arms around his neck. My skin beaded with sweat. It was so hot in here. So damn hot. The hottest summer on record.

"Rhiannon," he rasped out. Why was he saying that word? He repeated it, *"Rhiannon."*

Was that my name?

Of course it was.

My skin went cold, then hot again as I looked around, blinking back shock as I realized the position I was in. Why was I touching him like this? My heart beat so fast my chest ached. "Eryx?"

He nodded, standing so still I was sure he'd stopped breathing.

"Saints," I swore as I tried to push away from him, to escape the cage of his arms. "I…"

He hugged me to him. "Stop," he cautioned. There was no sultry edge to his voice now. Just slow, measured, even safety. "This place feeds off our distress, off strong emotions, remember?"

I didn't remember. That was the problem. I struggled to remember the conversation we had the first time we ended up here. Hadn't I just been thinking of it? What had he told me? *I'm not the kind of man people should have relationships with. I'm not good for anyone.*

The memory was fuzzy already, but I clung to it. Something was wrong. This place was wrong. Movement caught my eye out the window, snow falling in big puffy flakes. Drifts of snow filled the garden. The moon was gone. The night was cloudy with storms, not clear and still.

"It's winter?"

"Yes," Eryx reassured me as he gestured at the windows. "Record snowfall and everything."

Something vibrated in my pocket. My phone. It was my phone. For some reason that was odd, anachronous, though I couldn't say why. Eryx kept a tight hold on my arm, but allowed me to draw it out of my pocket. "Is it one of the Maere?" he asked.

I shook my head, and it cleared a little. It was the home office. The Consulate. They never stopped calling. Reality washed back in.

Returning to Orphium, and the pain of reuniting with the Maere. The heist that returned my sword to me. The truth that my mother had sold me out to prove her moral purity. The never-ending bad news mixed with victories that were barely enough to keep our heads above water. The ways I'd failed to keep my sistren safe. The way I was a danger to them all.

My thoughts morphed slowly into a riot of voices, all of them conflicting with one another, but only in ways that proved that I was the cause of so much suffering. On that, all voices, including my own, agreed.

The truth was overwhelming.

I pinched the bridge of my nose as my phone stilled. Then, almost immediately, it rang again. The same number as always. I answered, not waiting for so much as a hello. "Stop. Calling. Me."

The voice on the other end rushed to ask me not to hang up, reminding me that I had a job to do. An important position at the Consulate. Eryx held my eyes with his, his grip on me firmer now than ever before. His fingers pressed into the plush flesh of my hips. It felt like support, like solidarity.

"I said stop calling," I interrupted, not pausing to contemplate why the Necroline Dynasty's enforcer might want to support me. "My place is here, with the Maere. Don't call this number again."

I hung up, my body stilling as I tried to breathe normally. Eryx's grip on me didn't falter, but neither did he move closer. Because I noticed such things, it was obvious when the cadence of his breath matched mine. When my lungs sought to match the slowing pace of inhalation and exhalation that he set, surprise glimmered within me. But my phone sat in my grip, cold and heavy with the weight of the Consulate's call. I wanted to believe my own words.

For nearly my entire immortal life, I'd believed that our sisterhood of immortal warriors was the key to bridging the divide between the mundane human world and an ancient past that held all the secrets to magic. I'd stayed the course. I'd done my duty over and over, and it had all come to nothing. Yes, we had our swords back, and with them, access to the full well of our power, but our own people had stolen them.

My mother, my queen, had believed it was better to test my sistren for hundreds of years, to keep them without the full range of our power, to prove that allowing me to come to Orphium with Ember and the others hadn't been nepotism. As though my devotion wasn't enough. As though my unwavering commitment to the island didn't matter. Despite Eryx's grip, and his calming effect on me, I sank deeper into myself, into the spiral within me that led down, down, down into the dark.

Nothing mattered anymore.

Not the Consulate.

Not the island.

Not my mother.

Not the Maere.

And certainly not me.

Eryx watched me closely, his eyes narrowing as he

shook his head. It was as though he could read my mind. He finally stepped away from me, though he slid a hand to my forearm, keeping a tight grip on me. "They won't stop calling, and we won't stop ending up here, Rhiannon. We're on a path."

I had no idea what he meant. He pulled me across the kitchen, keeping his grip on me gentle but firm. Some part of me fought him, even though I wanted to leave. My eyes locked back on that wallpaper.

"I've always loved roses." The words slipped out of me, wistful and discordant with my thoughts.

Eryx looked back at me. "Roses? What do you mean?"

I pointed to the wallpaper. "Roses. The hedge maze."

He shook his head. "Rhiannon, those are oleander, not roses."

I blinked a few times before I saw what he meant. The entire room was decorated with the cottage's namesake flower. I blinked a few times, as though it might bring the roses back. I shook my head. This was all too much.

I stalked towards the mudroom, Eryx close behind. Snow fell, heavy and wet in the garden. I was going to need a bath to warm up by the time I got back to my bedroom in Hemlock House.

"I can't do this," I murmured, wrenching myself out of his grip, out of his magnetic orbit.

I was resentful of the comfort he lent me. It wasn't real, and it certainly wasn't for me to keep. Better not to get accustomed to such things, only to have them ripped away later. I'd had enough of that for six lifetimes. "I have to rest."

He nodded, letting me go. "Go get some sleep."

ERYX

HEMLOCK HOUSE. ONE DAY LATER.

THE SNOW HAD FALLEN thick and heavy overnight. And though we were practically snowed in at Hemlock House, I'd barely seen Rhiannon. She hadn't left her room much in the past day, but when I had seen her the circles under her eyes were darker, and her phone almost never stopped buzzing.

Calypso, the new Maere from Aradios, found an ancient warding ritual that Ember could use to shut Oleander Cottage off for a while. Briony, our teenage charge, had been found at the garden gate just this morning, glassy eyed and muttering about the hedge being too thick. It had sent a chill through me when she fought Sera, one of her favorite people, tooth and nail to return to the gate.

If we were going to live here, someone had to deal with the Cottage, and it couldn't be Ember and Ares. There was too much for them to do now. Ember had to reestablish the Maere's position with the Consulate, the Trinity, and the Authority. Now that Orphium's guardians had their swords back, the exciting work was over, and she would have to weave herself, and the other Maere, back into the evil fabric of our broken society—all with my brother by her side.

I didn't envy them the job—it was going to be intense work that would take months, if not years. But it was worth it to create a better world for our people. We couldn't have the new alliances we were trying to establish here disrupted by the guest cottage sucking people in and killing them.

So the warding would work as a temporary fix, though it didn't *solve* the problem of the haunting. Ember and Ares were going to close off the cottage today, and my hope was that now that winter had set in, I could spend it researching the cottage's history.

There had to be a reason the haunting had targeted Rhiannon and me first, and so doggedly. Briony hadn't been the first of us to hear its whispers, or to be drawn to the gate, but it hadn't pulled anyone else in—not yet, anyway. I was determined to find what had caused the haunting, and resolve it before things got any worse. I was on my way to the kitchen for a cup of coffee when I heard Rhiannon on the phone.

She was tucked into a dormer window seat in the hallway, and sounded nearly frantic. "I've asked you to stop calling me. What don't you understand about the word no?" She paused, then sighed. I was trapped. If I passed her, she would know I'd heard her. If I turned around, she would probably see me. I chose to keep walking. As I approached, she got up, saying, "I told you before I left that I want off the Blaire case. Permanently."

She walked into her room, and the door was still open as I passed. "There is only one person who gets to decide that I no longer belong here, and it certainly isn't you. For the last time, stop calling me."

The sound of her phone thumping against the plush rug in her room made me wince. Rhiannon was careful with her things. She treated all of her possessions with a kind of gratitude and grace that I rarely saw with people these days. I paused, worried that she might not be all right.

Sure enough, I heard her strangled sob. Then a shuddery breath. She did that, I noticed—buried any trace of emotion she ever let out. It hurt to know she did it when she was alone as well. I leaned against the wall outside her door, listening. I didn't want to be a creep, but Ember and Lara seemed unaware that she was hurting. Rhiannon needed a friend.

She was whispering to herself, "I just need a little break. Just a little one." There were muffled sounds, drawers opening and closing. "It can't be *that* haunted."

Was Rhiannon thinking of *hiding out* in Oleander Cottage? There was no way in hell I was going to let that happen. If she'd decided on something, I knew her well enough to know that arguing over the wisdom of taking a restive break in the city's most haunted house would do neither of us any good.

My mind combed through my options. *I could go too. Yes. That was the move.* Whether she liked it or not, I was going with her. I'd kept her safe from the cottage's spirits this far, and I'd keep doing it. She couldn't die, but neither could she go there alone. There were worse things than death, and being tortured endlessly by malefic spirits was most certainly one.

I changed direction quickly, heading back to my own bedroom. She was too busy packing to notice me passing her open doorway. Once inside, I glanced outside in the yard. Ember and Ares were out there with salt and coffee, getting ready to ward the cottage.

Rhiannon might not want me to go with her, of course. There was always that possibility. For a split second, I hesitated. But then I thought of the way she'd stifled that little sob. Even alone, she denied herself any opportunity to let out her feelings. Rhiannon Brontë was the most capable woman I'd ever met, fantastic at making sure everyone else got exactly what they needed, while she neglected herself entirely.

If I asked to go with her, she would say no immediately, and not necessarily because she didn't want me there; she had a terrible habit of denying herself even the slightest bit of comfort. But if I simply showed up, ready to go with her...

I packed quickly, shoving random shit into my bag before rushing after her. I meant to confront her alone, in the hallway, or her bedroom, but as always Rhiannon was quick, silent, and gone. She was already in the garden by the time I reached the back door. My brother and Ember were faced away from us. From the way their heads were bent towards one another, it was obvious they didn't notice Rhiannon moving towards them.

It was impossible to tell how she did it, but from my vantage point I could see nothing different about the way she moved from usual. It was as though her footsteps simply didn't make noise in the snow. How she'd managed to get her suitcases to quiet themselves was the real miracle.

Ares took Ember's coffee cup from her, and the movement was so sweet, so full of love, it nearly gagged me. I didn't want my brother to be alone, but watching him and Ember when I wanted Rhiannon so badly, and couldn't have her, was heart-wrenching.

Ares bent his head towards Ember and said, "Let's get this done and then we can sort Rhiannon out."

She was standing right behind them. I cringed as she replied, "No one needs to sort me out."

They both jumped, visibly startled. I smirked and took the opportunity to text my best friend. I needed to let Avaline know that I was following Rhiannon to Oleander Cottage. Her response was nearly instantaneous. She was at the cemetery today, having what she called her "office hours" for the restless dead that hung around there.

That is good, Av replied. *She is going to need your help*. Her first text was quickly followed by another. Av rarely texted all her thoughts at once. *Wish I could come help, but there's a problem with the ancient Necrolines and the renaissance Cognoscenti right now... and it's*, the text cut off. Another appeared: COMPLICATED.

I smiled, laughing softly before responding. *You're the best one for the job of sorting that all out. See you soon.*

Be careful, she cautioned. *The renaissance Cognoscenti say that you and Rhi should keep your wits about you.*

Will do, I replied, then shoved my phone back in my pocket. Ember was shouting at Rhiannon, who was, rather calmly from my perspective, explaining that the Consulate had been calling her for weeks. I had to get out there before there was any question of her going alone.

Rhiannon was still talking as I approached: "...they insist I can do both. I can't. I don't want to."

"You don't have to," I said.

Rhiannon turned; her blue eyes wide with fury at being interrupted. Her gaze fell on the bag slung over my shoulder. "What are you *doing*?"

I don't know what came over me—maybe it was how beautiful she was out here in the fresh winter air, maybe it was that she hadn't told me to fuck off immediately—but I grinned at her. "You're going to have them lock you in when they ward, right?"

Rhiannon blinked, obviously surprised. She knew exactly what I was up to, and instead of her earlier fury, she was merely shocked that I would come with her. She didn't have to say a word of what she was thinking; her feelings were written clearly on her face.

Her answer was simple: "Yes."

She hadn't refused me. She just answered my question, which in Rhiannon-speak meant that she wasn't going to say no. It was not precisely a *yes*, because she would never say yes to an offer of help. But if she truly didn't want me with her, I knew she would say so. There was only one bedroom in the cottage. She knew exactly what we'd be getting into.

So, I said what was on my mind. "Then I'm coming with you. The spirits like me."

Those azure eyes of hers narrowed for a second. She bit her bottom lip and I just about lost it. She was biting back a smile.

Fuck. I was in so much trouble.

But what had been true since the moment Rhiannon returned to Orphium was still true now: I would follow Rhiannon Brontë into the netherworld itself without so much as a second thought. She needed me, and if I wasn't mistaken, she *wanted* me with her. I stood my ground, waiting for her to deny me. We stood there; eyes locked on one another for a long moment.

Ember spoke first. "No. *No.*"

Rhiannon's gaze shifted away from mine, her head tilting slightly to one side. A charming expression appeared on her face. "Ember. Please. You know you can't just lock that place up and expect for things to be okay. That's not how warding works and you know it." She was going to let me come with her. There wasn't a word about me in what she said to Ember. "Let me go in and solve this. I can survive that place."

She didn't say "us" or "we," but her eyes flicked to mine as she spoke. That was all I needed. I started to pick up a few of the bags she'd discarded. My brother was about to say something—he was staring at me too intently to stay quiet.

My words were for him, not for her. She'd already said yes, in her own way. "Not alone. You need a clairsentient, and I'm the best pick."

Ares took a sharp breath in, and I had to wonder if he knew why Roman had been so adamant that I not be allowed to help exorcise the malefics in Oleander Cottage. Rhiannon spoke again before he had a chance to break in.

"Fine," she said with an imperious roll of her eyes. She stepped forward, brushed an elegant kiss to Ember's cheek, and said, "See you when spring comes. I'll have this solved by then."

Ember looked a little lost. But she was used to Rhiannon doing whatever she pleased, I presumed. "Do you… have your phone?"

Rhiannon shook her head. "No. It won't work in there anyway. EMF and all that."

It was a bit of a lie, but I nodded anyway. "She's right. But there's a landline. It's connected to the house. We saw it yesterday."

"*We?*" Ember demanded. "The two of you have been planning this?"

Rhiannon rolled her eyes again. "No. We just…" she glanced at me and frowned, probably remembering the heat between us last night. Or perhaps that was just me. "Keep ending up there together."

Ember sighed. "Did you talk to Briony?"

Rhiannon nodded, and I wondered how she'd had time for that. I needed to get quicker if I was going to keep track of her in the cottage. It was a small place, but she was sneaky.

"She's going to dig up some Cottage history for me. I gave her all my best Consulate hacks," Rhiannon replied.

Ember groaned. "Rhi… she is a *child*."

Rhiannon shrugged as she moved beyond the line of salt, stepping over it gracefully so as not to disturb the ward. "She is a genius. Let her be a genius."

I followed, carrying the rest of Rhiannon's luggage over the line of salt. Behind us, Ares poured out a bit more to reinforce the barrier. I heard him whisper to Ember, "They will be all right together. If anyone can solve Oleander Cottage's problem, it's them."

"We can hear you," Rhiannon said with a sigh. There was a hint of a smile on her lips. She was *happy* about this.

"Yes," Ares replied. He sketched a door into the salt barrier, using an old sigil of our mother's. I wondered if he remembered that, or if those had just been Calypso's directions. "I know. This should allow you to take groceries in, but you'll have to perform the ritual in reverse if you want out."

The four of us stood on opposite sides of the ward. I reached across the barrier to hug my brother before the barrier solidified. I was equal parts sorry I hadn't run this by him first and relieved to have a brief respite from my duties.

I hadn't realized until just now that when I'd heard Rhiannon whisper that she needed a break, something in me had echoed the sentiment. I needed one too. Ares never asked if I was okay with my job. It probably had never occurred to him that perhaps I might not like doing the Necroline Dynasty's dirty work.

"See you soon," I murmured, tacking on, "we'll be okay."

Ares nodded, clearly confident in that. It would have been nice if he appeared even a little concerned. He and Ember were cut from the same cloth though. They saw the big picture more often than the minutiae.

To them, we were both more than capable of solving the problem of Oleander Cottage. They loved us, but they only saw the endpoint, not what it would take either of us personally to get there. And that was what Rhiannon and I both needed a break from.

"Call as much as you can," Ember said, her voice blissfully calm now that she'd accepted that we were going.

Rhiannon stood right next to me—she'd moved closer in the past few seconds. She was close enough that I felt it in her shoulders as she tensed. Perhaps it bothered her that Ember wasn't worried. That she'd barely fought her on going, or even asked a follow-up question as to why she wanted to go at all.

I got it. I'd spent centuries with my brother, and he was the same, but that didn't make it any easier to swallow when Rhiannon replied, "Of course."

Her voice was a little too bright, her expression far too smooth. How did Ember miss that she'd hurt her? Rhiannon picked up the handle to her suitcase and we turned at the same time. I nodded, gesturing with my head for her to go first, and the two of us disappeared through the garden gate.

As it shut behind us, the world went silent. The ward was complete. Rhiannon and I were alone within the bounds of Oleander Cottage's garden. She turned to look at me, a faint smile on her face. "Sorry you got stuck with me," she said, before turning back towards the cottage and heading in.

If we managed even one thing while we were here, it would be making Rhiannon understand that all I wanted from here on out was to be stuck with her. Somehow, that seemed like a harder task than solving the problem of the malefic spirits that waited for us inside.

CHAPTER 4

RHIANNON

My eyes were bleary as I awoke. The ceiling above me slanted downward, rain drumming the roof. A briar of thick roses and greenery clustered on the walls around me, giving the room an eerie greenish glow in this light. Whether the effect was claustrophobia-inducing or cozy, I couldn't decide.

With a little trouble, I sat up in bed, confused and stiff. The room was nearly dark, but the lace curtains were open just enough for me to see outside. Sure enough, rain pelted the leaded glass window, obscuring my view. But I didn't need a clear view to see the green outside. *Leaves on the birch trees in the garden.*

That wasn't possible. I leaned forward, staying in bed and glancing about the room. The quilt that covered me was different shades of white fabric, pieced together in a wedding ring pattern. My suitcases were stacked neatly next to one another on one side of the room. Eryx's single duffle bag was nowhere to be seen, but a cable knit cardigan that was clearly his lay draped over a comfortably lumpy overstuffed chair in the corner of the room.

How had I gotten here? I wracked my sleep-addled mind. The last thing I remembered was being in the garden with Eryx. I couldn't help but smile at that as I swung my legs over the edge of the bed. My muscles were stiff, my joints aching just slightly as I rolled my neck and shoulders.

Footsteps on the stairs caught my attention. Eryx's head popped up over the banister, his dark expression brightening when he saw me. "You're awake."

The relief in his voice was palpable. I glanced down at my nightgown, frowning. I didn't remember putting it on. "What happened?"

The thought that he might have changed me into my nightgown, that his fingers might have touched my skin— that he might have seen me naked—should have been upsetting. But it wasn't. It was *thrilling*. My blood felt as thought it might burst through my skin, I flushed so hard.

Eryx came into the dark hallway, but stopped at the doorframe, leaning against it. It was as though he was afraid to come closer. Then I remembered. My nightgown was practically sheer. Why that was embarrassing when I'd just hoped he'd seen me naked was beyond my under-standing. I drew my feet back up into bed and pulled the quilt up, nodding to the chair.

He breathed what looked like a sigh of relief. It was hard not to take a little bit of offense to that. Was my body really that terrible to look at? A little inkling in the back of my mind said perhaps that wasn't the reason he was relieved. Men were typically rather predictable, but I couldn't read Eryx Necroline to save my life. Not that I had to.

When he was comfortable in the chair, he spoke. "When we entered the house, it put you into the same sort of daze it has every other time we've been here." He paused, obviously waiting to see if I remembered that. I did, so I nodded, not wanting to speak and derail this explanation. "You said you needed to rest. So, I carried your bags up here, you got your nightgown out, and that was that."

"That was… that?" I asked when I was sure there wasn't more to the story.

He nodded, but said nothing else. It was rather lovely that he never chattered on needlessly, but sometimes, one did wish he'd say a bit more. "For how long?" When he frowned, I added, "Was I asleep? For how long was I asleep?"

"Of course," he replied. "Sorry, I've just been so worried… for three days."

I stared out the window at the obviously warm, rainy day, rather than the snowy winter we'd arrived in. "Three *days*?"

"Oh," he replied as he followed my gaze. "Yes, that is disconcerting. It's summer in the garden." It was clear there was more to the haunting than I'd expected. "Maybe you should get dressed and come downstairs and see."

I nodded and he got up, but there was a faint hesitation in his movements. He glanced at the sloping walls once, his jaw clenching, but only said, "Be careful on the stairs. They're steep, and objects appear on them without warning."

There were sharp edges in his voice that made me nervous. Now that he was gone, I noticed a book next to the chair, topped with a heavy pottery mug. It was empty. He'd been watching me sleep. My breath caught for a moment—my head still blurry-feeling from my long sleep. As it cleared, it occurred to me that Eryx Necroline was nothing if not respectful. He'd never sit and watch me sleep for three days if he didn't have a damn good reason.

And there wouldn't be that edge in his voice either.

Something sank within me, a heavy weight I'd learned to pay attention to far too late in life. This place was more than it seemed.

When his head disappeared down the stairs, I got up. The air in the attic was warm and damp. Not at all what I'd expect from the first bluster of winter. I walked to the window and though rain streamed down it, wet from the angle of the wind, I could make out not only the green of the birch leaves, but the watercolor riot of flowers in the garden.

I nearly choked. That simply wasn't possible. I blinked a few times. I'd grown up in a time where magic was plentiful in the world—in a place where true mages worked incredible spells—and I'd never seen anything like this. The seasons were unchangeable.

Weather magic? Of course. On the island there had been women who made it rain when they cried. But to change an entire season was *impossible*. A flash of lightning broke through the gloom. Thunder rumbled through Oleander Cottage, and dread seeped through my clammy skin and into my bones.

What had we gotten ourselves into?

With my teeth brushed, my face washed, and a pair of navy parachute pants and a white tank top on, I was comfortable enough. I'd only brought winter clothes, of course, but luckily, I was a fan of layers. As I folded my nightgown, movement caught the corner of my eye.

I spun, expecting to see Eryx coming up the stairs, but there was nothing behind me. I tucked my nightgown into the top drawer of the nightstand. Eryx had left a glass of water for me, and I drank it down, suddenly quite thirsty. Again, something just beyond my range of vision moved.

Instincts I was born into my current life with stirred. The fact that the Maere couldn't die in this life had never made me fearless. In fact, it was my first life—which would have been immeasurably long compared to a human's, had I lived it—that built my instincts as one of the Maere. It had been part of the spell that made us, to keep us keen as warriors.

And now, my heart raced like something hunted me from within Oleander Cottage's walls. I breathed deep, getting my bearings, then turned. Once more, there was nothing to see behind me, but my eyes locked on the wall, just where the slope of the ceiling creased.

The thick briar of thorns there was interesting somehow, though I could not say why. As I watched, it began to move, as though one finger pressed into it behind the wallpaper itself.

I swallowed the immediate fear that flushed through me, hot and damp at first, then cold as a second finger and a third pressed through the wallpaper. My breath wouldn't come, stuck in my throat as a full hand pressed against the paper, straining to get out. My eyes went wide and unblinking. Someone was trapped in the wall.

"Rhiannon?" a voice said from the hallway. When I looked up, Eryx was standing there, his brows knitted in concern. He followed my gaze to the wallpaper and shook his head. "Come downstairs."

The hand was gone, the wall just as it had been. I opened my mouth to say something, but nothing came out. Gently, Eryx moved towards me, reaching for my hand, his fingertips grazing mine. "Come downstairs, Rhiannon."

I glanced behind me, at the evidence that he'd sat by me while I slept, as I followed him downstairs. He knew what I'd seen, and it had scared him too. The haunting at Oleander Cottage was more than whispers and spirits showing the living how they died. Of that much, I was sure.

From the kitchen window, I could see quite clearly that it was not winter outside. In fact, it looked to be full-on summer. I stepped into the mudroom, angling my head to see past the rain.

"There's a black cat in the garden," I murmured, squinting a little to try to see past the blur of water on the glass. "It will get wet." Eryx didn't reply. He just crossed those giant arms of his, quiet at my side. I sighed. "Well, you've been awake, I assume?"

He nodded, a muscle in his neck flexing slightly, as though something about his vigil strained him. He glanced sidelong at me for a moment, and when I returned his gaze, his cheeks flushed.

The frown on his lips cut straight to my soul. Truly, I didn't understand him. I turned to leave the mudroom. A heavy wooden butcher block sat at the center of the kitchen. "Was that there before?"

Eryx shook his head. "No. There are many things here now that were not here before." He stared at me, long and hard. It was impossible to discern what he was thinking.

He'd grinned just a few days ago in the garden. Grinned about coming with me. Where was that smile now?

My heart dropped as his words took on another shape in my mind. Many things that were not here before… "Like, *us*."

He nodded. "Yes, like us. The house changed as soon as you fell asleep. Objects appear and reappear. The cat —" he gestured towards the mudroom. "Comes and goes." His jaw clenched. "It looks like Stanley."

The poltergeist cat that often accompanied Avaline

Reyes and had attached itself to our protégé Briony? "Strange."

He nodded. "And the wallpaper…"

"You don't like it," I murmured, looking him over. He wore a t-shirt that was probably twenty or thirty years old. It was merchandise for a Necroline autobody shop that the Authority put out of business a decade ago for being a front for illegal exorcisms.

"Okay," I sighed. "Level with me. What are we dealing with here? Surely you have some idea."

"Yes," he answered. "I think this all has something to do with my uncle—Magnus, and his wife Cassandra."

I wracked my mind, trying to remember if I'd ever met Cassandra. Magnus was Roman Necroline's brother, and I'd certainly met him. He'd killed Roman to take the Dynasty from him. Cassandra though…the name was familiar, but my mind was fuzzy. "Wasn't she a Seer of some sort?"

Eryx hummed his assent. This was getting ridiculous. Why couldn't he just talk to me? Irritation mounted in me, but then I heard it. The whispers. I couldn't make out the words, but it was obvious he could. He swallowed hard, his throat bobbing slightly as his head turned slowly to look at me. Whatever he was hearing that I couldn't, was not good.

I needed to change the subject. A memory flitted across my mind; I caught it before it slipped away. "Didn't Cassandra predict some kind of natural disaster?" I bit my bottom lip and his cheeks flushed again, his eyes trained on my mouth. *Did he like that?* "A tsunami?"

Eryx nodded; the lines of his handsome face solemn as he dragged his gaze from my mouth to my eyes. He was so serious. "She did. Shortly before she met Magnus. It's what got his attention. She saved the lives of everyone in the northern peninsula. They evacuated and not one person died. She was a hero…" he trailed off.

Now I remembered her better, though vaguely, as though through cloudy glass. A woman about my height, with strawberry blonde hair and wide sapphire eyes, cloudy from her failure as a Seer, probably. "But it was her only clear vision, wasn't it?"

Again, Eryx nodded. "She disappeared a few years after they got married—he claimed she went back to Aradios, where she was from." His crossed arms tightened around his chest.

"But you don't think that's what happened?" I asked.

Eryx shrugged. "I think it's hard to say. What was easy enough to figure out is that there's a malefic energy here—"

"Not a malefic *spirit*?" I interrupted.

Eryx leaned against the butcher block. "Well, yes, but it's more than that… like a web, almost." He flicked a hand towards the window, bringing it immediately back to his chest. "That's not a trick, Rhiannon. It's really summer out there. I can't think of how that could happen without…"

"Magic," I finished for him.

He nodded. "But there's not real magic in the Three Cities anymore? Just what the Maere can do with their swords, right?"

There was a hint of suspicion in his voice, as though I, as the Orphium Maere's assassin, might know something he didn't. Or maybe he thought I'd learned something useful in my time at The Consulate. But I hadn't. I had no idea how someone could do real magic here, or how powerful they'd have to be to change a season.

Slowly, I shook my head, before asking, "Have you been outside yet?"

"No," he answered quickly, his cool eyes flicking towards the stairs. "I wasn't keen to leave you."

I took a deep breath, assessing our situation. This was more than a terrible haunting then. If someone was using magic here, I needed to let Ember know. "I think we should go back to Hemlock House for the night," I said. "It might give us some perspective on what to do next. How to solve whatever this all is."

He didn't answer. He did that a lot, I'd noticed. It seemed to indicate he was thinking, whereas I always had a quick answer. Though I'd cultivated the ability to appear patient, I never truly was. "What do you think?"

CHAPTER 5

ERYX

THE WAY SHE LOOKED, her hair still mussed from sleep, and those clothes—I'd never seen her in anything so casual. Rhiannon's sweats were typically matching cashmere sets, luxurious and elegant, just like her. But now... now I wasn't even sure she was wearing a bra underneath the white tank top that clung to her curves.

I was afraid to even look at her, for fear I might combust from the intense longing I had to touch her. All those days she'd been asleep, and I hadn't felt like this. I thought I finally had this attraction to her under control. I'd only wanted to keep her safe from what lurked inside this house.

But now she was moving, that long, curvaceous body graceful and strong. Her avid expressions, the bite of her words. Rhiannon was dynamic in ways that would have terrified a younger version of myself. But now? Now I wanted to be challenged, and more than anything I wanted the way she pushed me, pulled me—I wanted to let her tear me apart.

There had never been anyone like her. When I fucked

someone, it was typically because I had an urge. A need. I didn't screw just anyone; I did have some standards, after all. But I never had to be attracted to them… not anymore. I never had to want *them*. Just sex.

With her, it was different. I wanted *her*. I wanted the ferocity in her touch as much as what it might feel like to be inside her. No. I absolutely could not think of what it might be like to be inside her. My heart raced, my cock so hard I was sure she'd notice. I'd made a mistake wearing sweatpants. This had to stop.

She was right. Going back to the house was the right move. We needed to talk to Ember and Ares, and the others. With the Maere together, along with the leadership of the Necroline Dynasty, there was no doubt we could ferret out what the source of the seasonal shift here was. And yet… we came here because the Consulate wanted Rhiannon back. Ever since the heist to reclaim the Maere's swords, they'd wanted her to return to the home office in Aradios.

A part of me worried that if we left Oleander Cottage, they'd get their way and I'd never see her again—which elicited an ache in me I'd been trying to hide since the moment she'd appeared back in Orphium. I didn't allow myself to get attached to anyone but Ares and Av. We were a closed circle and that was how it had to be.

My job was wretched, and while I could handle it, my lovers could not. Rhiannon Brontë wasn't just anyone; in fact, she might be one of the few people in the world who could handle the particulars of what I did. But no one deserved to be exposed to the demons that lived within me.

All that aside, she was right. We needed to tell our people that the haunting here was more than we'd anticipated. We were going to need some serious help—and probably a lot of research into how something like this was possible. My mind raced with possibilities. Av would know more.

Finally, my thoughts in order and my cock under control after the sobering reminders of what we were up against, I nodded. "We can come back for our things."

Rhiannon's answering smile was a false thing, sending a cold, seeping dread through me. It was beautifully crafted, and I was sure it fooled most everyone. But I'd watched her closely since she'd returned to Orphium for her sword. I saw that smile for what it was—a gorgeous mask. "Great. I'm gonna order a giant pepperoni and mushroom from Pizza Queen as soon as we get back."

Rhiannon stood up, and I followed her through the kitchen, back into the mudroom, trying to keep my eyes off the gentle curve of her hip, the tight roundness to her behind… I *had* to stop. Rhiannon was not for me. I knew that.

She stared for a long moment at the floral print in the wallpaper. The flowers were supposed to be oleander; I remembered now. But they weren't. They were roses. Something here was powerful enough to shift reality.

Rhiannon glanced at me. Her smile had disappeared. As she slid her feet into the boots she'd left in the mudroom, all of her movements were deliberate and smooth, as though she worried she might disturb some trigger and set off a chain reaction of spirit activity. I couldn't blame her for that, certainly.

We had no idea what we were up against. I mimicked the quality and pace of her movements, which earned me an approving nod, a curve of her generous lips. I tried not to let it warm me too deeply as she opened the back door, her touch on the brass doorknob delicate—ginger, even.

We stepped out into the thick, humid heat of the afternoon. The rain stopped as soon as Rhiannon's feet hit the first step. She gripped the wrought-iron railing on the stone stairs, glancing back at me over her shoulder. The timing had been too precise, and the rain didn't peter off the way it should. It had simply stopped.

We went slowly down the back stairs to the house, a giant lilac blocking our view of the garden. The blooms were fragrant, but out of season for full summer. Lilacs bloomed in spring.

As we came around the bush, Rhiannon's breath sucked in with a sharp gasp that caused me to follow her gaze. In the garden, at a set of wrought-iron table and chairs, sat a woman dressed in a corpse's garb. A loose, black gown swathed her body. She stared at us through the dark veil covering her face.

For a long moment, we both froze, our eyes locked on the spirit, as hers were locked on us. It didn't seem to matter that Rhiannon couldn't die and that I was a necromancer, we were both locked in instinct.

The creature before us was a predator, and we were its prey.

My lungs felt as though they might burst. I'd been holding my breath. I attempted to breathe deeply, but my body wasn't mine to control. Fear had me immobilized, waves of it flowing over me.

Was it mine?

Was it Rhiannon's?

Was this all a part of the haunting?

"Do you see her?" Rhiannon whispered, so softly I thought I might have mistaken her question for my own inner monologue.

"Yes," I answered, as soon as my tongue loosened enough to move.

A voice called out, obviously coming from the dark figure, but ringing inside my mind, not my ears. The spirit's words were delivered in a discordant tone that immediately brought on nausea. *The next generation is the answer. Find the key and find the truth.*

She disappeared. Not a slow fade away, but a crisp break in the reality of the moment. The spirit had been there, and now was gone.

Rhiannon's chest heaved, as mine did, both of us gasping for air. The fear I'd felt a moment ago was gone. The haunting had the ability to affect our emotions. That wasn't good, but it wasn't entirely unexpected.

"Is it safe to go?" Rhiannon asked, her voice small as she recovered herself from the apparition's control.

More than anything, I wished I could reassure her. But I couldn't. Not honestly, anyway. Ghosts liked to show you how they died, but often had no awareness of their bodies after death. If a spirit appeared in corpse garb, necromancers considered it an especially bad omen. Spirits that had that kind of self-awareness were dangerous, and quite rare.

But she was gone now, and we had all the more reason to get back to Hemlock House. "Yes." I chose lies. The truth was that I had no idea if we were safe to cross the yard. But I was certain we weren't safe to stay here. "Go."

Rhiannon moved quickly through the garden. We were both on high alert. The stone patio where the spirit had been sitting was at the center of the garden. The wrought-iron table and chairs still sat in the same spot. As we approached, a glass of iced tea appeared, condensation beading on the bevels of the footed cup. Rhiannon glanced at me, pointing to a newspaper.

We stopped. I read the date at the top of the paper. "This is the year Cassandra went back to Aradios," I said.

A chill slipped down my spine. When we came to the cottage, I'd remembered that Magnus had lived here for a few years, of course, but I hadn't thought this might be about him. When Ares killed him, he'd bound his spirit, kept it to the netherworld. Now, I had to wonder if my brother's preemptive exorcism of our uncle had worked.

"What's wrong?" Rhiannon asked.

I was tempted to shrug it off. But I'd been the lead on too many investigations for the Necroline Dynasty. If I had to enforce our brutal rules, I always wanted to be damn sure that the person Ares was punishing really needed it. The small things were important to me. It wasn't wise to dismiss any one.

"This…" I fought the childhood stammer in my voice. "I think this might all be about Magnus."

Rhiannon's deep blue eyes met mine, searching. She was so close to me now, and her role as the Orphium Maere's assassin meant she had plenty of experience evaluating people, ferreting out their secrets. I was suddenly uncomfortable with what she might find in me.

Her tone was even with certainty. "Magnus hurt you, didn't he?"

I tore my eyes from hers. I wouldn't be able to stand it if I found pity in them. "Yes. He was cruel."

"Roman let him get away with that?" She sounded sharp, accusatory.

"No," I breathed. "He never knew. I never told him. I only told Ares after Roman was dead."

Her eyes narrowed. "It is good that he's dead," she said with a vicious edge that drew my gaze back to hers. There was a heat in her eyes I'd never seen. "Or I'd have to finish him now."

The sentiment was so primal, so earnestly spoken, it delved deep into my soul. No one I'd ever been involved with had spoken about me that way. Not even Frannie—

but I didn't think about Frannie. I moved to keep going, but she stepped towards me at the same time.

We nearly collided and my fingers brushed hers. Her hand slipped into mine, natural as anything. My heart raced. I fought between my desire to protect her from the truth of me and the pure pleasure of her touch.

If she thought Magnus was a monster for hurting a child, what would she think of me, if she knew all I'd done? What would she think of me if she found out what had happened to Frannie because I couldn't stop it?

Her touch was comfort I didn't deserve. I'd been my brother's enforcer for so long I barely knew what it meant to be a peaceful man. I was a monster in every way that counted but one: I'd never hurt someone I loved. But someone had hurt Frannie because I loved her, and I hadn't been good enough to stop them.

No one should feel safe around me. But her fingers laced through mine, and her eyes rested on me steadily, like I could bring her peace. And, if I was honest with myself, I wanted to. I wanted to bring *someone* peace with all this violence within me. She looked up at me, those long-lashed azure eyes wide with worry. And fear.

I'd seen Rhiannon Brontë fight with the grace of a dancer. I'd seen her move so fast and so quietly she might have been a spirit herself. She was lethal grace embodied, the only person in Orphium with as much blood on their hands as me. The fear in her eyes nearly killed me. But it wasn't directed at me. She showed me her fear because she *wasn't* afraid of me.

What was happening here wasn't possible, and I knew she'd seen the movement in the bedroom wallpaper, as I had. It's why I'd barely left her side. There was no telling what might have happened if she'd been alone.

The strongest of spirits ever recorded could possess a

parapsych for eternity. Malefics fed off fear, guilt, sadness —shame—and people like Rhiannon and I were lousy with those emotions. To think of something getting inside her, twisting all that drew me to her. It scared me. And I thought it might scare her too—she had that look in her eye, like she understood that what was happening here wasn't normal. It wasn't right.

My throat clenched tight around the thought, our combined fear nearly choking me. Was I allowed to take comfort in her? Was I allowed even one small measure of respite?

Slowly, so slowly it nearly stopped my breath, I let my fingers close around hers. As I did, she nodded, determination in her eyes. "What are you going to get on your pizza?" she asked, as though we were taking a walk around the neighborhood. She began walking again, drawing me close any time I fell even slightly behind.

"Extra mushrooms," I answered, knowing it was her favorite way to order her pizza.

"Excellent," she responded, weaving through the back beds of the garden, where foxglove and gladiolas waved in the breeze amongst the echinacea, allium and yarrow. They were all completely dry, as though it hadn't poured rain all morning.

It was a simple kind of oddness, something easy to miss. But in its simplicity, there was an eerie reality. Whatever magic worked here, it went against all natural order. Not even the strongest miracle worker could go against the weather, the seasons—the basis of life.

It was *wrong*.

I held tighter to her hand. The smooth silk of her skin contrasted with the worn-in calluses of a warrior's palms. That was Rhiannon in a nutshell, lethal silk. A rosy-pink

Elephant Hawk moth fluttered on to some honeysuckle as I relished the feeling of her hand in mine.

I frowned, glancing up at the sun. The moths were nocturnal, and by the sun's position, it was high noon. Before I could say anything, Rhiannon walked toward the place where the garden gate was. Or where it should have been. The closer we got, the thicker the hedge of white roses became.

Rhiannon's breath caught, and she made a little choking noise, her eyes widening, though her movements returned to that same slow, smooth cadence she'd used before. Then her molars ground together, her jaw clenching so tightly I thought she might crush her own teeth.

Her hand slipped out of mine as she rushed forward, apparently seeing something I did not—or perhaps could not. She tore at the hedge. I feared the thorns would cut her, but she came to no harm. Neither did she do any. The hedge was unchanged. Rhiannon glanced back at me, pure frustration in her eyes as she drew her sword.

I stepped back, letting her do her worst, but also admiring the miracle of her having pulled a sword straight from her spine. I'd asked her about that after the heist, and she'd admitted it wasn't always totally comfortable. Her face had gone so serious then. So guilt-ridden.

The Maere had not always left their swords in their metaphysical sheaths. There was a time, centuries ago, when they'd worn them at their waists. I remembered it. When the Orphium Maere's swords had been stolen, the rest of the warrior women in Palladiere and Aradios had all taken to keeping them hidden. And now that the Orphium Maere had their swords back, they did the same.

Whatever Rhiannon saw or sensed was beyond me at the moment, but I trusted her. Trusted her instincts. I'd done my research on the assassin. I'd read all of the Consulate's records I had clearance for that detailed missions she'd been a part of.

Ember Verona might be the most talented warrior in Orphium, but Rhiannon Brontë was a brilliant strategist. She missed nothing, and was so often several steps ahead of her opponents that it had piqued the Consulate's interests.

Too much. It was likely why they didn't want to let her go now.

If I was honest with myself, I'd admired Rhiannon from afar for years. I'd just never thought I'd have a chance at having coffee with her, let alone being in such close proximity to her. There was a part of me that didn't want to leave the cottage now, but we *needed* to go.

Rhiannon hacked at the hedge, but made no headway. I watched as she grew more and more frustrated. Something bothered me about the moth. I turned from Rhiannon, but only slightly, keeping her in my periphery as I glanced back at the honeysuckle. The Elephant Hawk moth was approaching the exact same bloom it had been a moment ago, rather than having moved on.

"Stop," I said. "It won't do any good. Look. The garden, it's on a loop."

Rhiannon did as I asked, her chest heaving slightly with the labor of her rage. She followed my gaze easily, watching as the little pink moth drew nectar from the honeysuckle, disappeared, and then appeared again, as though out of thin air. Her eyes moved over the garden.

"It isn't," she said after a moment of appraisal. That was not at all the conclusion I expected her to draw. "Not exactly."

"What do you mean?" It certainly looked as though the garden was looping. "Look at the moth."

"Yes," she agreed. "I see it. Now look at the tree branches. Focus on those white pines."

I watched as they followed the same pattern of movement, again, on a loop.

"Now look at the birches. See the raven that keeps landing on the branch near the birdhouse?"

I followed her line of sight. I saw the bird. "There shouldn't be ravens here, not in summer." Just like the moth should not be appearing in full day.

Rhiannon nodded. "Now," she murmured, stepping closer to me. "Try to watch them all at once."

I relaxed my gaze, trusting her. It took a few moments, and then I saw it. They *were* all looping, but separately.

"Wait for it," she whispered. "Watch the birches this time."

I saw it. The split second the leaves turned gold. It looked like a trick of light, but it wasn't. The birches looped through their autumnal color for the briefest of moments.

"Keep watching," she said. "I'm going to try something. Don't take your eye off the loops you've recognized." I nodded. Behind me, the sound of Rhiannon hacking at the hedge began again. "Now," she shouted, the sound of her hacking intensifying.

I wasn't sure what she meant for a split second, but then I saw it. Three more loops began. The noise behind me stopped. "The hedge is thicker than before," she noted as she came to stand next to me. "What happened?"

I pointed to the black cat slipping around the corner of the house, moving towards the front yard. Then the reappearance of the iced tea pitcher. Next, the shutter on one of the attic windows shuddered in the breeze, but made no sound.

"It's not one loop," I said, fear gripping hold of me,

finally. "It's dozens, and the more we try to leave, the thicker they get around us."

She sheathed her sword, her usually voluptuous lips pressed into a grim line. "Shall we try the phone?"

Both of us knew what we'd find, but I nodded anyway, following her back into the house. Rhiannon lifted the phone's receiver and dialed Hemlock House's number. I could hear the dial tone, plain as day. It was as though she hadn't made a call. She tried again, but still, nothing.

"Do you want to try?" she asked.

I shook my head, then had a hunch and opened the fridge. The food inside looked good, but I had a feeling about it. "What do you see?" I asked.

She stared at the fridge for a moment, then touched her back, her fingers going around the invisible hilt of her sword. "First, I see the fixings for a turkey dinner. Milk. Eggs. The usual for a fridge at the turn of the century."

I nod. It wasn't what I saw, but that didn't matter.

"When I touch my sword and focus, it's empty. The light isn't even on. But the rest of the room is the same."

My stomach, which had clenched tighter and tighter as we followed her experiments, now twisted into knots. This was why no one could get out once the Cottage had hold of them.

"Shit," I swore. "This is worse than I thought."

CHAPTER 6

RHIANNON

I DIDN'T UNDERSTAND the technicalities of what Eryx explained, about what was possible for spirits and what wasn't, which vexed me. This infernal secret-keeping between parapsych Dynasties was for our own survival, but it meant that in situations like these, when our survival depended on both of us sharing knowledge, I was at a disadvantage.

He leaned back against the blue tile of the kitchen counter, his back to the sink. The floral tattoos on his forearms moved as he talked. Eryx talked with his hands quite a bit. He was a patient teacher, ignoring my frustration as I asked question after question about the metaphysics of spiritual energy and what rules there were around Echoes. If the spirits weren't looping, then it was hard for me to discern what they were doing, or how magic might be involved.

Finally, something clicked in my head. "It's like a finger trap."

His pale eyes lit up. "Yes. Exactly."

That was the part that was magical. "All the different

loops have been woven together, and the more the living try to leave, the tighter they pull."

Eryx nodded, a sigh escaping him. The relief my understanding brought him disappeared quickly. He was puzzling through the same thing I was—who had enough power to do something like this? Even on the island, this would have been quite a feat.

"Was Cassandra Necroline capable of something like this?" I asked, remembering his theory that this had something to do with his uncle's wife. "Would she be able to orchestrate something of this magnitude?"

He stared up at the ceiling, a thoughtful look crossing his face. "It's hard to say, to be honest. My first instinct is to say no. She was a Seer, not a necromancer. Roman might have been able to pull something like this off in life, but in death? No. Most spirits don't have the ability to wield their parapsych powers after death, let alone the kind of skill it would take to weave these loops."

It might have been the most I'd ever heard him say at once. I hopped up onto the butcher block counter. At least nothing inside the cottage was looping. Not that I could see anyway. But the atmosphere here was weird.

The usual sounds that made up a house in the city were simply not present. The perpetual ambient noise of traffic, sirens, people talking, were all suspiciously absent. It was too quiet.

Eryx continued, his voice growing more thoughtful by the moment. "But Cassandra is a curious case. Why did she only have the one life-altering vision, and then never another?"

It was my turn to shrug. Somewhere in the house the whispering had stirred up again. The words were still indiscernible to me, but the voices of the dead sent chills through me. "Sometimes that happens."

I didn't say it, but we both thought it—that happened to weak Cognoscenti—but weak Seers didn't predict enormous natural disasters. In fact, most modern Seers, ones born in the last century anyway, didn't have the capability to predict such huge events at all.

They were excellent at short term visions, and had developed a variety of skills to hone their powers further, but if there were Cognoscenti with large-scale powers, they kept them quiet, and for good reason. The Authority tended to disappear Seers whose talent was too accurate.

Eryx frowned, pausing to listen to the whispers for a moment before continuing. "Yes, sometimes a parapsych has one powerful emanation, and then no others... but that's not what I remember happening to her."

He was right, now that I thought about it. There had been rumors about her for a short while—maybe when she married Magnus and moved to Orphium? That part was hard to remember, but now I recalled that Cassandra's terrible reputation had come from the fact that her subsequent predictions had been *wrong*.

The intensity of the whispers increased, and I finally understood where my fear came from. Though the dead couldn't truly hurt me, they could see into me, know me in a way that I didn't usually allow.

I shook my head. "I wish we could visit the Library of Amarante."

Eryx's shoulders slumped. The mood in the kitchen had darkened. A feeling of helplessness danced at the periphery of my mind, alluring in its promise that if I would simply give up, this could all be over sooner. Perhaps something similar took place in Eryx's mind, because he pushed off the kitchen counter, shaking his head.

"Why *can't* we visit the library?" he asked, turning quickly to look out the window. He peered out at the garden for a long moment. "We can't go back the way we came… but we might be able to go further in."

Further in. I wasn't sure what he meant, but the thought of it was a disconcerting idea. What other choice did we have, though? "All right," I agreed. "Let me freshen up a little and then we can try."

More than anything, I needed a few moments to myself. It was rare for me to feel afraid. I had been alive for so long, and seen so much, that very little scared me anymore. But this place… being trapped here… it frightened me.

And it wasn't just the way the spirit energy was too strong here. It was Eryx, being locked in here with him. I was terrified for him to see me the way the spirits did. Terrified for him—for anyone—to know me so deeply.

Terrified, yes. But despite that, some intrusive impulse within me wanted it. Desired it. Craved it. It practically burned within me, this idea that letting him in would *feel good*. But I didn't make decisions according to what would feel good. I made decisions based on what would be right to do, or most efficient.

Quickly, in the gleaming bathroom at the top of the stairs, I splashed my face with cold water. There was nothing efficient about being here. Why had I come? This had been a foolish, impulsive decision, and I so rarely made those. I took a risk and now both Eryx and I were stuck. When I raised my face to the mirror, the face that looked back at me was not my own. It was the spirit from the garden, dressed in corpse garb.

I bit back my yell of surprise, then blinked. It was just

me in the mirror. I knew better than to second-guess myself as my heart raced. The spirit had been there. It was trying to frighten me. I took several steadying breaths, then marched out of the bathroom. I wasn't going to be intimidated by a dead person.

In the bedroom, I grabbed a crossbody bag from one of my suitcases and slung it across my chest, then stared at the walls. Defiance rose in me. "Just try and scare me," I whispered.

I don't have to try, *Rhiannon,* said an unfamiliar voice in my head.

I did my best not to shudder. "You are dead, and I will never die."

There are fates worse than death, and if you're not careful you will find all of them.

It sounded like a threat, and I didn't take kindly to threats, and I most certainly didn't negotiate with bullies. "Well," I breathed, my heart racing. "Thank you for the heads up."

Without another word, I made my way downstairs. Eryx waited in the front hallway of the cottage. I stopped on the landing, using the gilded mirror that hung there to apply a swipe of deep rose lipstick with a blurring effect that made my lips look as though they'd just been kissed. As I stepped into the foyer, Eryx's eyes slid from the window in the arched front door to me.

"Gorgeous," he murmured, so softly I wondered if he actually meant for me to hear him. Before I could think too hard about it, he cleared his throat. "Did you know the front door opens to Eighth Ave?"

I frowned, trying to work the geography out in my mind. It made sense. The property Hemlock House and Oleander Cottage sat on had been the historical site of the Necroline Dynasty's first seat, back in Orphium's feudal days. The lot was huge. It wasn't out of the realm of possibility that the front door of the cottage might open onto one of the chicest streets in the district.

"Really?" I asked. "How close are we to the original Delicia's?"

A slow grin spread over Eryx's face. "If this works, we could go."

I nodded. "If this works, it should be our first stop."

Eryx took a deep breath, then opened the front door. I followed closely. The rose hedge was thick here, the heady scent of the blooms filling my nostrils as we walked towards the wrought-iron gate a short distance away. The sounds of the city street were more apparent the further we went. It was comforting that at least they existed here in the past, or wherever it was that we were.

It was obvious we'd gone through some kind of portal, but how much was real and how much was illusion was still a mystery. We paused by the gate. Like the garden, there was discord between what I saw and what I heard.

Sounds of the city bustled around us, but almost no one was on the street. No cars, no throng of people rushing to and fro. It was afternoon here, summer, which meant that it was hazy, not sunny but not cloudy. The sky was a faint shade of pale green, like it might storm.

That gave me no information at all. Orphium was always on the brink of a storm. It was bizarre though that there were no throngs of people, only the sounds they would have made if they were here. And then I saw her, the post-lady, coming our way. She had the gate open before she saw us. Even then, she recognized we were there, but only barely.

Eryx greeted her. "Good day."

She nodded, but continued moving past him to slide the mail through the slot in the front door. I stepped into her path. I wanted to try something. "Excuse me, has my copy of Women's Watch Weekly come?"

The post-woman stopped, her eyes flickering to a spot just past me. "No, Mrs. Necroline. They won't be in until next week."

Mrs. Necroline. I glanced at Eryx, who nodded once. He'd caught that too. The skin on my arms prickled with a sudden chill. I shivered, thinking of the spirit in corpse garb. Could that have been Cassandra? Was she dead? That didn't matter right now. We needed to find out how this worked.

"Can you see me?" I asked on a whim, despite the fact that she'd addressed my question. Her eyes flickered to mine, and then she was gone. Simply not there any longer. I glanced at Eryx, who shook his head. He had no answers for me. "Best not to address anyone directly, then?"

He held out an arm for me. "I think not."

As we stepped out onto the street, the mail carrier approached again. This time, her hair was pulled into a severe bun, her shoes a slightly newer style than the ones she'd worn previously. There were laugh lines around her eyes that had not been there before. She nodded briefly to us, but again, it was as though she hardly saw us.

Eryx led me onto the street. It was true, we stood where the residential section of Eighth Ave began, a block away from the old Delicia's. The air was neither warm nor cold. It wasn't like the garden; this was something else. Like there was no weather at all.

No breeze, though the trees that lined the sidewalk all moved. No warmth from the sun that finally peeked out of the stormy green haze. No whiff of petrichor from the plants. Nothing smelled of anything, nor felt like anything. The disconnect between senses disconcerted me almost more than the garden had. We walked for half a block without encountering another person. The sidewalks should have been bustling, but they were not.

We passed a haberdashery I remembered from a period long before this one. I stopped in front of it, watching as a salesperson inside showed a lovely straw hat… to no one. Eryx froze next to me, the bulk of his muscles clenched tight.

The next shop was a bookstore. No one was inside, but the books moved on their own. A cobbler was next, a shop from a century before Cassandra Necroline's time in Orphium. It looked as though it had been burned. I glanced at Eryx. I knew the story of how his parents died. Hundreds of years ago, the radical anti-parapsych sect known as the Chiorics had burned their parents' shop to the ground, killing the Necroline brothers' parents and their closest family friend.

What did Eryx see when he looked into the burned-out shop? Did he think of his parents? Or was he thinking of the time twenty years ago when he and Ares had given the order to burn our house down, so gravely injuring Sera that she was barely recovered, even now? I wasn't going to ask him, and he offered nothing, but his eyes were sad, if guarded.

We reached Delicia's, which was a pastel dreamland just as I remembered it, though no one worked the counter, nor were there any customers. There was, however, music.

The song playing on the old transistor radio behind the counter would have been old when Delicia's was new. The song had been meant to be playful at the time it was written, about a man who considered himself royalty and the woman he wanted to possess. As I stood there, listening to the lyrics, they sounded sinister, though the song had not been altered, as far as I could tell. Perhaps I was simply on edge.

Eryx stared at the pastries in the case with longing, apparently not as affected by the music as I was. "Are they real?"

I had to try not to let this place get to me. With a deep breath, I reached back and touched my sword, expecting it to be like the refrigerator at home, empty. But nothing changed. The pastries were real enough.

I didn't have to understand it; I just wanted to eat. I skirted behind the counter. "Which ones do you want?"

Eryx smiled. "I'd love one of those big buttery croissants, and some of that brie."

He peeked around the counter as I pulled pastries out of the glass case. The vintage espresso machine was complicated. I didn't know how to use it. But Eryx got right to work, and in moments he had the machine purring under his fingers. His hands were beautiful, his large, deft fingers moving with precision and ease.

A weak beam of summer sunlight cut through the green haze outside, and bathed him in otherworldly golden light. Every movement he made was pure, graceful precision. If I begged him to touch me, what could he make me feel? A flush of heat up the back of my neck nearly made me dizzy.

To stop myself from thinking about what other uses I could find for Eryx's fingers, I piled food onto plates, then cautiously placed a cheese puff in my mouth. It did not turn to ash, nor did it taste stale or rotten. It was perfectly soft and delightfully cheesy. I moaned softly as I swallowed.

Eryx glanced at me, worry practically living in his furrowed brow. "All right?"

"Fucking heavenly," I replied, licking my lips. "I was so hungry."

He watched me closely, his eyes tracing the place my tongue had touched my lips. The way he looked at me was calm, confident, as though he was perfectly fine with me knowing he was watching me. Slowly, he stepped forward, his eyes still on my mouth, and plucked a small eclair off my plate and popped it into his.

As he chewed, his eyes met mine. "Thank the Saints this is real."

The way he looked at me sent all thoughts out of my head.

Before I could think of an answer, he turned away and was steaming milk he found in the icebox. Questions about how this illusion could work raced through my mind. There were no true mages outside of the island that the rest of the Maere and I grew up on. Not anymore. Not after my mother drew the mists in.

Or at least that's what I'd thought for myriad years. Eryx picked up our mugs. "Lattes are ready."

I nodded, carrying our plates to the sky-blue laminate tables that lined the back wall of the bakery. The chairs were upholstered in a plush aquamarine velvet and a blush gingham wallpaper gave the bakery a soft glow that was eerie in the quiet nothingness of the day; the radio had stopped playing music. The coffee steamed and smelled real enough, and that broke through the unnaturalness of the rest of the atmosphere.

With food and coffee in front of me, I was ravenous. Apparently, Eryx was too, because neither of us spoke as we tucked into our food. Neither of us had to eat the way mortals did; parapsychs could go weeks without eating, and technically, I could forego food altogether and not die. But it wasn't a comfortable feeling. Our bodies were still human, despite our immortality. As such, they craved food, sleep, sustenance of all kinds.

I slowed down, not wanting to be sick from eating too fast. Eryx sensed my purpose and did the same, leaning back in the booth across from me. He took a napkin from the white enamel dispenser on the table and wiped a bit of foam from his upper lip. He did it slowly, watching me eat as though it were the most interesting thing he'd ever seen.

When he spoke, his voice was quiet, almost as though he was afraid someone might hear. "This reeks of magic."

I nodded. "It does."

A long silence stretched between us. It might have been uncomfortable for someone else, but I liked it when people took their time to think about what they wanted to say, rather than filling space with empty words. And now that I'd had something to eat, I could appreciate that Eryx wasn't a chatter. Not that he was silent as a rule. He talked plenty when he had something to say.

In that way, we were very similar. It's why I was all right with him coming with me to Oleander Cottage. He was an excellent clairsentient, probably the best in the city, and he didn't blather on unnecessarily.

And he fills out that shirt in all the best ways possible. I stared at his forearms, not registering the floral tattoos, but focusing on the musculature beneath them, my mind drifting to pleasant places.

Pleasant places I had no business imagining. I wasn't fit for a lover of any kind, and certainly not the brother of my commanding officer and oldest friend's partner. If Ember and I both got involved with the Necrolines it would look bad when Eryx and I returned to public life.

It might make people trust Ember less. Trust *us* less. Orphium's parapsych population needed the Maere more than ever. And they needed our alliance with the Necroline Dynasty not to turn into a shitshow of broken romances. Ares and Ember *seemed* solid, but who knew what had happened since we left. She might have murdered him in his sleep by now, for all I knew.

It wouldn't be the first time.

"What are you thinking about?" Eryx asked. There was a calm tenor to his voice. Not a hint of demand, just pure curiosity.

I let myself smile all the way. For the first time in a long time, the expression warmed me all the way through. It wasn't half-fake, or fake even a bit. It was a little too easy to smile around Eryx. *Dangerous.*

I kept smiling. "Did you ever hear about the time that Ember murdered the Duke of Westborough in his sleep?"

Eryx smiled back at me, shaking his head slowly. "The self-proclaimed Duke of the Wastelands?"

I nodded. "It was before the Accords. He was breeding *unicorns.*" Eryx's nose wrinkled in disgust. I nodded, agreeing with the sentiment. "They were wretched, stinky things. Sera set them all free." I let my eyes roll a little, though I kept smiling. "Lara helped her while Max lectured them both about the dangers of interfering with experiments gone wrong."

Now Eryx snickered. "Sera's a bit of a bleeding heart, isn't she?"

"Pure starshine, that one," I agreed. "Anyway, while they were doing that, Ember seduced the Duke." I paused. "He *was* quite handsome."

"But evil, I assume," Eryx added.

I nodded vigorously, the waves of my hair falling in my face before I pushed them back. "Oh, yes. No one spends that much time with unicorns and is anything but evil." I shuddered at the thought of the terrible creatures that roamed the Wastelands between the Three Cities in roving, murderous herds. "Anyway, she seduced him and killed him in his sleep. I was supposed to do it, but she said she couldn't stand the sound of him snoring another moment."

Eryx let out a loud laugh. "Ember Verona is quite a character."

I nodded, my heart softening at the memory of my sistren. We'd been together for so long. Had so many memories. So many stories. And once, I'd reveled in them.

Now all my memories were tainted with the knowledge that my own mother had thought me a burden to my cohort. So unqualified to be here that she and the Admiral orchestrated a massively complex plan to steal the Orphium Maere's swords, leaving us vulnerable and looked down upon for years so we could prove ourselves.

So I could prove *my*self—my sistren punished along with me. Shame filled me to the brim. My fork clattered to the table, emotion overcoming me. A hot tear slipped down my cheek. Every instinct in me told me to cast my eyes downward, to get myself under control.

But Eryx Necroline held my gaze. He did not look away. The mirth he'd given me so freely a moment before was gone with both our laughter, his face redrawn in hard, serious lines. "Are you thinking of your mother?"

I nodded, another tear falling. I would not look down, but neither could I speak.

"What made you think of her?"

"Every story I have is fouled by her deceit," I choked out.

It was strange to tell someone something so honest. Stranger still was having been asked. Ember and the others rarely asked what or how I was feeling or thinking. It wasn't their fault, not really. I'd discouraged such things for the majority of our relationship, not wanting to burden them unnecessarily with my thoughts.

But now I *wanted* to talk, and it seemed Eryx wanted to listen. "Every moment that I've cherished between the

Maere… now I wonder… were they all resentful of me being there the whole time?"

Eryx's eyes narrowed, but only slightly. "Have you asked them?"

I shook my head, finally averting my eyes as I took a shuddering breath. "No. I can't bear to hear the answer. I thought I had done enough before we came here. I thought the entire island believed I was qualified. But if she had to go to such lengths to force us all to prove ourselves…" I trailed off. The rest of the sentence was too horrible to think about, let alone say aloud.

"Maybe none of them ever wanted you," he finished for me. "Maybe they've spent every day of the past three million years hating your guts." He said it in a matter-of-fact way, not taunting, not sarcastic, just completely neutral, like he could read my mind.

"Am I so transparent?" I asked.

Slowly, he shook his head. "No. But it's easy to recognize those feelings in others when they live inside you."

I lifted my eyes back to his. "Why would you ever feel that way? Everyone loves you."

CHAPTER 7

ERYX

Everyone loves you. How was she so imperceptive and still so good at her job? She was Orphium's most successful assassin, after all. I saw her so clearly, and she didn't see me at all.

Or perhaps she simply sees the best in you, a small voice inside me said. *Perhaps she likes you more than she lets on.*

Foolishness. Rhiannon knew exactly what kind of monster I was and why it was a good idea to stay away from me. She'd always seemed like someone with her head on straight. She might be a little down right now, but she wasn't going to blunder into some kind of affair with me. Those thoughts were not helpful.

Outside, thunder rolled, sending vibrations through the shop, but none of the glass or china made a sound. I glanced out at the color of the sky. It had shifted to a darker green, a color I hadn't seen in Orphium since I was a child, pre-industrialization.

What *was* this place? It was difficult to believe we were inside a complex illusion, but nor could I believe we were actually in some pocket realm or shadow dimension.

I took a long last sip of my latte, swallowing my bitterness and worry. When I set the cup back onto the saucer, it disappeared. I scanned the open shelves behind the counter, and sure enough, it had reappeared next to the other cups.

I shook my head at the strange phenomenon, returning my mind to the conversation at hand. "There is a difference between people being attracted to danger and being loved," I said. "Ares is feared and hated because he makes the tough calls. People want to *fuck* me, because I'm the one who executes them."

That was the hard truth. People wanted into my bed for a few nights, maybe even a few months, but it never went deeper. Any time I tried, I hit a wall. It was humiliating. Another crash of thunder outside brought on the rain.

It wasn't much different with friends. Some wanted a taste of Dynasty life. A look behind the curtain of the upper echelons of Orphium's Trinity. But what they did not ever want was my *true* friendship. No one wanted to befriend someone who might someday murder them.

Rhiannon nodded slowly, staring first out the window as the light grew darker on the street, before her eyes turned to me. "What about Avaline Reyes? Does she feel that way about you?"

An Av-shaped hole in my chest made me shake my head. I missed my best friend. Avaline had never once judged me. Not when we were children, and certainly not now. But there were times that I dreamed about it. Sometimes I woke up sure she hated me, and I would jog to her place in the middle of the night and stand outside her door until she opened it.

I never had to wait long. She was the best friend a person could have. She never asked me to stop waking her in the wee hours. Av just put on a pot of coffee and we watched cartoons until the dream-feeling died down. Until I knew there was one person in the world who loved me for exactly who I was, not who I could trick her into thinking I might be.

"Av gets me," I answered. "I'm more than a tool to her."

"And your brother?" she asked, lightning striking so near that the thunder should have shook the cafe, rattled the china. But it didn't. The sound was loud, but the world did not react the way it should. Rhiannon didn't seem to notice. "Does he see you as more than a tool?"

I realized what she was doing. "Yes. I'm lucky we're close," I answered, then waited for one, two, three heartbeats. "Do you want me to ask you these same questions about the Maere?"

Rhiannon sighed so dramatically I thought she might feign a swoon. "Please don't be reasonable right now. I want to wallow."

It was the most adorable thing I'd ever seen. My fucking heart swelled a size or two in that moment, and I wanted nothing more than to pull her onto my lap and rock her against me until she'd cried every one of those unshed tears. It was all going to come out, eventually. It had to. She'd locked too much away.

And just like that, I'd made a decision. I came here to help her, to protect her. The more I observed her, the clearer it was that she was incredibly unkind to herself. She seemed to believe she didn't deserve the benefit of her own care. I was good at taking care of other people. It wasn't something I let myself do very often—not after Frannie—but this was different.

We were apparently stuck here together, and I was the only one who *could* keep her safe. For the time we had together, I was going to make sure she was rested and well-fed. If she'd let me help her unwind, I'd take that on too, risky as that would be for my heart.

Never one to hesitate once I'd made a choice, I stood. "Wallow on the move."

"We should clean up," she said, but as we stood, the dishes all disappeared. Her pale skin flushed pink, and for a dangerous moment, my mind drifted to ways *I* might elicit that reaction from her.

I cleared my throat, banishing that thought entirely. When she was ready, if she was ready, I would be there. But I couldn't go down those roads on my own. "This is witches' work, Rhiannon," I said as another crack of thunder made no impact on the cafe. "Whatever is going on here, it's deeper than spirits with unfinished business. This is *magic*."

A rash of gooseflesh raised on her bare arms, the flush subsiding. "I know. We should get to the Library."

I nodded, and we made our way towards the door. I wondered if we should find an umbrella, but Rhiannon had already pushed the door open. As soon as we stepped outside, we were back at the garden gate—as though we'd never left Oleander Cottage. The weather was calm, though the sky was still that old shade of green.

Without speaking, we both went through the gate and back to the street, only to end up back inside the garden again. Twice more we tried this. Twice more, we found ourselves staring at the wrong end of the gate.

"I don't think we can *intend* to go to the Library," she said. "But I'm not going hungry again. There's a grocer on Eighth and VanHausen, or at least there should be. It's been there for nearly a century."

I agreed to this change in plans. This time, the gate squeaked open, and we stepped onto the sidewalk. It was nighttime outside the gate. Rhiannon glanced up at me as we walked, the neon lights that had switched on in the dark illuminating her pale skin.

"There are rules to this, then."

The pervasive nothingness of the atmosphere was still disconcerting enough that I wanted to turn and face the horrors of Oleander Cottage rather than this barren city, devoid of life, but I nodded anyway. "Apparently so."

Steam poured out of the vents as we walked, but that made no sense. The night air was hot, there shouldn't be steam. The streets were just as empty as before, but there was no rain. We walked in silence, both of us obviously perturbed by the quiet.

Like Delicia's, the little market was full of food that Rhiannon determined to be real, but no one was working when we entered. The walls had last been painted a shade of green, but they were peeling now, revealing layers of other colors beneath, and traces of old wallpaper.

Rain pelted the windows, storms blowing through the city in rapid turns that weren't true to life. I stared at the way the green neon sign across the street for the local apothecary reflected in the raindrops splattering the window. An ominous heaviness hung in the humid air of the grocer.

"Do you think this is how people died in the Cottage before?" Rhiannon mused as she selected oranges, while I selected vegetables for salads and soups.

The oranges disappeared. The entire crate was simply gone. She froze. We both froze. Nothing else disappeared. Slowly, I shook my head at her. She drew in a heavy breath and changed the subject.

"What was this neighborhood like when you were a child?"

Rhiannon's question came wrapped in significance and it was my job to decipher its meaning. It was obvious this world behind the real world, this illusion the Cottage existed within, was listening somehow, almost sentient. There was no doubt that we were being watched, and that being cautious going forward was necessary if we ever wanted out of here. A few seconds ticked by as I sorted out what she was up to.

What did the question mean?

It was a test of whatever magic governed this place. Anything that might get us closer to finding a way out was not allowed, here in the deeper aspects of the illusion. We found that out by trying to go to the Library. But exploring our own pasts? Perhaps that would be permitted. I could wish she hadn't chosen something so painful for me to think of, but that too might serve a purpose.

"Busy," I said, feeling cautious. We both waited. The food remained. "My parents' shop was close to here." Still, nothing changed. "Would you like to see it?"

There was a slight thickening to the air. Not a change in temperature or quality, but a closeness, a contraction of sorts. Rhiannon's eyes widened slightly. "I would. Perhaps tomorrow? I think we should unpack."

We waited. Nothing changed about the shop, but neither did that oppressive quality of the air decrease. Finally, I nodded. "Yes, and then perhaps I could make you dinner."

The air returned to its normal consistency. *Go slow*, seemed to be the message. The oranges returned. Rhiannon put a few in her basket. "That would be nice. We might need to settle in."

Her words and tone were neutral enough, but the message behind them was hardly masked. She thought we might be stuck here for a while. Much as I hated to admit it, it was clear she might be right.

CHAPTER 8

RHIANNON

Eryx was an excellent cook—better than excellent, actually. He was good enough to be a chef. When I got drowsy at the table over wine, he sent me to bed early, offering to sleep on the couch. I let him, not really taking in what that would mean.

Now, I stood above him in the little blue sitting room, gloomy summer light filtering through the leaded glass windows, barely suppressing laughter. The "couch" was an uncomfortable looking divan and Eryx was spilling off it. His shirt was off, tossed to the floor, and I wasn't sure what he wore under the crocheted throw blanket over his lap, but it couldn't be much, because one of his muscular thighs was showing.

"This looks terrible," I whispered, in an attempt to stop my salivating over the sight of his thick, beautiful body.

His eyes flew open and he grabbed my arm, as though by instinct. "Sorry," he breathed, but he didn't let go. "You startled me."

I tilted my head to one side, unable to keep from smirking. "Are you comfy?"

There was a hint of amusement glimmering in his eyes. His eyes roamed slowly over me, assessing the situation. When he came to a conclusion of one kind or another, a bare hint of a smile played at the corners of his lips. "Perfectly. Do you want coffee?"

"Yes," I answered.

He let go of my arm and tossed off the blanket, revealing that he was dressed only in a pair of tight black boxer briefs. My cheeks flushed hot. Now, he grinned. This man that had hardly smiled in all the weeks I'd known him was laughing and smiling in my presence.

I did my best to hold my ground, to not look away, but also not to look too hard as the muscles in his chest and stomach flexed as he got up.

"Great," he replied, passing me on the way to the kitchen.

I caught sight of his absolutely perfect ass as he went and had to stop myself from groaning.

"You can look," he called out, over his shoulder. "I don't mind."

All I could do was giggle. I clapped a hand over my mouth, tears forming in my eyes. I hadn't giggled in decades. Laughed, sure. But this? This kind of mirth was something else. It was girlish. Sweet. Almost innocent.

All things I was not.

As much as he was changing around me, I was changing around him. Despite the pressure of being stuck here, of the incessant whispers, and the strange state of whatever haunted realm the house existed in, there was relief in feeling good. In accepting that even a few things could be good for me.

The sounds of water filling the kettle filled my ears, and I backed up against the wallpapered living room wall, clasping my hands to my chest. Tears flowed down my cheeks in earnest now. I had no idea why I was crying. Just a little bit of genuine, unguarded emotion had triggered a torrent of feelings in me.

Something loosened in my chest that I had not known was tight to begin with. As my tears slowed, I wiped them from my cheeks. A wave of exhaustion, tinged with relief, washed over me. When I looked up, Eryx stood in the doorway.

"Are you okay?" he asked.

I nodded, only barely noticing his state of undress. "Yes, I think so."

His face had gone back to its usual serious expression, but there was worry there too. "You're not."

"I—" There was no use in denying it. "No, I'm not. Everything has been a lot lately."

He nodded. "You need to rest."

"Yes," I agreed. "I would do that better though, I think, if you would sleep upstairs with me."

He raised an eyebrow. "Scared of the dark?"

I smiled. "The wallpaper up there is a bit disconcerting. I think it behaves better when you are there, and the bed is big enough for us both." I paused, but he didn't say anything in response. "We're grownups, after all."

Slowly, he nodded. "We are." And like that, he was back to business. "Do you want cream in your coffee?"

"Yes… I can make it, if you prefer," I offered.

He shook his head. "No, that's fine." He looked outside. "The rain has stopped. Shall we take our coffee in the garden?"

"Yes," I agreed, following him into the kitchen.

I gathered pastries while he finished the coffee and we went together to the stone patio in the garden. Nothing was on the wrought-iron table as we approached, but right before I sat down, I found a black silk scarf and a small leather datebook in the chair I was about to sit in. I set the plate of pastries down and picked it up, half expecting it to disappear.

Neither the scarf, nor the datebook dissolved. I sat down quickly, worried that the loop might end before I got a chance to examine them. Eryx took the scarf from me as I sat. "C.N.," he said, holding the scarf up to show me where the initials had been embroidered at the corner of the silk in bright pink letters.

I nodded, opening the datebook to the page marked with a green velvet ribbon. There was an address and a time, but no name. "This is close by, isn't it?" I asked, showing the address to Eryx.

He glanced at it and nodded. "And look at the opposite page."

I did, finding a brief handwritten note from the previous day that only said, "roses' first bloom." I glanced around at the hedges that had closed in on us and watched the white roses bloom in real time. The day was gloomy, but unbearably hot and humid. The datebook disappeared, but the scarf remained.

"It looks like we have an appointment to keep," Eryx noted. "At Triomphe."

I let out a nervous laugh at the name of the famous atelier. They *only* made intimate apparel—and a few silk scarves. "I think I am supposed to wear the scarf," I said, not knowing where the thought had come from.

Eryx swallowed hard, setting the scarf down across the table from us. "I don't know how safe it is to do that."

I took a deep breath. "I am practically impervious to harm, and you are a necromancer. The worst that can happen is that something frightens me."

He looked at me for a long moment. It struck me that the two of us were playing through a rather domestic scene, him in his underwear and me in my nightgown, taking breakfast in the garden. When he finally nodded, I smiled, taking a long sip of my coffee. It was perfect.

"For the record," he said. "I know that you are more than capable in a fight. It's just obvious to me that you haven't been taking care of yourself."

It was one of the most straightforward, frank things that anyone had ever said to me. I raised my eyes to meet his with the same candor. "Correct. I am no good at that." It felt good to be honest about it. "I could try to explain, but I think you understand my position better than most."

After all, Eryx was second to Ares, as I was to Ember. He might not have come from an ancient royal line of witch queens, but he had been raised by Roman Necroline, as his own son. As far as I was concerned, that came with the exact same amount of high expectations as my mother had for me. He and I were cut from much the same cloth.

"I do," he replied. "More than you might think."

I set my coffee down, keeping my gaze steady on his. "I think you understand perfectly."

He looked down at his hands, which were clasped in his lap now. "Then let me be honest with you, Rhiannon." My breath caught at my name on his lips. The trepidation in his voice was nerve-wracking. "I want you to let me help you."

I swallowed the lump forming in my throat, my heart racing wildly. "And… how would you do that?"

When his eyes met mine again, they burned with a particular intensity I'd seen only a few times, and only when he was looking at me. "*Any* way that I can."

The emphasis on the word *any* set my thighs aflame. My mouth went so dry, I had to take another sip of coffee. I knew I had to be blushing, because my cheeks absolutely burned. I never blushed because I was never embarrassed.

But with him, it wasn't shame that caused me to flush scarlet—it was desire.

I wanted what Eryx Necroline suggested so badly, my body threatened to combust there and then. The part of me that should say no was nowhere to be found. All I could do was nod.

"Thank you." The words slipped from my lips before I could stop them.

Eryx kept his eyes on me. "I am fairly certain it is me who should be thanking you."

My skin felt as though it might melt off in the heat of the garden. Was he saying what I thought he was? It was so hard to tell. A slight breeze caught the scarf and it blew across the table. I bent to pick it up as it hit the ground and glanced across the table. I hadn't meant to, but I caught sight of the erection Eryx couldn't possibly hide in such scant garb.

At least that cleared up where we stood. But now I was flushed so pink that all my feelings were obvious as well. When I sat back up, he just smiled at me. "Eat your breakfast, Rhiannon. We have lingerie to buy."

I couldn't die, but I was sure the anticipation was going to kill me.

Somehow, we managed to shower, dress and make our way to Triomphe without incident, or another word. For once, it wasn't raining, but neither was it sunny. That same oppressive, green gloom hung over the city.

I wore Cassandra's scarf draped loosely around my neck. The sidewalk was hot, and the sound of birds chirping surprised me as we approached the wisteria covered shopfront.

"It feels a little more real here," Eryx said.

I nodded, staring through the front window of the shop. An attendant, dressed in a gown that would have been fashionable during Cassandra Necroline's time in Orphium, stood behind a marble-topped counter. The interior of the store was a fever dream of seafoam green walls, white marble tile, and lush fabrics.

"Here goes nothing," I said, as Eryx pushed open the door.

Triomphe smelled like a blend of the most expensive perfume possible, mixed with the heady scent of the giant bouquets that graced the table at the center of the shop. While there were very few of the store's intimate wares displayed here in the front of the shop, there was a vast assortment of silk scarves like the one I wore.

The attendant, a slender woman with sharp brown eyes and porcelain skin, smiled at us. Her ebony hair fell down her back in cultivated waves, held back by mother-of-pearl combs. "Mr. and Mrs. Necroline," she said, in a deep, rich tone. I dared not look at Eryx to see what he thought of her misidentification of us. "Your order is ready for viewing."

"Viewing?" Eryx asked, not missing a beat.

"Of course," the attendant said. "We know you like to view Mrs. Necroline's items before purchase. There is sparkling wine waiting for you, and I shall show myself out."

"Very good," Eryx answered, following the direction she'd gestured in.

As I passed the attendant, who headed towards the front door with a set of brass keys in her grip, she touched my arm lightly. "Behind the mirror," she murmured so softly I wondered if I had imagined it.

Before she reached the door, she was gone. Disappeared, just as the post-lady had. Eryx shook his head, almost in disbelief.

"What do we do?" I asked, not wanting to shatter whatever this was.

This appointment had been significant to Cassandra for some reason, and so far, this was our only clue to what might be at the heart of Oleander Cottage's haunting.

"I think we need to do what they came here to do, originally," he answered. "If you feel comfortable with that."

"Try on the lingerie?"

A flash of tight discomfort passed over his face, a clenching of muscles. "If you are all right with it."

I nodded. "I am. I just don't want to make a mistake."

The tightness in his shoulders receded a bit and to my vast relief, Eryx took a shuddering breath. He was as nervous as I was. I could take the lead here. As I passed him, I brushed my fingers through his, pulling him with me.

"Come watch me, then." He frowned, glancing back at the front of the store, as though he could hear something I couldn't. "What is it?"

He held up a finger. "The clerk. She's on the phone."

I listened, but couldn't hear a thing.

Eryx's eyes went cloudy. When he spoke, he sounded like himself, but also like the clerk that had helped us. "They're here." A long pause. "I made sure of it." Another pause. "Don't worry, she'll find it."

He blinked a few times, then shook his head. I couldn't wait for him to tell me the details. "Could you hear who she was talking to?"

Eryx shook his head. "No, but I think you need to go

back into the dressing room alone. Magnus wouldn't have gone back there with her."

The tone he used chilled me to the bone. Though I wasn't entirely sure what he was implying, it was clear it wasn't good. Slowly, I nodded. "I'll go put something else on."

His hand caught mine, his pale eyes worried. Eryx didn't say anything, but I felt his unspoken words, *Be careful.*

CHAPTER 9

ERYX

THE DRESSING ROOM WAS ELEGANT, the ceilings lower than out front, giving the room a more intimate appeal. Sparkling wine was laid out on a low brass table with a glass top, and a lush velvet settee sat behind it, giving me a view of the curtained space Rhiannon had disappeared behind. Dim light from crystal sconces hanging on the walls reflected from the gold-leafed ceiling, giving the room a soft glow.

It was difficult to believe Magnus and Cassandra had come here for romantic trysts as a married couple. That didn't seem much like my uncle, who had never been interested in anyone romantically, unless he had complete control of them. But perhaps that was the answer—he'd wanted her to be uncomfortable trying on the lacy underthings he bought for her. My stomach turned at the thought.

"Is everything all right?" I asked. She'd been in there for a while.

"Oh yes," Rhiannon answered, from behind the curtain. "Everything is beautiful." For a long moment, she

75

was quiet. My heart began to beat faster. "I think I have to show you, though, for this to work."

I almost asked what made her think that, but then the crushed velvet seafoam curtains opened. Every thought I'd ever had left my body. Rhiannon wore a light pink camisole, edged with the finest lace I'd ever seen. There was a matching set of little shorts. Her skin glowed like a pearl in the soft light.

"Fuck," I breathed. There was nothing else to say. I couldn't find words anyway.

"Do you think it's nice?" she asked.

I nodded, unable to say more, but there was a shade of disappointment in her wide blue eyes, a slight knitting of her brow. "Let me try another. There are eight."

Eight? I had no idea how I would make it through this. My cock strained against my jeans. I readjusted slightly, but there was no hiding it. She'd seen me at breakfast when she picked the scarf up, anyway. Surely, she knew by now that she had an effect on me.

The curtain opened again. This design was similar to the last, but this time the silk was ivory and the lace was a soft green. "What about this?" she asked, her voice low. "Is this better?"

Had she thought I didn't like the first set? *Saints.* "They are all very good," I managed to spit out. Without think-ing, I asked, "Are they comfortable?"

Now she smiled. She knew she had all the power here —she had to. "This is the softest silk I've ever felt."

Yes, Rhiannon knew exactly how hard my cock was for her. She was staring right at it. It was so easy with other people. So easy to say all the cheeky things that made them want me even more than they already had. But now it was me who wanted her. It was me who was unsure.

And I didn't want to play with her. Not that way. I

wanted whatever she would give me, and I'd meant what I said at breakfast. I would take care of whatever needs she wanted met, in any way she wanted.

And I would be grateful for the opportunity.

Rhiannon took a step outside the curtain, towards me. "Would you like to feel the fabric? Make sure it's to your taste?"

Heat rippled through me. There was only one answer to that. "Yes."

She took two more steps and then she stood between my legs. Her nipples were hard under the thin silk of the camisole, and up close, I saw that the fabric wasn't exactly sheer, but it was not opaque either. The shadow of her nipples showed through, the hint of the hair at the apex of her thighs.

"Feel how soft," she said.

I sat up, my hands curling around the back of her calves. If she wanted this, I would give it to her. "So soft," I said, sliding my hands up the back of her thighs, pulling her towards me.

And then I saw her face. The faraway look. The way her muscles had gone suddenly too loose, even though tension strung through every line of her body. It was one of the first signs of possession.

"Rhiannon," I barked. She swayed a little. "Rhiannon!"

She blinked again. This time, the light in her eyes was her own. "What just happened?"

"I don't know," I answered. Something in me moved, shifting without my permission. I touched her cheek; she was still disoriented from whatever spirit had its fingers in her. "I want you to go get dressed. We're leaving."

It didn't matter to me if we were on the right track. I wanted her out of here. Rhiannon was more affected by the haunting than I'd have expected. Until I figured out what was happening to her, I wasn't willing to risk a possession. I didn't have Ares' power with aura, which meant there was only one avenue I had if she were to become truly possessed, to use the vox spiritus on her.

And that was a risk I truly wasn't willing to take. The spirit voice was not meant to be used on the living. There were consequences for that. Ones I wasn't willing to risk Rhiannon's immortality on without knowing the intricacies of *why* the Maere didn't die.

"The attendant," she breathed. "She said there was something behind the mirror."

"Do you want me to come with you?" I asked. "To come get it, and to get dressed?"

She frowned up at me, her beautiful face narrowing with suspicion. "Just what is going on here?"

I swallowed hard. "I am not sure that now is the time to discuss this."

Rhiannon crossed her arms, her hip bumping out to one side. She looked so wholly herself. So self-possessed that it was hard to imagine there being room inside her for a spirit to take hold. "Tell me what you're worried about. Now."

Saints alive. I loved the way she bossed me around. And from the way her eyes dragged over me, lingering just below my belt, she knew I loved it. It was a dangerous game we were playing, but I was determined to win.

I straightened up a little, flexing my hips, just slightly. A flush crept over her

moonstone skin, but her eyes glittered with wicked power. She liked the way it felt to be in control of a situation she could understand, and I wanted her to feel powerful. I wanted her to use me like a tool in her arsenal, to give her every moment of control she needed in private to be able to carry that confidence into her public life.

I made a choice. "I'm worried you'll become possessed. Whatever this is—this place, this haunting—it's having a different effect on you than it is me."

She nodded once, but didn't say anything. Clearly, she waited for me to say more. Something coiled tight at the base of my spine, sending warmth through me. The way she nodded was so imbued with natural power that I was desperate to get on my knees for her, to serve her in whatever ways she wanted. It was the nod of a General to her Executive Officer, and there was nothing I wanted more than to be Rhiannon's XO.

"I want you to let me protect you in here," I explained. "I want you to trust what I tell you."

Her eyes narrowed as she licked her lips. She stepped forward, pressing a hand to my chest. "And when the time is right… Do you want me to…" Her eyes flicked up to mine, her silk-clad body pressing into me, "...do what you tell me to?"

I stared down at her, relishing the way her soft breasts felt pressed against me. My cock hardened, pressing into her belly. She stood so still, those azure eyes locked onto me. And then I felt it. The way her back arched, so slowly, her lips falling open as her breath quickened.

Without thinking, I slid one hand onto her back. She took a sharp breath in and it seemed that the world disappeared around us. The lights had dimmed in the dressing room, down to a glow so dim it might have been night. This wasn't the effects of being aroused, though we both certainly were.

Whatever this place actually was, it was reacting to us. I pulled her against me hard, letting myself get swept up in it for a moment. "Yes," I hissed. "I want you to trust me enough to know when it's time to let go and let me tell you what to do."

"Give it a try," she breathed, arching further into me. "Now, just to see how it feels."

"Kiss me," I said without thinking.

And before I could consider the wisdom of what I'd just said, she did. She was up on her tiptoes in an instant, her arms around my neck, her body melting into mine as her mouth claimed mine.

Rhiannon's mouth was exactly as I had imagined it would be; silky and soft, with a wicked tongue that made promises I was desperate for her to keep. Every moment drew us deeper together. My eyes fluttered open and the entire store had gone dark.

Outside, it was night. It had barely been lunchtime when we came in. She noticed at the exact moment I did, and pulled away from me, but just slightly. "What is going on?"

I shook my head. "I don't know. I think you should go see what's behind that mirror."

Slowly, she unraveled her limbs from mine, still in complete control. Still watching me watch her. But she nodded, slipping away from me to disappear behind the curtain. She left my heart racing and my cock hard.

Whatever this place was or was not, the thing happening between us was real.

When she walked out of the dressing room, she was fully dressed again, and she carried a small jar and a slip of paper. She handed the jar to me first. I frowned as I opened it, then brought it to my nose. The scent was familiar to me, after years of getting patched up after a fight. "Arnica, I think, but something else as well. Definitely a healing salve," I said, setting it down next to the champagne.

She handed me the note, her eyes wide with worry. "There was also this."

I opened the note. *It's not in the crypt any longer. Search the house.* On the next line it read, *This should help if things get too bad. –L*

Her voice was quiet as she asked, "Do you think Magnus was hurting Cassandra?"

Old fear thrummed through me as I sank onto the settee. "I don't know." I shook my head, covering my mouth with my hand, averting my eyes from hers. This was what I'd feared, and eventually she was going to know it all. This place was dragging things out of both of us. "Probably."

She watched me carefully, and I watched her right back. Fury rose in her eyes, as she searched my face for clues. "Okay," she said, a forced steadiness in her voice. "That's information."

I nodded, my mouth pressing into a grim line. "I'm sorry."

She sat next to me on the settee, angling her body towards mine. The lights had come up, but it was still dark outside. "For what?"

I wasn't sure why I'd apologized, and I was suddenly unable to look at her. "I don't know... It's just..." My molars gritted together, all the old fear rushing in. Of childhood, of what happened after Frannie. Of all the ways I'd changed in the years after, of the man I'd become. "What if I'm just like him?"

She stared at me, her eyes widening. And there it was. The same fear I felt, reflected in her eyes. "You see it, don't you? What I do? My job? The only reason I can do it is because I'm *just* like him."

"It isn't the same," she breathed, but the fear still lingered on her face. "Surely you know that."

Some part of me wondered if it was about something else, not me. Some part of me warned not to jump so quickly to conclusions, but that would be embracing hope, and I learned from Frannie not to hope. "Isn't it, Rhiannon?" I got up, stepping away from her. "I don't see how it's any different."

She sprang up behind me. "Then what about me? Am I the same as your average serial killer?"

How could she say that? We weren't the same. And she wasn't some common killer. She had a mission. It was one of the first things you learned as a parapsych kid. The Maere had a mission from the Saints to protect us. To save us from the Authority in whatever ways they could.

How dare she speak about herself that way? "No," I shouted back. "What you do is *sacred*."

"Sacred?" she hissed, mad as I'd ever seen her. "It is *murder*."

"The Maere are blessed by the Saints," I ground out, wishing she would let me cling to just one Saints-damned notion. "I am cursed."

"Horseshit," she practically screamed. I looked at her, amazed by the power of her rage. She was all grace, even in her fury, all controlled rage, thrumming against her guardrails, begging to be set free. And then she let all her walls down, yelling, "If I'm blessed, then so are you. Tanith's fucking favorites, that's us."

"Tanith's fucking favorites?" I spat out, getting caught up in the river of her anger. For a moment, I thought I might stay there, but the humor of our situation hit me.

We were yelling at each other over what exactly? Who was the worst between us? Who was the best?

My shoulders began to shake, laughter bubbling out of me. It was all just so ridiculous. We'd come to a haunted house for her to relax—not just any haunted house, the most haunted site in Orphium—and the two of us had the audacity to be shocked by all the shit it was stirring up in us.

Rhiannon crossed her arms, glaring at me.

"You're something else, you know that?" I finally said.

"I could say the same about you," she spit back. Her shoulders slumped a little. "I don't think we're going to find anything else out tonight."

"I agree," I replied. "Let's get some rest."

She rolled her eyes, but her hand slipped into mine as I picked up the shopping bags she'd left in the dressing room. We were damn well bringing the lingerie back with us.

CHAPTER 10

RHIANNON

THE FACT that it had been lunchtime when we'd gone to Triomphe, and now it appeared to be the dead of night walking back was disturbing. Despite my immortality, this place was starting to frighten me. Maybe that was why I was clinging to Eryx Necroline like a helpless schoolgirl.

Keep telling yourself that, a voice in my head sneered.

So what if it felt good to hold his hand on the street. It had been years, decades, since I'd had anything more than a few nights with someone. Holding hands, even here, wherever *this* was, felt like an experiment.

I tried to focus on the street as we walked, rather than the way Eryx's big hand swallowed mine. The near-oppressive heat hadn't disappeared because the sun went down. It was humid to the point that I couldn't tell if the water beading on my skin was sweat or from the air itself.

Steam rose from the hot streets, billowing into unearthly mist. Old neon signs flickered in the fog. The sounds of the city were there, but it was as though I heard them from a distance, almost like hearing traffic on the other end of a phone conversation, in the background.

"Sound is strange here," I murmured, worrying that something might shift on us again. This place was making me anxious.

Eryx looked back at me, his hand tightening around mine. "It's the dead," he explained.

I looked around, but neither saw nor sensed any spirits. "Where are we?" I whispered. "Really?"

Eryx took a deep breath, and despite the heat, pulled me closer to his body so that our hips touched as we walked, his arm slipping around me. I tried not to sigh at the feeling of his fingers spreading over the small of my back. "It's hard to say," his deep voice rumbled, sending vibrations through me. "The best I can tell right now, is that the haunting is strong enough to conjure up a pocket realm of sorts."

I frowned. Things like that weren't really possible, even for mages. Not that I knew of anyway. "I don't know if you've read DeWitt and Bassey on this," I said, naming two of the most prominent necromancer scholars in Aradios.

Eryx chuckled. "Of course I have. I consulted on their paper about clairsentience fifteen years ago."

I stopped dead in my tracks. "*You* were the Necroline consult credited on that paper?"

He nodded, arching an eyebrow at me. "Don't look so surprised that they'd work with me, Brontë. I'm smarter than I look."

The way he said that infuriated me. Who'd been making him feel like he wasn't smart? I tightened my grip on his hand, yanking him back towards me. "I'm not surprised," I hissed. "I know you're smart."

It was his turn to look surprised. He took another step towards me, examining my face as though searching for evidence. Of what, I wasn't sure.

"I was surprised you'd work with *them*," I added. "The Aradios necromancers are assholes."

He chuckled softly, his eyes not leaving mine. His head bent slightly, as though he couldn't help but get nearer to me. "That they are. Everyone in Aradios thinks a little too much of themselves." He paused, his free hand rising between us, grazing my chin, just slightly before drawing back. "Not you, of course."

"I live here now," I reminded him. "I was never really one of them."

His head tilted slightly. "No," he murmured, almost as though I wasn't there. "You're too good for them."

"Don't do that," I whispered back. "Don't put me on a pedestal."

"Why not?" he asked, his face getting closer to mine by the second. "From where I stand, it's where you belong."

I grabbed his shirt, fisting knots into the thin fabric as I pulled him down to me. "I belong right *here*."

His face lost its sultry, languid quality, his eyes sharp now as he assessed me. That kiss in Triomphe had been more than good, it had been a promise of what might be possible for us. My heart raced with anticipation. So slowly, I almost didn't notice it happening, he unhooked my hands from his shirt, kissing one lightly on the knuckles, before taking the other and pulling me along.

"Let's get back to the house," he said, his tone a little too firm.

What had almost just happened between us? Disappointment flooded me, a touch of embarrassment stinging palpably in the flush of my skin, ringing through my chest. I hated how I couldn't read him. One moment it seemed clear that he wanted me, and then the next it was confusing again.

Was he sending mixed signals, or was I just broken? The

thought nearly broke my heart. By the time he was opening the front door to Oleander Cottage, I realized I'd walked the rest of the way back to the cottage in a haze of self-pity.

It was an ugly feeling, and I was all too prone to it these days. Second guessing myself so deeply that I simply lost track of what was happening around me. It was putting me off my game.

Eryx didn't follow me upstairs. It probably hadn't been five hours since I'd gotten out of bed, but it was dark out and I was utterly exhausted. Maybe I just needed to roll with this and start over. I changed into a nightgown after washing my face and brushing my teeth, and then crawled into bed, feeling so tired I thought I might pass out the second my head hit the pillow.

His footsteps on the stairs sent my heart racing. I listened as he showered. The light in the hallway went off, but I could make out the outline of his form as he walked down the hall, passing the stairs, coming straight for me.

My entire body tensed as he climbed into bed next to me. The bed was too small for two people as long as we were. The second his full weight was on the mattress, we fell into one another.

He wasn't wearing any clothes.

My brain nearly shorted out.

It was possible he was wearing another pair of those infernal boxer briefs, but I wasn't about to stick my hand between us to find out. I froze, unsure what to do. I didn't want to scramble away from him. That seemed rude.

But if I just cuddled in… what message would that send?

I'd said he should sleep up here, but…

His hands were gentle as he turned me onto my side, spreading the covers out evenly over us as he fit my back against his chest. And then one arm slid under my pillow, cradling my head.

"Is this comfortable?" he asked, the other hand sliding up the outside of my thigh, onto my waist.

Comfortable? It felt like my skin might burst into flames. All I could think of was how hard he'd been in the dressing room at Triomphe as he'd kissed me. "Yes," I whispered, my mouth gone bone dry.

Behind me he settled in, one of his legs twining through mine. This was not casual cuddling. As his thigh caressed mine, the hand on my waist slipped down to my belly. "What about this?" he breathed into my ear, causing me to arch my back, a soft moan slipping from my lips.

His fingers stroked long, slow lines down my abdomen, and then back up again, grazing the undersides of my breasts. There was no mistaking his touch for an accident. He meant to touch me exactly this way.

"Yes," I managed to answer, flooded with need.

His hips moved behind me as he pulled me closer, the hard length of him pressing into my ass. The messages weren't mixed now. I could feel how much he wanted me. He wouldn't touch me like this if he didn't, would he?

"Go to sleep, Rhiannon," he whispered. "You need the rest."

"I don't." I was practically begging.

And then his fingers stopped their teasing, pressing me harder against him as his breathing slowed behind me. My skin burned with need, but I willed my hips to stay still.

"You do," he murmured, his voice thick with sleep already. "Just let me hold you tonight."

I wanted to argue, wanted to make my case for ripping all our clothes off and fucking until the sun came up. But then he said just one more word, "Please."

There was so much need in his voice, and I remembered what he told me in Delicia's—about the lovers who used him for cheap thrills. I took a deep breath, allowing my body to relax against his.

A deep, satisfied sigh, accompanied by his rumbling hum of pleasure, vibrated through me. "You feel so good," he murmured, already half asleep as his hand dropped lower onto my belly, cupping the curve of my flesh as the rhythm of his breath rose and fell in even turns.

My eyes were heavy, though my body still throbbed with unmet need. It was maddening how tired I was, and yet all I could think about was having his hands and mouth on me. If his thigh moved even an inch more, he'd find out just how much I wanted him.

I hadn't expected him to follow me up here, and I almost never slept in anything at all. The nightgown had been a courtesy, in case there was an emergency in the night. There was nothing between the bare skin of his thigh and how absolutely wild the hand caressing my belly was making me.

But if he needed rest, I needed to let him get it. He was processing a lot of spirit energy, and that took a lot of effort. So I took another deep breath and shifted my weight slightly away from him to get comfortable enough to sleep.

He moved with me, his leg pushing between mine. Our combined movement at just the wrong moment sent him sliding directly between my legs. I couldn't help but gasp as his skin met the spot between my legs that was positively drenched with need.

Behind me, he froze, his breath suddenly ragged. "Fuck," he breathed. "Fuck."

I wasn't sure what to do. A moment ago, he'd acted like he wanted to sleep. But now all I wanted was to ride the thigh pressing into my pussy.

"Rhiannon," he groaned, his erection pressing harder into my ass. "I'm trying so hard to control myself."

Before I could say a word, he moved, the hand on my belly disappeared, then sliding onto the thigh he now had propped up with his own, spreading my legs. He pushed the covers back, letting the hot air of the attic bedroom kiss my bare pussy. I could feel him pull away from me, looking at me in the dim light of the bedroom.

"You are making this so difficult," he groaned. "How am I supposed to sleep knowing you're this wet?" Before I could answer, he whispered. "Were you like this when I was kissing you in Triomphe?"

"Yes," I answered, without hesitation.

He caressed my ass, brushing soft kisses down the back of my neck. His thigh moved back between my legs. "Ride me," he commanded. "I want to see you come on my leg."

It was all the permission I needed. In one smooth motion, I rolled away from him, repositioning myself so I faced him, pushing him back onto the bed. "If you want to look at me while I ride you, I don't think you can be back there."

His eyes shone with lust in the dim light of the bedroom. The glow of the city outside was enough to show me that he was, indeed, wearing those tight boxer briefs. It was hot in the bedroom, sweltering, in fact.

I crawled over him, straddling his hips, grinding my bare pussy down on the fabric his cock was straining against. He was bigger than I'd imagined and as my skin made contact with him, we both let out strangled noises. I pulled my nightgown off and he lost all semblance of control, pulling me down against him.

As my breasts grazed his chest, he thrust his hips up against me, our mouths meeting in a tangled frenzy. I clung to him as we moved against one another, frantic to touch as much of each other as we could. Slick sweat beaded over both our bodies, my belly and breasts sliding more easily over the firm planes of his body.

The friction between us was too much for me to bear as he dragged us into a seated position, his mouth closing around one of my nipples. I tumbled over some edge I didn't even know was possible this fast, my hips unable to stop seeking the intense pleasure I got from feeling how hard I made him.

He pulled my hair, his mouth unlatching from my nipple to suck gently at the skin of my neck. "You taste so good," he groaned. "I can't wait to taste the rest of you."

White light flashed behind my eyes as he urged me on. "That's it," he commanded. "Make a mess of me, baby."

A feral scream came tumbling out of me as he held me tighter against him, my body shaking as he pushed back against my still gyrating hips. When my body slowed, he smiled at me. "That's what you needed to sleep, wasn't it?"

I looked into his eyes, confused. "What about you?"

He brushed my hair back from my face. "I got everything I needed just now. Time to sleep."

I wasn't sure what he meant, but my body was going limp with spent energy. He lay me down gently, then got up. There were soft noises in the dark. The sound of running water in the bathroom, and the soft click of a glass being set down on the bedside table before he climbed back into bed with me.

This time, there was nothing between us as he gathered me to him. I stopped fighting sleep, letting it take me without thinking anymore about what any of this meant.

CHAPTER 11

ERYX

THE NEXT DAY, I sat on the patio with a bottle of whisky, while Rhiannon searched the house for more clues. Thick heat gathered around me, sticky and wet. The crystal glass I'd swiped from the bar in the sitting room was slippery with condensation. From inside the house, the sound of Rhiannon's sword meeting wood was an erratic drumbeat of fury and frustration.

I swallowed another gulp of whisky, trying not to wince as she let out a cry of rage. Too many doors were still locked, and though she'd tried breaking them down, it seemed Oleander Cottage was impervious to harm. Listening to her fight the house was confusing. A part of me wanted to help her, to step in and find a way to calm her down.

But somewhere deep within me, a wiser voice said to leave well enough alone. Whatever was happening inside her, she needed to work it out on her own right now. Last night, I'd helped her loosen the ties she had knotted up inside her enough that she'd let go a little.

The trouble was, I'd undone myself in the process, and woken up alone in bed. When I'd come downstairs, she was already hard at work trying to figure the house out, and I was moody about waking up alone, but also about what we'd learned the day before.

Something about knowing that Magnus had hurt Cassandra had sent me into a morning tailspin. It wasn't that I couldn't believe it. My uncle was a terrible man. It was an open secret in Roman's organization. Not that any of us bound to the Trinity of Dynasties were allowed to be *good* people. Being good was for rich humans, not for parapsychs of any persuasion.

We had people to protect, and as much as I railed against the way the dynasties and the Consulate had fallen short of my own ideals, I knew exactly how we'd gotten backed into these corners. But Magnus wasn't bad for a cause, or in the face of injustice; he was simply a bad man. And unfortunately, he'd been a useful tool for my father. For Roman.

I couldn't remember my real father's face anymore. My head hung as emotion rose in my throat, a ghost of ancient grief that I wasn't sure I recognized anymore. When I thought of my biological father all I saw was a blank space. My mom was the scent of lily of the valley, but not a face. They'd been gone too long, taken too early in my life to remember.

Soft footsteps approached. For half a second I tensed, and then I smelled her. Jasmine, roses, and something else, something warm and sensual. Like the smell of skin after a bath. I'd smelled it on her every time I got near her, but I'd had that scent on me all day after sleeping next to her.

After having her come all over me. But I couldn't think about that now, the feeling of her sweaty skin against mine.

The taste of her. The smell of her as she'd soaked through my boxer briefs getting off. It was more than I'd ever expected to do with her, though of course I'd hoped. I didn't want to push my luck by talking about it now.

She slumped into the other wrought-iron chair, her jaw tight with dissatisfaction. Her feet were bare and she wore a pair of tight leggings and a soft white t-shirt with a wide neck that slipped off her shoulders. It took everything I had not to stare at her. Every time I got a chance to look at her it took effort not to drink her in.

"What's vexing you so?" I asked, keeping my voice low and even.

"The house is impervious to damage," she explained, taking the bottle off the table. She uncorked it, then took a powerfully long swig from it, her lips closing around the shaft of the bottle like… no.

I cleared my throat, desperate to banish those thoughts before I tried to act on them. "Sure. But what's actually bothering you?"

Rhiannon sighed. "Nothing."

I raised an eyebrow.

She shrugged. "Everything."

"That sounds more like the truth."

A wry smile lit up her face. "What's eating at you?"

She had me there. "Everything."

Her bottom lip stuck out a little, barely a pout, as she nodded. "I guess I deserve that after the answer I gave you."

It was my turn to shrug. We were both playing it so cool, but it was all a sham. I saw the way she crossed her legs, her thighs flexing. She was thinking the same thing I was—how good it would feel to work out some of this pent up agitation on one another. What else did we have to do, after all?

One of us was going to have to broach the subject, but it wasn't going to be me. Or, at least that's what I told myself as she leaned forward to squint at the cat coming around the corner of the house. It gave me a look down her shirt that I wasn't expecting, and the sight of her bare breasts was enough to make my cock jump.

"Look, should we talk about last night?" I asked without thinking.

Rhiannon sat back in her chair, her eyes relaxing from the squinting she'd been doing. I couldn't help but wonder if she needed glasses. She'd look adorable in glasses. *Fuck.*

"I'm sorry I yelled at you at Triomphe," she said after a long moment.

I nearly snorted. "That wasn't what I was talking about. And you barely screeched."

Her mouth fell open, giving me a glimpse of that soft tongue of hers. Shit, shit, shit. I closed my eyes before I could think more about her mouth and what it would feel like—really, I could not think about that. I had to cross my own damn legs. I'd made the poor choice of a pair of cotton pajama pants, and my erection was about to pop out and say hello.

"I did not screech," she said as I opened my eyes again. "I don't screech."

"You do a little." I smiled, grinned really. She was flirting, so I could too. "I like the noises you make. Even the screechy ones."

Those pretty cheeks of hers flushed pink and I'd had enough torture. "Let me take care of you while we're here." I leaned forward, adding, "Let me make you make every sound known to man." She flushed deeper, and I couldn't help myself. "Give me all your screams, Rhiannon."

Those long legs of hers flexed again as she crossed her

legs tighter. I needed to slide a hand between them. I needed to lick her sweaty skin clean, and taste every bit of her that was heating with my words. I'd wanted inside her, and now she was in me, coursing through my veins like a drug I couldn't get enough of.

"What happens when we leave?" she asked, her voice and bottom lip both quivering a little. "You made it clear that you don't do relationships, and I don't really do casual. Especially with people in my life. And with…" she waved a hand towards Hemlock House, and I assumed she meant Ares and Ember. "With everything Ember and Ares are trying to do, you and I are bound together, no matter what."

Her words were like a cold douse of water. I sat back, frowning. That wasn't what I expected her to say, and I was stunned into silence.

She shook her head. "Yesterday was…" she paused, her eyes falling closed for half a second as her cheeks flushed again. "So good. But that's all I can manage without getting my heart all twisted up. And I don't think you want that with me. Maybe not with anyone, but especially not with me. I'm a messy lover."

Her words cut me to the core. I hated that something had left her with that impression of herself. Her mess was beautiful, and I'd gladly take it on, and more, if it meant getting to be near her. But that just wasn't possible. Not with me.

At the very least, I owed her the truth. Too many people had lied to her. "I can't be the man you deserve, Rhiannon."

Her arms crossed as her eyes narrowed, bitterness etched in the line of her mouth. The woman was *mad*-mad. "That's smooth, Eryx. Have you used that one before?"

She thought I was letting her down easy. I was fucking

this up. I stood up, took one step to get closer to her, and then knelt at her feet. "You're not understanding."

Her chin tipped down, her glare imperious. Saints, I would lick the bottoms of her feet if it would please her. "Explain then."

Explain? How? I stared at her hands, then slowly reached for them. She tensed, her fingers curling into fists. I pried them apart, and she relaxed, those big blue eyes so sorrowful. All I wanted was to erase that look, forever. But a man like me couldn't do more than be a good time. I only brought pain to the people who made the mistake of loving me back.

I swallowed hard, looking up at her. I brought each of her hands to my lips, kissing them so gently it nearly brought tears to my eyes. It would be so easy to love her. She was everything I wanted. Hell, everything I *needed*.

And I would make things worse for her. Worse at a time when she needed to heal. Bitterness flooded me. I set her hands back in her lap. "I am not a good man, Rhiannon. I tried to explain this to you yesterday, and I appreciate what you said, but I am not like you. The things I do get the people I love hurt."

A shuddering breath went through me as I exhaled. I couldn't think about Frannie. Not now.

But apparently I couldn't hide from Rhiannon. Her fingers grazed my chin. "Tell me what happened."

"No," I growled, standing up. Thinking about Frannie was bad enough. Talking about her wasn't an option. "I can't. You have to trust me. I am no good for anyone—and much as I want you, Rhiannon, I cannot be what you need."

Her expression flickered from analytical to something open and vulnerable. "And what is that? What kind of partner do you think I need?"

The bottle of whisky was in my hand before I could think, hurtling across the garden, disappearing into the hedge. Every memory I kept locked deep inside flooded out. Frannie's sweet smile. Her mean way of talking when she was mad. The way she looked when I finally found her, when it was far, far too late to save her from any ounce of pain she'd endured on my behalf. "One who won't get you hacked to pieces."

My voice was strangled, my eyes clouded with unshed tears. If I cried for Frannie, even once, I'd never stop. Rhiannon's voice broke over a gasp. "This is about Francesca Lyon, isn't it?"

I spit out the only words I could think of to protect myself. "Don't say it was hundreds of years ago."

She was standing in flash, moving in that silent, invisible way of hers, her arms around my waist. "Eryx," she whispered. "I would never say that."

My teeth gritted, but some tight thing around my heart came a little loose. I swallowed. "She was just fifty-three. Barely grown."

Rhiannon hummed, a deep, soft sound that vibrated through her and into me as her belly pressed into mine. "I don't know what happened, but I can see how deeply you cared for her. I can take it, whatever it is. Please trust me with your pain."

She wiped the tears from my face, her fingers soft as silk on my skin. *Trust me with your pain.* I'd never thought it took trust to let someone else hold what hurt before. It had never occurred to me. Maybe that was why I couldn't let anyone love me. I didn't know shit about this kind of trust.

But maybe for her, *with her,* I could try.

Slowly, I nodded. "They gave her every cut I made on their guy, and more ..." I choked out, unable to say more about the details. Rhiannon's fingers glided over my face, comforting and cool. "She died like that because of what *I* did, Rhiannon."

She let out a little noise, somewhere between a sob and a sigh, as though it hurt her to hear me in pain. Her voice shook a little with the rage that burned in her eyes. "She died like that because of the people who killed her, Eryx. Not because of you."

"If I hadn't tortured Vance Hoight, they wouldn't have—"

"What did Hoight do?" she cut in, her voice sharp as a knife. "You didn't torture him for fun."

I swallowed hard. This was too much. I didn't talk about this for a reason. Hoight was sick, one of the sickest shitbags I'd ever killed. "Raped and murdered six necromancers. He wouldn't give up the location of the last body."

Her long fingers closed around my chin. "Look at me, Eryx." It was too hard. I couldn't. Not when the memory of Frannie's cut up body flooded my mind. "I said, *look at me*."

The way she ordered me was so deeply urgent, it made me think she needed me to look for her, not for me. So I did. Her expression was all fierce grace and vengeful deity. Rhiannon Brontë was a fucking goddess.

"Did you get the location of the last body?" she asked.

I would have done *anything* to get that girl's body home to her parents. Her dad was a trash collector and her mom ran a daycare out of their house. The girl Hoight had taken was the first in her family to go to college. Her loss had shattered them. They were necromancers, and without a body, they believed her soul would never be at peace. Even telling them that Ares had sent her soul on hadn't been enough. They needed the body.

So I got it for them, and I wasn't a bit sorry for it. But

Hoight was one of O-Tex's finance whizzes. He cleaned up shit that nobody else could. And the Corps had sent mercs after Frannie to teach me, and Ares, who'd made the call, a lesson.

"Yes," I finally answered. "I got the body, and Frannie got what I deserved."

"Did you kill the men who did it to her?" Rhiannon asked.

"I killed the ones who tortured her. But I could never get the ones who killed her. Hoight worked for O-Tex."

Rhiannon bit her bottom lip, blinking back tears. "Corps scum. We're all at their fucking mercy." She took a few ragged breaths and then said, "First of all, I don't take the same view you do on who's to blame for Frannie's death." I opened my mouth to argue, but she shook her head. "Second of all, I understand why you think what you do about yourself, Eryx Necroline, but I don't share that view either."

When I didn't try to cut in, she smiled the grimmest smile I'd ever seen. "But I respect your feelings about what you're capable of. You're allowed to feel what you do." She shook her head, staring at Oleander Cottage. "Gods know I understand it."

And then she hugged me tight, laying her head against my chest. Like I was someone worth hugging. Like I deserved to feel her soft body pressing into mine, to smell that sweet, sensual, floral skin-scent of hers up close.

"Hug me back," she ordered. A sob rose up in my throat. "Hug me back as tight as you can and cry." I started to say something, but the woman was on a mission. "Cry for Francesca," Rhiannon whispered. "Cry for what you lost, Eryx. Cry for what those bastards took from you."

And because it was Rhiannon Brontë, and she could boss me around any day of the week, I clung to her like my life depended on it. I cried hundreds of years' worth of grief and guilt into her hair. Slowly, she pulled me down to the cool stone of the patio, keeping me pressed tight against her, rocking me and whispering, "Let it all out, love. Scream for Frannie."

And Saints damn me for it, but I did.

CHAPTER 12

RHIANNON

FOR NEARLY THREE WEEKS, Eryx and I made meals, visited the empty shops on Eighth Ave and continued to explore what we could of the house. There was a kind of pregnant stillness in the house after his confession about Francesca's death. It wouldn't last. I knew it wouldn't, but the way he'd given me his pain had changed something.

It was as though the house was waiting. Or maybe, maybe it was pondering. Pondering on who the two of us were. Sizing us up. If it was going to punish someone for whatever wrongs had occurred within its walls, I hoped it would be me. I was eternal, and I could take it. Eryx Necroline had been through enough. We didn't talk about Francesca again, but he seemed a little lighter. I'd catch him staring at me, occasionally, a soft look in his eyes.

But he didn't touch me at night. We did nothing more than sleep in bed together, and I wondered how well either of us were sleeping, trying as hard as we both were not to touch one another. I was glad he'd told me about Frannie, but now I was hesitant to make a move.

It was so obvious that he'd cared deeply about her and

I wasn't brave enough to ask him if he'd gotten over her. It had been a while since her death, but I never underestimated how serious things could be for those of us with these long lives. Parapsychs tended to work on one of two modes: completely casual or deeply committed. It took one or the other to make things work when you could live for hundreds, or even thousands of years.

I had only a vague recollection of Francesca Lyon. If I recalled correctly, she'd been a sweet-faced little necromancer with the power to help restless spirits cross over to whatever waited after death, beyond even the netherworld. I tried not to let my fury take me under for what had happened to her, and subsequently him. I'd never known they were even together, but I hadn't been that interested in what Roman Necroline's adopted children were up to at the time.

There were times when this horrible world was too much to bear. Times I wished I *could* die. It would do no good to tell Eryx that I was made of sturdier stuff than Francesca had been—that I could withstand anything his enemies wanted to throw at me, and probably end them myself. That wasn't the point. He knew who I was and what I was capable of.

He had to believe he was allowed something better. Something more. And frankly, I did too. So I let things settle between us. Let us get into a routine that was safe enough, despite the way the cottage seemed to grow hungrier by the day, even in its stillness. By the start of the fourth week in the cottage, the spirit in corpse garb hadn't showed up again, but Eryx and I found bloody evidence of Magnus' harm against Cassandra every day.

Sometimes it was nothing more than a stained handkerchief, but it was enough to chill the blood. I could kill thousands of people that needed killing. I was almost numb to the violence now. But there was something about knowing that the person who was supposed to love Cassandra Necroline the most had hurt her instead that disturbed me. And knowing what had happened to Francesca made it all the worse. I didn't know how Eryx could stand it.

Today had dawned gray and gloomy, the stagnant heat broken by a torrential downpour. When I woke, he was already downstairs. The faint hiss of bacon sizzling floated up to me, the smell of coffee not far behind. I crawled out of bed, still feeling exhausted, stiffness and a hint of pain lacing my every muscle. I stumbled to the bathroom and did the bare minimum of hygiene before making my way downstairs.

Eryx stood in the kitchen, tending to the bacon. That thick feeling was in the air, and I wondered if it was the house, or us. Tension had been mounting between us again for the past few days. Long looks, clenched muscles. I was starting to know Eryx's tells, and they were driving me wild with anticipation.

I leaned against the counter, stealing a piece of bacon from the cooling rack. It occurred to me that the grief he'd let out for Francesca was old, and I had no idea what was appropriate now. He'd been brave to share it though, and I wanted to offer him something of myself in return.

"Do you remember the night we met?" I hesitated, realizing the question was a little confusing. We'd actually known one another loosely for centuries. "I mean, the night we met for real."

He pushed his hair out of his eyes before looking up. The angles in his face were sharp, but sensual. His full lips twisted, just slightly, as though he was having trouble dragging himself out of his thoughts.

"Yes," he said, after a long moment and a turn of the

bacon while I poured myself coffee. He gestured to the toast he'd already buttered. I took a piece and ate it as he talked. "One moment Av and I were fighting and the next, you'd killed all of Fairchild's guard." He paused again, his eyes distant, as though he remembered every move I'd made. I licked a crumb from my upper lip and his eyes met mine, intensity building behind his cool gaze. "It was beautiful."

My heart thumped hard. "I murdered them," I said, my voice cracking a little as the words came out.

"Yes," he agreed. His eyes were steady as he watched me. The sizzle of the bacon went soft in my ears, his voice the only thing I could focus on. "With utter grace and efficiency."

He said it as though it were an easily acceptable fact. I stared down at my nails as I put my coffee cup down on the counter. I'd found a bottle of Cassandra's nail polish in the medicine cabinet a few days ago and painted them. It was a soapy pink shade with a bit of pearl in it. Something I'd have chosen myself.

"I had never killed another person before we came to Orphium as the Maere," I admitted. I had never told anyone that. Not in thousands of years. I don't even know if Ember or Lara knew. It wasn't what he'd offered me when he told me about Francesca, but it was a deeply vulnerable point for me.

A deep urge for something real to happen between us thrummed through me, urgent and hot. He'd told me the truth of him, or at least one truth, and I wanted to give it back. To keep exchanging truths until we knew each other inside out.

I'd never wanted that with a lover, other than Lara. But then, she'd been my friend first, in two lifetimes. And I wanted Eryx to be more to me than a good lay. I wanted him to be a real friend, and more, though I didn't know how much more yet.

So I opened up my heart, dangerous as that seemed. "The first time I killed someone, I wanted to die myself… but of course, I can't. When I agreed to do this job, I didn't know what that would be like, but it festers inside me. I've never gotten used to it… I feel like a monster."

He put down the tongs he held and reached for me, his fingers unfurling with a gentleness that elicited a dull, painful ache in my chest. I waited for several beats too long to move my own hand, but Eryx didn't draw back. My fingers stretched towards his before sliding into his much larger palm. He let me rest them there for a few heartbeats, his pulse throbbing through his fingertips, before his hand closed around mine.

It was nothing like the frenzied way we'd touched one another after the discovery at Triomphe. Somehow, this was more intimate. More real.

"I vomit nearly every time I murder someone," I admitted. "Later, in private. It just comes out of me."

"And after you puke?" he asked, still not letting go of my hand.

Would the bacon burn?

I shook my head. "I never think about them again. I don't feel guilty. I react, and then I just… don't care anymore. That's what makes me a monster."

"Probably," he replied, then paused, seeming to consider his words carefully. When he spoke, his voice shook a bit, but it was clear he'd been thinking this over. "But if you are, then so am I. I don't even puke anymore. I just shut it out. I kill them because I have to. Because this is our lives, this is what we've been pushed to. We are the monsters so someone else doesn't have to be."

His words cracked me open, laying me bare. The

bacon was definitely going to burn; I nodded towards it and he moved quickly, letting go of my hand. I didn't want to be the monster for others anymore. Working for the Consulate had been horrible. The years I'd been in Aradios were some of the worst of my too-long life, but coming back to Orphium, to the place where I'd wreaked so much havoc over the years—it was breaking me.

I couldn't tell the others. Lara would offer to take over for me. To become Orphium's assassin. She'd already hinted as much while she'd been working as the Angel; before we'd found out that her missions had all been orchestrated by the island. I knew she'd take this on now, if I asked her. But she deserved better than to feel this way.

She deserved better after all the years she put up with you. I tried to push the thought away, but it wouldn't go. No part of me missed Lara that way, not really, but old wounds opened too easily in stressful circumstances and I was already feeling much too sorry for myself. Contemplating all the ways Lara and I hadn't worked out might just break me. Besides, that felt like another lifetime now.

Everything did. It was like the world had gone gray around me. Tears streamed down my face without a sob or even a whimper. I tried to turn away from Eryx, but he caught my wrist in his hand the moment I said, "Sometimes I don't know if I'm even real anymore."

Slowly, Eryx lifted my fingers to his lips, so gently I barely felt the contact. "Seems real enough to me." He moved my hand to his heart, waiting for me to register the slow, steady thump before asking. It was a kind of opening —the kind I recognized. Vague and tentative, so that if I said no, he would recover. My heart ached at the thought. "What about me?"

"Very real," I breathed. I wanted him to touch me. To feel things for me. I wanted to feel things for him. To protect each other in this hard world. But maybe he was right, in a way. Maybe that wasn't for people like us.

He nodded. "Two monsters. Very real."

Too real. I swallowed, and then ever-so-gently pulled my hand back and said the thing I feared most. "I don't want to force Ember and Ares into having to tell us no," I whispered. It felt far too much like my heart was breaking the moment I said it.

Eryx swallowed so hard I could feel it in his hand. His jaw clenched. "You think they would deny us the happiness they have?"

I ripped my eyes from his. "Ember knows I am not capable of loving anyone the way she can. She knows I'm not good at this. That I'll hurt you in the end. That it will cause problems and Eryx... we have eternity to deal with one another. I just... I can't be the cause of more trouble."

He let go of my hand, the motion gentle, but it still felt like someone tearing at my soul. That had come out wrong. I was trying to say something else—something that might bring us both hope. But it had come out sounding like I didn't want him.

When I looked back up, his face was calm in that heartbreaking way he had of burying himself. "Understood."

A part of me railed against the ease with which he accepted my statement, but that was unfair of me. I couldn't expect him to fight for me after what I'd just said. All the same, despite the unfairness of it, I wanted him to. I didn't want him, of all people, to let me push him away.

But maybe it was a relief for me to do it. Maybe he hadn't realized that somewhere inside my foolish head, I thought the way he looked at me might mean he wanted more than a meaningless affair. And now he knew what I'd been thinking, and he was relieved.

I knew full well I was assuming too much, letting the worst of my thoughts get the best of me. It wasn't a healthy way to operate, but all my coping mechanisms had gone out the window the day we got our swords back.

The day I realized in a kind of horrible finality that my own mother not only did not love me, but didn't trust me. She'd never been able to see me as her child, just a tool, and when I'd disappointed her, she had even less use for me. It had fucked me up more than I ever imagined it could.

I might never get over it. Talking about my feelings had never been my strong suit, and I was still bad at it now. I ate the last of my toast, and drained my coffee cup. He finished the bacon, quietly making himself a cup of coffee, but not looking my way even once.

It was too much. I wanted to fix it, but I didn't know how. When I finally spoke, he didn't turn towards me. "I'm going to look over the library again. Maybe there's something we missed."

"Sure," he agreed. "I'll do the dishes, and then I am going to try Magnus' office again. Yesterday, I thought it almost opened. Lunch is already in the fridge. The bacon is for salads."

He'd made lunch as well? He'd been making most of our meals and cleaning up after them as well. It was odd, but such a relief. I wasn't a good cook, and he was excellent at it. If the world were different, he could open a restaurant, we would be free to fall in love, and I could do what Cassandra Necroline had always wanted to: garden.

What would it be like to feed people, to grow things, to nurture life, instead of all this death? I shook my head as I handed him my dishes and backed out of the kitchen before I hurt either of us even more. Eryx had been wrong about himself. He wasn't a danger to me. I was a danger to him.

It didn't matter that he was one of the most lethal men in Orphium. Under all that hardness and stoicism, he was a sensitive soul who blamed himself for far too much. And I was nothing but a selfish bitch who ruined people's lives with her arrogance. I choked down my bitterness and shame, trying to focus on the task at hand. If I didn't, I was going to drown in self-loathing.

The library was dark and gloomy, only a little brass sconce to light the way. Shelves painted a deep, dusky rose were filled with books on gardening, etiquette and cooking. There was not a single piece of fiction, nor was there even one book on any subject other than homemaking, which left me wondering who the hell Cassandra Necroline had been. The books were lovely enough. High quality. But there was a kind of studied sameness about the selection that was boring.

Too boring. Nothing a man like Magnus ever would have thought twice about looking inside. From what Eryx had told me so far, his uncle had held some kind of unreason-able disdain for his wife, dismissing her at every turn as unintelligent and useless. If she'd wanted to hide some-thing inside these books, she could have. I pulled one down. It was simply titled, *Entertaining.*

I paused, listening to the sounds of Eryx in the kitchen. The running water, the soft clink of porcelain as he washed them by hand. There was an early model of a dishwasher in the cottage, but he showed Cassandra the respect of treating her dishes carefully. The distinct memory of holding his body as he shook with grief for the woman he'd lost crossed my mind.

I'd been right to push him away. Hurt him now, so my sharp tongue and never-ending demands wouldn't ruin him later. He deserved a softer kind of love than mine. Someone who could understand the complexity of what he did and nurture his feelings with grace, rather than stomping all over them in an attempt to explain herself.

My cheeks were hot with shame. *Why do you always have to ruin things?* How many times had Mother hissed that at me? How many times had I fumbled through conversations as a young woman, not knowing what I'd done wrong—or even that I'd done something wrong until I found out later that I'd made someone uncomfortable, or been outright rude.

I'd seen a therapist that Lara had recommended in Aradios for a while a few years back. It had helped for a while—until it didn't. But I'd picked up a few tricks for moments like these. I closed my eyes and counted backwards from ten. Beating myself up wasn't going to help anything.

If I wanted to be useful, I needed to focus on the books, rather than feeling sorry for myself. There was nothing unusual about *Entertaining*, so I put it back. Methodically, I pulled each book down, looking inside and then replacing it. With the house watching, I didn't feel as though I could be haphazard with Cassandra's belongings. Somewhere near the middle, I hit gold. Inside a copy of a book called *Hothouse Flowers: Cultivating Rare Beauty*, a chunk of the pages were hollowed out and a single skeleton key sat inside.

"Eryx," I managed to croak out, feeling suddenly weak in the knees. "Come look."

He strode into the room in smooth, powerful strides, drying his hands, concern on his face. I held up the key. "I found this."

He stepped forward, taking it from me and examining it a bit more closely. "It might be to the basement door."

I nodded. "Go try it. I'm going to keep looking."

But there was nothing to find; a minute later he called up to me, "It's not to the basement."

I sighed, and kept searching as Eryx returned. He leaned on the secretary and watched me as I continued on. "Want me to help?"

I shook my head, turning. "I'm almost done." A few more books, but all were normal. "Nothing."

He handed the key back to me. "We'll figure it out."

"We will," I agreed, trying to inject some hope into my voice.

"Guess I'll finish the dishes," he said, pushing off the desk.

The desk. "Wait."

He raised an eyebrow as I pushed past him. The key was a little large for a desk, but now that I saw them both, I understood. Cassandra had changed the lock on her secretary at some point. She'd put a stronger one on it, one meant for a door. One that would require Magnus to destroy the desk, rather than just jimmy the lock, if he wanted to snoop through her secrets.

My breath caught as the key turned. I glanced up at Eryx. His expression was so open and earnest I nearly took back everything I'd said at the kitchen table. But my tongue wouldn't form the words, so I turned the key the rest of the way. The slanted cover to the secretary popped open.

The interior of Cassandra's desk was neat. Organized. A day planner and several pieces of correspondence sat in the usual spots, along with some lovely stationery with her monogram on it. Pens. A beautiful old tube of lipstick—the kind you could still buy inserts for.

Eryx ran his hand along an empty top shelf inside the desk's opening. He stopped suddenly, pressing a finger down very gently until an invisible panel popped up. The whispers that had gone so quiet for the past few days hissed like a den of vipers. Eryx and I glanced at one another.

I leaned towards the desk to get a look at what the panel had revealed, my head uncomfortably close to his. Inside the hidden space lay a plain black notebook. I lifted it out and opened it. I recognized Cassandra's handwriting immediately from the recipe box I'd gone through earlier this week looking for clues.

Both of us let out a breath, surprised that we'd found anything. We waited for the house to react. To disappear something, or for something in the air to shift. Nothing happened. Well, nothing happened to the objects in the room. The whispers were clearer now. *Swim in the depths*, some said. Others warned, *Beware the Ossuary*. And still others I could not make out.

A shadow fell over the library. I glanced up at the window. The woman from the day we'd tried to leave, veiled and dressed in corpse garb, stood outside, pressing gloved hands to the window. I was so startled, I nearly shrieked at the sight of her.

Eryx stood, crossing his arms and shaking his head. "Don't do that," he said in a strange, low voice. There was a tenor to it, just beyond what I could hear, some note that was not meant for the living. I'd heard stories about some necromancers having a voice for the dead, but never actually heard one use it.

The phantom disappeared, blinking out as suddenly as she'd appeared, the whispers silencing along with her. "Was that Cassandra?"

Eryx shrugged. "I don't know. It's possible, I suppose."

That wasn't particularly comforting, so I moved on. "What was that about the Ossuary?"

Eryx covered his mouth with his hand, his eyes widening. He looked around the house, as though he thought he might find something else. Or perhaps he *did* see something I couldn't. He pointed wildly towards the door we'd decided probably led to the basement, and then his eyes went straight back to the desk. To the place where he'd pulled the notebook from. "It's here."

I frowned. "What is?"

He laughed, but there wasn't a shred of joy in his eyes. "This is the City of the Dead, Rhiannon, and this property was once the Necroline Dynasty's seat of power." His arm reached past me into the hidden panel in Cassandra's desk. "During the Massacres, there were too many dead to bury, so Roman took what he could of them and laid them to rest deep beneath the fortress."

He pulled another key from the back of the hole and held it up before my face. It was larger than the desk key, simple and ancient, made of a metal that seemed to swallow light. "This is the key to the Ossuary. It's been missing for nearly a thousand years... kind of like your swords."

The parallel between the two scenarios was not lost on me. Had the two incidents been connected? And why did Cassandra have the key locked away? I chose not to ask those questions right now. "Do you think it opens the basement door?"

He shook his head, looking past me. "It's too big, but we're onto something. Do you want to read that while I look through Magnus' office again?"

I nodded, gazing down at the notebook. "I do."

He placed a hand on my shoulder, nearly hesitant with his touch. "We're getting somewhere, Rhiannon. Finally, we're getting somewhere. We should celebrate."

Relief flooded me at his words, though I couldn't tell why. I smiled. "Okay. What do you want to do?"

"Dinner. Out. Tonight. We've got the fancy clothes now, after all." He was right; we'd been "shopping" a lot to keep ourselves busy, and none of the things we brought home had disappeared. "You in?"

I nodded. "Yes, I'm in."

"Good. I'm going to finish the dishes and then try some of the other doors with these keys. I'll call for you if I find something. Want to go at seven?"

"All right," I agreed, my heart racing.

Was this a date? I tried to let the words form in my mouth, but he was gone, leaving me with the notebook—and the feeling that I wasn't ready to go back to the world just yet. As I looked up to pull the desk chair towards me, I found it occupied. A tall, blonde woman with a similar build to mine sat in it, arms crossed, nearly transparent, not a hint of corpse garb in sight.

Instead, she wore a pretty tweed suit, tailored perfectly to her curves. Her short hair waved gently around her face, which was twisted into a deep frown. "There's nothing of use in the notebook. Just my grocery lists."

I nodded, grateful for the tip. "Who was the woman in corpse garb?"

Cassandra didn't answer me. Not about the other spirit, anyway. "He isn't like his uncle, after all," she said, before disappearing from sight. Her voice wasn't quite done with me though. "You're a fool to let him go."

CHAPTER 13

ERYX

ALL MORNING, I'd been trying to find a way to thank her for what she'd done for me in the garden. To tell her that it had changed me to finally finish grieving Frannie. That it had shifted something fundamental for me. I wasn't sure if I could try again with someone, but I thought if I was going to risk it with anyone, she was the only one who was worth it.

And before I could, she'd said all those things... *We have eternity to deal with one another.* To deal with one another? It had stung to hear her describe us that way, as though we were doomed already.

But then she said the words that unlocked her heart for me, though I was sure she didn't know it—*I can't be the cause of more trouble.* Rhiannon wasn't saying no to being with me. She was saying no to herself.

In the time I'd taken to let my grief find its place within my heart, she'd been filling her head with the kinds of stories about herself that I was all too familiar with. I had to do this carefully. I needed to show her what things could be like between us. I needed to show myself.

That's why I'd asked her to dinner… and then spent the rest of the day avoiding her so that she couldn't walk her yes back. From upstairs, I heard the sound of the bathtub draining. My suit was hanging on the back of the downstairs powder room door. I'd just finished pressing it.

I listened carefully to the sounds of her getting ready from the couch I'd slept on when we first came to the cottage. Maybe if we both just let each other in a little, if we just tried, we'd find our way tonight.

We'd walked by the famous Paradiso restaurant several times over the past few weeks, and last week it had finally come to life. I'd even gotten steaks to-go one night last week, just to see. The steaks had been real, but the staff and patrons of the restaurant had barely noticed me. It was the same as it had been with the post-lady. If I spoke to them directly, they acknowledged me, but otherwise, they hadn't been able to see me at all.

It was the perfect place for us tonight. Somewhere quiet. Romantic. A place to start over. I heard the sound of the closet doors opening upstairs. She was getting dressed. I got up off the couch and did the same. Five minutes later, I was waiting for her at the bottom of the stairs.

When she came down, she was an absolute vision in a white gown, made from some light, diaphanous fabric. The sleeves were long, but the front of the dress plunged deep between her breasts, gathering and flowing in all the most alluring places.

The fabric was not transparent, but I could see the outline of her body through it. Her hair waved away from her face, pulled back partially by sparkling combs. As she made her way down the stairs I could see the reflection of her bare back in the mirror on the landing. I let a slow breath out.

"Is something wrong?" she asked.

"No," I breathed. "You are magnificent."

There was that blush I loved so much. My heart beat faster as she held out her arm as she reached the bottom of the stairs. I took it, lacing it through mine so that her body was tucked against mine, a perfect fit.

"You look lovely as well," she said, glancing up at me. Her teeth sunk into her rosy bottom lip for a moment, then she seemed to think better of that. She pressed her lips together again, likely to make sure her lipstick wasn't ruined. It wasn't, but I wanted to do things to her mouth that would muss it.

"I am so nervous," she finally said, her fingernails digging into my bicep. Even that was so sensual I suddenly wanted to stay home. The fact that *she* was nervous nearly unnerved me.

"Me too," I replied. "It's been a long time since I took anyone on a date."

Her eyes darted up, her brows furrowing slightly. "So, this *is* a date?"

I thought I might vomit. She didn't know this was a date? "I mean… I hoped it would be, but if not…"

"No," she said, practically breathless. "I want it to be."

Calm rushed over me. That breathless tone. The way her skin had flushed. She wanted this too. "Oh, good."

She let out a little laugh. "We're a pair."

I let myself get brave and slide my hand around her waist, my palm grazing the bare skin of her back. The sound of her drawing in a tiny little breath had me hard in an instant. I let my fingers slide down, feeling how deep that dip in the dress went. She made that noise again and her nipples hardened behind the thin fabric of her dress.

Her eyes raised to mine, her long black lashes fluttering a little as I dipped beneath the edge of the dress, letting my fingers graze the spot right above her ass. I bent down, letting my lips brush her ear. "You could stop a man's heart with a dress like this."

Her back arched and I had a flashback to her on top of me in bed. Saints it had been a trial to not touch her all these weeks, and now that my fingers grazed her skin I thought I might lose all control. It was that exact moment that I realized Rhiannon was wearing only one thing—the dress. She had nothing on under it.

As I thought that, she smiled up at me, wicked and lovely. "You're made of sturdier stuff than that, though, aren't you Necroline?"

I flattened my hand against the small of her back, pulling her against me, dragging her body against the evidence of how far gone for her I already was. She let out another of those whispery little breaths.

"Plenty sturdy," I assured her as I pushed her against the front door. "Now, if I kiss you here, we'll miss dinner, and I'll ruin your hair and makeup."

"Yes," she said, arching harder into me. "Ruin all of it."

I ran my thumb across her bottom lip. "Is that what you want?"

"Yes," she insisted.

"What if I want to eat out?" I asked with a smile.

Her tongue grazed my thumb, and she dipped her head to take the tip of it into her mouth. I growled in response, pressing myself harder into her. She was just so damn warm and pliable.

"Promises, promises," she replied, slipping out from under me to open the front door. I had to adjust myself before stepping out to follow her into the night, grinning. Finally, Rhiannon Brontë and I were on the same page.

The restaurant was crowded with glittering patrons, though I didn't recognize anyone. Everywhere I looked, there were flashes of sequins and furs, pinstriped suits from another age, gowns in styles popular just twenty years ago. It was as though time had collided at the Paradiso.

The spirits of Trinity luminaries were out in force. I was sure of it. This was one of those places. The dynasty higher-ups loved to come here to do deals. There'd been more political murders at the Paradiso than almost anywhere else in the city. It had always been a hotbed for depraved activity, and I was curious to know whose spirit still lingered here, but every time I attempted to focus on their faces, they blurred a little, or turned just before I could make out their features. It was an unsettling phenomenon.

Opera played in the background as the hostess seated us at one of the curved half-moon booths. Rhiannon moved towards the back of the high-backed, tufted leather seat, candlelight diffusing all her features into a warm glow. I slid in next to her as the hostess disappeared. There were bullet holes in the richly paneled walls, just behind her head. The blood of our people had soaked into the bones of the Paradiso over the years.

Ares and I had chosen not to come here very often. This was the kind of place that Magnus and Roman had frequented, and we were trying to do things differently. But being here now, I wondered if we'd made a mistake. Power thrummed through the walls of the restaurant. Even I could feel it.

There was a bottle of sparkling wine already open on the table, two glasses poured. Rhiannon took a sip from hers, scanning the room. "I've only been here once, twenty years ago."

I nearly spit out my wine. "The night Lara was taken to the Asylum?"

She nodded, a wan smile on her face. Perhaps this had been a monumental mistake if it was going to make her think of her ex, and what had happened to her when the Authority had hauled her off to the Asylum.

"I don't hold it against the restaurant, of course," Rhiannon said, her smile brightening a little.

"You and Lara stayed close after you broke things off," I said, changing the subject a little.

Rhiannon made a little noise. "In some ways. But she and Ember are really better friends with each other than either of them are with me." I frowned. That was not the impression I had of them. To me, it seemed like they both depended on her more than that. "It's all right," she assured me. "I've accepted that this is the way it is when you end things with someone and have to work with them for the rest of eternity."

She took another sip of her wine, and I tried not to draw connections between that and what she'd told me in the kitchen. Rhiannon was so perceptive about so many things, but she sometimes didn't understand how her words might affect others. I wondered if that was because she thought herself unimportant.

The only thing to do was to show her I cared about her, about her past. "Can I ask why things ended?"

After a long breath, she answered. "We were a bad fit. Everything that was good between us was ephemeral. The bad stuff stuck. We nearly ruined each other, and our cohort, with our fighting. We actually work a lot better as friends. When there's no sex involved, we seem to stay on the right side of things."

"Is that a struggle?" I asked, worried it might seem like I was interrogating her.

She shrugged, leaning comfortably into me. "No, I don't miss fucking Lara. It always came with the consequences of fleeting passion." The look she gave me was molten with desire. "We could never go deep as lovers. We didn't tell each other things—we never even seemed to want to. Eventually, it ruined the sex, and that was all we had left."

Her words were a bit blunt, but they were precise, cutting right to what I'd feared, that some part of her still ached for Lara Achilles. It was as though she'd thrown a door that had been closed between us wide open, and I was marveling at the invitation to walk through.

"Oh," was all I could manage. We'd told each other so many intimate things already. It was easy to talk to Rhiannon, to tell her things I'd never dreamed of telling another lover.

"I don't seem to have that issue with you," she said, her hand moving onto my knee. The way her dress was cut revealed that the cadence of her breath had gone from even to something quick and labored. My cock jerked at her touch and every muscle in my abdomen clenched. Her hand slid further up my thigh, a dark, sensual energy winding into every word. "When I talk to you, it's like my whole heart opens up. I fuck things up, the way I always do, but I still want to tell you things."

I glanced at the room. Not a single person looked our way. It was as though we were invisible. Rhiannon's hand was at my inner thigh now, and my legs spread almost involuntarily as she cupped my balls through my dress pants, then squeezed.

"Fuck," I breathed as her hand slid up to lightly tease my cock.

"Kiss me," she ordered in that sweet way of hers that she only used for my benefit.

"No," I replied, my head clearing just enough to think about what she'd said. "Why did you say you fuck things up?"

She drew back, her shoulder slumping as though I'd insulted her. I reached out to touch her face, to pull her chin so that she had to look at me. Her eyes were so sad. There was so much pain there. So much ancient pain.

"Because I do," she said with a horrific little laugh at her own expense. "That's what I do. Fuck other people's lives up. Stick around, you'll see."

Whatever she was thinking of went back further than her and Lara, further than even the Maere. Someone had torn her down from the beginning, made her feel small and worthless. I wracked my brain quickly, thinking about the blunt way she sometimes spoke. About the sharpness in her that drove me wild, and how that might be misinterpreted by some as rudeness, rather than refreshing honesty and clarity about what she thought and felt.

Before I could say anything, the waiter came by. His face, at least, wasn't an odd blur. "Good evening, I am Marcus. Have you dined with us before?" He was a tall human with pale skin, sprinkled with freckles and bright blue eyes that didn't quite focus on either one of us. In fact, it was almost as though he was looking at someone else.

"Good, good," he said before either of us could say a thing. "I'll get that right out for you."

Rhiannon laughed as he disappeared. "What do you think we're getting?"

"Who could tell?" I shook my head as the tension broke between us. "I don't think you fuck things up."

Rhiannon looked down at her hands. It was the smallest I'd ever seen her look. "Objectively, that is not true. Our swords, for example—"

"Your people made a grave mistake, Rhiannon. They

have hidden from the world for a long time. They don't know who you are."

"And who am I, Eryx?" she asked. Not defiant, not challenging, but curious.

I ran my thumb over the ridge of her high cheekbones, then pushed my fingers into her silken hair, winding them in at the base of her neck. "You are kind and capable. You do too much, and expect too little in return. You're the sharpest person I've ever met…" I breathed her in. "So damn smart, and so fucking sexy."

Her eyes widened, hearing me describe her. I bent closer, loving the way she reacted when I spoke into the sensitive shell of her ear. "You are the most beautiful crea-ture on the face of the planet."

She made that whispery gasping noise again, breathing just one word, "Eryx."

The way she said my name was so full of need that I stopped holding back. I kissed her. Gently at first, then hard as she melted into me. Her mouth opened for me, her tongue meeting mine as I drank her in. I folded her into me, not caring who watched me kiss her. There was nothing I wanted more than this woman. Her hands pressed against my chest, her fingers gripping the lapels of my jacket.

When my lips trailed away from hers to kiss her jaw, her neck, behind her ears, she gasped. "No one is watch-ing, Eryx. I don't think any of them can see us."

I glanced up. She was right. The entire restaurant went on just as it had when we came in. They weren't trying not to look as my fingers grazed her hard nipples, or as I dragged my tongue along her neck to suck the deliciously soft column of her neck. They simply didn't see us. My cock was so hard I thought it might burst.

"Would you care to test that?" I asked with a grin.

CHAPTER 14

RHIANNON

I NODDED, not taking even a second to worry that I might appear too eager. I was eager. It was thrilling to think that maybe they were all just pretending not to see us. That at any moment, the other restaurant patrons might look up and see him touching me.

Heat pooled between my legs. My heart raced as Eryx trailed a hand down the front of my dress. He played with my nipples as he kissed my neck, stroking them in light, lazy circles as they hardened, almost painfully.

The way he caressed me was full of deferred longing, as though he'd waited eons to touch me, and was afraid that after this he might not have another chance. The urgency, mixed with the slow, yearning desire in every breath he took, captivated me.

His mouth moved up my neck, his lips closing around my earlobe before he murmured into my ear, his deep voice sending vibrations straight into my aching core. "Are you wet for me, Rhiannon?" He didn't wait for me to answer, but began to pull my dress up, inch by slow inch, teasing my skin with the silky fabric. "When I spread your legs, what am I going to find?"

I moaned louder than was appropriate and no one turned. No one even paused or batted an eyelash. His fingers were running up my inner thigh now, pushing my legs apart, then grazing the curls of hair at the apex of my legs. He teased me, touching me everywhere but where I wanted him most. Doing everything but sinking his fingers into me.

"Please," I murmured. "Please touch me."

His free hand stroked my jawline as he looked into my eyes. Staring into those icy green eyes, now burning with the intensity of his desire, was so arousing I thought I might come just from the way he looked at me. Two fingers sank into me, sliding so deep that I gasped as he thumbed my lower lip.

"So fucking wet," he answered his own question. "I need to taste you."

Every thought I'd ever had disappeared, narrowing in on the feeling of him inside me so closely that I was little more than wet, throbbing need. He smiled before moving his head back to my ear, trailing hard, passionate kisses up my neck. He wasn't making a show of teasing me anymore. The fervor with which he kissed me, the hard strokes of his fingers inside me, all told me just how much he wanted this.

"Would you like that, Rhiannon?" he asked. "Would you like me to lift you onto the table and make a meal of you in front of all these people?"

His fingers drove harder into me, curling upward to find the spot inside that made me shiver with pleasure, as the heel of his palm pressed against my clit. My hips bucked against him, pushing him deeper inside of me as I ground myself against him.

"Yes," I begged, scanning the room as his free hand slipped inside my dress.

He laughed softly, then pushed my dress aside to expose my breast. Still, no one looked our way. As he brought his mouth to my nipple and sucked, no one turned. As he brought my other breast out, no one deviated from their conversations. I moaned louder as he stroked his fingers harder inside me.

"Are you sure you want to do this?" he asked. "Are you sure you want me to make you come in front of all these people?"

It was all I wanted. The kind of risk I'd never take in the outside world, but I could indulge here. I could lose myself in this fantasy, lose myself in him.

"Yes," I pleaded. "Yes."

In an instant, he pulled his fingers out of me, leaving me hollow and empty. He hooked his still-soaked hand around my knee and pulled me deftly into his lap. I ground myself into his erection, taking what pleasure I could while I was on top of him. He growled as he jerked into me, rubbing hard through his pants.

"I'll make a mess on your pants," I murmured.

"Godsdamn right you will," he groaned before pushing my skirt up to rub my clit. "And a mess on my face as well."

His huge hands were around my waist before I could think. I glanced behind me, but there had been no change in the dining room. Eryx lifted me easily, placing me on the table, right in front of him. Gently, he kissed between my breasts, trailing kisses down my belly as he pushed the cutlery and our glasses aside. Then he pushed me back onto the table, placing my heeled feet on the seat on either side of him. They barely touched.

My breath came quick and shallow as he lifted my

dress up, pushing my knees apart until I was exposed to him, the cool air of the restaurant caressing the wet skin between my thighs. I looked back, my heart racing. Any moment, it felt as though whatever phenomenon caused the spirits not to see us might break. But no one looked our way. Eryx's breath was hot on my skin as he kissed my inner thighs.

"I need you inside me," I begged.

"Let me look at how gorgeous you are," he said, spreading my legs wider.

His fingers parted my outer lips gently, exploring me, drawing my slick desire out to make circles around my clit with it. "So fucking perfect."

He waited until my eyes met his to slide a finger inside me, swirling it slowly around my inner walls, while his other hand stroked my belly. "Every part of you is so soft and silky," he murmured, adding a second finger. "So tight." And another, as he watched my clit swell with need.

His expression was rapt with lust as he pushed deep into me. "So responsive to everything I do to you. Will you scream for me when I make you come?"

I nodded, desperate for him to do as he'd promised. To make a meal of me. "Yes, I promise."

He looked like the cat who ate the canary at that moment. "You want my mouth on you, don't you?"

"Yes," I whimpered. "Please."

"I don't want you to beg, Rhiannon," he said with a smile. "I want you to order me to suck your clit." He smiled. "It makes me so fucking hard to hear you tell me what to do."

Heat flushed through me, and one glance down told me he wasn't lying, but this felt like something deeper than sex. More significant than playing out a fantasy.

Eryx sat back, watching me. "You are safe with me," he

said. "There isn't anything you could ask for that I wouldn't give you."

There it was. The reality of things. He wanted to take this thing between places I wasn't sure I could go. I averted my eyes. "There is. Everyone has their limits."

"I don't," he responded, leaning forward. "Not with you." Then he frowned. "You don't want me to dress like a chicken, do you?"

I shook my head, lifting it a little to get a better look at him. "No, do you want to?"

Eryx leaned forward, his breath grazing my thighs. "Please don't tell anyone, Rhiannon, but I am afraid of chickens." He pressed a kiss to my inner thigh as I laughed. "But for you, I'd be poultry."

The silliness of his words sweetened by the second. He wanted to care for me—wanted to give me what I needed. And he wanted me to ask for it.

"I want your fingers inside me," I said, feeling strangely tentative.

I'd been accused of being bossy plenty of times, but it felt difficult to ask for what I really wanted, let alone what I needed. If I told him what I needed now, would I ever stop?

His fingers slid directly back into me as an aria played over the restaurant's speakers. The power I felt at getting exactly what I wanted, just because I'd asked for it, was heady.

I tried again. "Suck my clit."

He grinned, bringing his mouth directly to me, rolling my clit between his lips before closing them around me, lapping and sucking in quick turns. Every movement was bliss, and he was right, I was safe with him.

Safer than I'd been in a long time. The perpetual tightness in my chest began to loosen as my breath came in quick pants, my abdomen quivering with each jolt of sharp pleasure he sent through me with his tongue.

"Harder," I demanded, practically breathless now.

Eryx moaned his approval against me, driving into me harder.

The waiter was coming towards us. Was his name Marcus? His eyes seemed to meet mine for the briefest of moments, then slid away as he set a basket of bread down at the table. Eryx glanced up at him, but didn't stop. In fact, he moaned loudly again, sending vibrations through my clit that reverberated through my body.

Marcus paused, as though slightly surprised, looking down at me. His eyes widened and he blushed as Eryx continued his ministrations between my legs. I watched as Marcus licked his lips. He wanted to be the one between my legs. Or perhaps he wanted to be the one being sucked. Either way was exhilarating to think of, sending a thrill through me that made me dizzy with power.

My back arched and I pulled the plunging neckline of my dress aside to reveal my breasts. Marcus watched as I played with my nipples, his cheeks flushing. He was hand-some, a strawberry blonde, with broad shoulders and a slim, but muscular build.

Eryx raised his head. "Isn't she beautiful?"

Marcus nodded, an erection sprouting in his pants. Eryx smirked as he noticed it, obviously pleased.

"She tastes incredible," Eryx said as he stroked deeper into me. "And she is all mine."

"Of course, sir," Marcus replied.

I was almost certain he wished he was the one being fucked, but it didn't really matter. His eyes slid back to me and his hands flexed. Maybe I was wrong. Maybe the dead waiter wanted to be with both of us.

"Do you want him to watch me make you come, Rhiannon?" Eryx asked.

I looked from my upside-down position at the dining room. Marcus was the only one who could see us, the only one who noticed. Like the post-lady, I imagined that if I talked to him too much, he would simply disappear, or start over in some way. My eyes slid to the growing hard-on in the waiter's pants, and I'd never felt so powerful.

"Do *you* want him to watch?" I asked.

Eryx grinned at me, curling his fingers into the spot inside me that *would* make me come if he did it too many more times. "I want to play however you do, my love."

My love. The words sent delicious thrills through me. But I wasn't sure. Eryx flicked a hand at the waiter. "Go away."

He pulled off the table, gathering me into his lap. "Are you all right?"

He was worried that Marcus seeing us had scared me. "Yes," I breathed, winding my arms around his neck, and repositioning myself so that I could rock my hips over his erection. "I only want you."

"I only want you too," he murmured. "But letting them watch isn't the same as having an orgy."

"Them?" I murmured.

He nodded to the dining room. I glanced behind me, only to find that a good number of the spirits were watching us, their faces clearer now. Many were intent with lust. Some at tables across the dining room were engaging in acts of their own. Slowly, I turned back to Eryx, heat flooding through me as I brought my mouth to his.

"Do you want to go home?" he asked, obviously still concerned.

I looked back over my shoulder. The dining room was

much as it had been the whole time, except now, eyes were on us. Hungry eyes that watched.

My eyes flitted around the room. In a dark corner, near the bathroom, Marcus had melted into the shadows, but it was clear he saw us. Clear that he wanted us both. I kept my eyes on him as I raised my hips and unfastened Eryx's pants. Like me, he was wearing nothing underneath.

His cock sprang out, hard and huge. I didn't bother to push his pants down further. "The waiter is watching us from the corner," I whispered.

"I can make him stop," Eryx said, his voice husky as I stroked his cock a few times, a bead of precum appearing as I squeezed.

"Let him watch us," I murmured, raising up onto my knees and rearranging my dress to take him in. "I want you to fuck me hard and fast."

"Yes," he agreed as I sank onto him, arching my back to press an exposed nipple into his mouth.

I moved slowly at first, making eye contact with Marcus as Eryx moved inside me, sucking my nipples so hard it hurt in the best way. I could feel the other eyes in the room on my back, but focusing on just the waiter gave my mind clarity. I moved my hips faster, getting wetter as it became obvious Marcus was going to watch as Eryx brought me to orgasm.

Marcus stepped further back into the shadows, his face open with wide, earnest lust. I nodded once to him, giving him permission to touch himself. I saw his hand move and he leaned against the wall, taking himself in hand.

"He's getting off to us," I murmured, moving my hips faster as Eryx thrust into me.

"Can you see his cock?" he asked.

I shook my head, squinting a little. "Not really, but I can see his hand moving, and his face... he's enjoying us."

"So is everyone else," Eryx growled. "They're watching you, love. No one can take their eyes off you."

"What are they doing?" I murmured, relishing the idea.

"Everything you're imagining and more," he whispered, before pulling me to him and kissing me deeply.

And then Marcus and the dining room faded away—not just because of the way Eryx kissed me. When I looked up, he was gone, and so were all the other patrons. Eryx pushed me off his cock, back onto the table.

"I need to come with you," he murmured before climbing onto the table with me. "Now."

"Yes," I agreed. "Fuck me so hard, baby. Right here on the table."

He let out a sound of feral desire as he thrust back into me. "Gods, you are wet, and so fucking tight." He watched as his cock slid into me, stroking my belly as he pumped into me.

"I love that," I moaned. "I love feeling you feel yourself inside me. Fuck me harder now."

He groaned at my words, grabbing my chin. "What else do you want, Rhiannon?"

"Kiss me," I ordered. "Lose control. *Ravage me.*"

The noise that came out of him was practically animalistic as he slammed hard into me, grinding his pubic bone against my clit as he kissed me. I wrapped my legs around his hips to take him deeper, and he cried out in my mouth, the muscles in his ass tensing as he thrust.

"You are going to make the prettiest mess all over my pants," he murmured into my ear. "I can't wait to see how wet you make me when my cum spills out of you."

My vision went white, and then I was screaming his name, as he roared with the pleasure of my release. His movements slowed, and then he started to laugh. "Shit, we broke the table."

I opened my eyes, which I had not realized were squeezed shut, and then began to laugh as well. The table was absolutely shattered around us. "Take me home," I said. "I want to be alone for real."

Without a word, or even a moment to fasten his pants, Eryx Necroline scooped me into his arms and kissed me as he stalked out of the Paradiso. "With pleasure, my love."

CHAPTER 15

ERYX

I DIDN'T KNOW how we got back to the cottage, only that she was in my arms, kissing me, saying the filthiest things imaginable, making me so hard again that I could hardly think straight. I got her up the stairs without really processing anything, until she lifted her dress above her head and the moonlight hit her skin.

"You are so beautiful," I breathed, kneeling before her. "The way you feel. I can never get enough of you."

"Take off your shirt," she said, running her hands through my hair. I did as she asked, practically purring under her touch.

But when she pulled me closer, I knew we had to stop. We hadn't had even the most basic of conversations about sex, limits, boundaries or anything of the sort, and we'd fucked in front of a restaurant of spirits—so hard we broke the table. Besides that, I knew she had to be sore, or she would be later, from how roughly I'd fucked her in the restaurant.

I took a deep breath and hugged her. "We have to slow down, love."

Her breath caught, and then she laughed. "That's probably a good idea. We never did get to eat."

I chuckled and stood up. "Why don't you draw yourself a bath, and I'll go scrounge something up?"

Rhiannon nodded. "That sounds good. Something light, I think."

"We have some strawberries, and there's a nice butterkäse, I think."

"Perfect," she replied, raising on her tiptoes. "Will you bring it to me in the bath?"

I kissed her again, just because I could, and was pleased when she melted into me. Before the kiss deepened, or rather, before I was tempted to deepen it, I trailed kisses along her cheekbones, her eyes, her forehead. "You were amazing tonight."

A flicker of something odd passed over her face. "You're not leaving, are you?"

It felt as though I'd been stabbed. How could she think that? "Of course not."

She nodded once, but didn't quite meet my eyes. "Just checking."

"I'll be right back," I assured her. "Unless you're not that hungry, and then I could stay."

"I'll be all right," she answered, but I didn't like the way she was retreating into herself. Had we done something at the restaurant she didn't like? Things had gone a bit farther than I'd have liked without a clear discussion of what her limits were.

"Why don't I run the bath and we can get in together?" I asked, winding a strand of her hair around my fingers. "And then when we're done, you can come to the kitchen with me, and you can watch while I make you whatever you please."

She nodded, her face solemn. I pushed my pants off so

I was naked too, with a bit of flourish. It had the intended effect. She laughed a real laugh, though it was a little softer than usual, her hand slipping into mine.

As my fingers closed around hers, and we walked to the bathroom together, she spoke so quietly I could hardly hear her. "When I was in Aradios, I was with a man who would disappear in the middle of the night. He'd say he had to go to the bathroom, and then just disappear."

I turned, whipping around in shock. "Why would he do something like that?"

She shrugged. "He was a human. One of those ones who called himself an ally to parapsychs. Wouldn't go to dinner with me either, or be seen in public."

My lip curled in disgust. "Someone should beat the living shit out of him."

She shrugged, smiling sadly. "Maybe someone will someday."

I walked ahead of her into the bathroom and turned on the light. Her breath drew in sharply. When I turned, her expression had shifted out of that wan sadness into what I could only describe as incandescent fury. "Who did that to your back? I will kill *them*."

I'd forgotten. I glanced back over my shoulder at her. "Magnus. After Frannie."

"Eryx," she breathed as I turned the knobs on the tub. "I am so sorry for asking."

I shook my head, then sat on the thick edge of the clawfoot tub, pulling her onto my lap. She curled into me so naturally, her head resting in the crook of my neck, her breath soft on my skin. I had to close my eyes to be sure she was real.

"It's fine to ask." I laughed a little, which was a surprise, but felt so good. "It is actually nice that you got so angry."

"Why did he do it?" she asked. "Did he care about Francesca?"

"No," I answered. "He cared that I fucked up. That I killed Hoight."

Her body tensed in my arms, her fingers closing into those precious little fists again. No one knew how adorable Orphium's assassin was. It was the most perfect secret I'd ever known. The City of the Dead's most lethal woman was actually a squish-ball of sweet fury.

She was waiting, I realized, for me to keep talking. Giving me space to speak, to tell her how I felt. A lump formed in my throat. Immediately, I understood why everyone in her life sought her out so frequently. It wasn't that she was a people pleaser, or that the Maere were assholes taking advantage of her. It was *this*.

I didn't actually know a secret about Rhiannon. They knew it too, knew just exactly how special she was. How intoxicating this mix of fierce and soft could be. And like me, they couldn't get enough of it. She was a person so unique that she made people see that they too were imperfectly perfect. However sharp her edges were, there was a depth of care to her that was addictive.

I held her a little tighter. "Magnus never let a mistake slide. Not when Roman was alive, and certainly not after he killed him. I was supposed to get the location of the girl's body, then Eli was supposed to perform some healing miracle and we were going to send him back to O-Tex raving."

"Eli *Cabot*?" she asked. When I nodded, she shook her head. "Is there anything that guy can't do?"

I didn't miss a beat. "Crack a fucking smile."

She snickered. The miracle worker was notoriously grumpy. Feeling her laugh against my naked body was the kind of familiar sweetness that threatened to get me hard again.

I brushed a kiss against her temple. "Tub's full. Do you want to get in first while I light the candles?"

She let me help her into the tub, and then I did as I promised, climbing in behind her. When she leaned back against my chest, it felt as though the world might collapse into a single point, a part of me existing in all times. In a past where I didn't know her—but I missed her, missed this. In a future where I loved her, and she loved me. In this moment, when the sum parts of our past and future moved between us, shifting to create some new reality.

Candlelight flickered over the surface of the water. Her head fell back against my shoulder and she let out a long, heavy breath, raising her face to mine to be kissed. The movement was so surreal, so familiar. As my lips met hers, the house itself went quiet, the whispers of the dead gone completely silent for the first time since we'd been here.

Her body slid against mine, her eyes falling shut as she curled against me. There in my arms, in a bathtub, inside the most haunted house in Orphium, I fell irrevocably in love with Rhiannon Brontë.

I let her sleep when the music started from behind the locked door of Magnus' office, a haunting melody creeping out into the hallway. My arms tightened around Rhiannon, but I had nothing to fear from the dead while she slept.

So I waited, watching, listening, as the water slowly chilled. When I feared she might be cold, I lifted Rhiannon out of the tub, and though she woke as I wrapped her in a towel, she fell asleep again as soon as I had her back in my arms. It was like the first nights in the cottage. Some uncanny force kept her asleep, while I remained awake.

It was possible that her deep sleep was triggered by

release and just enough comfort and relaxation that she could finally let go. I wanted to believe that, but I knew better. I knew spirits. The house was doing this to her somehow.

I helped her into bed, then sat back in the chair I'd kept vigil in those first few days. "Quiet," I whispered in the vox spiritus.

The music stopped immediately. Too immediately. It typically took a moment for the vox spiritus to set in and work. I rose out of my chair, moving to the bed by instinct. Some energy built behind the door of Magnus' office, but it was nothing like any of the malefics I'd ever encountered.

There was anger in it, rage, vengeful fury. But none of it was directed at me, nor at Rhiannon. It threatened to swallow us whole, all the same. I tried to focus my energy around it, to help bring it forward, to allow it to speak. When others watched me communicate with spirits, it appeared that they spoke through me, but my own perception of it was that of the vox spiritus being used in reverse.

To me, it was always a conversation, not the delivery of a monologue. I felt the spirit acquiesce to my request, a kind of relief in its energy that had not been there before. But something went wrong.

Rhiannon sat up in bed, her eyes open, but heavy. "Take me back to the gods of destruction. Tell them all I did in their endless names."

I shook her shoulders, begging her to wake, but she just repeated herself in that same hollow voice. *She was possessed.*

Panic nearly pushed me to a place where I couldn't think, but I forced myself to, for her. It was a grave sin to turn the vox spiritus onto the living. If she had been a necromancer, I would not have hesitated—necromancers can't be hurt by the vox—but the rest of the living might be. We could never direct it at them without unpredictable things happening. But she was a true immortal, and as far as I knew no one had ever tried to use the vox on one of the Maere. Her volume had increased, and she began to convulse.

I brushed her hair away from her face, pleading as I shook her. "Please Rhiannon, please wake up."

But she didn't wake. She just stared at me wide-eyed, repeating "Tell them all I did," in a hoarse, vacant whisper.

Her voice was already weakened, which meant the spirit would take over soon, adding its vocal intonations onto her vocal cords, as a final act of domination. I couldn't let this go on, a powerful spirit inhabiting one of the Maere was the kind of nightmare that Ares and I had discussed after midnight for years. For one to take over Rhiannon Brontë was the worst thing I could think of, on too many levels to count.

I had to take the risk of using the voice on her.

My heart raced, but I knew that she, herself, would insist on it. That's who Rhiannon was. So I steeled myself against the fear inside me, drawing the vox out of my soul, holding gently to her shoulders as I spoke. "Let her go."

Her eyes rolled back into her head and she went limp in my arms for a moment. Then her eyelashes fluttered and she shook her head. Her legs stretched out in the bed, almost languorously. My heart, which had galloped ahead of me a moment ago, slowed a bit now.

She yawned, then opened her eyes, smiling at me. "I fell asleep."

"You did," I agreed, my heart resuming its usual pace.

She was all right. I lay her back down on the pillows.

"We were happy tonight," she said as she snuggled back into the bed.

I climbed in bed next to her and shut off the lamp next

to my side of the bed. "We were," I said as my eyes adjusted to the dark.

She yawned again, stretching like a cat in the dark. When her body relaxed, her eyes snapped open. My heart stopped as her arm raised, moving with none of her usual grace. She smiled as she stroked my cheek and said, "Remember her this way."

What had I done wrong?

If the vox had worked, the spirit would be gone.

Rhiannon blinked and smiled more naturally. "I'm sleepy. Will you hold me?"

Possessed or not, there was nothing that would keep me from fulfilling that request. As my heart rate returned to a gallop, I pushed her hair back from her face. Somewhere along the way, we'd lost her sparkling combs. They were probably amongst the rubble at the Paradiso.

Rhiannon curled into my chest, kissing me one last time before turning over and tucking herself under my chin. She fit perfectly, and my heart sank. Had I made a terrible mistake using the vox on her?

"Please be all right," I whispered to the dark. Rhiannon's breath was steady and even. She was deep in sleep. "I can't lose you, Rhi. I love you."

In the hallway, the door to Magnus' office opened, a soft glow of lamplight falling onto the wood floor in the hallway. The house fell blessedly quiet. I listened to Rhiannon breathe, examining every bit of her aura that I could access. She was, as far as I could tell, intact. Herself. Unpolluted by any energy that was not her own. But I could not relax, nor retreat.

An instinct rose up in me. A simple observation of pattern, really. Spirits were just *people*, after all. Dead people, but at their core, they behaved the way they had when they were alive. And if I was right about this... well, it would open up a whole host of issues, but we would deal with that later. And if I was right, we would have another clue about who controlled this place.

So, I declared myself. "I would die to protect her," I said in a soft, clear voice, not wanting to wake Rhiannon. "I would never willingly hurt her, and as long as she wants me, I'll never leave her."

The light in the office shut off, and a deep peace fell over the house. Even I, who had been painfully awake a moment ago, was sleepy. Sleepy, but pleased.

As I sank deeper into bed I knew the answer to one piece of our puzzle: whoever was responsible for the complexity of the trap here in Oleander House *loved* Rhiannon.

CHAPTER 16

RHIANNON

I STOOD at the door of Magnus' office, frowning. Briony would say "the vibes" were off, which felt apt. The man's office radiated bad energy. Eryx had been quiet all morning, though we'd moved around each other with a kind of ease which had not been there before.

But something was worrying him. That much I was sure of. He was currently in the bathroom brushing his teeth. The air in the cottage had gotten so hot and stuffy it was tempting to open the windows, but—if possible—it was worse outside. As Eryx bent over the sink, I took a few steps back to appreciate the view.

Because it was so hot, he wore a pair of gym shorts so tiny, they were almost obscene. I was fairly certain he was mimicking the outfit I'd chosen for the day: a pair of hot pants I'd found at the local Thrifty Penguin on Ninth and a halter top. His eyes caught mine in the mirror right after he rinsed his mouth out.

"Whatcha lookin' at, Brontë?" he asked with a smile.

"Your ass," I admitted. "You can't blame me for ogling. Those shorts are delectable."

He came out of the bathroom, pushed me up against the railing and grabbed my ass, pulling me into his orbit with a kind of fevered energy. Instantly, I wrapped my legs around his waist, licking my lips.

"Don't make that face," he murmured.

"What face?" I asked, all wide-eyed innocence.

His head bent towards my neck, and a trail of kisses that ended with my earlobe in his mouth had me panting. "The face that makes me want to get inside you and stay there all day," he growled. "We have shit to *do*, Brontë. I can't live with my head between your legs."

There was a sound I made with him that I'd never made with anyone else. Something between a whimper and a sigh. I made it now, pushing my hips into him.

"But I want to," he added, his voice rough with as much needy energy as I had. He squeezed my ass hard, his erection pushing into my core. "Maybe just a little taste," he growled before his lips met mine.

His kiss was hungry, desperate, as he moved me away from the ancient railing to slam me against the opposite wall. Suddenly, the hallway was freezing cold. Eryx stopped kissing me, but didn't put me down. In fact, he held me tighter. When my eyes met his, there was something like panic in them.

I put my feet on the ground. The way he had me caged against the wall was protective, like he thought someone might snatch me from him, and he'd stop them by the sheer barricade of his enormous body.

"What's wrong?" I asked. He glanced behind him, furtive. Then towards the open door to Magnus' office. Mysteriously, it had been open this morning when we got up. Dread seeped through me. "Tell me what's wrong."

"Last night, after you fell asleep in the tub—there was music coming from inside the office."

I swallowed. "Music? What kind of music?"

He shook his head. "Old music. I don't know how to describe it. Not creepy, but creepy in context, you know?"

I didn't, not exactly, but I nodded anyway.

"And then the light turned on and the door opened." I sensed there was something else. Something he didn't want to tell me. I crossed my arms. The chill in the hallway was spirit activity. That was Ghosts 101. He sighed. "I had to use the vox spiritus on you."

The spirit voice. "Why?"

He shook his head. "It got inside you, Rhiannon. It spoke through you."

It felt as though I was falling, as though someone had simply pulled the floor out from beneath me. Eryx caught me, pulling me into him. "I'm sorry. I should have told you sooner, but... I."

His fingers clenched around me, and he opened his mouth, but no sound came out. It was a cowardly move to hide something like this from me.

"What did I say?" I snarled. My anger was so quick to rise to the surface. So full of frustration at not having been told something that happened to my own body. I was just so sick of people keeping things from me.

"I am sorry I didn't tell you first thing," he repeated. Again, he seemed to struggle with his words, finally saying, "It was a mistake."

I ducked under his arms, taking a few steps towards Magnus' office, trying to quell the rage within me. It wasn't all about him, or what he'd done, after all. As I stared inside, I insisted again. "Tell me what I said."

His head hung slightly, his shoulders tight. He opened and closed his mouth again, twice, and then forced out. "You said..." He paused, looking like he might scream or cry for the briefest moment. What was wrong with him?

The tone of his voice was odd, almost strangled. Something in my gut tightened. And then he said, "Take me back to the gods of destruction. Tell them all I did in their endless names."

I swallowed hard. The verbiage was hard to mistake. "You're sure that's *exactly* what I said?"

He nodded. "Yes, does it mean something to you?"

Fleetingly, I was tempted to draw this out and make it hard for him. But it was so obvious he hadn't told me because he was frightened of what might happen to me. There was no doubt in my mind that Eryx Necroline wanted to protect me. Somehow, some way, we had to talk about what that might mean.

"Yes," I finally answered. "The gods of destruction are Tanith and Amarante—their dark aspects, anyway. Death and immortality paired are either a healthy cycle of life and existence, or a recipe for destruction." I sat down in the doorway to the office, not wanting to set foot inside, especially now. "And only someone from the island would use the phrasing, *their endless names*. It is a common way to end a prayer."

He came to sit next to me, his body still taut with some emotion I couldn't discern, and together we stared ahead. "I suppose that explains how all this is happening then, doesn't it?" he asked. "Your people have power that para-psychs don't anymore. Real magic, yes?"

I nodded, knowing there was a limit to what I could say. Until he knew the island more personally, there were guard rails, magical boundaries against talking about it. "Yes."

He placed his elbows on his knees, and his chin in his hands. For a split second, he looked like a little boy, puzzling through a big problem. "The trouble is, how does it all connect?"

I pointed at the office. "I think we'll have to go in to find out." Eryx didn't respond to that, other than to look worried. Decidedly worried. I bumped his shoulder with mine, resting against him. "If it would help, I can go downstairs and look through the library again. Maybe there's something we missed yesterday. I'd like to have another look through the sitting room as well."

There wasn't anything there; we both knew that, but it would make him feel better if I went elsewhere while he determined the possible danger of me going into the office. He was, after all, the expert in these things.

"That would help, I think," he replied. "If you're all right by yourself."

I stood, first pressing a kiss to the top of his head before agreeing. "I am."

He took hold of the hand that rested on his shoulder. "I was very scared I might lose you last night, or hurt you with the vox, but I didn't know how to tell you what happened. Yesterday was so good. I just wanted to keep that feeling for a little while longer."

My heart ached for him. For me. For two damaged souls who weren't sure how to be happy. All my anger dissolved. "I get it. I was mad at first, but I'm not now." I offered him a hand and pulled him up. "Go figure this thing out, okay?"

He nodded, solemn in the mission I'd given him, then stepped inside the beast's lair. I took a deep breath and headed back downstairs, shivering from the chill that still hung in the air.

As predicted, there was nothing I missed in the library. Nothing to tell me who Cassandra was before she'd come to Orphium. Neither was there anything in the sitting room, the kitchen, or anywhere else that I could access downstairs.

I sat on the bottom step of the staircase, feeling discouraged. I let my mind drift, using a method that often worked at a dead end in an investigation. I closed my mind, and purposely thought of something else.

Fashion Week in Aradios, last spring. Everything I'd worn. The shows I'd gone to. The galleries I'd visited for parties. When my mind was clear of the track it had been on for the past hour, I opened my eyes and walked slowly through the downstairs of Oleander Cottage, trying to see it from a fresh perspective.

What did the choices Cassandra had made about decorating the cottage tell me? The wallpaper was nearly oppressive in its overwhelming mixture of patterns, and she'd deliberately chosen fabrics for furniture and window coverings that coordinated, but also were patterned.

"You felt trapped," I whispered to her spirit, wondering if she could hear me.

Yes, a voice in my head responded. *All the time.*

The voice was familiar, but not, at the same time. I wasn't sure how that could be. How could I know a voice, and yet also be so sure I *didn't* know it?

I stared at the painting in the sitting room that rested on the mantel, above the fireplace. It was a seascape, but rather melancholy. Most seascapes from the period represented the ocean in the many sheltered, sunny bays of Aradios, rather than the roiling thing that was the truth of our world, full of monsters, full of threats. This was neither.

It was familiar somehow, though. There was no signature on it, so I peeked behind it, hoping to find an artist's statement. The back of the frame revealed that it had not been professionally framed. There was no paper backing. But there was an artist's mark. A very clear CN.

Did the voice sound so familiar because it was Cassandra? We'd only spoken the one time, when she'd appeared in her office, and I barely remembered what she'd sounded like. But some part of me obviously did.

I was almost certain the voice in my head was her, so I asked, "You painted this?"

Yes, the voice answered, sounding just as sad as the painting felt.

"Is it a real place?" I asked, squinting at it. There was something about it that I felt I'd seen before.

Not anymore, the voice said. *It's all gone now. Maybe it never was true at all.*

I got the impression that she hadn't answered my question, but the question I should have asked. I repeated her words to myself a few times to commit them to memory before asking, "Was it you that possessed me last night?"

I am so many people, she answered. *I cannot remember them all. I cannot say if I have ever been you.*

I couldn't help but let out a wry laugh. That much I could identify with, though it was another cryptic answer. "Could you just tell me what's happening here?"

It was the wrong thing to do, to ask. The finger trap of the cottage contracted, squeezed hard enough on my windpipe that I held up my hands in defeat. "I'm sorry," I gasped, feeling as though someone had been trying to choke me. "I get it. I'm supposed to figure this out on my own."

Cassandra didn't answer. She was gone.

CHAPTER 17

ERYX

Why hadn't I been able to tell her all that had happened? At first, I thought I'd made the choice on my own. That fear had held me back. And perhaps it had. There wasn't any part of what happened after our bath that I wasn't afraid of. Maybe I had just gone cowardly.

I swore, clenching my fists, gritting my teeth, suppressing the urge to scream at something, to hit something. But I didn't do those things. If I needed to let my anger out, I did it with a punching bag at the gym. I pushed breath through my lungs, long and slow, forcing my heart to slow and my mind to refocus. There had to be an answer here.

Something good *had* to come from all this.

I had to find a way to help Rhiannon, to get us both out of here before anything else happened. There had never been a case of spirit possession from within the Maere's ranks. I hadn't even known it was possible, though after what had happened to Briony, Ares and I probably should have looked into this.

If only my brother or Av were here now to help me

think through this calmly. If the spirit decided to keep Rhiannon, to possess her forever … well, I wasn't sure what that would mean for the Maere, for us, but worse, I couldn't imagine what it might mean for Orphium. For the world.

Spiraling wasn't going to help, though. I took a deep breath and looked again, though I'd searched Magnus' office three times and found nothing of any real use. It wasn't as though I was inexperienced in finding things that were hidden, but Magnus' office had been carefully edited.

Too carefully edited, in my expert opinion. I'd been sacking other people's personal spaces since I was twelve years old, and it was my view that anyone without anything to find had something to hide.

Before I was twelve, I'd learned from Roman that the majority of us operated under the erroneous belief that other people saw the world as we did, thought the way we did, and did things the way that we did. When you searched a space, you had to try to come at it with a blank mind, rather than your own preconceived notions about what you would do. It had served me well for centuries, but today all I knew was that Magnus had something to hide.

I sat at the heavy desk staring at the familiar, identically bound books that sat against the wall: a fraction of the Necroline Dynasty's old ledgers. I'd already thumbed through them, looking for a hidden key or scrap of paper that would lead us to another clue. *Nothing.*

A sheen of sweat had broken out over my skin as my search had grown more fervent. Anything to keep myself from thinking about what had happened to Rhiannon last night. The danger she was in, just by being trapped here with me. My thoughts took a desperate turn, racing through all the ways we might force our way out. They were all reckless. All far too dangerous to try.

I needed to buckle down and get her out of here the reliable way. Solve the mystery of the cottage. Exorcise the primary spirit. Get Rhiannon out. Those were my objectives now, in that order. I turned my attention back to the ledgers.

If there was nothing obvious to find in the office, perhaps there was something less obvious to find, hiding in plain sight. Too often, in Orphium, violence was hidden under layers of bureaucracy or business.

I flipped through one of the ledgers, feeling frustrated and wishing again that Ares were here. Not only would he have solved this mystery already, Ares was truly good at numbers, and though I typically collected our raw data, he was the one that always made the finances make sense. It looked to me as though it had been the other way around between Magnus and Roman.

I tried to focus.

Though I wasn't much good at knowing what to do with a budget, I was plenty familiar with what the local tithes looked like, and what yearly patterns were for every neighborhood in the city. Some folks didn't have steady work, and their tithing to the Consulate fluctuated. Magnus had organized his ledgers in a similar system to what Ares liked to use.

The longer I looked through them, the odder they appeared to me, though I couldn't say why. I stood, calling down the stairs, "Rhiannon, are you any good with numbers? Budgets, I mean?"

There was a pause, and then the sound of her footsteps as she came to the bottom of the narrow staircase. "Yes," she answered. "I have a good head for figures. Want me to come up?"

"Please," I answered, before returning to the desk to lay things out for her.

"It's so hot up here," she said as she entered the office, pulling her ponytail a bit tighter.

Her face glistened with a sheen of sweat that matched my own. The heat, and her mere presence scrambled my brain, sending my ability to focus on anything but her skittering to realms beyond my grasp. I tried not to appreciate the generous curves of her body as she sat down.

The way her plush thighs pressed together as she crossed her legs, or the muscles in her back, honed from years of work with weaponry. Another faint glow of sweat created a sheen on her decolletage. I had the distinct urge to lick it off her. I had to focus, but she was a terrific distraction.

She broke through my lust-addled haze. "Why don't you sit for a few, and I'll look this over."

I nodded, sinking into the large leather chair in the corner of the tiny office. Being around her had me either frenzied with need, or perfectly calm. It was my desperation to enjoy every second with her, to drink it in so fully that when she inevitably pushed me away, I would have the memories of her.

Remember her this way. The words had felt like a threat, but were they? And why couldn't I tell her what had happened?

As Rhiannon worked, she turned the pages of the ledgers so methodically for a few minutes that I was lulled into stillness. A deep calm came over me. I never should have sent her downstairs. Something about her aura had this effect on me, steadying somehow—and I could examine the room from a different perspective now that I was settled.

There was wallpaper here, as in most every other room in the cottage. This pattern was a forest scene I recognized from old tapestries depicting a unicorn hunt. My eyes got lost in the leaves and pine boughs. The swirls of greenery changed, moved, the longer I stared. I watched, fascinated, as the leaves on the birches shimmered, the needles of the evergreens glistening with snow.

The soft sound of Rhiannon's even breath brought me back, the rustling of pages, the scratch of her pen on paper. She must have taken up one of Magnus' blank notebooks, but I hadn't seen her do it. I opened my mouth to speak, but found it stuck shut. There was something on it, something covering it.

I tried to lift my arm to touch my face, but could not. A shadow crept slowly across the long narrow corridor of floor left uncovered by furniture in the room. There was no trace of the usual chill in the air that accompanied a haunting. In fact, the room was hotter than ever.

Whoever, *whatever*, cast that shadow was corporeal. It had come up the stairs without me noticing. How had I not noticed? How had I not heard something coming for us? And what's more, how had Rhiannon not noticed?

The absence of a racing heart, or a pant of lungs was disconcerting. My mind fought against my frozen muscles to move my body. To open my mouth. Saints, even to simply turn my head. But I could not. The shadow crept closer, its arm raised menacingly towards Rhiannon, but I could do nothing but wait for the hand to fall.

All these years. All this violence. And in yet another moment it truly counted, I was useless. Powerless to use any of it for good. *Just like I had been with Frannie.* Though my body didn't react, couldn't react, my mind screamed with futile rage, burning through the fear that kept me bound up in panic.

I blinked. It wasn't much, but it was something, and it seemed as though my vision cleared, though I hadn't realized it was blurred. The shadow paused, a finger emerging from the amorphous mass that was its hand. It pointed to a spot on the wall above the desk.

"Did you fall asleep?" Rhiannon's voice, clear as a bell, woke me with a start. I practically gasped for air. She leaned forward in the desk chair, her hand touching my knee. "Bad dream?"

I nodded, suppressing the urge to grab onto her and keep her as close to me as possible. My head had moved of its own accord. I could sit forward, swallow my fear. She was all right; there was no one else in the room with us. No shadow covered the floor. And most importantly, Rhiannon was still herself.

Breath heaved through my lungs as the chemicals rushing through my body that screamed *Act! Act!* calmed.

"Did you find something?" I asked, trying to keep my heart from racing.

Rhiannon's eyes were concerned, but as my breath returned to normal her shoulders, which had been slightly hunched, relaxed a measure. Suddenly it occurred to me that I hadn't hurt her with the vox spiritus—the entity that controlled this house, this advanced spirit trap, had us both in its grasp.

Us, and how many other spirits? My heart ached for Cassandra Necroline's spirit. After what she'd endured in life, being married to my uncle, I hated that she'd gotten caught up in this now. I had to save them both. I had to get Rhiannon out, and set Cassandra free from whatever monster controlled this place.

"Yes," Rhiannon said slowly, obviously worried about me. "I think I did."

I nodded once, then tried to speak, tried again to tell her what I learned. It was impossible. Whatever force controlled what happened here would not allow me to tell her what I knew.

Rhiannon's lips pressed together as her eyes narrowed. I had to hope that she was sorting out that something was wrong, as I had no way to tell her. With her eyes still narrowed, she picked up one of the blank legal pads that had been on Magnus' desk, and showed me her chicken scratches. I could make neither heads nor tails of it. I shrugged, which caused one corner of her mouth to quirk up.

"Magnus was getting money from somewhere other than the tithes, and it was going somewhere else—not to the Consulate." I raised an eyebrow. Surely that would have been obvious, even to me. But I *had* thought something looked off about it. Rhiannon continued, "It was in tiny amounts. And so randomly done, it would have appeared to be someone over-tithing."

My breath caught. Of course. It would be easy to hide money in the tithes. Some folks gave more in abundant months, tiding them over for the lean times so the Consulate wouldn't send their people out to collect the difference. It was something Ares and I always made sure to look the other way on, and most of the other Trinity leaders throughout the Three Cities were the same.

The tithes weren't meant as a punishment for our people, after all. They were to make sure the Consulate kept running. Without it, problematic as it was, there would be no mediation between us and the Authority. That was too dangerous—imperfect as it was, the days before the Consulate grasped as much power as it had now had been harrowing for parapsychs.

I tried not to think about my parents, turning back to the figures at hand. Magnus had been smart to hide what he was doing in the tithes. Few people would notice the discrepancy there.

Rhiannon showed me a column of numbers, running

along the months of the year for three years. She had traced a red line to show the general shape of the tithes. "This is the real over and under-tithing," she said. "More or less anyway. Some months it was hard to parse out from Magnus' deception. But you can see, it moves in cyclical patterns over the years."

I wasn't sure I saw what she referred to clearly, but I caught enough to understand why I'd been suspicious. Rhiannon tapped one month in particular. "This was the year of the Cities' Fair. You can see how in the months before the Fair, tithing went down. Then, in the months during and after, it slowly went up. There are similar ebbs and flows in other years."

Rhiannon pointed out similar rises and falls in tithing patterns. "Now look at the way the lines change when you just look at what actually went into the bank before the tithes were delivered to Ember." She turned back to the desk and brought the ledger closest to her onto her lap and traced her nail down the new lines. "See?"

The shape of the tithes was similar, but not identical, and it no longer showed the natural ebbs and flows from before. The difference was very subtle, but it was there. Magnus had manipulated the numbers, but failed to recognize the real ways our people lived and tithed.

He'd made a mistake that almost no one would notice. But Rhiannon had. She was the kind of smart that could figure things like this out. It was like the push and pull between us. We knew when to let the other lead, and when to follow, almost by instinct. We made a good team.

Rhiannon closed the ledger and leaned back in the chair. "The unwise believe that life is random, uncontrolled. But people move in patterns. In waves. Every action elicits a reaction, and we move together, whether we believe we do or not."

She wasn't just smart, she had the wisdom of thousands of years, and two separate lifetimes. My admiration for her grew. I nodded, turning my attention back to the problem at hand. "Where was the money coming from? Can you tell?"

Rhiannon shook her head. "No. He was very good at hiding it. There's no evidence of the source here. We've run into *another* dead end." Her arms went around her waist, like she was hugging herself. The look of helplessness in her eyes troubled me. That wasn't how Rhiannon typically operated. She didn't give up.

When she spoke again, my concern was allayed, but only a little. "How do you think Cassandra got the key to the Ossuary? Shouldn't Roman have had it?"

I sucked a deep breath in, creating more space in my mind. Being around Rhiannon made me want to push the boundaries of how I thought about things. With Ares, I was always wary of being wrong. He was the one who'd brought us out of hard times again and again. It felt easier to simply leave the deeper strategy to him. To let him lead alone.

He didn't ask for it to be that way. Alone here with Rhiannon, unknotting the tangles in this mess my family had created, I wondered if I'd made a mistake by assuming he'd wanted to carry so much of the burden alone. My thoughts rearranged, but it didn't seem I had the answer she was looking for.

Typically, with Ares and Av, in a situation like this, I would step back. Let the two of them think things through alone, assuming they didn't need my interference. Now, I changed tack—after all, things were different between me and her—and maybe that was a good change to have in my life. "Maybe. But the note in Triomphe would suggest that she took it from Magnus, and that someone else knew that she was looking for it. Whoever the 'L' was from the note."

I held my breath, feeling the unhelpfulness of my words deep in my bones. *Why had I even said anything?* To my surprise, Rhiannon's eyes went wide and a bit soft. "Yes," she breathed, as though my words had unlocked some idea within her. "This must all connect somehow. I just can't quite see *how*."

It wasn't a breakthrough. Not in the traditional sense. We hadn't come to some stunning conclusion and solved the mystery, but something shifted within me. I felt different when I was alone with her, free to think more deeply, to offer my own opinion.

It wasn't Ares that stopped me from sharing my ideas —I'd been holding myself back. Unsettled by the thought, I stood, going to the window. It looked out over the garden, but also gave me a sliver of a view of Hemlock House.

A flash of the mansion's snow-covered roof reminded me that the real world was still out there. That it was the dead of winter, and the people we loved were probably worried sick about not having heard from us for Saints knew how long.

"Cassandra had the key to her desk hidden in the library," I mused. We didn't have a pinboard, like Rhiannon and the Maere had set up during the heist, but we could gather our information all the same.

"A library full of books that would have been utterly unimportant to a man like Magnus, if I am correct in my remembrance of him," Rhiannon added.

My stomach clenched. "You are."

"I think we can assume she stole the Ossuary key, *and* that she stole it from Magnus himself, since she hid it in the locked part of her desk."

"In a secret compartment," I added. She was right. *We*

were both right, I corrected myself. This was adding up to something. I glanced back at her.

Rhiannon's long fingers closed around the arms of the wooden desk chair, her knuckles going white. "The basement door is locked, but we can assume the door to the Ossuary is down there somewhere, or at least access to it is."

And that the access to it was what was important here. What was in the Ossuary? I turned back to the window. The trees in the garden moved into their usual pattern of looping. The black cat came around the corner. The newspaper disappeared from the table. "Yes," I agreed. "And Magnus was taking money from someone."

Rhiannon took a deep breath. "Typically, I like evidence-based hypotheses. In this case though, I am going to…"

"Speculate?" I offered, turning to look at her again. She stared at the spot on the floor where I'd seen the menacing shadow in my dream, humming an assent.

"Magnus underestimated Cassandra," Rhiannon continued. My eyes drifted to the place in the wallpaper the shadow had appeared to point to.

"Whatever he was up to, he never thought she'd figure it out."

There was nothing there.

"But she did."

My eyes returned to the floor.

"She figured out what he was doing and she took the key from him."

I connected the dots between the spaces where the shadow's head had stopped and where it pointed, in the air, and then let my eyes scan the room at that exact latitude. *There it was.* Right above the desk, an anomaly in the wallpaper pattern so slight I never would have noticed it.

Rhiannon's breath hitched as I leaned over, reaching over her shoulder to press the spot in the wall just beneath the anomaly in the wallpaper. "What are you—"

Another invisible panel popped open and my body warmed in the ambient heat of her skin. *Do not touch her*, I cautioned myself. Right now wasn't the time for that. *Do not even* think *of touching her*.

The sound she made was soft, her lips forming just one small word, "Oh."

Her arm moved beneath mine, and gently she reached inside the dark panel, pulling out a skeleton key that was just the right size for the basement door. She handed it to me. "I don't think we should use it yet."

I frowned. "Why not?"

RHIANNON

IT WAS JUST A FEELING. A gut feeling, to be sure, but a feeling nonetheless. I'd spent so many years denying my instincts, insisting instead on hard evidence because I never felt as though I could wholly trust myself. But my instincts were evidence unto themselves. When I went against them, I was usually wrong. When the evidence supported them, and I went with them, I was right.

Learning to trust myself again was part of the reason I'd come here. Even so, saying out loud that it was "just instinct" wasn't attractive. I liked to be able to explain myself clearly to others. Luckily, an answer came to me fairly easily. It was, after all, right there for the taking.

"In my view," I said softly, feeling both unsure and confident of my words and my instinct simultaneously, "understanding why we are here and why Cassandra took the key to begin with is the first task."

There was the slightest of tremors, and then a noise that rang from within me, so loud my ears felt as though they might bleed. Something in the magic that held the house together cracked open. And in the pain of the moment, I realized what had been bothering me all morning. Eryx had been trying to tell me something. Trying to tell me something the house wouldn't let him.

Information that would have let the two of us better understand what was happening here. Information that would let us out of this trap. I clapped my hands over my ears, knowing it wouldn't help. The noise wasn't a real sound.

There was no time to react. No time to cling to Eryx, or hold onto something in Magnus' office. It all fell away. We were hurtled out of the house and into the garden, like a video tape on fast-forward. Nausea nearly pushed me to the grass, bowling me over.

Eryx's voice cut through my confusion. "There are consequences for your actions, Cassandra."

My heart raced wildly, my head spinning as a cold sweat broke out over my skin. He didn't sound like himself at all. He didn't sound like my Eryx. A voice within me—*not* the voice I'd come to know as my own, but Cassandra's—said, *Please watch. Please see.*

Perhaps she spoke the words inside Eryx's head as well, because he did not intervene. Against all baser instincts, I released my hold on my body and gave into the vision, remembering that we'd likened this massive illusion to a finger trap. If I pulled too hard, it would just tighten. Hard as it was to let go—I had to.

All right, I responded. *Show us what happened here.*

My mouth moved, my voice working out of my control now. "You know."

Eryx's eyes narrowed. "I have known for months that you were plotting something. I just didn't think you'd be quite so vicious."

I laughed, sinking further into the vision even as I

struggled against it, some base instinct in me knowing what had happened here.

Cassandra hadn't died in Aradios.

She hadn't even *gone* to Aradios.

She'd died in the garden.

Yes, the mournful voice in my head responded.

Let us out of here, my mind's voice snarled back.

"Where is it?" Eryx growled. "What have you done with it?"

I smiled, knowing how much it would infuriate him. No, *I* did not. *Cassandra* had smiled at Magnus. "I gave it to Lourdes. She'll know just what to do with it, and with everything I've told her."

Infuriated as I was that she was using us as puppets, I understood her desperation. She needed some way to make us understand how she had felt. Was Magnus the one keeping us all here? The only way to find out was to try to talk to her. To try to get her to let us help her untangle these old knots.

You were lying, I spoke inwardly to Cassandra, trying to stay calm. *The key was in your desk.*

It was the only way, she replied.

To save yourself? I asked.

She didn't answer, but she didn't need to. I felt it, just as she had felt it. She'd known nothing could save her, and so she chose to protect her secret. To save something else instead. Something she cared about more than anything else.

But what was it?

Eryx stepped forward, fury in his eyes. Panic flooded me for an instant, countered immediately with the refrain that came from my deepest knowing: *It wasn't him. It wasn't him.* "What did you tell that bitch about me?"

His words broke any illusion I had that Eryx was

involved in this in any way. He would never speak to me like this. *Never.*

Eryx was nothing like Magnus. He might have been a monster. We both were. But this was what evil looked like. That wasn't Eryx at all. It was only Magnus.

Inside my head, I made one last, desperate bid to Cassandra. *Eryx is a good man. He was hurt by Magnus. Not to the same degree that you were, but you cannot force him to hurt me. You will ruin him.*

She didn't answer me. I had to keep trying. If this played out the way I feared it would, Eryx would never forgive himself. He couldn't actually kill me, but he would never let himself be near me again if she forced us to play these roles. It would shatter the man I knew.

Please do not ruin him, Cassandra, I pleaded. *I need him as he is.*

Still, she did not answer. The scene was stuck, almost as if someone had pressed "pause" on a remote control. She wasn't answering me, but she was listening.

I had to keep trying. *Please, Cassandra. Don't damn me to an eternity of loving a man who can no longer love me in return.*

As the words formed, I knew they were true. I loved Eryx Necroline now in a way that was fragile and new, but would someday be gloriously strong. The possibility of eternity spilled out ahead of me in a way I'd never experienced.

I never thought of the future, because before coming here, all I'd expected was more pain. More endless suffering. But beginning to love him had given me hope. It had opened more than just my heart. It opened up the possibility for the one thing I never dared imagine for myself: *a happy future.*

Eryx's face changed, and I was thrown out of the vision. Incorporeal as a ghost, I watched now from the outside. A slight movement in my peripheral vision put me on alert.

It was just Eryx. He stood next to me now, just as insubstantial as I was, but no longer inside Magnus. No longer in danger. Relief flooded through me, and I nearly fell to the ground with the magnitude of it. I had not known until this moment how much I needed him. How much I needed for us to have a chance at that happy future.

And now I had it.

I reached for his incorporeal hand, which flexed towards me. My eyes filled with tears as his diaphanous fingers, somewhat impossibly, closed around mine. My heart beat erratically as I forced myself to turn back to Cassandra and Magnus.

"I told her what you do to me. How you treat me," Cassandra lied.

I wanted to close my eyes. More than anything I wanted to disappear. To not see this. But I simply squeezed Eryx's hand tighter, moving closer to him, my cheek resting against the steady bulk of his shoulder. It defied logic that we could be incorporeal and touch, but I didn't have time to question it.

"How I treat you?" Magnus sneered, towering over Cassandra. "How I saved you from a life of infamy?"

"How you hurt me," she replied, straightening her spine. "The way you ignore my visions. The way I was *sold* to you."

He grabbed her arm first, pulling her towards him. His other hand closed around her throat. Cassandra didn't so much as struggle. Even then, she'd felt the futility of it all. The fact that struggling would only make things worse, trap her for longer. I covered my mouth with my free hand, stifling the sob that bubbled from my throat as I understood why the illusion felt like a finger trap. That was how she'd felt. Her struggle was her true demise.

Death had been her only way out.

This was the only end, she answered in both our heads. *I saw it the day I was sent to him. I tried to warn my family. No one cared to hear what I had to say.*

Eryx's hand tightened around mine. He pulled me closer, tucking me into his body, as Magnus' hands tightened around her throat. My chin quivered. I was the picture of calm when I took a life. Clean, quick, quiet. That was *my* way. *This* was cruel—what I always tried to avoid.

Cassandra smiled again. "You will never get the key back, Magnus," she whispered, her voice hoarse as he slowly crushed her beneath his fingers. "Lourdes will never..."

Her body spasmed then, an involuntary response to him cutting off her airway. But she still did not struggle away from him. Not purposely. Cassandra Necroline had made her peace with Tanith, and the goddess' gift had been this horrible death.

Eryx had averted his eyes, and I wanted to look away, but I couldn't. Something in me needed to witness her passing. I let go of Eryx and stepped forward.

I couldn't stop this. It had already happened. Even so, I couldn't let her die alone, even in a vision. When Magnus dropped Cassandra to the ground, the light had almost gone out of her eyes, but still her body fought for life. I lay belly-down on the ground next to her, slipping my incorporeal hand into hers as Magnus crouched to the ground to finish the job.

Her head lolled to one side, her eyes meeting mine.

Can you see me? I asked.

Yes, she replied, and I knew only I could hear her.

I am here. I won't leave. You are not alone.

A tear rolled down her pale cheek as his hands closed around her throat, a faint smile on her lips as he stole the last of her breath. Her face flickered in my mind, the woman I saw replaced with a face that looked eerily like my own before flickering back.

Thank you, she replied as my mind struggled to comprehend. *Thank you.*

My eyes fell closed. A murmur behind me caught my attention. Eryx. It was only Eryx. "She needs to see it again, Cassandra. I need her to see what you showed me."

I shook my head, crying now. "No," I said through choked sobs. "No, I can't."

Eryx's hands were on my trembling shoulders. "You won't have to watch that part. I promise." He pulled me to my feet, crushing my body safely against his as he turned me.

I shook my head, eyes squeezed shut. "No."

His arms around me were gentle. "Rhiannon. I will block your view. Please, open your eyes."

I didn't. I *couldn't*. Silent sobs wracked my body.

"Trust me," he whispered, his voice warm, his bulk steady behind me.

Trust us, Cassandra said at the same time.

The funny thing was, I did trust Eryx. He'd never given me a single reason not to. I opened my eyes. I faced Hemlock House. The conversation between Magnus and Cassandra restarted. I blocked it out.

Eryx brought his lips to my ears, his broad chest secure and steady against my back. "Watch the upper window," he murmured, his palm splaying across my stomach, pinning me to him.

If it had been anyone else, I would have cut off their arm for handling me so. But it was Eryx, and we'd forged something that allowed it. That allowed me to let him take me somewhere I didn't want to go, with the knowledge that with him, I was safe. I didn't need a single soul to keep my body safe. I could save myself in that way. But my mind was safe with Eryx—and maybe too, my heart.

"Look." His whisper was a dark rasp in my ear. "There."

The rose hedge had lowered slightly. Nor was it as thick as it had been the past few days. Now Hemlock House was actually visible. Or, at least one window was, in the upper part of the house, which had once been the principal bedroom. It was Calypso's room now. Ares and Ember preferred a suite of guest rooms downstairs so they could be near Briony.

Thoughts of my real life streamed back in. Thoughts I'd been surprisingly absent of during the time we'd been here. I suddenly missed Ember and the other Maere fiercely. Eryx held me tighter against him, the sounds of Cassandra dying a horrifying soundtrack to this moment. "Watch the window," he urged me. "Now."

A figure appeared: Roman Necroline. He looked more like Eryx than I remembered. But maybe I'd just never noticed it before. When he was alive, I'd had no reason to pay much attention to his adoptive sons. Every head-of-dynasty had heirs, after all. But now I saw it. They looked *related*.

Why had *Roman Necroline been so interested in saving Eryx and his elder brother from the streets?*

What an excellent question, Cassandra's voice said in my head. I felt her presence next to me. She wasn't on the ground, she wasn't being strangled to death by the man who should have been willing to do anything to save her. She was next to me. I *felt* her.

Roman clearly saw what went on in the garden—and

did nothing. He made no move to help, though it was clear from the expression on his face that he was horrified by what he saw. That he did not approve.

That look faded. His face hardened, and when the noise behind me stopped, when the garden went unnaturally silent, he turned away.

A rage deep as the ocean built within me.

How dare he watch her die and do nothing?

How.

Dare.

He.

The sky darkened, crystal blue fading away, oozing into gray. The thick grass of summer faded under our feet, the rose hedge receding until it was no more, and early spring appeared. The garden gate came next, and we stood in the last muddy remnants of rained-on snow, both of us dressed in clothes suited for the hottest of summer days.

Now you know what I know, Cassandra said, materializing next to Eryx and I, as she pushed back a black veil. She was dressed in corpse garb.

"No," I replied aloud, a strange sense of relief filling me that the malefic spirit *had* been Cassandra all along. Was it possible that she was also the one who had orchestrated all this? "We don't. What was Magnus doing? Why did you take the key?"

Cassandra laughed, her voice soft. *You will sort that out on your own. The two of you are clever. Go home now and use the tools at your disposal to understand Oleander Cottage. Learn what we know, and bring us peace.*

It had been her all along. But how? In life, Cassandra had barely any power. She was a failure as a parapsych—but even that didn't seem true now. My mind whirled, trying to make sense of all this. The stranglings that had taken place here. She'd been trying to tell people for all these years what had happened to her.

My stomach turned at the thought. I couldn't make sense of this. It was too twisted. All she'd wanted was for us to know that Magnus had killed her and that Roman had known… but why? She'd also wanted us to find the keys that she and Magnus had hidden—that much was clear.

But again, why? What had been worth all this death and destruction? We'd come here to solve the mystery, to rid Oleander Cottage of the blight that had killed other inhabitants. I wasn't sure we could just leave.

I glanced back at Eryx—maybe he had a better idea of what the right thing to do was—and he nodded. He gripped my hand hard, pulling me towards the garden gate. "We need to go."

I hesitated. This felt like undone business. "I—"

"Rhi." His voice was pleading. He'd never used the diminutive for me before. "Rhi, please. I have to get you out of here."

I glanced back at the house. We weren't abandoning our mission. We were only widening our scope of knowledge. We would solve this and return. "May we return to Oleander Cottage?" I cleared my throat. "Will it be safe for us?"

For you, Cassandra replied. *Only for the two of you.*

"We'll come back," I promised. "We're not going to ignore this. I promise. You promise too, don't you?" I asked.

Eryx took a deep breath. "Only if Cassandra promises in return that no harm will come to you, that she will give us both full autonomy from here on out." His voice changed, that eerie, unearthly quality coming back into it. "Can you promise us that, Cassandra?"

I promise that you will be free to come and go, and that no harm will come to either of you from my working, Cassandra replied. *Her* working. So she admitted that she had done all of this. She continued, *You are nothing like your father or your uncle. Make certain your brother has not fallen into the trap that Roman did.*

"And what was that?" Eryx asked.

Cassandra's voice was quieter now. *He believed fear would save us.* Her voice was far away, as though it came from directly inside the house. *But love is the key. Make certain Ares Necroline understands.*

CHAPTER 19

ERYX

LOVE WAS THE KEY. That was why she let us go. It had to be. I'd said I loved Rhiannon. I'd said I would die for her. I glanced back at Rhiannon as I practically dragged her through the rose hedge. She looked younger than I'd ever seen her, her lineless forehead creased with worry.

But those eyes. Those eyes were ancient, and when they met mine, I wondered if she had worked out what I had. If she suspected what I did. I didn't have the chance to ask her.

Ember Verona came rushing out of the back of Hemlock House as we approached in a wild fury, snatching Rhiannon into her skinny arms. I was about to slip past her when she caught my sleeve, and with her trademark strength pulled me into her embrace as well.

"Ares and Av had to go to an emergency exorcism uptown," she said, making eye contact with me. "The shit hit the fan while the two of you were gone. We have a lot to catch up on—everyone else is out."

The Orphium Maere's commander had tears in her eyes when she let us go, words tumbling out of her mouth in a torrent, like she'd been keeping them in for years. "The hedge… It made us forget you. And then yesterday Briony remembered the day you left…"

Rhiannon took her oldest friend's face in her hands and said in the calmest voice I'd ever heard, "Slow down. It's going to be all right."

I tamped down the immediate irritation I felt that after all Rhiannon had just been through, she had to comfort Ember now. This was their dynamic, and she didn't need me passing judgment.

Ember nodded, but it was clear that she might burst into tears at any second. She was holding back because I was here. Rhiannon turned to me, giving me a look I took to mean, "Could you give us a few?"

Immediately, I resented the way Ember relied on Rhiannon to be the calm one. My heart thumped. Ares and Av rarely knew how I felt because I kept it all from them. It was the same for her. We were the same, in so many odd ways, but I had to let her work this out on her own. I couldn't solve it for her, no matter how much I wanted to.

The important thing was that we were out. I'd done what I needed to: I got her out, and we'd found out the source of the problem with the cottage, though not the why of it. Right now, Rhiannon needed a friend who would help her investigate a whole lot more than she needed an overprotective lover. And I had somewhere I needed to be—someone who needed to answer for what had caused years of suffering at Oleander Cottage.

I could do this. I could leave her with Ember. I forced one foot in front of the other, squeezing her shoulder as I passed her. "I'll be back in a few."

She nodded, leading Ember into the kitchen of Hemlock House. I waited in the foyer, listening as they dialed my brother and the other Maere into a conference call so Rhiannon could tell them what had happened to us, and what we needed from them. I didn't wait to find out if she would reveal that Roman knew about what Magnus had done.

Before I spoke to my brother, I needed to talk to our father. Ares would want to handle things more respectfully than I would. I wanted to throttle a ghost, and if I wanted to, I was pretty sure I could find a way to do it. Ares would only try and stop me.

My motorcycle was in the garage. It looked like Av had been working on it. Fresh oil change, a tune-up and a wash. She'd clearly missed me, and now that we were out of the Cottage, I missed her too. I hated the way the Cottage had fucked with my head. Had fucked with Rhiannon's head.

Now I wanted to know the truth.

The cemetery where Roman was buried wasn't too far away. This was Necroline territory, after all. I didn't know how long we'd been trapped in the cottage, but it looked to me like the monsoons could start any day now. There were signs of life everywhere, but I'd been hollowed out in the last hour.

A tower of evergreens canopied the narrow street to the cemetery, neon city lights shining through the thin veil of trees. The smells of the city in early spring were pungent. Wet earth and trees, eclipsed by the ever-present scent of the industrial haze that clung to Orphium. The pavement was wet with melting snow, mist hanging over it in heavy clouds.

I'd never managed to talk to my parents after the shop burned. They'd been at peace when they went, and for that Ares and I had always been so grateful. Our mother's best friend Amanita, who had died with them, had not been. But it wasn't until the heist that Ares had found her.

Mist rose over the road, swirling around me. The air chilled as the vapor swallowed the motorcycle whole, dampening the world around me. I'd never admitted to Ares that Roman wasn't at peace. That I'd seen him at his own funeral. That he was avoiding us like the plague.

Spirits could lie, but they seemed to have a more difficult time with subterfuge than people did in life. Or perhaps, since they were dead, they no longer cared. Necroline philosophers and metaphysicists had debated this for centuries. But there was one sure place a restless spirit couldn't avoid a necromancer's summons, and that was their grave.

The mist parted as I approached a set of curled wrought-iron gates. This time of day, they were open and I rode through, feeling the change in atmosphere. Necromancers buried their dead in hallowed ground, a testament to the fact that this land was once imbued with magic. That once, parapsychs had lived in harmony with a world that needed us. Our abilities had not been "paranormal" then—they had been sacred.

The cemetery was dark, tree branches blocking out what little light we were getting on such a cloudy day. Skyscrapers loomed above this small sanctuary for trees and the dead, sharp neon cutting through the clouds, giving everything an eerie glow.

I slowed down, parked my bike at the base of an ancient redwood cedar, and walked up the hill to Roman's mausoleum. I sat down on the stone steps outside. There were rituals people did for this kind of thing, proper channels and all that.

As a clairsentient, I rarely bothered with such nonsense. I had a direct line to the dead and I'd never been afraid to use it when needed. It was needed now. "We have to talk about Magnus. Don't make me force you out."

I would use the vox spiritus, if I had to, but I'd rather he do this on his own. He'd hid from the truth for long enough. If he was even a fraction of the man I'd hoped he was as a child, he would do this for me now.

For a moment, nothing happened. I closed my eyes and waited, contemplating violence. And then he appeared, incorporeal and huge, right next to me. Like both Ares and myself, he was dark haired, with skin so pale he'd been nearly translucent in life. It was easy to see why many people assumed he was our biological father. We did look a lot alike.

"Hair's gotten long," he said as he materialized. "You look good, kid."

After what I'd seen in the garden, I couldn't pretend I wasn't angry. "You look dead."

He shrugged. For several heartbeats, he was quiet. I started to wonder what he knew about where I'd been and why I came. Roman had always seemed to know all in life, though I'd had secrets from him. Secrets a child never should have had. "So, Cassandra's message finally found you."

I nodded. He'd done a lot in life to keep me away from Oleander Cottage, and now I knew why. He hadn't wanted me to know that he'd seen it all and done nothing. He'd been afraid she'd show me.

But why hadn't he stopped all this in the first place? There were dozens of ways he could have prevented the subsequent deaths at Oleander Cottage, but he hadn't. The only way to find out was to ask. "Is it true?"

He rested his elbows on his knees, staring at his hands as he steepled his fingers. "Did you know that your mother was my cousin?"

This was not what we were meant to talk about. He was evading. I didn't answer him, but I had not known that. I tried not to sigh. Roman had been infuriating in exactly this way in life—I'm not sure why I expected this to go differently.

"When she met your father, she asked that we cut ties. She didn't want this life for herself. For you and Ares. She wanted you kept out of the Dynasty."

My heart sank knowing that. I wondered if wherever she was now, she was disappointed in me. If Roman was trying to make me feel better, it wasn't working.

Roman continued, "But they found her anyway, the Chiorics. And when they sent people after the two of you... I couldn't leave you to rot. You were all I had left."

The sinking feeling in my heart deepened. It felt as though I was being pushed into ice cold water. This wasn't what I came here for. I sank into the shadows the ancient pines cast onto the mausoleum, letting the chill permeate my bones. I rarely thought about the problems having such long lives caused, but this was certainly one. Everyone became a disappointment, at some point.

Everyone but Rhiannon. The thought swirled in my head, feeling something like hope in the muddy dark of this moment.

Roman sighed. Incorporeal as he was, he was the same as he'd been the last time I saw him. Larger than life. "Not helping Cassandra is one of my many regrets. I didn't want to believe what was happening right under my nose, and when it was too late, I was a coward."

"Yes," I agreed, my anger building. "You were. But why? Why did you let him kill her?"

Roman blew out a huff of air. Spirits were like that. They didn't have bodies any longer, but they remembered what it was like to be corporeal and still had their same mannerisms in death as they had in life.

"I wish I had a clever answer for you," he replied. "But the truth is that I was scared of Magnus. He loved her, Eryx. He loved that woman more than anything I'd ever seen him love."

Any*thing*. As though Cassandra Necroline were an object. My stomach soured at the notion. It didn't matter that it had been a different time. That the world's views had been different. My disappointment dug deeper in me, taking root.

Roman just kept talking, "Or at least that's what I'd thought. Now... I understand it was an obsession. She was a challenge, difficult and beautiful, much like your Rhiannon."

That got my attention. I wanted her name out of his mouth, immediately. With the way he'd talked about Cassandra, I didn't want him even *thinking* of Rhiannon.

He smiled, not sensing my hackles rising, in the slightest. Roman had always been self-centered to the point of hubris. "I've looked in on you when I could." He stared out at the misty cemetery for a long moment, as though we were having a heart to heart. "I didn't understand until it was too late that he was trying to break her. That he'd picked someone headstrong and brilliant like Cassandra because she *wouldn't* break easily..."

My stomach turned. "He was a psychopath."

Roman shrugged. The casual way he talked about this shit was terrifying. "You'd have to talk to a shrink about a diagnosis. But you are right that he wasn't balanced."

Logically, the next question should have been about why he didn't take the steps to prevent the kind of haunting that had happened at Oleander Cottage. The kind that came from a soul so tortured she couldn't help but draw others in and try to make them understand. Every death that happened after Cassandra's was on both Magnus and Roman's hands, not hers.

A spirit that died that gruesomely was not in control of their actions. And the worse things got, the more souls they dragged into their misery, the less conscious they became about what they did. Until their message was understood, they were little more than rage. I knew something about that.

"Did you know that he beat me?" I asked, my voice soft.

Next to me, Roman tensed. "*What?*"

"As a kid, your brother beat me for every little mistake. You didn't know?"

Roman tried to grab hold of my arm, but his fingers passed right through me. I shivered from the intensity of the chill. "Son, you have to believe me. I had no idea." His hands covered his face. I watched him swallow hard, his voice cracking. "I thought you were fighting with the other boys, like Ares. The bruises... I thought you were making your way with the Dynasty children..."

His words made sense. I did believe him, but it didn't help anything. "If you had known, would you have stopped him?" Roman paused, fear in his eyes. I shook my head, my lip curling in disgust. "Don't answer. I don't want to know."

At least he did me the favor of following my wishes. Any respect I had for my father disappeared. Disappointment dug deep into me, cutting through layers of fear that I'd been hiding behind in seconds. I saw the truth in the fresh, gaping wound—the way that fear had obscured so many realities over the years.

The way I'd gone along with shit I knew was wrong, over and over, hoping to preserve what little was left of our people's way of life. To keep our people safe, all of us had given in to fear and isolation, rather than binding ourselves closer together. Something had to change.

Roman placed a hand on my shoulder. I couldn't feel it, not exactly, but there was a kind of pressure there. "You say you're a monster, but you're not. You and Ares both have retained your integrity in a way Magnus and I never could manage. We lost ourselves to power and immortality."

It was too little too late. His compliments rang hollow. I understood what he was attempting, but I no longer wanted it. I could forgive him, eventually. But I didn't want anything he had to offer anymore.

He stood, pushing off my shoulder. "I am sorry Cassandra was collateral damage to my cowardice. You tell her that for me, all right?"

Did he think that was all it took to make things right? Something was fundamentally wrong with Roman Necroline. The world had taken too much from him, and he'd never bothered to fill himself back up with what was good in life. I didn't pity him. He'd had the same choices to make that Ares and I had, and he'd chosen wrong every time.

Even now, with all the wisdom of death at his fingertips, he didn't see what he'd done. I'd never wished for Ares' ability to grab spirits by the aura. Not in all my long life. I knew the toll it took. The way it connected him to them in ways that damaged him. But in this moment, I wanted that power. I wanted to thrash Roman Necroline into a second death, if that were possible.

"That's it?" I cried. "You don't have anything else to say?"

He shook his head, so calm it was eerie. "I knew he was hurting her, but I didn't want to know. I knew he was plotting something, and I didn't want to know that either. I loved my brother, Eryx. It never occurred to me that he wasn't capable of loving me, or anyone, back. I *am* sorry he hurt you, though."

But not sorry enough to have ever done anything about it. "And what about the people who died there because neither of you took care of her spirit?"

Roman shrugged. "That fault lies with Magnus. Not me."

My blood sang in my ears. The last time I'd been this furious was when Frannie died. He took no responsibility for *any* of this. I spat at his feet, making the ancient Necroline gesture that translated loosely to *may your spirit never rest.*

My adoptive father bent down, his eyes gentling. Perhaps *he* was the psychopath. "You came here for a confession, and that is mine. I wish I knew more, but Magnus made sure I stayed in the dark, and I made it easy for him. I'm sorry to disappoint you, kid."

Disappointment wasn't the half of it. The rage I didn't allow to the surface bubbled in my gut, threatening to boil over into my fists, my legs, my teeth. I couldn't remember another time when I'd had the urge to rip someone apart with my teeth.

But now, here in what should be the most peaceful place in the world, I wanted to do an incredible amount of violence. For me. For Frannie. For Cassandra. For all the lives that Roman Necroline had failed to save when he let his corrupted brother live.

By contrast, Roman Necroline pressed a kiss to the top of my head. "You'll probably never know how sorry I am to have disappointed you."

Tears stung the corners of my eyes as I clenched every muscle in my body so tightly that I was immobilized. When he faded, I felt him go. He wasn't gone-gone. He wasn't at peace, but I doubted very much that we'd ever see him again.

And that was just fucking fine with me.

I'd come here for closure, or at least something new to go on. Not a confession of cowardice. Roman had finally come clean, and it gave me *nothing*. Coming here had been a waste. All it had done was rile me up.

I rested my head in my hands, sitting on the mausoleum steps in the same position Roman had, breathing shallow, panicked breaths. The spiral out of control was tightening, the slide to the center of chaos frustrating, infuriating even. What did all of this *mean*?

Tears streamed down my face, sobs wracking my body. I cried for the child I'd been. For the man who'd lost his first love more horrifically than anyone should have to live through. For Cassandra, who'd needlessly lost her life. I screamed into a void that could never be filled. I screamed until my throat gave out, until I was hollow inside, but for the endless quagmire of disappointment that was this wretched world.

Would there never be enough cruelty or violence?

I rocked back and forth, shaking with helpless anger. Somewhere a raven squawked at its mate. Sparrows chirped. A few little crocuses peeked out of the fading patches of snow, turning towards the soiled sky to face another spring of struggling to find the light.

It was a terrible reminder that this had all happened before in myriad ways, and it would probably all happen again, because *this was people*. We were horrible, wonderful, good and bad. There was no escaping this, and if you had the misfortune to live long enough to see the cycles of it ebb and flow, it would run you ragged. This would never end, and I didn't know how to bear it.

"There you are." A familiar voice broke through my

sorrow. I looked up to find Av standing before me, spritely, but not a bit cheerful. "Cassandra Necroline said I would find you here."

Av's amber eyes were soft, concerned. Her tiny fists were clenched into balls. She was worried about me. From the hunched set of her shoulders, she'd *been* worried for a while. As my eyes met hers, I smiled through my tears. I was just so damn happy to see her.

This was how we bore it. This was how we survived. The people we loved, and who loved us back. This was all that mattered—all there really was in this abattoir of an existence.

I laughed—a shaky sound—grabbing her hand and pulling her down next to me on the steps. She wore her usual suit and tie, though she'd cut her black hair into a severe bob with a thick fringe of bangs across her forehead. The style gave the sharp angles of her face so much gravitas, I was nearly intimidated by her.

"I like the new look," I murmured.

"Scarier than ever," she said, miming claws with her fingers and baring her teeth to me.

It was so silly, I smiled. It was good to be near her extremely specific mix of terrifying and goofy. My heart needed this. Av knew the darkness in me and it had never once scared her.

I asked the question I hadn't dared think about. "Did you kill my fish?"

"Yeah," she admitted. "Kind of."

I raised an eyebrow, waiting for her to admit she was joking but she shook her head. "I'm sorry, Eryx. I'm good with the dead, not the living. The little guy is a great spirit though, I think he'll find you when the time is right."

"For fuck's sake," I snorted. Only Av would charm a

goldfish into sticking around as a spirit. "Where's your poltergeist, by the way?"

Av shrugged. "Stanley's probably getting snuggles from Rhi about now. He hasn't been himself since the two of you left. Did you know that hedge made us forget you?"

"No," I answered, letting the familiar feeling of talking something through with Av wash over me. "Why don't you tell me all about it?"

I leaned back on the steps of the Necroline mausoleum and let the cadence of Av's storytelling soothe my tired soul. If there weren't going to be answers, at least I could have comfort.

CHAPTER 20

RHIANNON

LARA RAN wiry fingers through her short, dark hair, sending it flying in all directions as I told them what Eryx and I had learned. The one-time love of my life looked good, but wan, like she'd been fading while I was gone. It occurred to me that she too had been going through a lot. Both of us thought we'd found an answer to the Consulate's decline in the mysterious Mother and her organization.

Learning that we'd been manipulated up and down, in dozens of ways, by the island hadn't just fucked *me* up. What the Admiral and my own mother had done turned Lara into a veritable serial killer. And while the people she'd killed needed killing, I knew all too well what a toll it took on the soul to do that work. *And I'd just left her.*

I braced myself for the guilt I was sure would come next. But it never came. Yes, I'd left Lara, but she'd known I was going and she hadn't offered to come with me. Eryx had.

"That's so fucked up," she said when I finished speaking.

Ember nodded. "It really is."

I was glad Briony wasn't home to hear this story. Perhaps we'd be gone, back to Oleander Cottage, before she could find out just how bad things had been. The hedge of roses had affected them as well. It had caused all of them to forget we existed for over three months. The math didn't add up. By my count, we'd only been at the Cottage for a few weeks.

Calypso, who had been making tea while I told them what had happened, finally set the tray down on the table. "Kara and I ran into something like this a few years ago."

We all looked up at her, rapt with attention at the mention of the Aradios Maere's commander, Kara Asterion. Calypso was the newest among us, and we were all still getting to know her, though everyone else had more of a chance to do that than I had, at this point. She pushed a strand of her long auburn hair back behind her ear before pouring the tea.

"It wasn't as complex as what you've described at Oleander Cottage," she said as she handed out teacups, fixing everyone's tea just how they liked it. "But the way you described the finger-trapness of it all... that's the same as what we encountered. It was a house, like the Cottage, built over a significant site to the Thaumas."

Aradios was the City of Miracles. The miracle workers were strongest and most plentiful there. It made sense that the spirits there might retain the kind of power to form something like what we'd seen at the cottage.

"Was it a burial site?" I asked, wondering if there was a connection to the Ossuary.

Calypso shook her head. "No, but it was the site of one of the first Massacres. So in that way, it was very similar."

There had been several years of mass murders when the Trinity lost control of the Three Cities and the

Authority rose to power. Humans had been keen to weaken parapsychs permanently, though they had stopped short of eliminating us altogether. The ostracization came later. First, they'd murdered us in droves. It made sense that those places would be deeply haunted in similar ways.

Lara shoved her other hand through her shock of dark hair, mussing it irrevocably. "Why did anyone build over those spots? Seems like a recipe for disaster."

Ember sighed. "There was so little space for us after the Massacres. You know that."

Lara shrugged, grief heavy in her eyes. "I guess I can't blame people for making do with what scraps the Authority gives us."

Sera padded into the kitchen, still wearing an oversized pair of lavender silk pajamas. She looked better than she had when she and Max returned to us in some ways. Healthier. But from the way Calypso frowned at the sight of her, I could tell there was more to her appearance than just sleeping late.

"Is there a cup for me?" Sera asked.

Ember nodded, fixing Sera's tea for her. The petite Maere came to sit next to me. She was the shortest of us. So short, in fact, it was almost comical. Her fingers barely fit around the mug Ember handed her.

When we were reborn into human bodies, the majority of us had grown to be nearly as tall as we'd been in our first lives, and our people tended to be on the taller side in comparison to humans. But Sera had not been reborn exactly as she had been before. Later, we'd learned there was one in every cohort that had turned out to be a bit different than in her first life. It was an odd phenomenon, and we'd never quite puzzled out the why of it.

When the five of us were seated around the kitchen table, a restless energy in me settled. The magic of our swords connected us to the island, but also to one another. It always felt right to be together.

Tears welled in Ember's eyes, a softness there I hadn't seen in centuries. She had the same chaotic energy she always had, but it was tempered now with a depth of feeling I couldn't quite identify. Her hand stretched towards mine. She wiggled her fingers, her long oval nails shimmering in the light until I took her hands.

"I am so glad you're here," she murmured, the sound of tears lingering at the edges of her voice.

"Me too," I replied. And I was. "But I can't stay. Whatever this is with Oleander Cottage, we have to solve it."

Calypso nodded. "We do. The house in Aradios... we waited too long." Her teeth bit into her full bottom lip and she swallowed hard. "The spiritual energy there. It opened a door that shouldn't be opened."

Everyone's eyes snapped to her. None of us knew why Calypso had been so willing to trade places with Max and come here. Was this why?

"What door?" Ember asked, letting go of my hands. Her eyes were alert, sharp.

Everyone at the table had shifted position, even Sera. Time contracted, and I felt the way we'd been throughout the ages, sitting around tables just like this, in castles and cottages, in taverns and libraries. Max had been there then, but that did not take anything away from the rightness of Calypso being here now.

"A door to the underworld. To Tanith's domain," Calypso replied. Her voice dropped lower. "On the island, we never knew each other well."

That was true. In our past life, the rest of us had mostly moved in circles with one another. We were friends. But Calypso had been a cloistered priestess in Tanith's temple by the sea. She had been one of death's handmaidens. She likely understood the metaphysical aspects of the underworld much better than the rest of us. If that had been the case, why had she gone to Aradios?

Calypso continued. "But during my time in the temple, we learned that doors between the underworld and the living must stay shut, as the condemned dead long to return to the world of the living."

The condemned dead were the ones whose souls were taken to perform penance for the ills they'd done in life, or so legends said. But Calypso spoke about it as though it were true. "Necromancers' power comes from the under-world, from their soul's connection to it. They are what keeps the balance between the realm of the living and the underworld."

I groaned as I understood. "If a necromancer wanted more power though... if they were unscrupulous..."

Calypso nodded. "Yes, they would want more access to the underworld, to the essence of their power. But that would require opening a *door* to the netherrealm. And once open it wouldn't just be the condemned that would come through. It would be *all* of them."

All of the dead there had ever been. The idea was confounding.

Sera's mug slammed down on the table, her eyes bright with fury. "The living realm would be overtaken. There are too many dead." I hadn't seen her look so alive in a long time. Even before the fire, something in her had faded, I realized.

Ember and Lara both stared at her as well. We saw it, the Serafine we'd known before. Before she'd fallen in love with someone who could love her, but never return her feelings in kind. My heart broke for the two of them. Max and Sera hadn't meant to hurt one another so deeply, but they had. These long lives we had were riddled with mistakes.

"What did you do?" Sera asked, and the strength in her voice was reassuring. "To stop the door from opening? I assume it was about to open, or you wouldn't mention it."

Calypso nodded, smiling faintly. It was standard practice amongst the fifteen Maere of the Three Cities to never reveal the foibles of their cohort. What happened in our own cities stayed there. We complained about the Trinity not sharing information, but we'd grown just as secretive.

"The house had been a problem, much like the one we have here. Sucking people in, not allowing them to leave. Pulling them into the underworld, which to the living appears fractured, though to the dead, I think it is more whole, more real. The magic of it is…" she shrugged. "Somewhat unknowable. It's not *for* us to understand."

My heartbeat nearly stilled, my skin going ice cold. The world beyond Oleander Cottage's front door… it was not a loop. Not really. Nor was it a spell or an illusion. It *was* the underworld. We had gone into the netherrealm. Fed it with our energy.

And it had fed us in return. We had eaten the netherrealm's food. There were all kinds of stories about that kind of thing, but they all had one thing in common. Once you ate of the underworld, you became a part of it. I couldn't think of what that might mean for us now. The stories were just that, *stories*.

This was real. With or without the key, Oleander Cottage was a portal to the underworld—and sooner or later, the dead were going to get out. Even now, they were barely contained. "The Ossuary," I breathed, horror dawning on me. "Magnus was trying to open a door to the underworld, through the Ossuary."

Ember's eyes fell shut. "*Fuck.*"

Lara snorted, smirking at me in that old way. The way she had before we'd fallen for each other and nearly ruined each other's lives. It felt like the most worn-in sweater in the world—cozy, completely unsexy, but pure comfort. My throat caught on emotion. Being here with them was good. Everything worked just a little better when we were together. When we were in sync.

Sera drained her mug, frowning. "It seems obvious why he'd do it. He was morally bankrupt and power hungry. But what about the payments he was receiving?"

All five of us were silent. It didn't immediately make sense. Movement out the corner of my eye distracted me. Stanley, Avaline's poltergeist cat, came around the corner from the butler's pantry, making his way into the kitchen, his black fur gleaming in the lamplight of the gloomy day. He hadn't shifted into any of his more disturbing forms today, and looked like an ordinary black cat. Like most poltergeists, he was practically corporeal.

"Stanley," I murmured, the pieces clicking for me. "Did you die at Oleander Cottage?"

The cat stopped in his tracks, right in front of the dishwasher and sat down hard on his big furry butt. He yowled piteously. Somewhere towards the back of the house, a door opened. Avaline and Eryx entered. Eryx's icy eyes were worried.

"He says Magnus killed him." Eryx looked to Avaline. "Did you know that?"

I'd never seen Avaline Reyes look truly sad, but then I didn't know her very well. Her red lips turned down, as she bent to scoop the ghost cat into her arms. He rubbed his face against her cheek as she hugged him close. "It was brutal," she whispered. "Magnus Necroline was a monster."

Eryx turned away, having gone a shade of green. It

took something quite terrible to turn a spirit into a poltergeist, and whatever the little soul had shown him disturbed him.

"Don't tell me," Ember whispered. "Please."

Avaline and Eryx both shook their heads, but she was the one who spoke. "He doesn't want you to know the particulars. Not any of you. I don't think he really even wants *us* to know." She stroked the back of the cat's head. "You wanted to tell Ares, didn't you?"

Stanley yowled again, then sprouted bat wings and an additional head, which hissed. Av smiled. "Yes, we'll tell him when he gets back. You promise you won't show Briony this? The poor kid'll have nightmares for months."

The cat growled, as though to say, *I would never do such a thing.* He loved our little teenage Maere-to-be.

Eryx glanced at Av, his face going a little green again. "Did you see it?"

She nodded, setting the cat on the kitchen counter. "I did."

Eryx didn't keep us in suspense. "The money he was taking... Stanley saw several of the exchanges. He was taking money from Archibald Blaire the First." My heart sank as he paused, frowning. "They're onto a third one now, I think."

It was always going to come back to this, wasn't it? No matter how I tried to run from my problems, they always caught up with me. Archibald Blaire the Third was a concern for the Consulate, and for good reason. Blaire's family had been connected to nearly every case of para-psych exploitation for nearly three centuries.

And that was just what the world knew about. What happened in secret, in the Aslyum, but elsewhere as well—Blaire operated dozens of black sites—was so horrendous I'd about lost my mind in Aradios. It was important work, but I was no longer equipped to do it. Not if I couldn't actually do anything about it.

The Consulate had never wanted to use my skills as an assassin. All they wanted was information. Always more information, and never any action. I'd grown to hate my job as Orphium's assassin, but working for the Consulate without actually doing anything about the shit I learned had been worse.

Lara swore. "The Senator that founded the Asylum. That *fucker*."

"But why?" Calypso asked. "What does that have to do with all of this?"

Eryx's eyes met mine, and I knew he'd clocked me. He knew I knew more about Blaire than what I was saying. "We won't know the answer to that until Rhiannon and I return to the Cottage."

CHAPTER 21

ERYX

A CACOPHONY of opinions broke out, but Rhiannon stayed still, her eyes locked on mine as the rest of them spoke over one another about a door to the underworld and the key Rhiannon and I had found. *That* was at least part of what Cassandra had been hiding—what she'd been trying to show us.

It was obvious to me that she knew something about Blaire she wasn't saying, but why? The memory hit me. The day we'd left for the cottage, I'd heard her on the phone. *"I told you before I left that I want off the Blaire case. Permanently."*

It couldn't be a coincidence that Stanley had brought Blaire up now. The family was practically Orphium royalty, generations of wealth going back centuries. The Blaires had been among Orphium's First Families, humans who'd overthrown their parapsych kings and formed the Authority.

Archibald Blaire wasn't just one of Orphium's oligarchs, he was an integral part of the Authority. Beyond reproach. Beyond any law. Beyond what even the Maere could do something about.

I tried to keep my thoughts straight, tried to think of what to do next, but the azure depths of Rhiannon's eyes held me captive. No wonder she'd wanted to hide from the Consulate. If they were having her look into Blaire, but she hadn't been allowed to do anything to stop him… that would eat her up inside.

For weeks, all I'd wanted was to get her back here, where I thought she'd be safe from whatever dangers Oleander Cottage posed. And now I wanted to march her straight back there and lock her in, where no one could reach the woman I loved.

Ember too stayed silent, her gaze shifting from me to Rhiannon, understanding lighting her eyes. When they rested on me, her hazel eyes were warm, her mouth curving into a small smile.

My earlier frustration with Ember fell away. Perhaps I'd judged the situation too harshly. Or maybe it was just more complicated than clear lines of good and bad actions. We were all a tangle of emotions and behaviors.

Still. Whatever Rhiannon thought Ember might have to say about the possibility of us, it was obvious to me that she'd been wrong. Rhiannon's fear stood between her and the truth. Ember wouldn't stop us from falling for one another. She wanted the people she loved to be happy.

Ares would have a whole diatribe of cautions and warnings for me, but in his own way, my brother was the same as the partner he'd chosen. Being here, being surrounded by his family, had changed him. Cassandra Necroline didn't need to worry. My brother had already chosen love. This love that surrounded us now, even without his presence.

As though called forth by my thoughts, the back door

opened and closed. Briony's chatter about what had happened at school died, as the sounds of the Maere arguing over what would happen next reached her ears. When the two of them joined us in the kitchen, they were silent observers, though Briony rushed to Rhiannon's side.

Rhiannon opened her arms for the teenage Maere-to-be and the girl fell right in. In no time, she was whispering happily in Rhiannon's ear, grinning like there was no tomorrow. The kid wasn't the smiley type. She was a clever girl, but not cheerful. Rhiannon murmured something to her, an obvious aside from the conversation at the table that had Briony's eyes sparkling with humor.

The woman could make anyone feel like the center of the world—but she was the true center. The bright star around which everything rotated. It was a quiet power, subtle, but I wanted to stay in her orbit for as long as I could.

My brother bumped my shoulder with his, a sturdy weight reminding me that Ares and I always fought to stay on the same side of things. We weren't Roman and Magnus, and we never would be. "Glad you're back."

Stanley yowled at him, and to my surprise, my brother picked the little poltergeist up and closed his eyes, nodding as Stanley caught him up. "Saints," he murmured when the feline disappeared. "What a fucking mess."

His voice was low. The Maere were still arguing over whether or not it was safe for us to go back to the Cottage. Briony had joined in, loudly proclaiming her opinion that there were mysteries to be uncovered at the Cottage, and that Rhiannon was the best person to uncover them. The teenager was a prodigy hacker, and I had no doubt she'd spent the time since we'd been gone doing all sorts of nefarious snooping.

"This is good," I said, feeling better already.

Ares raised an eyebrow. "What's good about it?"

I shook my head, a rare grin finding my face. "What *isn't?*" I asked, gesturing at the room full of people we both loved.

We had been alone so long, he and Avaline and I. To navigate the mess Magnus had left behind, we'd had to isolate ourselves, even from our own people. But working with the Maere to get their swords back had given us family, and in turn had also given us our community back.

Nothing had changed in Orphium. Not really. The Authority still ruled in every way that was meaningful. But we were here arguing over what to do about a problem that would seem ancient to most humans. *Together.*

We all had our roles to play, and we would have to break off for each of us to do our part. But we'd do it together. The Authority could make any rule it wanted. It could make life harder for us in innumerable ways. But it couldn't stop us from loving one another. That was why Cassandra had wanted me to warn Ares about the dangers of ruling through fear.

Fear kept us from this. From this lifeline our people needed. That *we* needed just as much. Love really was the answer. Rhiannon's eyes had drifted from mine as she spoke to Briony, but now, the teenager was settling into her own seat, opening her laptop, and Rhiannon's gaze returned to mine.

I wondered if it were possible that she thought along the same lines I did. If she wondered, as I did, right now, what it would be like to love each other. Saints knew the two of us needed someone to love.

Not someone.

Each other.

Rhiannon Brontë and I needed each other.

I broke eye contact with her, keeping my voice low.

"They'll be arguing about this for hours. Can I speak with you?"

He nodded and gestured towards the back door. We'd made our office in the space above the carriage house's garage. I followed Ares out the back door and into the damp chill of the dark spring afternoon. It was hard to tell if it would rain or snow, at this point. We entered the carriage house through the back door, trailing up the narrow staircase to the bright office with its wainscoted walls and vaulted ceilings.

Ares worked to start a fire. "Stanley caught me up pretty well, I think. What did you want to talk about?"

"I spoke to Roman this morning," I said, cutting right to the point. "He didn't give me much, but he knew that Magnus killed Cassandra. He said he was a coward about the whole thing. That he'd intentionally looked the other way."

Ares blew out a sigh, settling into one of the leather chairs we'd brought from our old office in the Carlyle. I sat in the one opposite. Someone had found a beautiful antique rug from Palladiere to spread under the small semicircle of chairs and chesterfield couch that were set up in a cozy arrangement around the hearth.

Ares seemed at home here. He'd replaced his usual suit with jeans, though he still wore polished brogues, shirtsleeves, and a tweed vest. "Roman was an enigma," he murmured. "Since I took over, I realize how hard things must have been for him. The ways leading fucks you up."

I nodded, settling into my chair. Ares was a deep thinker. It was necessary to let him talk through this, to work whatever he needed to out on his own. My brother leaned forward, his green eyes narrowed and intense. "But I need you to know that I wouldn't look away. No matter how hard the truth is, no matter how disappointing, I won't look away."

It was a promise to me. Ares always understood. He knew how rigid I could be about doing what was right. Even when we had to do something rotten, deep in the muck of the moral low ground, I'd always maintained that we had to be sure we were doing it for the right reasons.

I'd held back my hopes for myself for too long. Now was the time to let Ares know what I wanted. "When I'm done with this job. When the cottage is safe—we have to change the way we do some things. We should have done it after Frannie died—"

"You're right," my brother agreed. "I'm sorry I didn't see it. When she was killed, there was just so much going on."

I'd always avoided thinking about that time. It had felt like I was so alone. But when I looked at the deep lines etched on my brother's ageless face now, the places his brow creased that were familiar with his sadness, I realized I'd been understanding it wrong.

When Frannie died and Magnus nearly beat me to death over it, Ares had started planning our uncle's demise. And it had taken years to accomplish. Years for the two of us to mature, for our talents to ripen, to become strong enough to stand against Magnus. And we'd had to bring Avaline up with us, making her strong enough to withstand anything that came next.

Ares had managed it all.

I'd always thought he moved by instinct, but in retrospect, it had all been carefully orchestrated. My brother was strategic in a way I hadn't given him enough credit for, because I was in too much pain to see it. "You killed Magnus for me. For Frannie."

My brother's jaw clenched, old rage burning in his

eyes. "You're damn right I did. And I'd do it ten more times if I could. Killing that fucker once wasn't enough."

"Thank you," I whispered. "I'm sorry it took me so long to understand."

He smiled. "What is immortality for if not taking our time?"

It was so easy to filter everything in life through our own singular perspectives, to put ourselves at the center of the world, and miss that other people's lives were as complex as our own. I'd lived inside my own head for far too long. I hadn't meant to do it, but I'd lost sight of all the ways that my brother had shouldered the responsibility of the Dynasty on his own.

The way he'd sacrificed for me and Av for so long, so that the two of us would have some semblance of a life, while he'd had nothing but himself to rely on. Something loosened inside me that I hadn't known had been knotted tight.

I managed to laugh, and then so did he. Resentments I hadn't quite known existed dissipated in a moment of clarity that felt like letting go and growing, all at once. "Are you happy with Ember?" I asked. "You love her, she loves you, and you're happy?"

Ares just nodded, but the smile in his eyes was all I needed to see. "And you?" he asked. "Will you tell Rhiannon what you feel for her?

"I'll try," I replied. "And if she'll have me, I'll be with her for the rest of my life."

Ares let out a long breath, his jaw clenched with emotion, covering his mouth with his hand. It was rare for him to get choked up. He was still processing it all. Still working through what we'd learned.

"I am happy for you," he finally said, a glimmer of tears in his eyes. "I worried after Francesca that you'd never be whole again. But now." He took a shuddering breath, nodding his approval. "So, you'll go back to the Cottage?"

I nodded. "We told Cassandra we would."

Ares frowned. "Is there a need now, though? If she took the key to keep him from accessing the door to the underworld, couldn't you just leave it alone?"

I shook my head, sure of something now that I hadn't been before. The door to the underworld wasn't in the basement, or the Ossuary. Oleander Cottage *was* the door. Cassandra didn't steal the key to keep Magnus from the power the dead might wield. There was something else down there.

Something Archibald Blaire and the Authority had wanted. And if they'd wanted it then, there was no way they didn't want it now. "Listen," I said to my brother, as I leaned forward. "I think there's more to it than that."

Ares' eyes took on that gleam they did when he was about to come up with a brilliant scheme. His body bent towards mine. "Tell me everything you know."

CHAPTER 22

RHIANNON

THE AFTERNOON WORE on with a mix of familiar arguing. Terrifying as being trapped in Oleander Cottage had been, at least it was quiet. My eyes were heavy with exhaustion that ran soul-deep. Without thinking, I looked up, expecting to find Eryx waiting for me, but he and Ares were still out in the office. Likely, they were still combing through everything that had happened with a fine-toothed comb.

A wave of fatigue hit me so hard I thought I might be ill. Somewhere between extreme nausea and the urge to let out an endless shriek, I felt profoundly unwell. If I didn't get somewhere quiet soon, I was going to end up in a puddle on the kitchen floor. I begged my pardons from my sistren, Av, and Briony, claiming I needed a nap in my own bed.

Really, I just needed to be alone with my thoughts. The way Eryx had looked at me in the kitchen was more than I could bear. We hadn't talked about what would happen once we got back. He hadn't made me any promises, and I hadn't made him any either. And maybe it was just fear taking the wheel, but something deep inside me felt sure things would fall apart out here.

After all, I had only been here for a little while and I was already falling apart. There was no way I could manage a relationship. I hadn't solved any of my own problems. Like always, I'd focused on someone else to avoid dealing with *me*. And if I didn't deal with my own bullshit, I was never going to be good enough for him.

A terrible spiral of fear and doubt caught me in a dangerous undercurrent as I trudged up the stairs. When we were locked in the cottage together, everything had seemed so easy, so obvious. Out here, things felt complicated—hard in a way my mind couldn't currently handle or think through.

There had to be a way to solve this. To fix it so this didn't all hurt so much. I was just too tired to see it. Too tired and shortsighted to figure it all out. Once I was shut inside my room, I set my phone on its charger and crawled into bed, pushing throw pillows onto the floor.

Someone had done me the favor of washing my sheets recently. They still smelled faintly of the lavender essential oil that Ember drizzled onto the felt dryer balls she favored. I buried my face in them, pulling the duvet over my head.

My phone buzzed softly, letting me know it was back on, but I couldn't bear the thought of going to get it. *Someone was always calling.* I'd forgotten what that was like in the time Eryx and I had been at the Cottage. Always calling, always texting. Always needing something from me.

It wasn't their fault. I'd let everyone close to me do it for years without setting a single boundary, or even waiting until I had time to talk with them. I answered every call, responded to every text. The second I saw them, I answered. And if I didn't, I felt guilty.

If I let Eryx in, would he become another person I dreaded intruding on me? Would he be another thing to feel guilty over?

My breath came in ragged gasps, as my phone buzzed again. I dragged myself out of bed to look at it. It was Calypso, and she'd just remembered that I'd promised to recommend a shampoo to her before I'd left... and did I remember which one it was? I did, but I couldn't bring myself to answer her. Instead, I opened the settings of my phone and turned off my read receipts.

This had to stop. I had so few pieces of myself left. I needed them for me. I closed my eyes and tried to clear some of the noise from my mind, letting my thoughts order themselves a bit more logically.

There was a number I could call to get my job with the Consulate back. All it would take was one phone call, and I'd be back in my posh little condo by the sea. In Aradios, everything had been quieter, but so, so painfully lonely. And they would expect me to get back on the Blaire case, and I *couldn't*. I pushed that out of my mind. Right now, the quiet was all I could think of.

My thoughts overrode my desire for just a few minutes of peace to gather myself. Now that I was out here again, I couldn't stop thinking. But one thought repeated itself: I couldn't go back to working for the Consulate. And it wasn't just the Blaire case. It was everything.

When I'd gotten the job, it made sense. I'd traded information that was completely useless to the modern Consulate about how magic worked in exchange for contacts. First for the best doctors for Sera, and later, for information about the mysterious "Mother." And, I thought, good information about who might have stolen our swords.

But "Mother"—the Admiral—had been too good at

hiding herself and what she'd done. I'd never once suspected her, or the island, and as a result, I'd probably given the Consulate more than was good for them to know. I couldn't go back to working for them, but I *could* go back to the warm quiet of Aradios. There were other things I could do there. Antiquities dealers who'd be grateful for my expertise.

Anything to get the distance back between myself and the people I didn't know how to say no to. Anything to get away from Eryx before I hurt him. After everything that had happened with Francesca Lyon, he deserved someone who could love him wholly.

If I went back into that house with him, I would lose control. I would let myself sink into him, and I'd lose myself further. I'd let myself love him and destroy us both. But the thought of leaving him left me nearly bereft. I didn't know how to fix this or change it. I'd made too many mistakes, let myself get too tired. All I knew for sure now was that the way he looked at me was dangerous, and I couldn't trust myself with him.

My phone buzzed again, and then dinged. How had the sound been turned back on? Every vibration and ring from the phone felt like a shot to my frayed nerves. I shook, unable to move to shut it off, unable to stand the sound of it.

A horrible thought occurred to me. What if I couldn't leave Orphium? What if eating the food of the dead had bound me to this place forever? I'd be trapped here. Trapped with all this noise I didn't know how to stop.

I had to try to get out. I had to know I could escape, if I needed to. Just for a little while. I could call Marv at Sanctuary, the top antiquities firm in Aradios. I could call him and be gone in an hour.

Six months of easy work identifying old shit and

sleeping for twelve hours a night might just do the trick. Six months of pure quiet would fix me. And then I could be the person everyone needed me to be again. My heart beat faster as my legs swung about, and my feet touched the floor.

The only way to stop this constant, soul-crushing exhaustion was to leave. It was never going to get better here. All I needed was my suitcase and summer clothes and this would be over.

My body moved without much thought, gathering my things. I was practiced at this, at running from my problems to solve them. It was the only thing I was good at anymore, and coming back here was never supposed to be permanent. Ember had Calypso now and they'd fared just fine without me, so far. They would be fine for another few months.

I *had* made a promise though. To Cassandra. I would stop by the Cottage before I went to explain. I told myself she would get it. That out of anyone, she'd understand why I was running from a Necroline man.

"What the fuck are you doing?"

I glanced up to find Lara glowering at me. She'd used my methods for silence and managed to sneak up on me.

"Leaving," I said.

She snatched a bikini from my hand. "No."

I snatched it back, feeling instantly resentful. This was the problem. This idea that I wasn't allowed to make my own decisions about things. That I owed them some part of me. "You don't get to boss me around anymore, Lara Achilles."

She smacked the bikini out of my hand and shook me by the shoulders, all in a lightning-fast movement. "We need you, Rhiannon."

It was the wrong thing for her to say. I didn't want to

be needed. Or noticed. Or even loved. I wanted to disappear. To find the endless peace of being unknown again. Aradios had been so quiet. Lonely, but so quiet. Tears pricked at the corners of my eyes. I didn't fight back. I just looked away, my hands shaking as I shook my head. "You don't. You never have."

"Holy fuck," she breathed, her grip on my shoulders tightening. "You don't get it, do you?"

She had no idea what I meant. She wasn't understanding me, because I was failing to communicate myself correctly. Again. This was how it always was with us. It was like we were having two different conversations, one hundred percent of the time.

"You are the fucking glue, Rhi," she murmured, shaking me again. Hard. "You know how to handle every single fight, make sure we come to the right conclusions… You are *irreplaceable*."

Her words slid off me as easily as if I was made of glass. It was hard not to laugh. She understood, but still didn't get it. Still didn't get *me*. I'd never wanted to be irreplaceable. I just wanted to be *one of them*. "You've all been fine without me."

She let go of my shoulders, only to grab hold of my chin, forcing me to look at her. "Don't be a fool, Brontë. We survived it, but no one is ever *fine* without you."

I pulled out of her grip. Anger was all I had left. This was a misunderstanding of some sort, but I couldn't be the one to solve it. Not this time. "Well maybe you need to learn to mediate your quibbles without me. I'm not your fucking mother."

Lara bit down on her bottom lip, shaking her head and raising her hands in surrender. "Fine. Do whatever you want."

She spun on her heels and I grabbed the bikini off the

floor and shoved it in my bag, marching down the back stairs in the opposite direction from her. Before I knew it, I was downstairs, slipping into my shoes by the back door of Hemlock House. Tears threatened, but I couldn't let myself cry. I had to get to Oleander Cottage and talk to Cassandra. Then I could leave.

Then I could find rest somewhere. Peace. All I wanted was quiet. My head ached with too many overwhelming emotions. If I didn't get quiet soon, I was going to implode. I sat hard on the bench by the shelf for shoes, fighting back angry tears.

My shoes had been put away in a cubby with my name on it. Briony's bubbly teenage letters were sweet, cheerful. Why couldn't I find peace here? Going back to Aradios would only cause more problems. I *knew* that. My head fell into my hands, and I tried to focus on my breath, but nothing helped.

Every second, trapped without respite, made things worse.

The sound of Lara following me infuriated me further. Why could she never let me be? Without looking up, I growled. "Leave me *alone*, Achilles."

When she didn't answer, I raised my eyes slowly. Eryx had changed his clothes—now he wore a pair of dark gray sweatpants, and a Pizza Queen baseball jersey that hung over his hips in a way that was far, far too tantalizing. His face was twisted with emotion.

"Lara says you're leaving?" He framed the words as a question, but they came out as an accusation. "Were you going to go without saying anything to me?"

I crossed my arms over my chest. I was fairly certain I was scowling. It was different with him than it was with the others, but I was too deep into my fury to say the right things. Now I wanted to make everything worse. "I don't owe you anything."

He took two steps across the mudroom, his eyes blazing. "The fuck you don't. You can't just *leave*."

"Why not?" My words sounded like a child's dare. This was wrong and I knew it. I knew it and I was going to push him harder. Hard enough to break this thing between us once and for all. I stood. He was so close I could feel the heat radiating off him. "Why. *Not?*"

I wasn't sure what I wanted him to say, but I expected bravery I didn't have at the moment. It was an unfair desire, a selfish one, even. But I was backed into a corner, embarrassed, exhausted… My knees buckled.

Eryx's arms were around me as darkness clouded my peripheral vision. "I can't do this anymore," I whispered, as the room slipped out of focus. Nothing felt real. I was going down, my lungs unable to take in air, my eyes unable to stay open a second longer. Words tumbled out of me, meaningless or meaningful, I knew nothing more than that I was speaking. "I need to take a nap."

My eyes drooped shut, but I didn't pass out. It wasn't that type of swoon. It was as though I was dropping slowly off a cliff, into a dark abyss. I felt Eryx's arms close around my body, strong and safe as he gathered me into his arms.

Suddenly, breathing was easier. My eyelids weighed a ton. Darkness seeped in, close and comforting as Eryx's body heat. "Then it's a nap you'll have," he murmured, his voice gentle now as I nuzzled against him. I'd forgotten why I wasn't supposed to. "You'll have all the rest you need."

CHAPTER 23

ERYX

IT WAS difficult not to chastise myself. I'd seen this coming, but she'd been better when we were alone. Rhiannon Brontë was burned the fuck out—and returning to Hemlock House and the realm of cell phones and constant communication had overloaded her fragile healing process. It was easy to forget because she was so damn capable that she was not, in fact, a goddess.

She might not be mortal, but Rhiannon was still fallible, still vulnerable. And despite the fact that everyone badly needed her help, she was worn out. If she didn't rest, none of us were going to make it through this. Anyone was free to argue with me about it, but I was sure of that fact. So, I took her to the only place I knew she might get the quiet she needed. Oleander Cottage.

Cassandra had known when we arrived that what Rhiannon needed most was sleep. For some reason, she was invested in her wellbeing. When I had Rhiannon tucked safely into our bed, I found Cassandra waiting on the stairs. She was dressed in the white linen dressing gown she'd died in, and had barely a wisp of corporeality. As I walked towards her, she gazed past me, looking at Rhiannon, I assumed. She pressed a finger to her lips, motioning for me to follow her downstairs.

When we got to the kitchen, she pointed to the garden, where Lara Achilles and Ember Verona sat in the wrought-iron chairs, waiting for me. I would deal with them in a moment.

For now, I had a question for my uncle's bride. "Who are you, really?"

Cassandra shook her head. "That is a conversation I am only willing to have with *her* and I will have it in my own time."

Fair enough. The woman had been through more than her share of being forced to do things by Necroline men. Still, I needed her help. "If I go out there and talk to them, what will happen here?" I was, I had to admit, a little afraid that Cassandra might not let me back into the Cottage.

She placed a ghostly hand on my shoulder. "She is safe with me, Eryx. I will deepen her rest, make it more effective. You should have let me help her more before."

My hands clenched into fists at my side. For Rhiannon to be truly safe, she needed more than just promises. "Please don't possess her again. Don't frighten her with whatever you're keeping from me."

Cassandra nodded. "It has been a long time since there was any hope at all. I made mistakes when she first arrived, when you came with her. I... wasn't myself." I already knew that. Tortured spirits lost who they were in their grief and pain. "She will rest now. Will you help her?"

The question was so tentative all my irritation bled away, remembering what Cassandra had endured in life. And now she had to deal with the fact that she had caused irreparable harm with her rage in death. "Yes," I promised.

Cassandra nodded then, fading away, then reappearing on the kitchen stairs, where she sat down, a sentinel between Rhiannon and the rest of the world. "Make them go away," she said. "They'll only bother her. They want too much."

The way she said it had an odd quality to it. She spoke as if she knew the Maere personally. I shook my head. "We need help for what's next. You have to let them help."

Cassandra shook *her* head, a mirror of my movements. "Not until I talk to Rhiannon. Not until I know they are safe for her—that they won't betray her, like my family betrayed me."

Now we were getting to the heart of it. There was no record of Cassandra Necroline before the year she prophesied the tsunami. The family she'd claimed sold her to the Necroline Dynasty was nowhere to be found. Ares and I had looked through the dynasty's records, but there was nothing there.

My hope was that she might just tell me. "Safe? In what way?"

The answer was a determined set to Cassandra's jaw. She'd said she would only talk to Rhiannon and apparently, she meant it. I sighed, walking out through the mudroom and into the garden.

Lara's eyes were wide and worried. "I didn't mean to upset her so much."

A third chair appeared. For me. Ember made a vicious noise at the sight of it. "Magic," she hissed. "*How?*"

I believed Rhiannon was safe with Cassandra, or I wouldn't have left her. But there was something about her story that didn't add up. "When Magnus and Cassandra were married, did you know her?"

Lara and Ember both shrugged, but it was Ember who answered me. "They weren't married for very long."

"Five years," I countered.

She and Lara both laughed. Five years was merely a blink of an eye to most of us, but to them—who would live forever—five years must have seemed completely inconsequential.

Lara's laugh died away. "Truth be told, we were busy renovating the house."

"You know," Ember added, "The one you burned down."

I blew out a huff of air, feeling razzed. "Everyone has apologized for that several times."

She shrugged, flipping her hair over her shoulder. "I don't think there's a limit on being sorry for arson."

Lara snorted, and I realized they were teasing me. And suddenly, it felt good to be teased. It felt like I belonged with them, that they'd accepted me into their realm. My shoulders came down from around my ears, as I sank into the chair the Cottage had offered me.

"I need to know something, and I know you're not supposed to tell me." Lara and Ember exchanged glances, but I continued. I wasn't sure why I felt the need for such secrecy, but this moment felt a little like when we'd been lost in the unreality of the underworld, like if we didn't move delicately, the whole thing might fall apart. "I need to know the way your immortality works. Why can't you die?"

Ember blew out a breath. There was an odd quality to the air, all the magic being used, I assumed. Perhaps she was familiar with what it signified and understood even better than I did why exercising caution might be wise. "It would be better to show him."

Lara nodded. They were on some wavelength I couldn't see or understand. "I'll stay here—with her."

Ember nodded. "I think that would be best. She needs a shield while she rests."

"Cassandra won't let you into the house," I cautioned.

Lara grinned at me, then stood. "Guess I'll have to climb onto the roof, then." She clapped a hand on my shoulder. "Gotta protect my girl."

I swallowed hard, something awful shaking loose inside me. *Jealousy.* The way Lara said, "my girl" nearly drove me to my knees. All the history between them, the love. It wasn't that I was worried Rhiannon might fall for Lara again. I knew her well enough to know that when she was finished with something, some*one*, she was done. I wasn't jealous of their friendship. I admired that.

The problem was that Rhiannon *wasn't mine.*

"Come on," Ember said, placing her hand on my arm. "Let's get a cab. I don't want to deal with parking downtown."

The cab ride had been quiet. I got the feeling I was being inducted into some deeper aspect of the Maere's lives, and that Ember wasn't altogether comfortable being the one to show me.

She hadn't bothered changing clothes before we left, and neither had I, so we were both wearing sweats to the very formal Library of Amarante. The woman who worked the front desk pursed her crimson lips at our casual dress, but said nothing when Ember checked us both in. The Library was private, members only, and had the air of a place where secrets were buried.

I followed Ember through white marbled hallways, up a stately set of stairs, and into a hallway where brass animals marked each door. Ember stopped in front of a door with two intertwining snakes, each consuming the other's tail.

"So," she said as she pushed the door open. "You'll stick your hands on that stone plinth and it's gonna try its best to consume you."

I raised an eyebrow, and she shrugged. The room was empty but for the plinth. We'd come for this?

"It's old magic. And as such, it requires a price," she explained. "It's a doorway to the island."

I knew there was an island the Maere hailed from. It was legend, after all. But not much else was known about where they came from, or why there were only fifteen of them. Ember opened a nearly-invisible panel on the wall, revealing a white, corded phone.

She picked it up and spoke softly to someone. "Eryx Necroline. Mission critical to our alliance with the Necroline Dynasty," she said in response to what was obviously a question. "I'll take him to the lyceum and that is all."

There was a long pause, and then Ember hung up without saying goodbye. Her mouth pressed into a tight line. None of the Orphium Maere were on particularly good terms with their higher-ups, currently. I was a little surprised she was willing to do this for me. "Your visit has been approved."

I nodded. "So, I just put my hands on the plinth?"

"Yep," she replied. "The trick is getting them off it when we're done. But you'll figure something out. You can talk to Rhi about what you've seen, any of us, but Briony… And Ares. He's seen it too. No one else, though, or bad shit will happen to your brain. Got it?"

"What kind of bad shit?" I asked.

Ember looked down at the plinth for a long moment. "We were told that the worst would be that we'd forget the island… and none of us want that… but once, long ago, I had a contact—a Duke that I needed to question, and I, er…"

I raised an eyebrow, wondering if this was part of the story about the Duke of Westborough Rhiannon had told me at Delicia's. "Killed him?"

Ember smiled. "So you've heard. Well, it turned out that he wasn't precisely dead. Just very injured, and I needed more information from him. So I brought him to the island. When he was returned, he promptly tried to tell the Authority where he'd been."

Her face had gone slightly pale. She swallowed. "I doubt they believed him. He'd gone quite mad. I have a theory that without true immortality's protection, the working that protects the island is more severe."

I nodded. It wasn't as though I was going to tell anyone the Maere's secrets. "Does Rhiannon know this?"

"No," Ember replied. Then she pursed her lips. "The other Maere don't know yet. I've been in the habit of keeping too many of the island's secrets."

"You should tell them," I said. "The island hasn't been completely honest with you about a lot of things."

"You're telling me." Ember's sigh was long suffering. "We need to move along if you want to see the big show. If you're not too chicken to go, that is."

I rolled my eyes at her gentle ribbing. "I'm going." It was important that I understand this. If what I suspected was true, it was going to be a difficult thing for the Maere to process, Rhiannon especially. I had to be sure. "And you can trust me not to scramble my brain by telling your secrets."

"Stick 'em on there," Ember replied with a wry grin. Then she whispered. "I like you a lot, Eryx."

Despite the fact that she was a little dense to Rhiannon's feelings, I liked Ember Verona too. And what's more, I trusted her. I pressed my hands to the marble plinth and everything went dark for a moment.

When I opened my eyes, I stood on a stone patio, a twisted pine casting shade over a tiny amphitheater of seats carved into alabaster. Huge waves crashed onto the dramatic black rocks of the shore below.

I'd never seen the sea so unfettered, so *close*. In the distance, a serpentine body rose out of the waves, its maw gaping as it closed over a smaller animal I could not make out at this distance.

The Ceti were out there. The monster crashed into a wave so high it would cover a skyscraper. Perhaps this was why no one had ever found the island. Calling those seas dangerous would be a wicked understatement. But they were beautiful. And this place—it shimmered with power.

But it was more than that. An ache built inside me, brick by brick, a longing to be close forever with that undercurrent of power. This is where magic was. This place was my heart's true home. My jaw tightened, my throat constricting as I swallowed the onslaught of pure sadness assaulting me.

"Rhiannon brought your brother here once," Ember said, her voice softer than usual. Her hazel eyes were wide, compassion shining in them. We didn't have to discuss what I felt. "She wanted him to know me, to know why I am how I am. Maybe I can do the same for you—and her. By now you've figured out that she needs more help than she lets others give, haven't you?"

The timbre of her voice was hesitant, like she was afraid she was telling Rhiannon's secrets. I nodded, hoping she would keep talking. Ember touched my arm lightly, pointing to the impressive stone structure behind the patio. "This is the lyceum."

The building was impressive, larger than most of the Three Cities' temples to the Saints—or the gods, depending on what you believed. Behind its enormous columns were several frescoes. Ember beckoned to me and I followed her to the one on the furthest end of the building from us.

"This depicts the last of the parapsych refugees making their way to Otrera," she said, standing in front of an enormous painting of ships battered in the waves. The painter had depicted one ship being swallowed by a Ceti, another being dragged under by the angry sea, a hint of a Kraken's tentacle showing under the water.

Ember walked to the next of the frescoes. A blonde woman, statuesque with familiar features, stood on a rocky outcropping, her arms raised. She looked like Rhiannon. Behind her stood a host of people. I recognized many of the faces: the Admiral, who had masqueraded as Mother; Ember, Rhiannon and Lara, standing close to one another.

Ember tapped the woman on the rocky ledge with her arms raised. "This is Rhiannon's mother, Silea, our queen. This shows her closing the mists, trapping magic here, forevermore. Protecting it from unscrupulous humans."

I raised an eyebrow. I had some idea after the heist that Rhiannon was from a powerful family, but I hadn't fully understood that she was an *actual* princess. For a moment, I felt the expanse of what we didn't know about each other stretch out before me.

"This is what you came to see, I think." Ember said, moving on to the next painting, which showed a series of events.

"First, we see the cloistering of true magic. What once was abundant in the world lives on here, protected. And these are the scholomages and the smiths, the women who created the spells that allow for the Maere to be reborn off the island, with their swords fused, metaphysically, of course, to their spines."

I marveled at the detail in the frescoes, a cool sea-breeze ruffling my hair. The salty air smelled of sharp evergreen and something faintly citrus. "There are more Maere than just the fifteen of you?"

Ember shrugged a little. "That depends on how you look at it. The word "Maere" was used to mean the warriors that protected Otrera for eons before the particularities our role was conceived of, or even needed."

I sat down on a stone bench that faced the frescoes, frowning a little as I sorted this information with my theory. "Otrera was the first of the Maere, correct? And the island is named for her?"

Ember sat next to me, staring at the frescoes along with me, a deep longing in her eyes. "Yes. Otrera was a goddess herself, Tanith and Amarante's daughter. The gods are not a metaphysical concept, Eryx. They are real entities, and Otrera is Rhiannon's ancestor."

My eyes nearly popped out of my head. "She *is* a goddess, then."

Ember chuckled. "I can certainly understand why you'd think so. And yes, some part of her is divine. All of the island's original inhabitants are demigods, technically, and parapsychs all carry divine blood. It's what gives you your powers."

My head spun with the information. I had been devoted to the Saints my whole life, but they had been a vague concept. Something distant. If they were real entities, they'd abandoned us. Abandoned their children to this wretched world. It was a slight I could hardly forgive.

As my heart hardened against gods who could abandon their progeny to the world, Ember's voice dropped to a low hush. "It is the swords, of course, that make us truly immortal, not just long-lived like the rest of you. All Maere have sacred swords, but not all of the warriors on the island have been purified by their blades, as we have." With her last words, she gestured towards the last frescoes.

I drew a sharp breath in, needing to process what she'd told me. "Does that mean you could have been killed when you didn't have them?"

Ember shook her head, a dark smile in her eyes. "No. Unfortunately not. Once the swords were fused to our souls, they might be stolen in physical form, cutting off our connection to the well of magic here, but the immortalizing effect was permanent."

I stared at the paintings that showed the apparent steps that had been taken to create a soul that might be reincarnated as truly immortal. It was bizarre to see it, all the way to the end, where those who now guarded the Three Cities were run through with their swords, losing their first lives to the magic that would bring them back on the Continent and doom them to a life of duty.

"We cloistered magic," Ember said, "but we also promised ourselves to the world. It was the best we knew to do in the face of everything."

Rhiannon, as I knew her now, had been created out of this purification, this brutal ritual. She'd died to protect parapsychs as well as she could from the evil of the Authority. How she could think of herself as a monster was beyond me.

Suddenly, I knew I wouldn't be sad to leave this place, though I was glad I came. It was time to go home. More than anything, I needed to be where Rhiannon was. Gods and Saints were nothing to me now. They'd abandoned us to the cruelty of the world. If there was anything truly divine in this world, it was Rhiannon, and the rest of the Maere. They did the work the gods had refused.

I nodded. It all made sense now. "So those of you who have not undergone the ritual, the purification as you call it, you live and die as others do?"

Ember smiled. "The people of this archipelago have always been a bit sturdier than the rest of the parapsychs— and because we are demigods, extremely long-lived, but yes."

I moved away from the frescoes, going to the amphitheater as my mind raced. I stood at the stone balustrade facing away from the sea, looking out over the island. Beyond the lyceum, in groves of evergreens, was a temple district. Further beyond that, the terraced cliffside was dotted with bright white buildings, some with colorful domed roofs. People moved about, dressed in an ancient style, tiny dots in the distance.

Everywhere I looked there were new marvels. Overhead, great birds with the faces of beautiful women flew in flocks, their ethereal songs echoing through the valleys. And then I saw the spirits. They flitted in and out of the underworld with no friction, no unhappiness.

My eyes locked onto a woman, far below us, sitting on the side of the road, eating a piece of fruit I could not quite make out. She braided a spirit's hair, without actually touching it. She was a necromancer. I was sure of it.

A necromancer, who seemed to be having an amiable chat with a happy spirit. Rage and hope battled within me. The entire world could have been like this. Peaceful. If only humans had known how to accept us. If only we had known how to stop lording our power over them. It wasn't a simple matter of which group was good and which was bad. We were all both, circling around one another in an endless loop of violence and sorrow.

I gestured to the woman, and Ember, who'd come to stand next to me, followed the motion of my arm with her eyes. "There are parapsychs here, then? Necromancers, thaumaturges, cognoscenti?"

Ember nodded. "Some here, many on the other islands. There was room for more, but so few came." She shook her head. "Many believed staying would stop the Authority from winning, that they could turn the tide from within."

"And what do you think?" I asked, wondering if the same battle that waged itself in me lived in her as well. I turned away from the island, barely able to contain my emotions.

Ember shrugged. "I chose to be reborn in a world I knew wanted to see my spirit broken, didn't I?" She stood next to me, all skinny, gangly limbs, throwing an arm back out at the frescoes. "I'll never know if all this was worth it. It's been centuries, and the world is different—better than it was in those days in so many ways… and in others, I think it may be worse."

She covered her mouth with one of those long-fingered hands, shaking her head. "I don't know, Eryx. I've never been one for the big picture. People like Rhi, your brother, fuck, even Lara, are all better at seeing ahead than I am. What I am good at is *staying*."

Ember and I were not so different from one another, in that way. There was a power in staying. In refusing to move in the face of a storm. Cleverness, foresight, even vision all needed one thing to be truly effective: endurance. Change was not a flash in the pan, it was a test of spirit. A horrific battle of persistence.

"They need us," I murmured. "The Areses and Rhiannons. My brother needs someone who is deeply grounded to pull him out of his head and into the world."

Ember's smile was wicked now. "I suppose he does. And she needs you, Eryx. She just can't admit it yet. This place fucked her up. Her *mother* fucked her up."

I nodded, my reason for being here surfacing. I needed to know who Cassandra really was, and I was sure that Rhiannon's mother knew the answer. "That is why I need to speak with her."

Ember shook her head. "Buddy, you've got a set on you." I had no idea what the Orphium Maere's commander would do next. When she pushed off the balustrade, I was surprised. "Come on, then. If we're storming the castle, we don't have a lot of time."

CHAPTER 24

RHIANNON

I WOKE to Cassandra sitting on my bed. My head was bleary and my very bones were brittle, exhausted by the weight of simply being. She was less corporeal than she had been the last time I'd seen her. Her appearance flickered slightly, between the corpse-garbed malefic and the ways I'd seen her present other times. The dressing gown, the various suits. She was struggling to keep herself steady now that her message had been sent. I stretched my hand towards her, palm up.

Cassandra's form solidified somewhat. Her smile was soft as she placed her hand in mine. "You are very kind, Rhiannon."

Still exhausted, I shrugged. "Maybe once, but not now."

Silently, she nodded. "Perhaps that is for the best. You have a visitor."

Cassandra went to the window and opened it before fading away.

Lara's dark head popped in through the open window. "Heya, Princess."

I shook my head. "Don't call me that."

Her long, muscular limbs came crawling in with the grace of a boxer. She was in bed next to me before I could tell her not to. "Okay."

She leaned against me, and I breathed her in. Lara always smelled like fresh air. It was comforting, familiar. And we'd be fighting within ten minutes if either of us got too cozy. There were some patterns that were doomed to repeat themselves.

"You always saw the worst in me," I whispered, pulling the quilt up around my chest. It wasn't an accusation. More of a question as I rested my head on her shoulder.

"And loved you more for it," Lara answered. "If only your worst and my worst hadn't been so diametrically opposed. I do love a difficult woman."

Tears clouded my eyes as she looped an arm through mine. "You do."

She pressed a kiss to the top of my head. "And I *still* love you. I always will. You know that, right?"

I nodded, knowing exactly what she meant. Somehow, hard as we both were to deal with, we'd managed to keep that. It had taken years, but we kept fighting for it. Fighting to stay for each other, to find a new way.

"You get that Eryx is falling in love with you, right?"

Her voice was soft, almost cautious. It was a version of her the world rarely saw. To everyone else, she was the rough and tumble Maere who kicked ass and took no prisoners. The parapsychs of Orphium had named her after mythological avengers of lore. They called her the Angel, and I understood why. But with me, she had always just been Lara.

My Lara, who never lied to me, who never tried to hide things so I wouldn't be mad. So, when she said that Eryx was falling for me, I knew she wasn't putting me on. But I couldn't hear it. I didn't answer, turning my face to inhale her scent of clean skin.

"Let him help you, Rhi. Let someone in."

I glared up at her. "You're one to talk."

She smiled. "I came back, didn't I? This, being one of the Maere again, for real—it's what I needed. You've isolated yourself since the beginning."

"Not from you," I murmured.

"That was a disaster," she replied with a wry laugh. "And then you retreated again. You always fall back. You have to let us love you, Rhiannon."

Tears slipped down my cheeks. "What if I don't deserve it?"

She shifted in bed, turning towards me, cool fingers cupping my chin. "What if you do?" I shook my head, but she gripped me harder. "Rhiannon. Saints spare me for saying this, but your mother is a fucking cunt. You have *always* deserved to be loved and respected. No one has worked as hard as you. That's why you're tired now."

I opened my mouth to say something. To protest. Lara shook her head, a mischievous smile lighting her face. "Nope. Not gonna hear it." She shut my mouth. "Close your eyes and take a damn nap. I'll watch for ghouls."

The problem was that she was right. I had been fighting it since before we underwent the ritual to become immortal, but it was true. Nothing I'd ever done was good enough for my mother. She'd always preferred someone else's behavior over mine, someone else's sense of style, or way of speaking.

When I'd ask if she cared that I forfeit the throne to join the Maere, she'd only shrugged. I could see her face perfectly in my mind's eye, so much like my own. She hadn't even looked up from the scroll she examined. It had meant so little to her one way or another. Her only words had been, "It will not be difficult to choose a replacement for you as heir. Do as you like."

It was the first time I'd allowed myself to *really* think of her in years. To picture her face brought a bittersweet edge to my exhaustion. In some ways, her dismissal had been a relief. She'd said aloud what I'd always known—she had no use for me. I meant so little to her that she could shrug off millennia of our line.

For so long, I'd carried that in my heart, believing that I had been such a bad daughter, such a bad princess, that she saw no future in me. But the truth was that *she* was a bad mother. On the island, in my first life, and all the years since, she'd been finding ways to punish me for not living up to her ideals.

Lara leaned against me. "Whatever you're thinking about, let it go, babe."

I sighed. "I was just thinking that maybe I wasn't such a bad daughter. Or princess."

Lara's laugh was soft. Gentle for me in a way it rarely was for others. The sound of it warmed me. She really did know the worst of me. "Rhiannon, you were beloved by all. How did you not see it?"

I frowned. Had that been the way it was? All that was left was the exhaustion from how hard I'd tried. From how hard I was still trying, even now. "I don't know about that."

"I do," Lara whispered. "The only person besides your mother who doesn't know who you are is *you*."

I considered that for a moment. "But if I let myself believe I am good, that I've done well, or even enough… what if I just stop trying?"

Lara's snicker was dry, but not cruel. "What if you do?"

The thought perplexed me. I frowned.

Lara readjusted in bed so that we faced one another,

her head on the pillow next to mine. "Are you afraid you'll turn evil the instant you stop trying so hard?"

My chin shook, and I was tempted to shut my eyes against the intense vulnerability of this moment. "Maybe."

Lara's left eyebrow arched. "Seriously?"

I shrugged and she grimaced. "Do you hear how silly that sounds? Your theory is *actually* that if you stopped preemptively being there for everyone but yourself that you might suddenly turn evil?"

My cheeks flushed. When she said it like that, it did sound ridiculous. Panic rose up in me, all the webs of cognitive dissonance I'd woven around me over the years collapsing. "It does sound a little silly."

Lara reached out for my hand, pressing a chaste kiss to my knuckles. "*You* aren't silly though. You are brave and smart. Very good with the murders, which I adore about you."

I rolled my eyes, but she tugged on my hand. "Rhiannon. No one loves you for what you do for us. We love you for who you *are*."

"That might take some time to believe," I whispered.

Lara's smile was dazzling. "You take all the time you need, Princess. You've got a whole family here who loves you, and who's going to keep reminding you."

With her words, the last of the fight left in me died. My body lost all tension and a great yawn stretched from my mouth, deep into my soul. Lara knew me better than anyone in the whole world. I could believe what she told me. My eyes were heavy as she pulled the quilt up over us.

"I won't let anything get you. Go the fuck to sleep."

I laughed, warmth traveling from my throat, deep into my belly. Tears seeped from my eyes and I cried. Lara leaned against me, knowing just what to do. She didn't shush me, or try to comfort me, but let the heavy weight of her dense body be a rock for me.

And then she hummed an old hymn, one from the days of our childhood. Windswept cliffs and alabaster hallways. Dragons on the wind, and monsters in the sea. Gardens, lush with magic. Gods, who would someday be Saints, still walked in the world.

Waves crashed on the shores of Otrera, the ocean's fury no match for my own. Wind whipped my hair around me, my feet bare to the rocky shore. I turned from the familiar coastline to see my mother arguing with a cloaked woman. From where I stood, they should have been able to see me, but of course they could not.

The wind carried their words far from my ears, but my mother's face was twisted with a rage I felt deep in my soul. She had turned that anger on me more times than I wanted to acknowledge—her eyes narrowed in the belief that she had the superior opinion. I saw now what Lara had meant.

It had been so long since I let myself remember my mother as she actually was, as my mother and not my queen. But that cold rage, that fury she made into my responsibility, so easily brought everything back.

She was the reason I'd run myself ragged.

She was the reason I could not be at peace with myself.

My heart shifted with these thoughts. She was the origin of my problems. The place where my relationship with myself had shattered into thousands of pieces, so many times. But I knew the way out of this, and I'd chosen not to take it. I hadn't been brave enough until now, and I thought I knew the reason why, though I couldn't admit it to myself just yet. Not fully.

The wind changed direction, and I heard the two

women's words clearly. The cloaked woman was speaking. "... ever *believe* me? We *must* prepare ourselves."

"I have said what needs saying," my mother responded. "My decision is made. The scholomages were clear; the mists are the only way—and you shall go to the continent and await my orders."

This was the past, not the present. I wracked my brain to do the math. If the idea of Otrera's mists had only just been conceived, then I was barely out of infancy. The Maere were naught but an idea. This was no memory, no recollection of some long-forgotten incident, brought back in a dream.

This was something else altogether.

My heart raced as the woman screamed at my mother. "I don't want to do this!" She lowered her voice when my mother drew back, as though she might slap her. "The Necrolines are not our enemies. We could just talk to Roman about this."

My mother scoffed. "You are so quick to trust. Roman Necroline will never give us the portal key, he sees it as his failsafe in case he can never get Orphium back." Silea sighed, some of the harsh lines of her face softening with what I knew to be exhaustion. "Surely you see that we cannot let the humans know about the path here."

I couldn't see the effect her words had on the cloaked woman, but I felt them deep inside my own soul. If humans could find a way to the island, they would destroy magic forever.

The woman pulled on my mother's arm. "If you make me do this, you will be dead to me."

"Then I will be sorry to lose my sister." My mother's eyes were cold once more as she spun on her heel. "But you will still do as I say. You will infiltrate the Necroline organization, and protect Otrera. The gods have spoken, sister. This is your fate."

Silea's gown billowed behind her as she stalked back up the beach without another word. And I stood stunned, too stunned to think, let alone speak.

My mother had no family. That is what I had always been told. The wind picked up, and the woman left on the rocky shore turned to escape its bite. As she did, her hood fell back, caught by the gale. Strands of her pale rose-gold hair broke free from the braid that crowned her familiar face, and she finally saw me.

She didn't look as she had in the cottage, but then, she'd likely used some bit of magic to alter her features. A good Thaumas could have even altered her permanently back in those days. But the lines were all there. I saw her for exactly who she was.

Cassandra's eyes lit on mine, and she frowned. "You should not be here, Rhiannon. Close the door between us. Close it now."

I woke to Lara's steady breathing. She had fallen into a deep sleep, but I had fallen through time. I sat up, cold sweat breaking out over my hot skin, fear coursing through me. *Close the door between us.*

There was only one place in the world that I might have had that vision. Here, in Oleander Cottage. I knew why Cassandra had kept the key from Magnus—and it had nothing to do with the dead.

CHAPTER 25

ERYX

EMBER MARCHED me through the halls of the lyceum, moving quickly, her eyes furtive. It was obvious that what we were doing was not allowed, that we should not be here. Somewhere in the distance, from within the building itself, there was trouble brewing.

The sound of voices raised with alarm came from within. Though no extra footsteps sounded next to me, a figure appeared. I reached out to touch Ember's arm. Her head swiveled, eyes wide as she tried to focus on the noise from inside the building and what happened here at the same time. I placed one finger up, the signal to hold. She nodded.

"Cassandra?" I whispered.

The spirit turned to me. She was dressed as the people in the frescoes had been, a flowing white gown and heavy gold jewelry adorning her. Her face was a bit different now, the lines of her features more defined somehow, as though I'd always seen her through a blurred lens before. She looked like Rhiannon. She smiled faintly as she materialized. Ember took a sharp breath next to me.

"You must go," she murmured. "You and Rhiannon must close the way. Even now, the humans grow closer to finding it. The third Blaire is not so foolish as the first was. He has been tracking your progress."

Ember's mouth fell open. "*You* are Cassandra?"

The spirit nodded. "I masked myself as much as I could the few times we met. I have a bit of a way with magic."

Ember took hold of my arm. "This is the queen's sister, Eryx. Rhiannon's aunt." Ember glared at Cassandra. "She doesn't have a *bit* of magic; she's one of the most powerful mages that ever lived. And she disappeared when Rhiannon was just a little girl."

I knew it. I knew she was connected to Rhiannon in some way. The signs were all there, but it was so unheard of for there to be Maere that were unknown to us, that I'd dismissed it as some sort of mirroring. Some feature of the trap to make both Rhiannon and myself feel affinity for her. But the truth was that she'd needed both of us all along. Her niece and Magnus' nephew.

The first time we'd encountered Cassandra in her corpse garb, she'd struggled so hard to tell us this. *The next generation is the answer. Find the key and find the truth.*

"What is Blaire looking for?" I asked.

Cassandra gestured to the walls around us. "He is looking for this. He is looking for the answer to immortality. To find magic and release it. To keep it for his own.

"But he cannot do that, not just because it would destroy the world—and it would. But because humans were not made to bear the weight of magic. It is a blessing that they cannot wield it—but they have mistaken it for a curse."

Ember's eyes widened. Her hand closed around my arm as Cassandra's words sank in. I nodded at her as I fully understood. Our powers, our talents, they *were* a burden.

Humans were jealous of the things we could do. But they didn't know the ways it harmed us. They didn't understand the sensitivity it created, the way the world and all its cruelty were all the harder for it. The way that even light could hurt us, or too many sounds or smells. They had no idea that to carry these talents meant allowing the world to hurt us, with absolutely no barrier.

They thought we felt nothing. That our power shielded us, made things too easy for us. But it was the opposite. We felt it all. That's what our powers were. Us feeling the entire world, all at once.

And Blaire wanted to unleash that onto humanity. To live forever, because he saw it as a way to gain more power. This had never been about overwhelming the world with the dead. The first Blaire had let Magnus think it was because that is what my uncle had wanted. But Cassandra had seen through that.

"You tried to tell Roman, didn't you?" I asked.

She nodded. "Hundreds of years before I married Magnus, I came to your father and told him how important it was that we make sure no doors to the underworld were allowed to go unprotected. I didn't know that telling him about the island would cause us both to forget."

Ember looked as though she might cry. "You didn't know about the spells? About what they would do to you?"

Cassandra shook her head, as though in slow motion, staring into Ember's eyes. "Because I was not sanctified—because I had not gone through the rituals you did, it did more than just make me forget. It ruined my ability as a Seer, destroyed my magic."

"But you did remember, eventually," I said, wondering how she'd known to protect the door to the underworld.

Cassandra smiled, though there was so much grief in her eyes, I wondered what she'd had to sacrifice for her memory. "Yes, though that is a story we don't have time for. Eventually, I remembered, and regained some of my power.

"And I returned to Orphium, having changed my appearance so much that no one recognized me." Grief lined her face as she closed her eyes. She looked so much like Rhiannon in that moment that I would have done anything to prevent a future where the woman I cared for was so marred by the past. "I married Magnus to protect the island, but also to protect humans. They are not so bad as we sometimes make them out to be."

Ember sucked in a breath. "No group of people is as bad as those who misuse their power."

Cassandra nodded. "You are wise, Ember Verona. You and my niece have the power to change this world for the better. To be better than the Authority, the Consulate, and even the Trinity." The sounds from inside the lyceum had turned from urgent to panicked. Cassandra gripped Ember's arms. "I wish we had more time. You must get to my sister, and to Myrine. They must prepare a host here. They must hold the line."

Ember nodded, glancing at me. "You okay with her?"

"Yes," I agreed. Ember broke into a sprint, her footsteps loud on the marble floors as she disappeared. "What do I do?"

Cassandra's relief was palpable, but she wasn't finished. "Magnus hasn't crossed over, Eryx. That is why I stayed, originally, it's how what you and Rhiannon called the 'finger trap' of Oleander Cottage was made. I never meant for so many to perish." Her eyes were wide, her mouth turned down with the weight of so much guilt. She looked behind her, as though seeing something I didn't. "I will deal with him as best I can, but I may need your brother's help."

I nodded. "Of course. If Ares can end him, once and for all, he will. I don't know how Magnus got around him to begin with."

Cassandra looked behind her again, and this time there was terror in her eyes. "You have to go. Use the key to the basement. Cut off the passage to the island in the underworld. Rhiannon will know what to do."

Rhiannon will know what to do. She would, but that didn't mean I did. I had a vague awareness that my body was not here, that I was only here in some sort of facsimile. I also understood now that the people of Otrera were the mages of lore—they were the witches—the originators of all parapsych powers.

"Wait," I gasped. "I need to get back to Rhiannon. My body is in the Library of Amarante."

For the briefest of moments, Cassandra looked confused. Her forehead wrinkled as she worked things out, then smoothed. Her arms stretched towards mine. "Take a deep breath."

I nodded, not wanting to distract Cassandra from what she did. Corporeal fingers wrapped around my hands, warm and comforting. Somewhere, in a distant place in my mind, they tore my hands off the plinth in the Library. The hallway melted away, and I stood at the bottom of the stairs in Oleander Cottage. Rhiannon was racing down them, Lara close behind her.

She practically tumbled into my arms, startled by my sudden appearance. But she didn't miss a beat. "Blaire is going to invade the island. He's looking for the secret to immortality. There's a door somewhere in the underworld."

I nodded. "It's already happening."

Lara, who had stopped on the stairs, shook her head. "Ember took you to the Library?"

"Yes," I said as I steadied Rhiannon. "I've been to the island, and I saw Cassandra there."

"She's my aunt." She didn't look up at me. "I never even knew she existed."

But Ember had. What would Rhiannon do when she found out? Now wasn't the time for telling her, I knew that much.

"She said you'd know what to do," I replied.

Rhiannon held up the keys we'd found. "We have to get to the basement."

So, we were going through the door to the underworld. Behind Rhiannon, Lara had the sense to look concerned. "Calypso is on her way to help Ember. Sera needs to stay here with Briony. She's still not strong enough to go."

I nodded. "What about Ares?"

Rhiannon smiled weakly. "He's afraid of what might happen on this side, if the dead get free. He's assembling a team to make sure that doesn't happen."

Our bases were covered. All we could do now was go help. "Let's do this, then."

CHAPTER 26

RHIANNON

THE FIRST KEY—FROM MAGNUS' office—was easy enough to use. Nothing even remotely strange happened when Eryx fit it to its lock and pushed open the heavy door to the basement. Of course, it felt as though we were in the rising action of a propagandist's film about haunted houses, but that was the point of those films, after all. To make humans fear the dead.

To make humans fear death itself.

So that when a solution was offered, they would be ravenous for it.

It was all so obvious now. Blaire would *sell* immortality, damn the consequences. Apprehension rose in my chest. I feared we were too late. It felt like we'd been out of time for far too long.

Eryx went first, then me next, with Lara bringing up our rear guard. The basement was, at first, exactly what I would have expected. Dark, musty, and uncomfortable. Though the last was more because something odd was happening between Lara and Eryx. Or rather, he seemed ill at ease around her, while she was doing that thing where she smirked too much.

Cardboard boxes moldered in unstable stacks, giving off a sour smell that turned my stomach. Was it only damp, or was there something else that caused the basement to smell so bad? This wasn't, as far as I knew, a common element to spaces where the world of the living bumped up against the underworld. I wished Calypso were here to ask, as it didn't feel like the right time to ask Eryx.

I was suddenly shy. He had been to the island. He knew what I was: a revenant. A monster, made, not born.

To distract myself, I glanced back at Lara, who grimaced as she pried a stack of boxes very gently away from the wall. A corpse fell out from behind them, oozing bright white maggots, oleander flowers springing from the rot.

"Disgusting," Lara muttered, as flowers burst from the rotting corpse. Her lips pressed into a hard line. There were no more smirks now. She was at her best, sharp as a finely honed blade.

I frowned. For a moment, oleander was all that was left of the corpse and then hemlock and white roses bloomed around it. I felt nothing associated with Cassandra attached to the vision of this odd bouquet. "Does it feel like Cassandra to you?"

"No," Eryx murmured, crouching down. "Spirit auras are like a signature. This isn't her doing, it's someone else."

"What does the oleander stand for?" Lara asked. "In floriography, I mean?"

Eryx rose from his crouch. "It is a warning to be cautious."

Lara was onto something. My mind jumped ahead of me. "What about hemlock?"

Eryx raised an eyebrow. "Death. It's the most common

floriographic symbol of the Necroline Dynasty." Lara and I both nodded. "But it is interesting—paired, hemlock and oleander, I mean—they would literally mean: beware death. But there's an older tradition, one that dates back to human cults of Tanith."

He stared at the spot on the floor where the rotting corpse had been, frowning. His eyes slid to me. "There was a combination of hemlock and oleander that loosely meant to beware the union of Tanith and Amarante—not literally of course, their union is considered a blessing—but more the emulation of it. To beware the creation of eternal life, you would add a rose, a white rose."

I drew in a slow hiss of a breath. It had been there the whole time. I'd seen the roses over and over, rather than the oleander. The house, the dead, they'd all been trying to warn us. It hadn't just been Cassandra. I only had one question left. "Do the dead experience time as we do?"

Lara's eyes widened; though she didn't know the details of why the roses were so important, she obviously followed my train of thought. Eryx shook his head. "No, and though we don't know exactly how it works, Necroline scholars have always thought that the dead might see into the future."

They had known what might happen. The dead had known, and had tried to keep everyone who came here from finding the door to the underworld. These were not the condemned dead.

These were the restless, the unquiet—the dead who still loved the living and who had wanted to protect them from the doors to the netherrealm opening, to protect them from the island's cloistered magic. From its secrets of eternal life.

And Blaire knew all of that. He knew the power of the white rose, and he wasn't going to the island for the scrolls or the frescoes. He was going to the one person still alive who could wield the magic it would take to create immortality. Blaire was going to take my mother.

"We need to hurry," I said. "Blaire means to kidnap the queen. This isn't about stealing the knowledge, or the process. He'll get her to give him eternal life."

"Everything Cassandra warned me against," Eryx murmured. He shook his head, staring at the floor. The whispers had gone quiet. Now that we knew what the dead did, they had nothing left to say.

Eryx turned slowly from where the flowers had grown out of the corpse, his eyes tracing the wall behind him. I knew the look on his face by now. He saw or sensed something we did not.

"What is it?" I asked.

He startled. "Give me the key."

My chest was heavy, something constricting with each breath I took. I handed him the key. He took it from me, staring at my fingers for a long moment as they brushed his. His jaw clenched.

Something inside me paused. It wasn't my breath catching, or my heart stopping. It was something else. Some essential part of me that reached out for some essential part of him. I wanted to know why he was upset, what he heard that I didn't. I wanted Lara not to be here right now.

As he took the key from me, I glanced back at her. Had she said something to scare him? She winked. Amarante take her, she was a pain in my ass. I would have to deal with that later.

Right now, Eryx had pressed the key to a spot only he saw in the wall, and a door began forming out of nothing.

"Magic," Lara whispered.

I nodded. It could be nothing else, and seeing magic manifesting here, in Orphium, was unsettling.

When the door had fully materialized, Eryx pulled the key back and handed it to me. "I think you should open it. Cassandra left this for you to find."

His words hit me harder than I might have expected. My aunt had looked ahead. She'd seen me. The dream I had, the day on the beach. *That had been real.*

Somehow, I'd slipped through time, and Cassandra had known that I would end up here. That was before she'd fractured her ability to See. It was the day she'd had the vision of her own death. She'd known what would happen and she'd still tried to stop it. She'd tried her hardest not to die, and lost her memory of the island instead. It was more than I could bear to think about as I slid the key into the lock.

I twisted it, and the door opened to a dimly lit, arched hallway. The whispers increased in volume as we stepped inside, our footsteps creating hollow echoes down the long hall. This felt like the old world, the places that the Authority wanted humans to forget.

What I first assumed to be carved limestone immediately revealed itself to be the bones of the dead. The spine of the arched hallway was crafted from the vertebrae of Orphium's fallen, the walls encrusted with skulls barely peeking out of the plaster, their prominent eye sockets all that showed. The dead whispered from within the hollowed-out windows to their souls.

But this time their words were not a terror or a mystery. They whispered benedictions ancient as the stars. Blessings on our path, wishes for our safety. The dead here were not frightening souls. They loved us, they wanted us to succeed.

As we moved further, the benedictions turned to warnings. To cautionary tales. The skulls embedded in the wall appeared to emerge, to seek out life. Our footsteps echoed amongst their howling alarum.

Lara, Eryx, and I moved in closer formation, as the warnings changed to whispered laments. Now, the skulls were not just skulls. They were skeletons in various states of assemblage, looking as though they fought to escape from the plaster, their bony mouths gaped open in screams. The sounds of their massacre, entombed for eternity. It was a gruesome path to walk.

A reminder that the dead were us. That we were the dead. That someday, most would join them. But not the Maere. Never us. We couldn't die here, or anywhere, and that scared me more than anything. Lara glanced back at me, the same bone-deep exhaustion that lived in me hollowing out her eyes. I was not the only tired one. I'd seen that same expression on Ember's resting face dozens of times.

Eternal life was killing us, but we could not ever truly rest. We'd given that up when they killed us with our own swords. If we had known this was the price, I doubt any of us would ever have paid it. Regret that we had not found another way filled me, weighing down each step.

The sound of the dead's terror grew in intensity as we reached a crossroads of sorts, an opening in the way. Five spirits in corpse garb materialized in the doorways to other paths as we stepped over the threshold into the crossroads. Eryx threw an arm out, pushing both Lara and I back into the tunnel we'd just come through.

Lara opened her mouth to protest, and I knew what she would say—that he didn't have to protect us that way. It was easy to forget we couldn't be killed, but I didn't think that was why Eryx had stopped us. He spoke in a low, almost guttural tongue—the vox spiritus, but also another language I didn't recognize. The syllables of the dead were lyrical. I could hear the rhythm of the words, though I couldn't understand them.

Whatever he said to the guardians was poetry. The whispering coalesced as Eryx spoke, lowering to a dull roar, a kind of humming. It didn't take me long to realize the song was the one Lara had hummed to me earlier.

A hymn of Otrera. A hymn to the union between Tanith and Amarante. Death and immortal life, embodied, their union one we considered most sacred on the island. Amarante and Tanith both had to bless the creation of the Maere before my mother would perform the ritual.

Very few people actually knew that. But the dead knew. The dead knew more than we gave them credit for. My blood chilled at the thought.

The spirits in corpse garb disappeared. Eryx turned to Lara and I and beckoned us forward. "I told them what we were here for."

"Thank you." Lara nodded, gratitude shining in her eyes. "Which passageway takes us to the island?"

Eryx smiled at me. His gaze was steady, confident. "Well?"

He thought I should know. He trusted me to choose.

As I'd done many times in the past few weeks to see the truth of things, I reached behind me, grasping the hilt of my sword. It sang against my spine at my touch, so I drew it.

Lara's eyes lit with interest as I did. "Yes," she hissed. "Like a dowsing rod!"

My smile was faint, my eyes still locked with Eryx's. "Yes."

He nodded, clearly agreeing with me about my course of action. I began to rotate at the center of the room. At the third opening from my left, my sword began to hum.

At the fourth, it lit up. To experiment, I kept going, Eryx and Lara both nodding as they tracked my movements. At the fifth opening, my sword went dark.

The fourth it was, then. "This is the way," I murmured.

There were no sconces in this part of the Ossuary, and the light from the crossroads disappeared as the tiled floor gave way to a crunching gravel beneath our feet. Lara drew her own sword, breathing some inner power I didn't understand into it until it glowed faintly red and shed light onto the ground.

I had to suppress the gasp that rose up my throat, chased by bile. We were walking on bone shards. We were walking on the bones of our people.

Lara's eyes met mine, tears welling. "So many," she whispered.

Eryx hung his head, turning his face slightly away from us as he wiped his eyes. "Too many. Always too many of us, and not enough of them."

Lara gripped his shoulder, her fingers digging into the thick, corded muscle. "Always."

He looked up, first at her. They nodded to one another like comrades in arms. Then his gaze moved slowly to me. "But never you."

And then he smiled, as though the thought that I would never die was the one comforting thing he could think of. Every part of me stopped. My heart, my breath, my mind. That smile was the purest thing I'd ever seen in my life—and it was for me.

Lara grinned, wicked as a fox, and then laughed as she continued walking, holding her sword out in front of her. Her shoulders shook with mirth. Always such an asshole. My cheeks flushed with embarrassment as I followed, but I felt a little better.

The passageway we traveled down was musty, smelling

of mildew and something else, stale and sweet. A sound of footsteps startled me. Eryx grabbed me by the shoulders. "Don't look back."

Lara moved behind me, covering my rear before he'd even finished speaking.

"You either," he cautioned.

"Got it," she agreed.

"What is it?" I asked.

He was staring behind us, drawing us slowly forward. "Nothing," he said. "Keep moving."

Lara sighed. "Necroline. We're not babies. We've seen our fair share of scary shit, okay?"

"A malefic spirit," he murmured. "A strong one. I can't make it out, but I feel it. It will appear differently to all of us, and once you see it, it will have power over you."

Lara scoffed, but she didn't sound sure. "*You're* looking at it."

"I'm special." Eryx grinned at me, but there wasn't a hint of joy in his face. He was playing a part to get through this. "Come on."

We walked faster, but the footsteps matched our pace. A man's voice began to sing an old song, from the year Cassandra died, about a woman who couldn't be trusted. It was meant to be sung to a much faster beat, but the voice sang it to the tempo of a funeral dirge. Sinister didn't begin to describe the sound.

Eryx took hold of my hand. "Don't let go."

Lara walked faster, walking next to me now. "Who is it, Necroline?"

"Magnus," he hissed. "It's Magnus. I'm afraid he's going to try to take Rhiannon."

"I'd like to see him fucking try," Lara snarled.

Eryx nodded resolutely.

Despite the particular intensity of the moment I

snorted, snatching my hand out of Eryx's grip. I lifted my own sword. "The two of you should remember that I am perfectly capable of fighting him myself."

No one answered me.

The air had changed, the scent now of brine and pine air. We were nearing the island. How that was possible, I didn't know. Somehow, coming through the crossroads in the Ossuary had been a kind of shortcut. But magic was thick in the air now. "The swords can do more here. Even banish a spirit."

Eryx glanced down at me, nodding once. "That's a blessing I hope we don't have to use."

All three of us tensed as something approached us, running at full speed in the dark. Lara and I fell into defensive positions on instinct, but relaxed when two familiar faces emerged out of the murky dark. Ember and Calypso.

"They have the queen," Calypso breathed, panic in her eyes.

I could barely register what she said, my heart racing. We were too late. We'd been too slow, and now they had her.

Ember gripped my shoulders in her hands. "I'm sorry, Rhi. They have your mother and Myrine both. We need to split up. We need to find them."

CHAPTER 27

ERYX

Rhiannon drew a slow breath in, her eyelashes fluttering against her cheeks in the dim light of the Maere's swords. I could see panic flooding her body. It was obvious she'd expected this, but the news was coming hard to her nonetheless. I longed to hold her hand again, but with Ember and Lara both here, I sensed I wasn't needed.

Before I could give it another thought, Ember dragged her into a fierce hug, giving the rest of us commands over Rhiannon's shoulder. "We have to find them before they make their way to the upper world. Before they get into the city." She pushed Rhiannon back, capturing her gaze. "Do you understand, Brontë? We have a mission."

Rhiannon drew in a deep breath, the panic draining out of her eyes. I hated the way she could pull composure around her like a cloak—that she could go from being a frightened daughter whose mother had been kidnapped to a seasoned warrior in an instant. No one deserved to have to live this way, least of all her.

Ember nodded slowly, taking in Rhiannon's revised

stance. "Calypso, you double back towards Otrera. Get as many of the guard here as you can."

Calypso nodded, her eyes dark in contrast to her bright hair in the lamplight. The murk that had clung to us on this trip seemed to avoid her—an odd discrepancy. She touched Rhiannon's arm lightly. "We'll find them, Rhi."

Rhiannon nodded, and I saw what it took to keep a leash on her emotions.

Ember glanced at Lara. "You're with me." Lara nodded as Ember's eyes turned to us. "The two of you, head towards the streets. We'll try and catch them in the tunnels, but if they've already found a way out..."

Rhiannon cleared her throat. "We understand."

"One more thing." Calypso's voice held a warning. "We've seen Roman Necroline in the tunnels. He's hunting something."

Perhaps something I'd said in the cemetery had actually affected my father. Maybe he needed to make amends, though they were scarcely enough given what we now faced. "Magnus is here," I said. "He wants Rhiannon."

"Maybe Cassandra crossed over," Rhiannon whispered. "I'm the next best thing."

Ember clasped Rhiannon's face in her spider-leg fingers. "He can't have you, Rhi. No one can have you without my permission. You understand?"

Tears filled Rhiannon's eyes, but she nodded. A part of me wondered if that was my line. If I was supposed to be the one to say no one could have her without my say-so. But that felt wrong somehow.

Rhiannon wasn't *mine*. She wasn't anyone's but herself. Ember knew that too. Her words were a reassurance, a commander's reminder to her soldier that some hierarchies were protective. That *this* hierarchy protected its own.

Ember and Rhiannon shared a long look. Their ability

to silently communicate was born of lifetimes of friendship, and rather than feeling jealousy or resentment, I was glad she had a life so full of love.

"See you soon," Ember whispered.

Rhiannon nodded, her hand slipping into mine as she turned. "Let's go." As we moved in the opposite direction, she murmured, "There's magic in the air, can you feel it?"

I couldn't, not the way I'd been able to on the island, but I trusted her. It was just another way she was extraordinary. "Not really."

Her smile was wan. "It's not as strong here, but I think I can use it to help us."

I wasn't sure what she meant, but when she squeezed my hand, I squeezed back. There were so many mysteries connected to the island that I wanted to understand now that I'd been there. So many questions I wanted to ask.

Suddenly, my feet were moving faster, and my flagging energy had gone up. "Are you doing that?" I asked.

Rhiannon's face was drawn. She was concentrating, but she nodded—she was using a power typically attributed to the Thaumas Dynasty, which made me wonder just what the Maere could actually *do*, given the right source of power. We covered the same ground we'd previously trodden in half the time, as we reached the crossroads in the Ossuary. She was breathing hard, the effort that it had taken to use magic obviously wearing on her.

I pressed a hand to her back, knowing that asking her to conserve her energy would be useless. All I could do was be supportive. She took a few deep breaths, and then stood, the light in her eyes gone dim. "Can you sense anything? I don't think I can draw my sword right now. I used too much energy getting us back here."

The corpse-garbed spirits reappeared as she spoke, and

relief flooded me. I drew out the vox spiritus, directing it at the sentinels. "Can you sense the location of this woman's mother?"

Rhiannon's eyes were wild with wonder. She stepped a little closer to me, rotating as she watched the spirits carefully, our backs touching. One stepped forward, raising a bony arm to point. *That way*, its creaking voice replied in my head. *Your queen is that way.*

And then we were running again, down the tunnel the spirit had pointed towards without another question. I knew Rhiannon would hate to go in without a better plan, but we had no time for that. We had no time for anything. If Blaire's people got the queen and Admiral Myrine to the surface, we might very well lose them.

We raced against that possibility, our energy—and hope—draining by the second. There was sound ahead, the noise of struggle. The sound of someone dying, and then a terrible howl. Rhiannon moved faster than I thought possible, and I knew this time she was unable to spare any of the magic she had left in her for me.

I had to trust that whatever happened, she would be fine on her own 'til I caught up. I pumped my legs harder, working to deserve her. To deserve her admiration and love. To be as strong as she was so she didn't have to be alone anymore. There was a dim light ahead. Rhiannon's phone flashlight, I realized as I approached.

She'd laid it on the ground and was cradling a deathly pale woman in her arms, rocking her slowly, tears streaming down her face. The tunnel was littered with bodies. I feared the face I would see when I stepped closer. Feared that my love was holding her dead mother in her arms.

But no, the woman she held still drew breath, and she looked nothing like Rhiannon. In fact, her face was familiar to me, though I'd met her only once a few months prior. She was Admiral Myrine, the woman who'd posed as Mother for so many years to manipulate the Orphium Maere, and Saints knew who else. The queen's second-in-command. And she was still alive.

Her wiry body was outfitted in modern tactical gear. Lightly padded armor, made from the finest new materials. Strapped to her back were two antique guns, which was confusing—why hadn't she drawn on her captors?

"They got away," Rhiannon cried. "They got to the surface."

"Was she conscious when you found them?" I asked, bending down to unfasten the harness so the Admiral could breathe better.

Rhiannon shook her head. That, at least, explained why the Admiral hadn't drawn on them. There was a ladder right behind her, and green neon light from above shone down in a dull glow.

We had been too late. Rhiannon shook her head, helpless and in distress. "How could they have taken them?" She choked on a sob. "They're *human*."

Myrine coughed in Rhiannon's arms. "Blades of adamantine," she spit out. "And shackles of the same. For her—they just stabbed me."

Under the spot where the harness wrapped around her torso, a wound bloomed, wet and sticky. Rhiannon helped her out of the harness, tearing a strip of fabric from her nightgown to wrap around the wound. The Admiral looked as though she might protest as I picked up her guns. Slender as the woman was, the harness was adjustable enough that it fit me.

The Admiral closed her mouth as I stared back at her, wincing when Rhiannon tightened the dressing. The mineral Myrine named was fictional. A boogey-tale to scare parapsychs, adamantine was said to steal powers from us. But it didn't exist. "That's not—"

"It's possible," Myrine bit out. "Everything is possible, you fool. Or haven't you figured that out yet?"

"Don't speak to him that way," Rhiannon said.

The tenor of Rhiannon's voice was rich, resonant as ever, but there was a chill to it I'd never heard. Rhiannon was always strong, always. Even in what she probably considered her weakest moments, her fallibility was what made her unbreakable. She was always warm, pliable—no, she was flexible. She made room for others.

This tone was closed off. Imperious in a way that expressed a kind of authority I never imagined she wanted. It was the voice of a tyrant. The voice of a *queen*. I looked at the woman I loved and saw the mother who had harmed her spirit, who'd taken away her confidence in herself, and I understood why she ran.

It was effective, though. Myrine bowed her head. "My apologies."

"Are you well enough to walk?" Rhiannon asked, sounding more like herself again, to my relief.

Myrine nodded, standing. In the dim light of the tunnel, I caught sight of her face. She was much as I remembered, a woman with strong features that carried the expectation that others did what she told them to. "I can walk. But I can't use magic. It'll be a while 'til I'm useful to you again."

"You're useful to me now," Rhiannon growled. "I need you to tell me everything you know."

"Rhiannon—" I kept my voice as calm as I could, given the circumstances. "We should take her back to Hemlock House, tend to her wounds. And you should rest."

Rhiannon's eyes turned on me, angry and sorrowful. I

thought she might argue, but her shoulders slumped. "Yes," she agreed. It was the last syllable she was able to utter, I realized. She'd overdone it and was holding on by a thread.

I glanced at Myrine, who looked back at me with suspicion as we moved back through the tunnel, towards Oleander Cottage. Rhiannon didn't want Myrine to know what bad shape she was actually in. Now I understood what Cassandra had meant about Rhiannon's people wanting too much. It was the kind of understanding that didn't come in clearly articulated thoughts, but a marrow-deep instinct.

Rhiannon's mother, Admiral Myrine, the island itself, they expected the Maere to act as gods in their stead. Fifteen women against this entire miserable world, while the island retreated behind the mists.

The Maere were incredible. There was no doubt about that in my mind. But they were still just people, immortal and powerful as they were. The expectations the island had for them weren't just unfair, they were unrealistic.

Rhiannon walked ahead of us, and to someone who didn't know her well, she appeared fine. But I saw the exhaustion she was hiding in every careful move. Did Myrine? How well did she actually know Rhiannon?

The Admiral stumbled. I grabbed her by the elbow. She gritted her teeth, shaking her head. "Thank you, young man. I am not used to being incapacitated."

I nodded, pulling her a bit closer to me so she could rest her weight against me, if needed. "She's been through too much," I said in a low voice. "You and her mother put her through more than a person should ever have to deal with."

The Admiral scoffed. "The girl is one of us. There is no 'too much' for *our* people."

I tightened my grip on her elbow. "You've barely lived in this world. You certainly haven't spent centuries navigating its complexity the way she has. The way I have. You know *nothing* about what you put her through."

Myrine glared at me, her pale eyes cold as steel. It was clear that she thought to argue with me, but I shook my head, stopping in my tracks, keeping the Admiral at my side. "I respect you, Admiral. But don't push me on this. I'll protect her from anyone that tries to hurt her, or make things harder for her. Do you understand?"

Slowly, the Admiral nodded, a glimmer of something in her eyes that I didn't recognize. "You are a warrior, then? Like her."

"Worse," I replied. "I'm her underboss now. The guy who'd rip out the entrails of anyone who so much as hurts her feelings. You feel me?"

The Admiral laughed, a loud and hearty sound that caused Rhiannon to pause, glancing back at us, her brow furrowed. Myrine shook with mirth. "So, a warrior then, as I said. Like her."

Rhiannon's eyes narrowed. "What are the two of you talking about?"

Myrine grinned at her, white teeth flashing in the murky depths of the tunnel. "Your lover's honor," she shot back. "He's got as much as you." She glanced up at me. "Maybe more."

Rhiannon nodded. "You have the right of him, then. Move a little faster. *I know you've got it in you.*"

The Admiral laughed again. "Well, I deserve that."

We drew closer to Rhiannon, who'd slowed for us. She nodded, pursing her lips. "Indeed."

The Admiral winced, clutching her side. The wound she'd taken wasn't seeping blood anymore, but it obviously still hurt. She shook her head, swallowing hard before letting out a breath. "Don't get stabbed with an adamantine blade, children."

"Where did they get it?" Rhiannon asked as we came to the crossroads again. "*How* did they get it? I thought we'd destroyed the last of the deposits in the war."

The Admiral shook her head again. "I don't know, child. The trouble is that they have it."

Rhiannon stared off into the dark tunnel back through the Ossuary. The spirits were quiet now. Perhaps their lament was only for those going in the other direction. "Is there a deposit of it somewhere we missed?"

The Admiral shrugged, leaning against me once more. "Truly, Your Highness, I have no idea. If I'd thought it was possible, I'd have taken more precautions. You need to make peace with the fact that Blaire got the drop on us."

So, Blaire had come to the island himself? "How did he do that?" I asked. "Get to the island, I mean? How did he figure out how to get there?"

The Admiral shrugged. "Your guess is as good as mine, child."

I was about to ask another question, but Rhiannon growled, ducking under one of the Admiral's arms. "You need to move faster so we can figure it out." I glanced at her, wondering just how she thought she was going to do that, but I didn't have to wonder for long. "The Maereling you wanted to take from us is a genius, Myrine. *She'll* figure this all out."

The Admiral coughed. "You'd trust this to a *child?*"

Rhiannon's laugh was dry. "You've always put your trust in the young, Myrine. Don't stop now."

I glanced at her over the Admiral's slumped shoulders, looking at her 'til she looked back at me. I wanted to tell her I loved her, right then and there. But it probably wasn't the moment. Not with Myrine between us. I wondered if she knew. If she could read it in my eyes.

The Admiral coughed, and this time she spit up blood. "I don't think I'm going to make it up those stairs on my own," she said as her eyes rolled back in her head. Rhiannon caught her before she could fall, scooping the Admiral easily into her arms.

"No," I said, holding out my arms. "She's out. You let me do it."

For a moment, I thought she'd resist or argue. But then she sighed, pushing the Admiral's body into my waiting arms. "Thank you, Eryx." She looked up at me, exhausted tears in her eyes. "I love you."

I nearly dropped the Admiral, I was so surprised. Had Rhiannon Brontë just said she loved me?

CHAPTER 28

RHIANNON

THE WORDS JUST SLIPPED OUT. I was so tired. So weak. And when he shouldered the weight of Myrine's form, so much relief coursed through me that I wasn't in complete control anymore. But I didn't want to take them back. They were true.

I loved Eryx Necroline with my whole heart.

We still had a lot to do to get to know one another, to find a way to work together, but I loved him, and I was too tired to pretend I didn't. Saints, I was too tired to even worry that he might not love me in return. The upside to not having overthought this to death was that I hadn't had a chance to consider the possibilities.

There was rarely a time when I hadn't explored all the possible scenarios before acting, but today was a day for it, apparently. I waited, knowing that Eryx needed time to process. I could wait, I decided, nodding. "It's okay," I said. "You don't need to say anything back."

"I need to find a place for the Admiral," he said, his words taking obvious effort. "I can't tell you I love you properly holding onto her."

I did the only thing I could do—laugh so hard that I cried. "Okay," I nodded.

I moved aside to let him go up the stairs ahead of me, crying with every step. Letting out all the hurt and anger I'd kept inside for so long. I had no illusions that one good cry would solve this. It would take time. Years maybe, but I could come back to myself now. I could come home to myself, and trust my instincts, and trust this man who loved me too.

"Am I going to have to put her down?" Eryx asked. We were almost to the top of the stairs. "You're crying a lot and I'm worried."

The simple, clear way he said it left no room for misinterpretation. No room for inserting my own bullshit that could make it mean something it did not. "No," I sobbed. "I'm just so happy."

Eryx snorted softly. "Sounds like it."

"I am," I insisted, as I cried harder through my smile. Too many emotions coursed through me now. The floodgates were open, and they were all free.

Like me. My mother might be captured, but I was finally free. A few days ago, I might have felt guilty thinking that way. I was supposed to love her. But the truth was, I'd never known her. She'd never let me. And though I would do whatever it took to rescue her now, I would do it for my people. I would do it as one of the Maere, not as Otrera's princess, or Silea's daughter.

I wasn't either of those things anymore. I was just Rhiannon Brontë now.

We reached the top of the stairs, and Eryx pushed through the barely closed door. The cottage was different than it had been in the time we'd lived there. Everything was similar to what we'd lived with, but faded. Older. *Dusty*.

The wallpaper that had been so vivid, just hours ago, was peeling, torn off in many places by what looked like clawed hands. Had the people trapped here before us been literally tearing at the walls to get out?

The undisturbed, thick layer of dust over everything made me wonder just exactly where we'd been living. There was no evidence that anyone had been here in years. Eryx shook his head, as obviously perplexed as I was. "I think we should take her to the house. This isn't... sanitary."

I tried not to think about that, but nodded. We made our way through the garden quickly, as it was raining rather hard. Sera and Briony met us at the door.

"Myrine?" Sera asked as she moved aside.

I nodded. "We need somewhere to put her. She's been stabbed with adamantine."

Sera went into healer mode. She'd been to medical school at least four times, as far as I knew, but hadn't practiced in years.

"Bring her this way," she said to Eryx.

Briony stood next to me. "What is she doing here?"

The teenager's body was tense. I took her hand. "She's not here to take you, darling. I promise. No one can take you from us."

Briony looked up at me, her brown eyes so trusting. "Okay. What do we do next?"

The way she simply accepted that none of us would let her be removed from our care warmed me. We had all suffered under the treatment of our human families, before ascension. And so had Briony, but unlike us, who'd had another fifteen years of mental torture before we'd learned who we really were, she already knew why she was different. She already knew, and she had a family who loved her, however unconventional.

I spared a quick glance for Eryx, who shot me a smile as he followed Sera upstairs. We were already doing what we were meant to do, fulfilling our true purpose, I realized. We'd broken the cycle all of our parents had created. We were here, necromancers and the Maere, all living in one house together.

Trusting each other.

Finding love.

I glanced back down at Briony, who still waited for an answer. So many different kinds of love. We were the promise we'd needed as young people. I took a deep breath. "We have to find out where they've taken my mother."

Briony nodded, gesturing for me to follow her. We made our way to her bedroom, where she had an impressive setup at her desk, with multiple screens and two separate computers and a tablet running, while her phone performed some other task I couldn't identify.

"I've already got your mom," Briony said, shaking her head. "They've taken her to the Asylum."

That was bad news, but I nodded. At least we knew where they were going, and it made sense that Blaire would take her there, at least. It was something.

"Good work." I hugged Briony around the shoulders. "I'm so proud of you."

She smiled, shrugging me off. "I know. Don't go all gushy on me like Ember though, 'kay?"

I laughed, nodding. "Okay."

"What else can I figure out?" she asked.

"Have you already found the schematics for the Asylum?" I asked.

Briony nodded slowly. "I'm on it. Should have what we need in a few hours. I'm sorry it'll take so long, but the Authority has that shit locked down."

I sighed. "That figures. Did you ask Eli for help?"

Briony hummed. "Of course. That's how I'm getting what I am. He cleared the way for me, and I—" she stopped. "You don't really want to hear the details, do you?"

I shook my head. "I don't think I'll understand, and I have another job for you, so long as it won't slow all this down."

Briony smiled, pulling another laptop out of a cubby in her desk. "I've got you covered. What do you need?"

"We need to find out where they got adamantine, and I don't have a single thing to go on."

Briony shrugged. "What do they have?"

I frowned a little.

"Like, what kinds of implements? It'll help with the search."

"Oh." I nodded, understanding a little better. "Shackles, for my mother, apparently."

"Good," Briony said with a smile.

"How is that good?" I asked

"Because, if they had an endless supply, the Admiral would have been shackled."

"Ah," I breathed, seeing her logic. I really was exhausted. I should have caught that right away. "You're right. They had at least one blade as well. Though we'll have to ask Myrine for the specifics when Sera brings her around."

Briony waved a hand. "Not an issue. I have what I need to get started." I smiled. "Please go," the teenager said, pushing me away from her desk. "I don't work well with anxious people hanging around."

"Fine, fine," I laughed as she shoved me towards the door.

I looked around her room for a brief moment. We'd

painted it a dark rose color before I'd gone to Oleander Cottage, but now there were posters on the wall of bands I'd never heard of. Collages of photos of all of us together, and some with peers from her sports teams.

Her bed was piled high with stuffed animals, and a jewelry box open on her dresser spilled over with bracelets she'd obviously made herself. "Will you make me one of these?" I asked, realizing how hard the cottage had clamped down on my mind. Suddenly, I missed Briony fiercely, though she sat just feet from me.

The teenager glanced at me over her shoulder, pointing a neon-yellow nail at the box. "Already did, it's the purple sparkly one."

I dug through the pile. All of the bracelets had words on them, spelled out in bubbly gold letters, surrounded by sparkling faceted rondelles. I found the one she meant and smiled. It read, "Murder Queen." I slipped it onto my wrist and turned it, watching the light from Briony's screen catch the facets.

No one had ever given me something so heartfelt before. I bit my bottom lip, trying to keep myself from crying again. Briony glanced up, caught my expression and blew me a kiss before waving me off. My heart was so full it ached as I moved towards the door.

"Give me two hours," she called out to me as I started to close the door. "Two hours and I'll have everything you need to get Queen-Mommy back."

"Please never call her that again. She has a name," I insisted with a groan. "You can call her Silea. That would make her mad."

Briony flashed me a grin. "With pleasure. Grandma LeeLee and I can have a real heart to heart about what I think about her parenting skills when you get her back."

My mother would hate that. I just hoped we could get

her back in time for me to see her face when Briony mouthed off to her.

I found Eryx waiting in my bedroom, his shoes off, the harness from the Admiral's guns draped over the couch at the end of my bed, and he was sprawled on top of the covers. I kicked off my own shoes and climbed in next to him, feeling old as the sea. "We're alone now," I said as he stretched his arm out to create space for me next to him. I crawled slowly into the nook of his arm, resting my weary head on his shoulder.

"We are," he breathed. "Let's take a nap, shall we?"

I glanced up at him. His eyes were closed but he was smiling. I slapped his massive chest.

"Careful, careful," he said, catching my hand in his, and pressing a kiss to it. "Try to remember that I'm just a delicate man, immortal warrior woman."

I snorted as he turned over, pushing me into the position of the little spoon. He pulled me into him, fitting me against him so that we fit together like puzzle pieces. It felt delicious to be here, in bed with him, but we had an unfinished conversation ahead of us. He'd promised.

His breathing was deep and even. "Eryx," I whispered. "Don't you have something you want to tell me?"

He hummed behind me, pulling me even closer, one hand slipping under my nightgown to caress my skin. "What do you mean?" he asked, so obviously teasing me. His mouth came close to my ear as his fingers grazed the undersides of my breasts. "Did you want me to tell you I love you?"

"Only if you want to," I shot back.

His hand drifted lower, gliding over my waist and hip. "I want to," he breathed. "I want everything with you."

My breath caught as heat built everywhere his fingers touched. My mother had been taken, but this was all I cared about. I wondered for the briefest of moments if that made me a bad person. I sat up, suddenly realizing there was a potential battle happening that we were missing.

"Rhiannon," he whispered, coaxing me back down to him. "It's covered. I spoke to Ares. And Ember. They know everything we do. You're to rest until it's time to get your mother. Everyone needs you to recharge for that part."

"Oh." I glanced back at him. "Thank you."

He nodded, his green eyes crinkling with his smile. "Now, because I know you won't be able to sleep. What should we do to get you recharged?"

I glared at him for a moment, until I spotted the hard length of his erection pushing against the fabric of his sweatpants. My mouth watered. Everything else melted away. There was just me, and him, and this. In a few hours, we'd do whatever we had to, but for now, this was all that mattered.

The thought crossed my mind that with adamantine weapons, the humans still couldn't kill us. Only the thrysos could do that. But the adamantine could subdue us. Imprison us. If they had more, they could do real damage with it.

"Stop thinking," Eryx said, his fingers tracing the lines of my face. "Be here with me now."

The heat building in me flared, and I twisted around, climbing on top of him. I'd almost forgotten that I'd gone into the Ossuary in just my nightgown. Now I was acutely aware of the fact that there was very little between me and Eryx. "Remember the night at the Paradiso?" I asked.

He smiled up at me, his hands running up my thighs, under the draping fabric of my nightgown. "How could I forget?"

His hands moved further up my thighs, one thumb grazing the spot I needed him most. I tilted my hips forward, moving quickly enough that his thumb dipped into me, sliding easily with the wetness gathered between my legs. Beneath me, his hips jerked as his thumb sank deeper into me, his hard cock pressing into his hand.

"Fuck, you're wet," he groaned.

"All for you," I practically purred, moving my hips to ride his thumb. "But do you remember telling me you wanted me to make a mess of your pants?"

"Yes," he hissed.

"Well, you forgot all about that, and let me leave the job undone."

"Do it now," he insisted. "Fuck me through my pants, Brontë."

I snarled, practically feral for him now, pulling my nightgown off so he could see me move on him.

"Yes," he growled, moving his hand so he could see me push against his erection. "Take what you need."

He gripped my hips, pushing and pulling me over his cock, a wet spot forming on the fabric of his pants. "Do you like that?" I breathed. "Does that make you hard?"

He pushed harder into me. "You know it does," he growled. "Fuck, I thought I could do this. But I need to taste you."

"No," I insisted. "You need to fuck me."

In a flash, I raised my hips, and pushed his pants down around his hips, sliding my wet center onto his hard, waiting cock. I pushed his shoulders back when he tried to raise up to turn me over. "Do as I say, Necroline. Tell me just how much you love it." I fell forward, angling myself so the head of his thick cock was fitted against my entrance. And then I pushed down on him. "Tell me just how much you love *me*."

He let out a noise that sounded like losing control. I raised my hips and then slid back down slowly, letting him watch as he filled me. Then I leaned back, touching myself as I moved on him, giving him a full view of my body.

"Tell me, Eryx. Tell me."

His eyes dragged up from where our bodies met to my eyes. And then he thrust hard against my bucking hips, his thumb on my clit. "I love you more than anyone in this life," he growled as he pushed deeper inside me, every muscle in my body pulled taut as I took him.

"I love you more than anything I've ever loved. Nothing you could ever do or be could scare me away. If you choose me, you're stuck with me."

I gasped. His words were everything I needed to hear.

"Do you understand me?" he asked. "Do you understand that if you love me back that I will never leave you, never betray you?"

"Yes," I gasped. "Yes, I understand."

"You will always be free with me, Rhiannon," he said, just before he brought his lips to brush mine. Against my mouth, he made his vows. "I will never cage you, never stop you from doing exactly what you need to, and I will always be waiting when you come back home."

CHAPTER 29

ERYX

RHIANNON'S EXPRESSION went so soft, I thought she might cry. She leaned forward, placing both her hands on my face as she moved slower and slower. "Home?"

I nodded. "I thought we did all right at the cottage. When this is all over, if you want to, we could go back together."

She threw her body against mine, sobbing. But she was nodding, clenching around me with such intensity that I nearly came. She clung to me, kissing me through her tears. Lust and love mingled in the sweetest way.

Her back arched as she raised up to take me at a better angle. I wiped the tears from her beautiful face, but more streamed down in their place. It was as though every emotion she'd pent up inside her was spilling out now. Her mouth fell open with little gasps of pleasure.

"I want that," she whimpered. "I want this, every night. Every morning. Forever."

Something in my chest contracted at the word forever. I shut my eyes against the onslaught of emotions. It triggered a fear in me I didn't even know I could have. Not after Frannie. Not after so many years of denying myself all true intimacy. I was afraid of losing her. Afraid to be alone again.

"Look at me, baby," she murmured. "Look at me."

I did as she asked and saw the tears in her eyes. "No one can use me against you. Do you understand? They can take me, torture me, rip me to shreds, and I can take it." Sobs choked me as I wrapped my arms around her. It was everything I needed to hear. "There isn't anything anyone could ever do to me to make me leave you. You understand?"

If someone had told me six months ago that a woman would say that to me. That *this* woman would say that—I might have been angry. I would have railed against anything that implied that Frannie should have been sturdier. But that's not what Rhi was saying. She was saying she'd never leave me. That I could grieve what happened to Frannie with the knowledge that not only could it not happen to her, but that if someone tried, they couldn't turn her away from me.

Nothing and no one could take her. It was the closest thing to reassurance that I was ever going to get. I was safe with her. For the first time in my very, very long life, I was safe to love someone. "I will never leave you," I promised. "I will always be there for whatever you need. Always."

She smiled and it was the gentlest expression I'd ever seen. And then she kissed me, so thoroughly and so deeply that the way we moved shifted into something I'd never done before. I had always thought of intercourse as fucking. But this wasn't that. It wasn't just bodies pleasing one another.

This was love, the kind of love that needed words, but that also needed these oaths we made right here and now, with our hearts, our minds, and our bodies. Every bit of her tightened around me as I moved in her, her face shifting into a state of bliss I hoped to recreate every day for the rest of our existence.

As she came apart around me, my determination solidified. Rhiannon and I were forever, and I would accept nothing less. That thought sent me hurtling over the edge, pouring every bit of my love and commitment into her.

When our bodies slowed, she lay her head down on my chest and I stroked her hair. "Does eating food from the underworld bind you to it?" she asked, her voice heavy with sleep.

I smiled. "No, those really are just stories. The food was magic, probably from the island."

She sighed, her eyelids fluttering a bit as she settled in to sleep. "That's too bad, it might have been nice to be stuck in the underworld with you forever."

"You're stuck with me forever either way," I promised her, closing my eyes as well.

A knock at the door woke us. I jumped up to answer, wrapping the flat sheet around my waist as Rhiannon found a robe. When I opened the door Lara stood outside, dressed in close-fitting black tactical gear.

Her smile was grim. "Hey," she said, nodding to Rhiannon, who eyed what Lara was wearing and headed straight for her closet.

"Can I come in?" Lara asked. I nodded, moving aside for her.

My heart sank as I watched Lara sink into a chair, dead-eyed. She wouldn't make eye contact with me. I leaned against the bed, my heart rate increasing steadily by the second. "What is it?" I asked. "Has something gone wrong?"

Lara shook her head, sighing as Rhiannon emerged in her own version of gear. "No," she said, sharing a look with Rhiannon. "But you won't like what I have to say."

Rhiannon held up a hand, before coming to kneel in front of me. She took my hands in hers. "Lara's going to tell you that Ember's decided we're going into the Asylum alone."

"No," I said, shaking her hands off me. "I'm coming with you."

Rhi and Lara exchanged another look. "Give us a minute, okay?"

Lara nodded. "I'll be waiting downstairs. Max is flying in, and we have to wait for her to get here. Take your time." She placed a hand on my shoulder. "Try to understand, Eryx. This isn't an insult."

When the door shut, Rhi smiled sadly. "She's right. It's not an insult. It's strategy. We can't die."

It felt as though every piece of me had shattered apart. I'd only just told her I loved her, only just convinced her that I could be as good for her as she was for me. Losing her now would be too much.

"I know that," I insisted. "But it's not like Ares and I are a liability. Hell, even Av is so scary that—"

"Baby," she breathed. "It's not about any of that. It's about the fact that some of us might not make it out of there—we can't die, but they can capture us, and with that adamantine..."

She was right. I knew she was right, but it still felt wrong.

Rhiannon saw me relenting and continued, "If we have any chance of getting my mother and all of us making it out, we cannot be worrying about one of you being left behind." She stood, stroking my cheek with her silky soft fingers, the worn calluses on her palm a reminder that while she was soft, she was also experienced at all of this. Lethal in her own right. "This is what we were made for, Eryx. This is why we're here."

Slowly, the pieces of me fit back together. All the times I'd thought of her as a goddess, only to find out that she was a direct descendent of one. I knew who the woman I loved was. And I trusted her to come home.

She stood and wrapped her arms around me. It killed me that she could smell so good in this moment. I mustered a smile for her, trying to use a light tone. "There's probably shit for me to do, anyway."

Rhiannon nodded, pressing the sweetest kiss to my lips. As she kissed me, she reached for my phone, and unlocked it as she pulled away. I sighed as she turned it towards me, revealing ten missed messages from Ares.

"Looks like there's plenty that needs doing," she murmured. "What's he say?"

I took the phone from her with one hand, letting my other arm snake around her. Lara said we had a minute and I was going to take every second of the time I had with her. I scanned through my brother's messages, shaking my head. I tried to smile. "Looks like Ares, Av, and I are going to finish closing the path in the Ossuary. Apparently, Cassandra's illusion has crumbled now that she's gone, but the door to the underworld is still cracked open."

Rhi nodded. "The things Calypso warned us about could still happen, even though that was never the point of all this."

She was right, and Ares and I were uniquely positioned to close the door to the underworld, now that we knew what we were up against. Especially with Av's help, we might be the only ones in the city who could fix this.

And if it had been Magnus' goal in life to open a door between the worst parts of the netherrealm and that of the living, surely in death, with his turn as a malefic spirit, those ideas had only intensified.

Necromancers had theories about the underworld and how it worked, and occasionally we could even visit parts of it, as Rhiannon and I had in Oleander Cottage. But only the first levels, the surface levels where spirits who existed in the liminal space between the living and the dead could travel to. The places beyond were unknown to us—though from what little we knew, there were places of torment for the condemned and places of peace for those at rest.

If Magnus opened the doors to the parts of the netherrealm where the condemned resided, there might be no way to close the door. Spirits in torment were some of the most powerful, as they fed on the misery of the living. And in this day and age, misery was in no short supply.

That could not happen. And Rhiannon was more susceptible to the machinations of the dead than I would prefer. She might not be able to die, but there were worse things than death. I didn't even want to imagine what a malefic horde of the condemned might do to her.

"Okay," I agreed, seeing the wisdom of splitting up more acutely now. "Let's do this."

Rhiannon raised up on her tiptoes as I slid off the bed, our bodies fusing together as she kissed me long and hard. "So, wanna meet my mom tonight?" she asked as she pulled away, keeping hold of my hand as long as she could as she walked towards the door. I wanted to follow her downstairs, but I could tell from the pleading look in her eyes that she needed me to stay put.

"Sounds perfect," I replied, no snap in my reply. Hollow banter was the best I could manage. "She a Pizza Queen kind of girl?"

Her fingertips and mine pressed together. "No, baby," she whispered. "But you get extra mushrooms on mine, okay?"

I closed my eyes. I couldn't watch her go.

"Don't say it," she whispered from the door as I started to call after her. "Tell me again when I get back. Tell me every day when this is all over."

I opened my eyes. "Extra mushrooms. I promise."

"Good boy," she murmured as she shut the door between us. I heard her deep breath, her forehead pressing against the door. And then she was gone. Off to do her part, and me to do mine.

My eye caught on the Admiral's guns. I drew one, my breath catching. *How was this possible?* I recognized the carvings on them. These didn't belong to the Maere. Why had the Admiral had them? How had she gotten hold of them?

I shook with anger. The woman had so much fucking audacity. To steal the Orphium Maere's swords, to steal from the Necroline Dynasty. When this was over, I was going to find a way to make her pay for it all.

As I took a moment to steady myself, the priority notification on the group chat between Av, Eryx, and I blared— a single siren in the quiet house. It was only supposed to do that in an emergency. I lunged for my phone, unlocking it as fast as I could. There was a message from Ares. *Underworld breach on 8th Ave. The condemned are escaping.*

Ares didn't need to say where the breach had occurred. I already knew. Magnus had done this—the breach was right in front of Oleander Cottage. As Ares and Av went wild discussing plans, I dropped the sheet, grabbed the stolen guns, and headed straight for my room. We had a job to do, and not much time to do it.

CHAPTER 30

RHIANNON

RAIN PELTED the SUV that barreled down narrow side streets and back alleys towards the helipad. The spring monsoons had swept in overnight, pummeling the city with a near-constant downpour. At the very least, it provided a bit of natural cover for us.

Some part of me listened as Ember briefed Lara, Calypso and myself, with Max on speaker phone. We were meeting her at the helipad, since Sera was still a few months out from being cleared to fight. I understood the plan well enough. Get in. Get my mother. Get out. There were complications galore, security that was going to be a pain in the ass, but we weren't finessing this.

Ember's plan was going to be an absolute shitshow, a carnival of chaos that only she could have come up with. I understood *exactly* why the Necrolines and Sera weren't coming with us. We were going to take heavy fire doing things this way, and we needed to move with confidence.

We needed to move like the immortal warriors we were, not what the Authority had forced us to become to protect our people. Orphium needed a swift, brutal reminder that while parapsych numbers dwindled, we were still powerful. And our people still had *us*.

The howling wind shifted directions as Calypso pulled into the helipad parking lot. Max was already here, already in the helicopter. She threw open the door, shouting over the wind, "We've got a window, let's go."

Calypso got out immediately, giving the rest of us a second. I sensed that she was still getting used to our dynamic, and wanted to respect anything private we needed to say to one another.

As the door closed, dulling the sound of the wind, Ember grabbed my hand. "I love you."

All I could do was nod. The reality that humans had gone to Otrera and known their way around well enough to steal my mother and Myrine was mind-boggling. If I thought about it for more than a few seconds, I froze with anxiety. There were so many possibilities about what this all meant. It was enough to scramble my mind.

Ember squeezed hard, bringing me back to the present moment. "I need your worst today, babygirl. You can give me that, can't you?"

I fought back tears. I hadn't let myself think about what it might mean for humans to have my mother until just now. The things they might be doing to her. I had a whole dossier on Archibald Blaire that I hadn't dared think about. The things the old man had done to get what he wanted went miles beyond heinous, but now what I knew all rushed back in.

"Brontë," Ember hissed. "Pull your shit together."

Lara pushed the door open against the wind, and jumped out of the SUV, apparently not caring that Ember and I were having a pep talk. She turned back smiling, that wicked gleam in her eyes. "Rhi's got this, Ember. Remember Abritus?"

Ember grinned, and there was none of the soft woman I'd seen helping Briony with homework at Hemlock House left in her. She was all ancient warrior, battle worn and wiser for it. "I sure do. You made them pay for what they did to that sweet little cognoscente."

The human contingent had martyred the Seer they'd stolen and forced to serve them. She'd been a friend of Sera's, and when Sera was devastated, we all felt it, especially back in those early brutal days of the Authority's grip on us. I'd killed them all in a haze of fury, not caring a whit for the consequences.

But now there was more to worry about. The world was more complex. Our ties to the parapsychs of Orphium deepened with every passing day. There were people that the Authority, that Blaire and people like him, could use against us.

It had to end somewhere.

The world might be different now, but this was a tale older than even us. Human men taking parapsych women, forcing them into service, only to use them up and murder them. It was always the same story. It didn't matter how powerful the victim was, these men found yet more ways to stoop to new lows.

A memory of the island, from when I was just a little girl, sprang to the forefront of my mind. I had been playing music by the lake with Lara, strumming a lyre and singing bawdy songs to make her laugh, when a fox had tried to nab one of the spring cygnets from under their watchful mother's eyes.

It had been over in seconds, the swan clobbering the fox to death in four elegant beats of her wings. Not a single feather on her family's heads were harmed. She had protected them with a ferocity that had inspired something in me. I'd never seen anyone behave that way before.

Otrerans weren't precious with their children. We were raised to be valuable to society, not the other way around. After the mists closed the island off, some of that changed, but neither I, nor any of the Maere, benefited from that change in views.

Our childhoods were brutal. It wasn't until I met Lara and Ember that I found family, that I found home—and now we'd created a complex web of love, a place for us to be our true selves. To be safe with one another. And if Blaire accomplished what he meant to with my mother, they would come for us. It seemed a foregone conclusion that he would use her up, kill her, and start a war with the Maere.

I had seen too much war already. The Battle of Abritus had been our last victory as parapsychs, and it hadn't mattered one bit. The humans still won. The Authority still prevailed. I glanced at my wrist, Briony's bracelet shimmering from just under the sleeve of my tactical jacket.

Thinking of her having to endure what we had as children—both times—was too much. The Authority needed to know that the Maere still had fight left in them. An ancient anger mounted in me, wrapping its way around my heart—a swan hissing at those who threatened her family.

Whatever they were doing to my mother, this is where Archibald Blaire's last chapter ended. "Let's go."

Ember and Lara nodded, and the three of us jogged across the helipad to join Calypso and Max, fighting the downpour. We were soaked by the time Max closed the helicopter doors behind us.

Kara Asterion, the Aradios Maere's version of Ember Verona, turned as the door closed, her dark brown eyes glittering with the same feral energy that snapped around the rest of us. She pushed back her ponytail of microbraids as she nodded to me in greeting.

I nodded back. "Thanks for this."

Kara glanced back at me. "Not a problem. Palladiere's dealing with their own issues, but my team is disabling as much of their communications network as possible right now."

I only had half a second to wonder what was going so wrong in Palladiere that their Maere couldn't come to help their queen before Ember spoke. "Did you bring the cuffs?"

Kara grinned. "Sure did. Took 'em straight from the armory."

My heart nearly stopped as their words sunk in. "You *didn't.*"

Max laughed, unzipping a duffel bag at our feet. "We sure as shit did."

Finely wrought metal arm cuffs sat inside, shimmering with unearthly power. There were just five sets. All the osmium left in the world. No one wearing it could be harmed by adamantine. The island had determined that they'd say when we were allowed to use it. Since the general belief had been that the adamantine problem had been dealt with, the island had decided we couldn't have it.

Each of us took a set, clamping them around our wrists. As we did, they changed size to fit us perfectly. The metal came from a meteor, and when the humans had found we could use it to protect ourselves against adamantine, they'd done everything they could to destroy what little of it there was.

This was all that was left. At the bottom of the bag was my mother's osmium torc. She hadn't worn it since the days when she led us into battle to protect our people. I couldn't help thinking that if she'd been wearing it they couldn't have taken her. I handed it to Ember.

She shook her head. "You wear it until we get to her. In theory, it should counteract the shackles."

Kara nodded. "It will. We tested it."

I leaned forward in my seat as the helicopter took a sweeping turn towards the center of the city. We were heading straight for the Asylum now. "How?"

She glanced back at me, her brown cheeks flushing a bit. "We confiscated a set a year ago." Her eyes met Ember's. "I'm sorry. I should have told you."

All the softness Ember's face had taken on over the past few months disappeared. "When this is over, shit has to change between us."

Kara swallowed, the same hardness in her own eyes. "I know. We've made mistakes. We'll fix them."

Ember clapped a hand on the other leader's shoulder. "We will, sister."

Watching them, I was glad they were in charge. This isn't what I'd ever wanted, and they were perfect for their jobs. Kara's hand gripped Ember's in return. We knew what we were up against, and it wasn't each other. Too many years had gone by of us not trusting one another. Of the Three Cities parapsychs keeping secrets from one another so there were fewer chances for the Authority to gain access to knowledge we didn't want them to have.

Enough was enough. This too had to end now. We had to be together, or we'd never succeed. The Chiorics last fall with their god-killing thrysos. Blaire kidnapping my mother. It was obvious. The Authority was done tolerating our existence. They were planning to wipe us all out, once and for all.

Ember sat back, her face still set in grim lines as she looked out the window. "We're here," she said. "Time to fly."

Below us, Asylum guards broke through the barrier

someone had created on the roof. As they streamed out, Max threw the door to the helicopter open and simply jumped out. Calypso and Lara followed her.

"Kill them all," Kara shouted as Ember and I leapt into freefall.

CHAPTER 31

ERYX

I CREPT around the perimeter of Oleander Cottage in the pouring rain, keeping out of sight as much as I could. In the distance, the sound of shouting sent me sliding into the shadows. Right now, I had the advantage of surprise to help Ares and our people. Monsoon season in Orphium was a bitch, but at least it provided good cover.

The harness I'd taken from Myrine fit a little too snugly around my chest, but the guns belonged with a necromancer. I readjusted as well as I could, giving myself a bit more breathing room. I'd known, of course, that Myrine liked to steal things. After all, she'd stolen the Maere's swords.

But how she'd gotten a hold of a pair of spirit pistols, I didn't know. The Authority had confiscated them all two hundred years ago. But there was a time when nearly all Roman's people had them. If I was correct, these were my father's.

I was fortunate they'd come properly loaded with bullets that would send even the most malefic of spirits into oblivion. The guns wouldn't destroy them the way Ares could, but they would send them to the depths of the netherrealm.

I didn't feel the slightest bit bad about having taken them from Myrine. She was fast asleep at Hemlock House, knocked out by some fell draught that Serafine had brewed up for her. The guns belonged to me or Ares, regardless of whether the Admiral was awake or asleep, and I would likely need them before the day was done. There was too much going on now for me to indulge in the multitudes of questions I had about how Myrine came to have Roman's spirit pistols. When the time came, she was going to answer to me.

The group chat had gone eerily quiet just after Rhiannon left, and I'd used the geo-tracking app Ares had installed on both my and Avaline's phones to find them. They were, as I'd suspected, in the street in front of the cottage—or at least their phones were. Neither of them had answered me, so I stopped messaging.

As I moved towards the front gate, I *felt* the reason they'd gone silent, rather than seeing or hearing it. Even through the torrential downpour, the air was taut with the electric deadlock between Ares and Magnus Necroline's malefic spirit.

I hated to be right, but here we were. Magnus was wreaking his revenge on Ares for killing him, as well as fulfilling his deepest wish in life: to feed off the energy of the dead's release from the underworld. Only now, if he got his way, it would make his spirit a monster.

As I reached the gate, I found my brother with his arms flexed tight, wrapped up in Magnus' toxic aura. Ares wore an expression of unmistakable determination, one I'd seen my entire life. He'd given up so much to protect others, and now his efforts were a losing prospect. The street in front of the cottage had caved in, leaving a yawning hole that glowed with a sickly green light.

Despair nearly immobilized me as I watched spirits clawing their way out of the hole, and they weren't peaceful souls. Magnus had breached the barriers between the living and the malefic dead, the condemned. All of their attention was locked onto Magnus, and the struggle between him and Ares.

My mind struggled to process the chaos, to determine where to insert myself best. I was tempted to rush in, but reminded myself of one of our father's most salient lessons about battle, slow is smooth, smooth is fast. So I took a deep breath and reassessed.

The spirits emerging now came by the hundreds. Still breathing, slow and even, I moved to get a better view of the breach. What had to be thousands of malefic spirits teemed in the bottomless pit that yawned open on Eighth Ave. My stomach turned at the magnitude of our problem.

No emergency vehicles rushed towards us. If the Authority had any clue what was going on, they had no immediate solution. This was why the Consulate should have made better moves—done more negotiating than capitulating. The entire city was in danger now—and if we couldn't contain the breach, it wouldn't just be Orphium. The breach would swallow us all whole. All because the Authority believed we were an abomination of humanity.

Movement across the street caught my eye. Avaline and the new members of the Phoenix team, the Necroline Dynasty's special operations unit, channeled peaceful spirits, creating a barrier around the breach between realms, but it was no use. The malefics were pushing back, overpowering them.

And then the screaming began. I fell to my knees, uselessly covering my ears against the eldritch noise. The sound wasn't simply aural, it was subaural, coming from the underworld itself, and as a clairsentient, it was nearly overwhelming. Hot liquid squeezed out of my eyes and nose. I touched it, and my fingers came away bloody.

Across the street, Av and the Phoenixes strained against the subaural sound, but none were affected the way I was. I was fucking useless. I couldn't help Rhiannon, and now I couldn't help my brother or Avaline either. My clairsentience was a hindrance, rather than a help right now.

My mouth opened in an impotent scream, but no sound came out. And then the pain in my ears, my head, receded a little. It felt as though cool waters soothed over the burning pain of the malefics.

Son. A familiar voice spoke in my head. *I am with you. Will you let me help?*

Roman. *Dad?*

Yes. Let me help you help Ares.

The cooling sensation seeped through me as I submitted to Roman's spirit, letting him block out the screams of the dead. He had not possessed me—not fully, as I could still move of my own accord, and think clearly. But something was different. My hands sparked with the same power Ares wielded.

The power to touch spiritual aura. To control spirits.

Roman's power.

I have searched for Magnus since my death, but he's never dared return to Orphium until now, my father said from within me. *This is the only way to atone for the mistakes I've made. You must use all of the power I have left and close the breach so that Ares can destroy him.*

I took a sharp breath inward, shocked by his words. Did he mean what I thought he did? *If I do that, you could cease to exist.*

We didn't know what happened to spirits whose energy

was completely extinguished, but the prevalent, and most sense-making theory, was that there was nothing left of them to return to the underworld.

Inside my head, Roman sounded peaceful. Calm. *Perhaps that is what I deserve.* Before I could argue that no one deserved that, he continued. *Eryx, my brother has always been out of control, and in life I failed to do what was needed. Let my last act be one you can be proud of.*

His reasoning was hard to argue against. If these were his last wishes, necromancer tradition said it was my duty to honor them. "You are sure?"

I am, my father replied.

"This is honorable," I murmured.

Roman didn't respond, but the warmth I felt in return told me all I needed to know. He was doing this for me, and for Ares, and the mess he'd left my brother when Magnus killed him.

Can you get around the back of the breach? Roman asked as I shifted positions to get a better look at our situation. *If you can, then we can hold Magnus while Ares banishes him.*

"Yes," I agreed, grateful for his centuries of battle experience. "I'll get there; you tell him what we're planning."

The feeling of being occupied dissipated immediately. Roman had gone. I moved quickly, thankful yet again for the rain as the wind changed direction as I ducked behind a parked car in the street.

All of the neon signs in the area, set on sensors to turn on when it got dark enough, buzzed to life as the storm worsened. In my sensitive state of heightened clairsentience, I heard each and every one. As I skirted the breach, trying to reach a place where I could get a good visual on the malefic without being seen, I saw that he'd given the last of his sentience over to keeping the breach open. He no longer emitted the kind of energy that suggested nuanced reasoning or discernment.

He was nothing more than pure hatred now, and he'd directed all that energy at my brother. Ares' expression of concentration flickered for a moment—probably as Roman told him what we planned. I found a spot behind a rusting olive-green van to crouch down.

Avaline stood at just the right angle to see me. She pushed a hand through her sopping wet hair to keep it out of her mouth, nodding once. Her guides were keeping her abreast of our movements. Her hand went to her walkie and the new Phoenix team tightened their formation around the breach.

Ares was plotting then, and I saw the lines of his logic as his plan moved into motion. Av and the Phoenixes would hold back the dead, while Ares and I made one last attempt to destroy Magnus.

CHAPTER 32

RHIANNON

Rain blew sideways in sheets as we dropped through the sky. My feet hit the roof with a heavy thud that reverberated through my bones. I drew my sword as I recoiled from the impact. The Asylum guards hadn't had a chance to prepare, so they weren't wearing armor.

This was going to be just like the swan and the fox. They stood no chance against us. They were humans playing war with the descendants of gods. If they had armies, that would be different. But these were just men. Just a few fragile, mortal men, with egos as big as the sun. A sinister smile spread over my face as I moved into formation with my sistren.

The guards tensed. I'm sure when the helicopter dropped out of the cloud cover, they were perplexed, but they could not have expected *us*. The trouble with binding the Maere to the Consulate had always been that our parapsych overlords felt a little too free to make deals that tied our hands. The Authority and all its nasty institutions hadn't felt the bite of our swords for centuries. Now, the humans stepped back as Ember let out a low laugh.

"Do you want to reconsider your choice of jobs?" Max called out with a dry chuckle.

"There's still time to run," Calypso added. Even with her auburn hair plastered to her head by the rain, somehow her makeup was perfectly intact.

"I need the name of your setting spray," I said casually as the first of the guards ran forward.

She cut them down with a happy little roll of her neck. "Breedlove's Facial Fix."

"Damn," Lara said with a look of admiration. "You split him in half."

A few of the guards did turn back as the rest of us moved. The slaughter was a macabre ballet, and the guards hadn't been to rehearsal. Bullets traveled down erratic paths, missing their mark every time. Fear made them weak, and they were drowning in it.

Humans had forgotten who we were, but we were here to remind them.

My sword glowed as I fed it blood, the humans' life-force flowing into me, giving me strength. It had been too long since I had this feeling. Nearly drunk with power, I moved faster, batting bullets out of the air with my sword as I butchered my way to the stairs.

When the swords had been forged, many on the island had called them evil things. And perhaps they were. The magic that fused them to our souls made us immortal, and it connected our three cohorts in unimaginable ways. When we fought together, rather than alone, the more we killed the more invincible we became. It was ugly business, and I'd never been more grateful for it than I was now.

Guards kept coming as Max kicked the door to the stairs open, let out a wild cry, and dove into the fray with an acrobatic flair I hadn't seen in years. The high of fighting together, *really* fighting, without holding back to appease the Consulate, was getting to us all.

Lara sliced through the first guards up the stairs, pushing them towards Calypso who shoved them towards the remaining guards who made to follow us. The blood of their comrades splattered over their faces, and several wailed in horror.

Lara grinned at us, stepping up onto the steel stair rail. "See ya at the bottom." As she disappeared, Calypso, Ember, and I readjusted, fighting our way down the stairs. We were silent as the new wave of humans coming up the stairs found themselves trapped between us and Lara.

Ember smirked. "You've got a choice, babes. Take your chances with a jump, or let me kill you."

They opened fire on us, but humans in this day and age had no idea how our power worked. They had no idea that our swords had been crafted to siphon lifeforce off each drop of human blood they ate, a sacrifice that created a feedback loop of power between us and the island's magic.

This was a secret we'd kept so well, many in Consulate leadership had likely forgotten it. The night we'd gotten our swords back, we'd been fractured. Calypso hadn't arrived yet. But now we were a true cohort again, and the swords' power reactivated.

The reason the Maere were feared in the beginning was because human blood, killing humans, made us nearly as strong as our gods. And because we could not die, we were that much more divine. Humans were lucky we'd never wanted revenge. All we'd ever wanted was to be left in peace. For our people to be left in peace.

All these fools had to do was be happy they'd won. All they had to do was leave us alone and turn their vile machinations on one another. But instead they'd massacred their way through innocent people, and when that hadn't been enough for them, they had ostracized us. Made our people poor. Forced us into the shadows. Humiliated us, villainized us, until we were criminals. They'd taken almost everything from us, and now they wanted the scraps of what we had left.

The words, *this has to end*, repeated in my mind, a low drumbeat of terror, as I cut through the last of the guards. When we got to the bottom of the stairs, no one slowed down. Ember and I stepped over the bodies at the bottom of the stairs and headed straight for the elevators.

I looked back. Blood seeped out of our victims, but I felt none of the old remorse. There wasn't a single urge to vomit left in me. Calypso pressed the "down" button on the elevator.

A soft ding played as it rose towards us. *All they had to do was leave us alone.* Ding. I took a shuddering breath, steadying myself for whatever came next. Ding. *This has to end.* Ding.

"They're keeping her in the basement," Lara said as the elevator crept towards our floor, breaking the thrum of the only two thoughts I could manage in my head. Her jaw twitched. "That's where they do the worst shit."

Instantly, guilt washed over me. I hadn't even thought of what it would be like for her to come back here. She'd spent twenty years in this place, biding her time to do what we now knew was the island's dirty work. Whatever she'd endured here, it had to have left its scars on her heart, if not her body.

I reached for her hand, but she sidestepped me, flinching a little. "You okay?"

Lara smiled, but the expression didn't make its way past her lips as her fists clenched tight. "Sure. This is fun."

Calypso and Max both rolled their eyes as the elevator

doors opened with a cheerful chime. There was nothing to do but play along with Lara. If we broke open the feelings box now, we were all fucked.

We'd done this together long enough to know that.

"To the basement, then," Ember said as the five of us, covered in blood, crowded into the tiny space.

CHAPTER 33

ERYX

FROM MY POSITION behind the van, I took Roman back in, let his power flood me. We didn't have time for platitudes or goodbyes. If I was right, we had seconds, maybe minutes before the condemned horde crawling out of the netherworld overpowered the Phoenixes.

What I wouldn't give for Tanith to show up right about now and save us. As usual, the Saints had no time for me, but Roman was ready. I could feel it. *Let's do this*, he said from within me. *Lock onto Magnus, and Ares will do the rest.*

I took a deep breath, allowing Roman's power to mingle with mine, feeling it infuse me as I let him take the wheel. I was still here, but it was better to let Roman direct his own power, using my auric energy—my spirit as a living, breathing being—to channel it.

He pushed my aura outward, and I felt a surge of power go through me like a wave as rain beat into my body. I closed my eyes against the extra stimuli, feeling only Roman's power, searching for Magnus' aura. When he found it, my aura locked onto Magnus. There was a brief moment of struggle while Ares adjusted to my aid, recalibrating his efforts to allow me to hold, while he prepared to strike.

The dead's screams increased, and from within the pit, a new noise emerged, a bone shaking growl. With the noise a putrid stench curled out of the pit. My eyes flew open.

The smell and the noise could only mean one thing—one of the fiends had come loose. But that was impossible. As I'd told Rhiannon, they were legends. Scary stories to scare necromancer babes.

Ares had been distracted by it too, and Magnus had the upper hand again. I moved quickly, letting Roman stay focused on helping my brother. For now, it seemed we could split our focus well enough.

The van I hid behind had a ladder on the back that allowed access to the roof. I climbed it for a better view. The breach was widening, and now there were only a few feet between me and one ragged edge of the opening to the pit.

Atop the van, I could see all the way down. The view was dizzying. The dead climbed over one another in various states of monstrousness and decay, lit by the neon glow in the rain, and the unearthly light of the nether-realm. Deep in the vast hole, a figure moved, tossing the dead aside as it climbed over them.

Legend came to life before my eyes, dripping in gore, mouths in haphazard locations all over its thorax, full of razor-sharp teeth. It had eight spindly legs, giving the impression of the world's most heinous spider.

My heart slowed as I watched the teeth rotate in its mouths. As far away as it was, the creature was still huge. Mind-bogglingly huge. If that thing got out, we were going to have bigger problems than Magnus.

I raised my face to the rain and shook my head. "If a single Saint wanted to pitch in, now would be the time."

Inside me, Roman's laugh was wry. *They'll never come.*

"They came for Ares before," I murmured.

They came for his woman, Roman answered. *The gods haven't a care for us—but the Maere are their daughters.*

Perhaps he was right. Still, I whispered an old prayer to Tanith. What I was going to do was foolish, but like Roman, my soul needed cleansing. Rhiannon had helped me to see things differently about Frannie's death, but I could never move on until I'd done something worthy of wiping my ledger clean.

Don't do this, son, Roman cautioned. Our connection must allow him some view into my mind.

"Tell Ares to explain to Rhi if I don't make it out," I said, drawing the Admiral's guns and leaping straight into the pit.

As I fell, I heard my brother's roar of anger above the din. Roman left me then, and I was on my own, rain hammering into me as I aimed for the fiend. There were thirteen bullets in each of the pistols. I had exactly twenty-six shots to make this right and get out.

I shot from each gun simultaneously as I fell, aiming straight for the fiend's biggest mouth. Two shots. Four. Six. Eight. They were landing, but it wasn't disappearing the way it should.

It was possible it was too big to exterminate this way, or that more time was needed for the bullets to penetrate. I had no way of knowing, but I had to keep trying. When my feet slammed into the roiling dead, it took everything I had to stay upright. I stomped hard, shooting one of the dead who extended something that looked like a tentacle to wrap around my ankle. The embodied spirit disappeared, leaving only a puff of aura behind, like a wisp of smoke.

The bullets and the guns weren't faulty then. I shot another and another, as the dead turned their attention my way. Twelve shots. Fourteen. I had twelve left and I had to make them count. The dead hung back, wary of me now. Even in the state they were in, they clung to existence. It wasn't life, but it was something.

The fiend didn't have eyes that I could see, but it seemed to turn its attention my way as I scurried beneath its hideous legs. Up close, the stench was unbearable, and it was nearly twice as large as I'd thought, probably closer to fifteen feet tall. From this vantage point, I got a view of its undercarriage.

Deep inside the fiend, a sickly green light pulsed. For a moment that felt precariously long, I tracked the pattern of the pulsing. Was that its heart? I thought of Rhiannon, of the way she moved when she fought. How it always seemed that she was three steps ahead of her foes.

How did she do it?

The dead were coming, and I had to wonder if they could sense that I was outnumbered. There was no time to contemplate more. I aimed and fired. Sixteen. Eighteen. Twenty.

The fiend's abdomen burst open, that putrid gore spilling down on me, but I didn't stop squeezing the triggers of my guns. Twenty-two. Twenty-four. The fiend exploded, but before more of it could spill onto me, it turned to auric smoke.

The dead screamed. Above me, Roman and Ares were getting the better of Magnus, but still he fought them. The fiend was dead, but there was so much more to do and I was exhausted.

Suddenly, I understood how Rhiannon had become so good, so proficient at killing. She never stopped. For thousands of years, she'd been relentless, burying herself beneath a greater good. And though I had my issues with what it had done to her, I couldn't deny that persistence was what counted.

My energy felt renewed as I centered myself in her spirit of resilience, of never quitting, even when shit was dire. I began to climb. At first, the dead fought me. And then, it was as though they bent purposely to become like steps for me.

Avaline. My best friend was working the dead like only she could.

My smile was grim as I climbed faster, every muscle in my legs and arms screaming with the effort. But I gained ground. I was almost there. One of the Phoenixes' hands shot out as I neared the edge of the pit, and a face I couldn't put a name to yanked me out.

"Thanks," I shouted as I sprinted for Ares.

When I reached my brother, Roman flooded back into me. Without a word, I nodded to Ares, taking aim at the cloud of writhing hate that Magnus had become, and shot, right as Roman held him steady, and Ares flooded him with the only power in the world that could destroy the dead.

Avaline shouted for one last push from the Phoenixes as Magnus' spirit began to scream. *Goodbye, my sons*, I heard Roman say. And then there was a flash of light, and a boom so loud it knocked the torrential downpour back into the sky.

Ares and I collapsed against one another, both of us holding tight to each other's arms as the world seemed to vibrate off its axis. I didn't realize I'd shut my eyes until Ares laughed. "Would you look at that?"

I opened my eyes and turned back towards the breach. The street looked as though nothing had happened. And then the rain, which had stopped with Magnus' banishment, fell doubly hard, washing all of us clean of the battle.

Ares and I scrambled towards Avaline and the Phoenixes. Av was on her walkie. Ares clapped her on the shoulder, smiling, but her face was grim. "Team Two just got to the house."

"What's wrong?" I shouted over the sound of the rain.

"No one's there," Av shouted back.

My heart, that had lifted with relief only moments ago, plummeted through my body into fathomless depths. We'd saved the city from the dead, but it wasn't enough.

"Move out," Ares shouted. "Back to Hemlock House." He grabbed my arm. "We don't know that anything bad has happened," he added. "Sera might have made a tactical decision."

I nodded. Ares might be right. She might have. But we didn't have time to discuss it, or the gut feeling I had that he was wrong. No matter what had happened, or how tired we were, we had to get there. One battle was won, but the war to keep our family safe had just begun. I broke into a sprint behind our people, Av and Ares right by my side.

CHAPTER 34

RHIANNON

INSIDE THE ELEVATOR, a classic bossa nova song that had been massively popular about sixty years ago played. Ember swayed slightly to it. Calypso glanced back at her, raising an eyebrow. Max just sighed.

Lara grinned at me, then started to sing. Her face was covered in blood. Ember joined in, wiggling her hips. Max shook her head, looking back to me for a rebuke, I suppose. I shrugged and lent my voice to Ember and Lara's. We hadn't done our usual ritual of singing to a mixtape on our way here.

"It's good luck," I hissed at Calypso between verses.

The redheaded Maere shrugged, adding her voice to the rest of ours.

"You have to sing," Ember added, shooting a mock glare back at Max as the chorus started. She rolled her eyes, but sang along anyway. We didn't fuck with tradition.

The six of us sang as the elevator crept to the basement at a glacial pace. At around Floor Two, when the song started over on some bizarre loop, she looked at Calypso and said, "This is why people don't take the Orphium Maere seriously."

Calypso giggled, but she didn't stop singing. Admittedly, she had the prettiest voice of all of us. The elevator doors opened up on dozens of armed soldiers with guns trained on us. These were not the guards from above.

This was one of the Authority's elite forces. Lara looked to Ember for direction. There was a crimson glow to her eyes that should have sent the soldiers running, but of course they didn't know better. "Can I go first?"

Ember made a gallant gesture. "But of course."

Lara stepped out of the elevator, beaming at the soldiers with her most dazzling smile. I wasn't sure how they didn't all fall instantly in love, but they kept their guns pointed squarely at her.

"So," she said amiably. "Unfortunately, we are here to kill you all. Fortunately, we're not the monsters you are. I'll give you the same offer I gave your dead friends upstairs— run while you still have the chance, and live another day."

They opened fire on her as an answer, but she moved too fast for them, her sword slicing through the kneecaps of the first row of soldiers like a hot knife through butter. The rest of us moved, pushing the fallen towards the elevator.

Bullets hit me, but they refused to enter my body as my sword drank more and more blood. There wasn't time to think or even time to strategize. It was just us butchering them. More streamed towards us from the teed corridor at the end of the hallway. A few stumbled backwards as our bloody footprints left their fellow soldiers behind, the same bossa nova song from the elevator repeating again as we walked towards them.

"We're just going to keep killing you," Max sneered. "Don't you get it? You can't beat us."

A pale elderly man in an obscenely expensive suit pushed a hooded figure through the crowd of soldiers. He'd had expensive hair plugs put in, when he would have looked better going bald. His face had been tweaked and altered many times, but he still wasn't remotely handsome.

Recognition slithered through me, bile rising in my throat at the sight of his face. I'd never seen him in person, but I knew my enemy: Archibald Blaire, the Third.

As for the hooded figure… it didn't matter one whit that her face was covered, or that he'd stripped her of her royal vestments, leaving her only in a slip of an undergarment. I would recognize the set of my mother's shoulders anywhere.

I pushed past Ember and Lara. "Absens haeres non erit," I said in a low tone.

It was the last thing she'd said to me before skewering me with my own sword. *An absent person will not inherit.* From underneath the bag over her head, my mother laughed, the sound throaty and arrogant.

Her head twisted backwards, as though she could see through the fibers of the bag over her head and wanted to see his expression when she insulted him. "Perhaps you should end things now, Archie. You have the right kind of face for a cowardly death." Her bagged head tilted to the side, raptorial even at a disadvantage. "Like a dead fish."

Max snorted at her insult. Calypso covered her mouth as my mother laughed with them. Blaire struck her hard across the back of the head, but she kept laughing. "You'll have to hit harder than that if you want to silence me, darling."

He did have a face like a dead fish, I decided. It twisted into some perversion of a smile. Then he drew a syringe from inside his jacket pocket and jabbed it into her neck.

Rather than plunging liquid into her, he drew out an entire vial of blood.

In what felt like slow motion, he pushed her towards me, then spoke a single soft word as the group of soldiers parted for her to stumble through: *Fire.* I lunged for her as my sistren instinctively flanked their queen.

But it didn't stop the bullets from finding her. The white silk of her slip was blossoming crimson when she fell into my arms only seconds later. This had all been theater. A trap.

As she slumped into my arms, my mother gave an order from beneath the bag I pulled from her head. "Destroy this place."

Ember heard her and nodded. "Get her out of here."

I pulled the torc from my neck and placed it around hers. The adamantine shackles fell from her wrists. My mother looked up at me, her skin far too pale. I raised an eyebrow at her. "Don't you dare pass out. Work on healing yourself."

My mother had been adept with magic for thousands of years—even this far from the island, she would be able to access her power. Until I met Cassandra, I'd thought she was the most powerful scholomage to have ever lived.

A bit of color came back to her skin, and her lips curled into a familiar wry smile. "I shall live."

Her words were confident, but there was nothing reassuring in my mother's eyes. Ember's gaze met mine, and I knew. My friend was a brilliant leader in battle, but her strategy for getting the most people out alive was unmatched primarily because she had an uncanny way of identifying those that would live, and those that would die.

Ember's slow inhalation told me all I needed to know. My mother wasn't going to make it. She'd been hit too many times. "How long?"

"Maybe an hour," she said. "Make the most of the time you have left. We'll clean up here." I could hardly hear my heartbeat over the roar of my blood. Ember turned back towards the fray, calling, "Lara, go with them."

But Lara was beyond us now. She sprinted after Blaire. Ember didn't have to give another order; Max was by my side. Ember nodded to her and turned back to the fight, while Max covered me as I lifted my mother as gently as I could over my shoulder and prepared to run with her. "Kara and the Aradios Maere will meet us at the back door," she said into my ear. "Follow me?"

A pang of worry went through me. This wasn't how I was used to doing things. I'd have preferred my own people take care of this, and though I loved Max and always would, she was no longer part of my cohort.

She seemed to see my hesitation, her dark eyes going soft. "Things do have to change with us," she murmured as she pushed me back from the fray. Our friends were slaughtering the remaining soldiers. "I have a feeling we're going to need each other more and more in the coming days."

Whatever this had been, Blaire had baited us in the worst way. I glanced up at the cameras in the hall. Footage. He had footage of all of this. Of us breaking in and massacring humans. Without context, this would end us.

I'd worked with the Consulate for long enough to know what they could clean up and what they couldn't. If this footage got out, we were fucked.

"Fine," I agreed. "Let's move."

And then we ran. The halls were empty, so strangely empty. But the cells were full of our people. I stopped, setting my mother gently down on a plastic chair outside an office. I gripped her chin. "You understand what's happening here?"

She nodded once. It was all I needed. My mother was nothing if not cunning. She probably knew more than I did.

"I cannot let our people die here." It wasn't a request for permission, nor was it the kind of meek admission of ambition that I typically gave her.

A slow smile appeared on her face. "Do what you need to. I could use a moment to bolster myself." She took my hand in hers. Her skin was freezing cold. A ring appeared in my palm. "You will need this."

I looked down at the ring in my hand, a simple gold signet, with symbols of our house carved into it. What my mother suggested by giving me this ring was impossible, but I had never been one for denying a truth when one was presented. If this was the end of Silea Hyperion, who was I to deny her last wishes?

"You owe me at least a few hours," I ordered her, staring straight into her eyes. "After all you've done, you owe me that."

My mother nodded again. "Do what you must. But wear the ring."

I slipped it onto my righthand index finger, and felt a surge of power like I'd never known. Suddenly, I was connected not just to the island's magic, but *everything*. For a brief moment, magic seemed boundless, endless, filling me with the deepest, most comforting darkness, and the warmest golden light.

In my peripheral awareness, Max stepped back from me, kneeling. "Domina."

"Get up," I snapped. "I'm no different than I was a moment ago."

She shook her head. Max had always understood the

mysteries better than the rest of us. "That isn't true and you know it."

I did know it. But I didn't want it to be true. Because if I were to be Otrera's queen, it meant everything I held dear here was over.

From her plastic chair, my mother said with a prim smile, "Do ut des."

I give that you may give.

She knew she was ruining my life—any chance of happiness I ever had. Queens of Otrera did not marry. They did not even take long-term lovers, for fear of being corrupted by love. They ruled alone. I wanted to slap her silly, but thought better of it.

I crouched down and took a long, deep breath. Perhaps the feeling of real magic coursing through my veins made me arrogant, but I wasn't cowing to her ever again, even if she was dying. I pressed my hand to the wall beside her head, staring into her sapphire blue eyes.

There were many secrets of Otreran queens. One was that in the first few hours of official queendom, when the ring was passed from one sovereign to another, the new ruler was imbued with a surplus of power. The rules that normally governed magic did not apply.

Otrera hadn't had a new queen in tens of thousands of years. If the outer world had ever known this secret of ours, it had most certainly forgotten now. I stared into my mother's eyes, smiling defiantly. If she wanted me to have her power so badly, I would take it, and I would do the last thing she ever would.

I felt for the innards of the building. Felt the modern wires and tech that operated the locks, the security systems, that connected them to the Authority's servers and stores of data. I kept my eyes on my mother's as I sent a surge of precise magic through every wire that connected the Authority and the Corps to their precious data.

Every record, every prison, every aspect of the infernal stock market, every bank account for every oligarch, the list went on. I was connected to it all. Blaire had trapped us, but whatever it was he'd gained, I would take back tenfold.

I was not a blunt instrument the way my mother had always been, governing by broad measures that took no nuance into account. I had always parsed things out too far for her. Been too precise for what made a good ruler. She'd always accused me of missing the bigger picture for the details.

But the details were what mattered. The small things were what counted. And as my mind sifted the bank accounts of common folks from those of the multi-billionaires, I knew this was only a temporary fix. It would do no more than cause chaos.

But the chaos it caused would be a wedge. A lever. If we used it correctly, it might provide a way back from the misery parapsychs suffered under the Authority's boot. And not just parapsychs, but poor humans as well, for there were more of them than there were rich.

I let my eyes fall closed so I could concentrate. It didn't take much, as I was already so dialed into the complex web of information. Briony could have done a better job of it, but we didn't have time for that. What I needed to do had to be done now, before Blaire had time to wield what he had on us. It only took a little push now that I was connected.

I was fairly certain I'd done it—erased all traces of us having been here. I'd erased the things Blaire had done here as well, and that would have consequences of its own, but desperate times and all that. Still, I could do just a little more, so I pushed harder with the magic, sending the surplus far and wide over the continent, throughout the Three Cities, and then back into the many mechanisms that governed this very building.

The surplus of power was gone. All used up, but the doors in all the hallways, throughout the building, opened at once. And then the lights went out. The HVAC went quiet. Throughout the building, there was exactly three seconds of perfect quiet. We wouldn't get more.

In silence, I scooped my mother out of the plastic chair, and without hesitation, Max moved. Behind us, pandemonium broke out as the Asylum's prisoners realized they were free. Our boots fell heavy on the worn linoleum tile as we ran. Some that were released were a true danger to the world, but most were just people the Authority had been determined to hurt.

No move that destroyed this corrupt system would ever be perfect or clean. All we could do now was try our best. Backup power came on, illuminating the way. Max seemed to have memorized the schematics of the building, because she took turn after confident turn. We were out of the wings where they housed "patients" now, passing through a pair of heavy doors that were likely always locked. A glass atrium was ahead of us.

Bodies littered the floor, pools of blood everywhere. Kara Asterion stood at the center of the massive entrance to the building, covered in blood, her sword still drawn. When she saw us, she smiled, but the expression dropped off her face when she saw the state my mother was in.

Her dark brown eyes met mine. I shook my head. Ever observant, the leader of the Aradios Maere's eyes went straight to my finger, where the signet ring now rested. "We have to go," I said. "Time is important now."

My mother murmured something, her head muffled against my back, as we raced through the atrium. I couldn't hear her, and couldn't pause to ask her to repeat herself. Outside, an armored SUV waited on the sidewalk. The doors opened and three familiar faces waited inside. Titania Kabeiri, Ishtar Aina, and Ama Inari—the rest of the Aradios Maere.

"She is dying," I explained as I let my mother's body fall forward, catching her into my arms as I passed her into the car. "Be careful with her."

Ama nodded. She'd always been the best with healing amongst the fifteen of us. She'd helped Sera make great strides after the fire. It might have been decades more of recovery if it hadn't been for her. Her hands glowed crimson as she pressed her hands to my mother's chest.

Silea took the Maere's hands in her own when some vitality returned to her face. "Save your strength, child. Don't waste it on me."

Ama sat back, her gray eyes wide with worry. She glanced up at me as I climbed into the SUV and shut the doors. Kara got into the driver's seat, while Max rode shotgun.

"What have we got?" Kara asked. "Where do we go next?"

My mother held up a hand. "Where is Myrine?"

I smiled. "Don't worry. She's safe with Sera, at Hemlock House."

Silea's eyes darkened. "You left her alone with Serafine?"

I nodded. "And Briony. They'll take care of her."

My mother's fingers closed around my forearm, panic in her eyes. "Rhiannon. Myrine is working with Blaire."

Every atom of my being screamed in terror. I'd left

Sera and Briony with a traitor. With the most dangerous traitor possible, in fact. I'd left the most vulnerable of us with the strongest soldier in the Authority's army.

Kara's eyes met mine in the rearview mirror. "Hemlock House it is."

CHAPTER 35

ERYX

ALL WAS DARK. It seemed power was down all over the city. After the Phoenixes cleared the house, Av sent them off to coordinate their own teams. If the power was down, that meant subways were trapped. People needed aid and the Authority was always slow to provide.

Immediately, she was on the phone, making dozens of calls while I stared at the black landline phone hanging on the kitchen wall. I wanted to call Rhiannon, but didn't want to distract her. I'd failed her.

Sera, Myrine—Briony. They were all gone. Something soft brushed my ankles. Stanley. The little poltergeist looked mostly normal at the moment, just an extra pair of glowing eyes in his soft head. I sighed, reaching down to pick him up, hoping he'd seen something.

But when he pressed his face to mine, there was no memory of what had happened. Only the worry that Briony was gone. I hugged him to my chest, murmuring, "Look for anything out of place," before I set him down on the kitchen floor.

Ares came into the kitchen. "I can't find any clue to where they've gone."

"What about the cottage?" I asked.

Av shook her head, hanging up the phone. "The Phoenixes checked it. It's locked, Eryx. They couldn't get in. I think when we closed the breach, we might have shut the house off too. Maybe for good."

I nodded. That made a certain amount of sense, I supposed. But then, where were they? I had a terrible feeling about all this. I watched as Stanley sniffed the air, as though he'd caught wind of something.

It was just as likely that he was sniffing the remnants of lunch as an actual clue. The beast was just about as useless as I was. He jumped onto the counter, scratching at the pen by the notepad, hissing.

"For fuck's sake," Ares sighed, grabbing the poltergeist and handing it to Av. "Do something with him."

The feline howled at him, glaring with all four of his eyes. Ares crossed his arms over his chest. "That's not helpful."

Av frowned, watching as Stanley squirmed out of her arms to jump back onto the kitchen counter by the phone. He hissed at the pen again, and then head butted the pad of paper. Avaline moved to look at it.

"Don't encourage him," Ares said. "He's already too much of a pest."

Av grabbed a pencil from the mug that Ember kept next to the phone, and ran it lightly over the pad of paper. Ares smiled at her, obviously charmed by her efforts. It was hard not to love Av when she gave her all.

"Have you been watching Ghost Detective again?" he asked, naming Avaline's favorite among reruns.

"Yes. Of course." She raised an eyebrow, holding the pad of paper up. "But it worked. It's an address."

Ares scoffed, but he took the pad of paper, then frowned.

"Do you recognize the handwriting?" she asked.

My brother's mind was the kind of steel trap that held information like what every person in this house's handwriting looked like. "No," he said. "Has anyone but us been here for the past couple days? I used this three days ago to take the Taco Paradise order, and you can see this was written on top of it."

Av shook her head. "No, just us…"

"And Myrine," I groaned.

Ares gritted his teeth. "She's betrayed our girls before."

I pushed off the counter. "We have to get to wherever that is."

Av held up a hand, as she took the pad from Ares. "Let me make a call first." Ares glanced at me as she walked into the back hall, shaking his head. "Eli?" her voice called out before she disappeared. "It's Avaline."

Ares turned on the battery powered radio that sat just under the phone. He had to adjust the station several times, but a clear channel came in.

… ago the grid went out. The stock market has plummeted as billions of dollars went missing. The radio crackled, static obscuring what the host said… *ports that the Asylum is on fire.*

Ares' phone buzzed. He answered immediately. "My love," he breathed, stepping out onto the patio. Through the door he mouthed to me, *Rhiannon is fine,* but his eyes were dark with worry as he asked, "What happened?"

Rhiannon was alive, but I'd known she would be. The real question was whether or not she was all right. She certainly wasn't going to be if I couldn't find Briony and Sera.

Avaline returned, nodding towards Ares, a question in

her eyes. "Ember," I answered. "Sounds like they're mostly all right."

"Good," she murmured. "Eli says services are down throughout the city. Someone cracked into every major electronic system in the Three Cities and overloaded it. The damage is…" she shrugged, raising her dark eyebrows. "Huge."

"Okay," I said slowly. "And what about Eli?"

"Right," Av said, nodding quickly. "He's going to meet us a block from the address."

"Why?" I asked, feeling snappish and impatient.

Av's face drew in. "He got a message from Briony right before the power went out. All it said was, 'AM 2 rendvs w Blr'."

It felt like my brain was going to explode. I needed to know where Briony was, *now*. "*What?*"

Av flipped the notepad pages over and wrote down the nonsense she'd just said. As soon as I saw it, my heart stopped. "Admiral Myrine to rendezvous with Blaire."

Av swallowed. "That's what he thought too. He's headed there now."

The miracle worker had spent a lot of time with Briony since we rescued her from Mike Fairchild and his rogue branch of the Authority. They played chess online frequently, and talked about computers. It didn't surprise me that he'd step in now to help us.

Ares stepped back into the house. "They're headed back here. Max and Rhiannon aren't with them. She sent them on with the queen. They should be here now."

My heart stopped. I know it did. I closed my eyes. "If they came back here, and Myrine had betrayed them—she might have taken them all to Blaire."

Av put a hand on my arm. "Eryx, she might be fine.

Power's down all over town. We don't know that there's not traffic. Obstacles."

I shook my head. "And we don't know that she's not at this address, being handed over to Archibald Blaire."

Ares held up his hands. "I will stay here and wait for Ember and the others to get back." He paused, waiting to see if the two of us were going to keep arguing. When Av and I both crossed our arms, like children in a momentary truce, he went on. "They're five minutes out, and we'll be right behind you."

Av nodded, grabbing my hand and squeezing. "Let's go."

The address Myrine had written down was a warehouse in the Slaughterhouse District. Av and I parked three blocks away, and walked through the rain to the address across the street we'd agreed to meet Eli at.

A rat scuttled into the alley we'd ducked into, and without warning, shifted into a hulk of a man. Every time I saw the miracle worker he looked angrier somehow. He stepped under the awning Av and I were huddled into, the collar of his canvas jacket flipped up against the rain.

Av smiled cheerily at him. "That was a fun trick."

Eli glowered at her. "It was an illusion."

"It was a good one," Av said, her tone encouraging.

The Thaumas second-in-command shrugged, but something around his eyes softened a little. It was hard to stay impervious when Avaline turned her sparkling personality on you. "Blaire's inside. He's got a girl with him I don't recognize. No sign of our people though."

"A child?" I asked.

He shook his head. "No, she's probably in her late twenties. Early thirties, maybe. Young looking—pretty. Human, I think…" Eli seemed to stumble over that idea, but kept going. "He's got her strapped to some kind of gurney. She's asleep, wearing a hospital gown."

Av shook her head, huddling closer to me. "What the fuck is he up to? Is she an inmate from the Asylum?"

Eli threw his hands in the air, as confused as the rest of us. "What do you want to do?"

I took a deep breath. If the young woman was human, she was not our concern. But then, why had a human been in the Asylum? "You're *sure* she's human?"

Eli grimaced. "Sort of."

"What does that mean?" I nearly shouted. We were losing time. If Myrine wasn't here—if Rhiannon, Briony, and the others weren't here—we had to figure out where they'd been taken.

Eli sighed. "It means that she seemed human, but there's something weird about her. Something off."

"We don't have time for this," I growled, turning back towards the car, stepping out into the rain. The streets were empty in this part of town. It was quiet now, with everything down, but soon people would start to panic. I didn't want to have to fight in the streets. "If they're not here, the best thing we can do is get home and figure out what to do next."

Av grabbed my arm. "Eryx. Blaire may know where Myrine is. I think we need to make a plan and go in."

Eli nodded. "I agree with shorty here."

Av slapped him, her hand barely reaching his chest. He smiled faintly at her and I realized she might be one of the few people, other than Briony, that he actually liked. "I'm not *that* short," she hissed. "Sera's shorter."

Eli Cabot flushed red at the mention of the smallest Maere. If we weren't in the middle of an epic shitshow, I might rib him about it. "So what do we do?"

Av's eyes lit up. "Can you make me look like Myrine?"

Eli frowned, thinking it over. "It's hard to create an illusion over an actual person that moves and speaks, but I can give you ten minutes."

"Great," she said, grinning like an elf. "You two sneak in behind me, and if anything goes wrong, you can bop him on the head."

I blew out a wry laugh. "Simple as that."

She squeezed my arm again. "I can do this, Eryx. We'll find them."

"Okay," I agreed. "Let's do it."

Three minutes later, Eli and I were sneaking inside, behind what looked like Admiral Myrine. The illusion extended far enough that Av even moved like her. Eli had explained that even though he'd never seen Myrine, what was necessary was that Av had, and Avaline Reyes was nothing if not observant. We had ten minutes to find out what had happened to our people.

Eli and I kept to the outer walls of the building. We could see Av, but it would take effort to get to her if things went sideways. As she moved further into the warehouse, a dim light cut into the deep shadows. Above us, rain still poured on the metal roof.

Despite the noise, I heard Blaire speak before I saw him. "You're early."

I moved behind a stack of crates. I could see Eli across the warehouse because I knew to look for him, but otherwise, he blended into the shadows almost seamlessly. Av shrugged.

"Where are the scrolls?" Blaire snarled. "You were supposed to bring them."

So, she'd meant to go back to the island. It was all I needed. I knew where Rhiannon was—she had to be at the cottage. Myrine had probably tried to break back into the underworld through the basement. Hauntings could end, but they left residual energy, and Cassandra had promised the cottage would only open for Rhiannon and me. But I had a feeling Myrine knew ways to get around such details.

I crouched down, taking my phone out to text Ares to tell him we'd be there as soon as we could and where they'd find the others. When I had a reply that they'd turn back, I shut my phone off.

"I wasn't so stupid as to bring them here," Av said. "I want insurance."

We needed to get Av and go. Now. But I couldn't risk blowing her cover. As I peeked around the stack of boxes I hid behind, I realized that Blaire was armed. There was an adamantine blade on the table next to the gurney, along with an array of medical instruments and a device that looked like it was something for brewing potions. We needed to move carefully here. We also needed to get that blade.

Blaire sighed, picking a syringe up from the table and moving towards his potions device. Av or Ares probably knew what all that equipment was called, but I wasn't sure. "You're not rethinking things, are you?" he sneered. "We agreed. A new race of immortals will shift the balance. It will, as you say—" he gestured towards Av. "Normalize parapsychism somewhat, and make things better for your people."

"But you'll control them," Avaline murmured, not sounding much like Myrine.

But Blaire didn't seem to notice. He just kept talking while he drew liquid out of the device, into the syringe. "It's only fair. It evens the playing field. And then you and the others can come out of the mists. With Silea out of the way, our plan will work."

I'll never know what Avaline was thinking, but she said, "You don't need the scrolls. I lied."

Blaire turned, his buggy eyes narrowed. "What do you mean?"

Av smiled. "I've always known it all."

Blaire smiled, walking towards Av with the syringe in hand. "Just one more dose, my love." The two of them were in a *relationship*? I struggled not to gag. "One more dose and the ritual, and she'll be the first true immortal since you made the Maere." He slid an arm around Av's waist. "Are you as excited as I am?"

"Yes," Av breathed, somehow managing to sound like she was taken in by the idea. I still wanted to vomit, and apparently, so did Eli, because he appeared suddenly behind Blaire, and hit him so soundly on the head that he crumpled, the syringe in his hand shattering as it hit the concrete floor.

The sound caused the woman on the gurney to stir. Av pointed to Blaire's gun. "Get rid of that," she ordered, moving towards the human woman.

Eli had been right. She was human, but also not. Whatever Blaire had done to her, he was obviously trying to turn her into an immortal, like the Maere, somehow. She was a pretty thing, tall, a little thinner than Rhiannon, but voluptuous. Her head had been badly shaved so that sensors could be attached to her scalp, but her hair had been brown at one time.

From the table, Eli gathered all of Blaire's papers into a file folder. "We need to get out of here," he murmured.

The girl was waking up as Av freed her from the restraints. She sat up, gasping, then stared at Blaire on the floor. "Is he dead?" she asked, not really looking at any of us.

"No," I answered her, though our next move should probably be to kill him.

"I have to get out of here before he wakes," she said, her voice hoarse, as though she hadn't used it in a while. "He wants to make me a monster, like the rest of them."

Eli spoke gently to her from the table, not moving any closer. It was obvious she was upset, traumatized. "What's your name?"

The woman shook her head. "I'm not telling you anything."

Av nodded. "That's wise of you."

The sound of a door bursting open came from the back of the building. Soldiers in tactical gear streamed in. Eli pointed at Av, "Get her out of here."

But the girl was gone, as though she'd simply disappeared into thin air. I wasn't sure how she'd done it, but it didn't matter. What mattered was that we'd wasted time and let Blaire live.

I ran, following Av and Eli towards the front. As we slipped through the back door, I looked back, dread curdling my gut. Behind us, the soldiers gathered around Blaire, picking him up. A tall figure emerged out of the shadows.

Eli turned back to grab me, but his eyes arrested on the thaumaturge who'd been set to take over the Thaumas Dynasty in Aradios before coming here last fall. "Fucking Leo Atrior," he swore dragging me to to the door. "Rotten to the core. Let's go."

But the thaumaturge's dark eyes held no trace of triumph as we made eye contact. If anything, the man was so full of self-loathing he could hardly breathe. I recognized the feeling easily. I carried it with me wherever I went.

CHAPTER 36

RHIANNON

HEMLOCK HOUSE WAS SILENT. Too silent. The six of us spread out, though Max took charge of my mother. I headed straight for Briony's room, but it was empty. Throughout the house, as we moved back towards the foyer, where Max and Silea waited for us, came the soft calls of "Clear."

Kara shook her head at me as she came up from the basement. "They're not here."

Mother's head lolled a bit, but she was still breathing, her eyes still bright. "She needs the scrolls," she said, her voice fading. "No one but me knew the entire ritual. We kept the knowledge of the many parts of it separate, but there's a record—it's in the scrolls. She'll get them for Blaire."

The six of us stood silently, all of us waiting. It took Kara nudging me with her elbow for me to remember they were waiting for me. Coronations didn't matter to Maere. The ring was all that counted. I was the highest ranking Maere in the room.

"Move her to the living room," I ordered.

Max nodded, and the six of us moved as a unit, supporting Silea until we got her lowered into Ember's favorite reading chair, next to the hearth. The room was dark—the power was out here too.

Titania slid her phone out of her pocket. It was a thick, satellite phone, not a typical cell. Her bright green eyes flitted over the screen as she tapped away. "Power's down all over the city—and in Aradios too. No word from Palladiere yet. Consulate's called eight times in the last ten."

The ginger Maere was Aradios' communications expert. She raised the phone to her pale face, her deeply freckled cheeks flushing with amusement as she listened to the messages. When she hung up, she grinned. "Whatever you did, Rhiannon, you wiped everything clean. The Consulate has hard copies of everything, as you know." I shrugged. I did know, all too well. "But the Authority is in chaos. All the CCTV records are gone, and the banking?"

Titania laughed so hard that Ishtar placed a strong hand on her back. "Are you well?"

Tears of laughter streamed down Titania's face. "Rhiannon disappeared billions of dollars. They're already getting it back, but it's going to be a mess for months—maybe years."

Ishtar stood. "Do you have a generator? If I can get power running, I can use Briony's computers to find out more." The dark-haired Maere was nearly as competent as our Briony with tech.

I glanced at Max. "Show her where everything is. I'm going after Myrine."

My mother looked up at me. "Do you know where she is?"

I nodded. "I have a pretty good idea." I took a deep

breath, and looked around the room. "Thank you for all of your help. Keep her alive 'til I return."

Ama knelt next to my mother, a duffel bag in her arms. She must have gone and gotten it from the car, and she was drawing out various syringes and vials of liquid. She nodded as she took my mother's pulse before she glanced up at me through her long, thick lashes. "I can give you a few hours, at most."

"I won't need that long," I said, as I spun to leave.

If I looked back, my mother might say something to make me think I should stay with her—and not rescue my real family. As I reached the kitchen door, I heard her voice, clear and strong as ever. "You're doing the right thing."

I spared a single look back at her. "I know."

Traces of the struggle were evident in the thick, wet grass in the garden. Sera had fought Myrine. I found her slumped next to the garden gate between the cottage and the house and broke into a sprint. She had no obvious injuries, her breathing was regular, and her heartbeat was strong.

I felt the back of her head, where a giant lump was already receding. I pressed my hand to it, giving her as much of the abundance of royal magic I now possessed as I could. Her eyes opened, shining silver. She smiled, but faintly. "That feels good." Immediately, her eyes darkened. "Myrine… Rhi, she has Briony—"

"I know," I whispered. "Do you feel strong enough to come with me? We have to get our girl back."

Sera grinned at me, nodding. Tiny as she was, before she was injured in the fire, she'd been the most vicious of all of us. The light that gleamed in her eyes now was one I could use. "Yes, we do."

"Let's go," I whispered. "Be as silent as you can."

Sera nodded at me, and we crept through the gate, stealing across the wet paths in Oleander Cottage's garden. Movement in my peripheral vision stopped me in my tracks, just outside the mudroom door. Sera gripped my arm, pointing.

It was Stanley, but he wasn't a spirit. He was fully corporeal, and a fairly average looking, if large, black house cat. I glanced back at the garden, and found the hedge of roses as high as it had been when Eryx and I were trapped.

But there were none of the whispers. None of the finger trap feelings that I'd come to associate with Cassandra's illusion. Stanley didn't blink out, either. He came to brush against my ankle, transferring a bit of magic straight to my mind.

Cassandra stood next to me, the golden light of true afterlife clinging to her. She was dressed as she would have been as a princess of Otrera, in a loose indigo gown with intricate beading at the hem, heavy gold jewelry adorning her ears and wrists, a diadem in her mass of rose-gold hair.

She smiled, softly. "I almost left, but then—" it seemed she choked on her words. "I—is she?"

"She's in the house," I said, knowing that Cassandra had stayed to see her sister into the afterlife. There was something comforting about knowing that they would go together. That perhaps they could mend things between them enough that neither would be held back from eternal rest. "Go to her now. You've done all you could here."

Cassandra smiled as the sound of someone hacking at wood rang out from inside the house. She pulled a fully corporeal key that I recognized out of the pocket of her dress and placed it in my waiting palm. "I locked the door," she said, as she dissolved into golden light.

Sera gripped my arm, whispering, "A bit of luck, then."

I nodded. "A bit."

The hacking noise grew louder. I motioned for Sera to stay close, murmuring. "Get Briony out the second you can."

When I had her assent, we moved as one, creeping through the mudroom and into the kitchen. I could see Myrine hacking at the basement door through the back hall, and Briony tied up in the living room. Even with the extra power I had from my initial moments as Otrera's queen, I couldn't fight Myrine and win.

She'd taught me everything I knew about fighting on the island. But everything I knew about killing, I'd learned here. There was only one way this ended. I held up a hand to Sera, then signed for her to stay down. Her eyes widened when she realized what I was to do.

Briony caught sight of me as I moved, and I pressed a quick finger to my lips, my Murder Queen bracelet catching the dim light that came through the kitchen window.

I took one breath in and envisioned my movements. The trick, for me anyway, was to know exactly how I would move, where I might have to deviate if something about the conditions changed, and where I would strike. Three locations to step into, four quick movements to my kill, depending on the potential outcomes.

Planning ahead for problems was what made it seem as

though I murdered silently. I could kill Myrine quick and clean—she'd be dead before she even turned. But I needed a moment with her before she died, and that made things trickier than I'd have liked.

I moved quickly, without another thought, now that I'd decided. And as I crossed the threshold of the kitchen, I put the last bit of the island's power into my movements.

"Myrine," I called, my voice a sharp, staccato note in the cacophony of her incessant hacking at a door that was obviously spelled to be impervious to harm. She never had been particularly observant about how magic worked. Perhaps that was why she wasn't given the kind of information that would have benefited Blaire most.

She turned, her eyes wild, ready to hack at me next with the hatchet. But she hadn't seen me draw my sword. She hadn't felt it slide into her chest, pinning her to the basement door. I put the last of Otrera's borrowed power into the thrust. The magic would keep her pinned to the door until her death.

The sound of the hatchet clattering to the ground was what seemed to catch her attention. The spell over the house slid away. It was a dusty, dark mess once more. I didn't want to think that meant Cassandra and my mother were gone. Perhaps it only meant that Cassandra had pulled the last of her own power back to her.

Myrine frowned, so obviously confused. She tried to speak, but I held up a hand. "Don't waste much energy on asking how or why. I'll be happy to explain."

I kicked the hatchet away from her and stepped back. There was no telling how well armed she was. She couldn't hurt me now, but I didn't want any measure of violence affecting anyone else.

"Sera," I called, not taking my eyes off Myrine. "Take

Briony out the front door." I didn't want the teenager anywhere near Myrine if there was a chance she might have a weapon on her that she could throw.

Behind me, there were soft noises of Sera moving. I found a kitchen chair at my fingertips. "Milady," she murmured as she swept past me, into the living room.

Vaguely, I sensed her releasing Briony's bonds, whispering to her what they were going to do. When they were out the front door, I dragged the kitchen chair to face Myrine.

"Is there any chance you're going to tell me all of Blaire's nasty plans?" I asked. There was no use in trying torture or any other means of ferreting out information. Myrine had taught me every method I knew.

Her cold eyes were filled with resolve. There were no more snarky jokes. No more banter. She simply didn't answer.

"Fine," I breathed on a heavy exhalation. "Will you at least tell me why you did it? What was the point of all this?"

Myrine laughed, harsh and cruel. "For all the same reasons you do anything. For Otrera."

"Oh," I sighed. "You don't know me at all, do you?"

Myrine frowned, clearly trying to identify where she'd miscalculated.

I sat forward in the chair, crossing my legs. "I haven't done anything for Otrera in centuries, Myrine." I sat back in the chair. "Since my sword was stolen, I've been scrambling to survive. To help others survive."

The creases in Myrine's frown deepened. She was confused by this. For a moment, I was perplexed by her confusion. My mind raced over the information I had, and it was all there, so terribly clear.

"The night we got the swords back," I explained,

shaking my head. "You claimed that stealing them made us who we are." A laugh escaped me, understanding rattling my bones. "You were right."

"How so?" Myrine asked, gesturing to the sword buried in her chest. She coughed, blood trickling from her mouth. "It would seem otherwise at the moment."

I smiled. "You did make us who we are now. Stealing the swords drove us apart—and then back together again. You gave us a compass that didn't point toward the island anymore. Your actions forced us to stop thinking of Otrera as home. *This* is our home now, Myrine. *These* are our people."

"Oh," was all she said.

"Why did you do it?" I asked again.

She glared at me. "Because your mother was weak— hiding behind the mists was a cowardly move. An alliance with Blaire could have made us strong again. Could have brought Otrera back to the forefront of power."

I raised an eyebrow. "Are you actually this foolish?"

She gritted her teeth. "I had everything in hand, you twit."

Had. That meant Blaire didn't have what he needed. She hadn't delivered. It was why she was in here hacking uselessly away at a door that couldn't open.

"He'll kill them all, now," she said. "The parapsychs in the Asylum. Even his own—" she seemed to think better about what she was about to say, her mouth clamping shut.

"His own what?" I hissed.

But Myrine just smiled. "You're so clever, Rhiannon. Figure it out for yourself."

She wasn't going to give me anything else. Three movements. Four possible deviations. I had the blade at my thigh out and through the bottom of her throat, straight into her brain before she could say another word.

"I will," I whispered, as her heartbeat slowed, then stopped.

My body was heavy, so very heavy as I pulled my sword from her chest. She fell to the floor with a heavy thump and I wiped my blade off on her clothes. It faded into incorporeality as I sheathed it, my muscles heavy with effort.

I couldn't think of the last time I was this exhausted, and that was saying something. The thought occurred to me that this might have pushed me too far, though I was uncertain what that meant for me. I stumbled towards the door, through the kitchen, the maze of oleander in the faded wallpaper swimming before my eyes.

All the magic was gone now, and I'd taken dozens of hits during the rescue, despite the sword's magic. My adrenaline was crashing, and my body was trying desperately to put me to sleep so it could heal, but I didn't want to be here when I fell.

I couldn't fall until I knew what had happened with Eryx, 'til I knew he was all right. My steps were slow, and more awkward than I ever thought possible as I pushed the mudroom door open. The stone steps to the garden swam before my eyes. I didn't want to tumble down them, but I saw no other way.

As I pitched forward, bracing inwardly for the sting of stone meeting my body, strong arms caught me. "I'm here," my love said in that voice that could heal anything. "I've got you."

I looked up into his crisp green eyes, some strength returning just from being near him. "Want to meet my mom?" I asked. "I don't think we're going to have time for pizza."

"Absolutely," he said as he swept me into his arms. I searched his face for any signs of pain or injury, and found none. He was tired, just like me. Before he pressed a kiss to my forehead, he whispered into my ears. "But we are getting extra mushrooms later, I promise."

I wrapped my arms around his neck and closed my eyes, just for a moment, smiling. "That's why I love you."

CHAPTER 37

ERYX

THE WALK across the garden was quick, and we were lucky that the downpour had relented somewhat, and was now a mere drizzle. Ember met us at Hemlock House's back door. Rhiannon slid out of my arms and into Ember's.

"The queen doesn't have long," Ember whispered before turning to me. "She'd like to talk to you first, Eryx."

Cassandra appeared at Rhiannon's side, glowing with the golden light of the afterlife. Her form had turned translucent, and she was little more than a beam of light. Even still, she managed to take Rhiannon's hand. "Come, love," she said in a voice so far removed from the spirit we'd interacted with, I wondered if she might not be the same person.

But as I watched her sit with Rhiannon in the kitchen, I understood. She had one foot in whatever world came after this one—and in that world, she was happy. Cassandra was finally at peace.

As Rhiannon bent her head towards her aunt's, some of that peace seemed to transfer to her. It was the calmest

I'd seen her in weeks, and it helped me to leave her so soon after the horrors of the day.

Ember took me through the house, back into the living room, where Rhiannon's mother lay on a velvet couch by the bookshelves. She was deathly pale, but she still looked almost exactly like Rhiannon. Ember's hand rested on my shoulder for a moment, and when I glanced back at her, there was a warning in her eyes. But she said nothing, only closed the door softly behind her.

"So, you are the man my child has fallen in love with," the queen said from the couch.

Even a day ago, I never would have dreamed someone would have described me that way, let alone Rhiannon's own mother. "Yes," I finally answered.

"Come sit by me," the queen commanded. "My sight and hearing seem to be failing me. Without Cassandra here, it is worse."

I went to her, sitting next to the couch so I faced her. She smiled faintly as I got settled. "You are quite handsome. And a Necroline prince, I hear."

My head bowed, but I couldn't manage to keep the smile off my face. "We don't have Dynastical royalty anymore," I explained, knowing full well that she already knew that. "But a thousand years ago, that would have been true."

"Of course," she replied, sharp as a honed blade. "I don't ascribe to these modern ideas about the dynasties. You are Roman Necroline's child, which makes you a Necroline prince. That would be a fitting match for my daughter, if Otreran queens could marry."

Though I would have borne it if she had not approved of me, I would be lying to myself if I didn't admit that her words warmed me. I wasn't worried about the implied threat that Rhiannon's new role would take her from me, and I got the feeling her mother would only argue if I brought it up.

"Thank you," I replied, not knowing what else to say.

Her eyes narrowed. "Cassandra tells me that you lost someone, your first love, due to your work for the dynasty."

I had no energy to be angry with Cassandra for telling business that was not her own. "Yes," I answered honestly.

"Did you love her more than my child?"

I noticed that the queen continued to refer to Rhiannon in reference to herself. Many things made sense that had not before. All the ways that Rhiannon had burned out so fully were clear now. She had never been allowed to exist outside her mother as a child, that much was obvious. Her way of understanding herself was based on how others felt about her. That was changing, but it was good to see where those feelings came from firsthand.

The question the queen asked me was inappropriate, but I answered it truthfully. "No. She was my first love, but had she lived, it's very likely we would have ended things quickly. We didn't agree about much."

"And you and my daughter agree about many things?"

I had to laugh then. "We agree about what matters, I think."

The queen pursed her lips. "You think me impertinent for asking such prying questions." I didn't answer that. There was no need. She sighed. "As you know, I haven't much time, and as Rhiannon will likely tell you herself, I am not a good person, nor am I a good mother. But I do love her."

I nodded, slowly. "Of course you love her."

The queen's eyes narrowed further. "What does *that* mean?"

I rested more fully against the couch. The day was finally taking its toll. "You know Rhiannon. You raised her.

It is impossible for me to believe that anyone who had ever met her wouldn't love her."

The queen let out a little huff of disapproval. "Men in love are so emotional."

"Yes," I agreed. "But it is the truth."

"She is weak," the queen snapped. "You will have to take care of her for the rest of your lives."

The laugh erupted out of me before I could stop it. My head fell back as it reached my belly. When I managed to open my eyes to wipe them, the queen glared at me, obviously scandalized. Perhaps no one had ever laughed at her before.

"Rhiannon Brontë is the strongest, most resilient woman I've ever met," I replied. "Of course I will care for her. I adore her. But it's a pity you don't know who she is."

Before the queen could muster up a response to that, the door opened. Rhiannon rushed to her mother's side, as Cassandra appeared behind Silea's head. She smiled gently at me as Rhiannon sat back, her back resting naturally against my chest. Just that small show of trust was worth more to me than anything her mother might have said.

"I'm sorry it took so long," she whispered, taking her mother's hand. "Myrine is dead."

Silea nodded, closing her eyes. "Stealing the swords was a mistake."

"Thank you," Rhiannon said, gracious as ever.

Silea's eyes opened, sharp and cruel as ever. "It was a *tactical* mistake, Rhiannon. Had I seen her treachery earlier, I would have guessed that fracturing your cohort was meant to ease her way into the wider world, to keep you from catching onto her as she betrayed us."

Rhiannon sighed. "All that is true. It was also a mistake for you to make choices that manipulated and hurt me."

Cassandra placed a hand on her sister's shoulder. "Remember what we talked about."

Silea nodded. "Yes, that was also a mistake." Unexpectedly, the queen's eyes softened. "Now, we must talk about what happens next. Cass, please help me finish."

Cassandra closed her eyes, and golden light flowed into the queen. "Despite all that passed between us before you took the rites, you must be queen when I am gone."

Rhiannon opened her mouth, but Silea shook her head. "I do not mean for you to go home or to renounce your love. I mean for you to stay here. With our people. Melanippe Asterion will make an excellent regent, and you can trust her to handle things in Otrera until you can all return. And when you do…"

The queen paused, her eyes sliding to me. "You will do things differently than we have in the past. I understand this. I don't approve of it, but I am realistic about who you are."

From the surprise on Rhiannon's face, I gathered this was a more generous offer than she ever expected to receive. And from the relief on her face, and the ring she wore on her finger, I understood that she had meant to accept the responsibility no matter the consequences.

I couldn't be angry with her. This was who Rhiannon was, and I'd had no doubt she'd already be putting her beautiful mind to work to find a way around whatever obstacles might have been in our way before the queen had clarified.

"Is that someone related to Kara?" I asked, wanting to move the conversation along. I sensed from Cassandra's worried face that we didn't have much time left.

"Her mother," Rhiannon replied to me. "Melanippe *will* make an excellent regent. But how do you propose that I be queen to our people from here? There are no queens outside the mist. There are only corporations, and corrupt politicians."

The queen smiled. "I am aware."

My blood ran cold at that smile. The queen pointed to a folder that sat on the coffee table across from the couch. I reached out for it and passed it to Rhiannon, reading over her shoulder as she opened it.

Rhiannon gasped. "*You* are O-Tex?"

My heart nearly stopped. Had she known about Frannie? Had she given the order to kill her?

The queen's smile widened. "Yes."

"Did you know?" Rhiannon asked, and I knew she had my back—that she never meant to leave me behind. I loved her more than I could ever imagine possible that she would think to ask this first. "Did you order the hit on Francesca Lyon?"

The queen frowned. "Who is that?" Before either of us could answer, she shrugged. "I don't run the day to day at O-Tex. I don't have anything to do with the company itself. I've let it run exactly as the other Corporations have. It's how I've kept such a secret, and created this opportunity for you."

A hollow place inside me ached for Frannie, for myself. For the truth being revealed now. It was such a near miss that I finally got it—nothing could have stopped what happened to Frannie. Not even Silea.

Rhiannon shook her head. "No. I don't want this. The Corps are evil."

The queen scoffed. "The Authority is evil. The Consulate is evil. And yes, O-Tex is evil. But you, my darling, are not. Change it all, if you want."

Her mother was right. If anyone could make this work to their advantage, Rhiannon could. She swallowed hard, and I hated to see her so lost. "What am I supposed to do with this?"

The queen coughed, and blood trickled from the corner of her mouth. Rhiannon sat forward, using the handkerchief her mother gripped to wipe the blood away.

"She doesn't have long," Cassandra whispered. "Say your goodbyes."

The queen let out a long, shuddering breath. Rhiannon and I had both seen that before. We were intimate with death's myriad ways.

"Do whatever you see fit, Rhiannon. I built it all in secret, knowing that someday you would rule it all. That you were eternal. That you would change things from within the beast." She nodded towards me. "And you've found a partner who knows as well as you do that ruthlessness will never win the day. The old ways are useless in this modern world."

The queen's breath came in shallow gasps now. She laid her head back on the pillow, her arm raising to stroke Rhiannon's cheek. "Be the island in the storm, my child."

Her eyes fell closed, and Cassandra's light enveloped her. "Remember, children," Cassandra's voice said as she disappeared. "In the face of all we've endured, love is still the answer."

Rhiannon clasped her mother's hand to her chest, silent tears falling on her cheeks. "Goodbye," she whispered.

And from somewhere just beyond where we were, her mother's voice answered for the very last time. "I love you, my girl."

CHAPTER 38

RHIANNON

It had taken a full day of sleep, and another two of silence, for me to process all that had happened enough to even speak. On the fourth day, Ember insisted I talk with Calypso, who apparently had a head for business. I'd given her the go ahead to quietly look into every bit of information we now had about O-Tex. The Board of Directors had no idea who owned the company—and for now, we'd decided to keep it that way.

In a month, there would be a funeral and official coronation on the island, but I couldn't think of that now. I rolled over in bed. Eryx sat next to the window reading. He smiled when he noticed I was awake. "Hello."

"Hi," I whispered. "Thank you for staying with me."

He closed his book and got up, climbing into bed next to me. He'd hardly left my side for five days, leaving only to take food and trash away, and forage for sustenance. Ember had assured me on one of her brief visits that everything was being handled.

"I feel better this afternoon," I said with a sigh, leaning

into Eryx's chest. "And by better, I mean I can keep my eyes open."

His arms went around me. We'd slept in bed together every night since the day my mother died, but hadn't had sex once. Once the grief had set in, my exhaustion had bottomed out into an endless pit. Even walking to the bathroom was almost too much for me.

Physically, nothing at all was wrong with me. Sera had looked me over top to bottom, tested my blood every which way possible, and I was in near-perfect health according to the numbers. But I'd finally stopped fighting rest, and now it seemed I was incapable of anything else. It was awful. I leaned against Eryx, worrying.

"I can practically hear you thinking," he whispered. There was a laugh in his voice. It might have been infuriating that he found my fury at being so tired adorable, if I hadn't loved it so much. "Would you care to share what you're worrying about?"

"No," I said, feeling even more anxious now.

"Please," he whispered in my ear.

A few weeks ago, that would have sent us into a frenzy of lust. Now, every muscle in my body felt as though it was made of lead. Better to rip the bandage off though. Since I'd started speaking again, Eryx had encouraged me to be honest with him, and I believed that's what he wanted.

"I'm worried you'll lose interest in me because I'm not able to have sex right now."

"Oh," he said, his deep voice vibrating through me. He moved back a little so that I fell back into his arms, but he curled over me so that he looked me in the face. "That is not a problem for me."

I blinked several times, then frowned.

He only smiled. "We have a lot of years ahead of us for sex. Right now, you need rest. You need to heal."

I flopped back onto the pillow dramatically. "It's taking too long."

He mimicked me, spreading out next to me. "It's taking as long as it needs to."

"You really don't care?" I asked.

"No," he replied, getting up and pressing a kiss to my forehead. "I love you, Rhi. And I've been asking you to rest for quite a while now, as you well know."

"Where are you going?" I asked.

He moved towards the door. "*I* am going to have burgers and watch scary movies with Briony, Ares, and Eli. *You* are having a girls' night with your sistren—and Avaline." Eryx opened the door to show all four of the Orphium Maere waiting outside, each of them carrying armloads of supplies. Avaline brought up the rear, carrying a pitcher of what looked like sangria.

"Have fun," Eryx said, waving as he disappeared into the hallway.

An hour later, I'd been caught up on gossip. Sera had already fallen asleep next to me in bed, which was comforting. She'd always fallen asleep easiest with the rest of us chatting around her, and the familiar feeling of being surrounded by my loves, knowing Eryx was just downstairs with the rest of our family, made me so happy I could cry.

Lara was spread out on the couch at the end of my bed, peppering Av with questions about how Blaire's prisoner had simply disappeared. But there were no satisfying answers, apparently.

"And no one has seen her since?" I asked.

Ember, who sat at the end of the bed painting my toenails a shocking bright pink, shook her head. "No."

Calypso sat in front of Av at my dressing table, who was braiding her long hair in the most intricate fishtail braid I'd ever seen. Avaline sighed. "It's the strangest thing. I looked through every one of the photos from the inmates' files from the Asylum." She paused, smiling. "Briony managed to get a hold of them after you fucked with everything."

I laughed and Ember glared at me. "If you don't want this all over your foot, hold still."

I bit my lip to try to comply. She was my commanding officer, after all. "So we don't know who she is?"

Lara shook her head. "Nor a clue what Blaire's relationship to her was."

It was an odd way to put it, or rather, it tripped something in my memory. "Wait," I breathed, sitting forward.

Ember looked up, and I thought she was going to scold me again, but instead she capped the nail polish. She knew when I'd made a connection between things, and waited for me to speak again.

"Myrine said something before I killed her. Something like, 'not even his own…' but then she stopped and told me to figure it out myself." It wasn't even really a question why I'd forgotten it. My mother's dying revelations, in conjunction with her actual death, had wiped everything else out of existence until now.

Calypso picked up her laptop and opened it. "I wonder if the end of that sentence is…" she trailed off as her fingers flew over the keyboard. The room was silent but for her typing. And then the sound slowed.

Avaline leaned forward, gasping. "That's her. With hair, but that's her."

Calypso's eyes narrowed sharply. "This is an obituary from… this can't be right."

Avaline's mouth fell open. "From nearly thirty years ago. But… she didn't look even a day older than this."

Calypso turned the laptop around to show a photo of a pretty young woman with skin pale as porcelain, and dark brown hair. Lara sat up a little to look at it. "She's cute. And dead?"

Calypso shook her head. "It says here that Vesper Blaire was Archibald Blaire's 'natural' daughter. Her mother was some model he had an affair with. And then she died in a horrible car accident—apparently the body was so mangled that they had to have a closed casket funeral."

Ember sat back, sighing. "Or she's one of us, and she ascended."

Sera rolled over in bed, her eyes open. I wondered how long she'd been awake. "If she ascended, then why did he need to give her whatever all that stuff was that he was making? Why wouldn't Myrine have just told him what she was?"

Ember's head tilted to one side. "Those are good points. Do we think he found out she was a parapsych?"

Sera sat up. "Maybe the mother was. Sometimes if a talent is small, people go their whole lives without anyone knowing they're not human. People just think they're awkward."

Ember shook her head. "I don't like this. We don't know what he did to her before that night, and she's just out there on her own."

Lara sat up, sighing. "*Fine.* I'll find the cute girl."

Ember glared at her. "I didn't ask you to."

Lara threw her hands up in the air. "No, it's no trouble.

I don't have anything else to do. I'll just go find Blaire's love child and bring her over to the right side of things."

"Saints, you are annoying," Ember said with a snort. But she laughed.

We all did.

Lara's eyes met mine, a question in them. I nodded. It was okay. We were okay. Her smile in return was a little sad, but it was a volume closed in both our lives. Things had been over between us for decades, but neither of us had ever completely moved on, or fallen in love.

It was time now. Next to me, my phone buzzed at the same time as Ember's and we both got photos of the movie night happening in the basement. Stanley had transformed into several different versions of monster cats to amuse Briony, and all of them were laughing.

Sera's fingers laced through mine as she looked at the photos, her eyes lingering a bit too long on Eli Cabot's handsome face. I didn't say a thing. She was still raw from things with Max, and I knew my friend. It would take her a while before she could move on.

But the fact was that we all needed joy and love of all kinds in our lives. My eyes fell on Calypso, who was closing her laptop. "So," I said with a deep breath as her eyes met mine. "Are you ever going to tell us what you were running from in Aradios?"

All eyes turned her way. Calypso sighed, staring at the ceiling. "Too much sunshine." She grinned at us, gesturing to her pale skin. "The cost of sunscreen was bankrupting me."

As the six of us devolved into giggles and storytelling, it occurred to me that everything I'd told Myrine before she died was true. This was where my allegiances would be for the rest of my life. Here, with these people. In this house.

O-Tex didn't matter. Being Otrera's queen was irrelevant. This was my entire world. It might be messy and imperfect, and I needed to create boundaries for myself that let me rest better, but I wanted every silly text message, and every long intimate talk.

The world outside was grim at the best of times. But in here, inside these walls, we were safe. And I would cherish every moment of it for as long as I was allowed.

CHAPTER 39

ERYX

THREE MONTHS LATER. OTRERA.

THE WIND WAS WARM, and smelled of lemons. Bright purple bougainvillea wound around the columns that supported the arched openings to the covered porch. I set down my book, watching as Rhiannon finished Briony's hair in the sunshine a level below me. She kissed the teenager's forehead before Briony rushed down the ancient stone stairs to meet her new friends.

In the distance, the midsummer sun glinted off the sea. My love leaned back in her chaise, smiling up at me. It had been nearly two months since her coronation, and we'd decided to spend the entire summer here with Briony. It had given Rhiannon time to rest and recover, as well as time for her to reacquaint herself with the Otreran court.

That had been a complex project, but they respected her, and understood that she was here for healing before returning to the outside world. I was surprised at how easily they'd accepted the changes she wanted to make, especially the fact that she'd invited all of the Trinity leaders to come here, along with everyone closest to us.

Quietly, she had been moving the former Asylum inmates here, disappearing them from the outside world in a series of small moves the Authority wouldn't notice. Both the Authority and the Corps were still struggling to get back on their feet after the chaos she'd caused.

All in all, though things were not perfect, they were good. Below me, she'd closed her eyes, stretching her long legs out on the chaise as she breathed deeply. The white gown she wore was pulled up to her waist, so her legs could feel the sun. Being on Otrera seemed to have revitalized her. Showing the island to Briony had healed something in her that changed my girl for the better.

Rhiannon's eyes opened and she grinned up at me. "Want to go for a swim?"

"I'll be right down."

I stood, stretching before taking the stairs to the level below us. The queen's quarters weren't huge, but they were luxurious, and had access to a private lagoon. With Briony gone 'til nighttime, and nothing else on the agenda for the day, I was happy to take advantage of the privacy.

Rhiannon met me on the stairs, unclasping the pins that held her dress up. She let it fall behind her as she gazed back at me, love in her eyes. I caught the dress as I followed her down the winding stone staircase, shedding my own clothes as I went.

At the bottom of the stairs, she was already in the warm, crystalline blue water, waiting for me. I placed our clothes on one of the two chaises on the swim deck, and then dove into the water. She screamed in delight as I splashed her, scrambling away from me as I swam towards her.

She let me catch her on the lowest level of the sea stairs, wrapping her legs around my waist. We were three-quarters of the way submerged under the water, and her body was warm against mine as she kissed me.

"Autumn will be here before you know it," she whispered when she pulled away. "I'm not ready to leave."

"We're still six weeks out from the Board of Directors meeting," I reasoned.

She sighed. I knew she was nervous about this, but we had a plan. A plan I had no intention of discussing today. It was a good plan, solid, vetted by everyone who could possibly weigh in.

Rhiannon had done well these past months. She'd done more to change the ways things worked than her mother ever had, and she'd managed to do it all while getting plenty of rest, eating real meals, and overseeing the renovations of Oleander Cottage from half a world away. And parenting a teenager. I'd helped, of course, but it was remarkable what she could do when she was feeling better.

Rhiannon opened her mouth, as though to argue with me about the plan, then shut it. Instead of fussing, she kissed me again, deeper this time. When she pulled away again, I expected her to suggest we make love on the sea stairs again. We'd done it a week ago, and it had been exhilarating.

Instead, she shocked me with her words. "Will you marry me?"

I brushed a teasing kiss to her jaw, near her ear, tasting the salt of the ocean and her sweet skin. In her ear, I whispered. "You are ruining my surprise, love."

"Oh," she said softly, her breasts pressing into my chest as she breathed. "Oh!"

I wound one hand into the wet mass of her hair, pulling her head back so her blue eyes met mine. "Briony and I had this all worked out. The ring is upstairs. I was going to ask after dinner tonight—under the stars."

"What are we having for dinner?" she asked, as though I hadn't just told her I planned to ask her to marry me.

Rhiannon moved in her own time. This was something I'd learned to roll with in the past months, loving the way her clever mind worked. If I answered her, played along, I would be rewarded. So, I answered her. "All your favorites."

She hummed against me. "Under the stars, you say?"

I nodded.

"Well," she answered, pulling closer to me. "You should know that I will be saying yes."

I laughed, and her soft belly pressed into mine, stirring my cock. "That takes some edge off my nerves then."

"Now," she said. "What should we do in the meantime?"

I lifted her higher. "I think I'd better make love to you."

"Oh yes," she breathed as I fit myself to her entrance. "I agree."

An hour later, she was in the bath, drinking a glass of white wine, staring out over the ocean. I watched from the doorway of the bathroom as she took one deep breath, and then another.

It took me a moment, but I realized she wasn't looking at the water at all, but the cypress below the window as they swayed in the wind. When her breath returned to normal, she set her glass on the windowsill and sank deeper into the enormous tub.

"Can I wash your hair?" I asked.

She smiled at me. "Yes."

I gathered her shampoo and conditioner, pulling the

rustic wooden stool from the shower next to the tub. She made the most delightful noises as I rubbed the floral-scented shampoo into her scalp. Her skin had deepened to a light bronze after so many days swimming in the salty lagoon.

Her skin was too tempting. I ran a soapy hand down her neck and decolletage to cup her breast. She moaned a little, her back arching. I pulled her head back and kissed her, tasting salt on her lips, mixed with the sweet taste that was all her own.

I moved slowly, rinsing her hair with a pitcher that sat next to the tub for this exact purpose, then conditioned her hair. When the thick liquid was in her hair, I reached down with both of my slippery hands to massage it over her breasts, pinching her nipples lightly as I kissed her again.

"You're teasing me," she said when I moved to rinse her hair again.

"Yes," I agreed, motioning to my cock, which stood at attention, bare in the warm light of the bathroom. "And myself."

She took the pitcher from me and stood, turning to face me as she finished rinsing her hair. And then she stepped carefully out of the tub, placing her feet on either side of the stool so she hovered above me.

Rhiannon slid down my body until my cock fit perfectly at her entrance. She sank down on me slowly, not taking her eyes from mine. "I love you," she said as I filled her.

Her words brought out an intense reaction in me as she moved slowly on me. She knew I would ask her to marry me tonight. And I knew she would say yes. We were here, in the most beautiful place in the world, and for even this short amount of time, we had respite.

I pulled her tighter against me, emotion catching in my throat. "I love you, Rhiannon. Now and forever."

There were tears in her eyes as we found release together. I cleaned her gently, wrapping her in a towel and carrying her to our bed. "Wait here?" I asked.

She nodded, her face soft with love, relaxed from an afternoon of swimming, lovemaking, and bathing. Rhiannon was always beautiful, but I loved her like this. I walked to the wardrobe, feeling more certain than ever. Under the stars would have been lovely, but this was perfect.

I found the little velvet box and made my way back to the bed, my feet warm on the cool terracotta tiles. Once in bed next to her, resting comfortably in a cloud of impossibly soft white linens, I showed her the box.

"I have loved you since the night you returned to Orphium. I have seen you do wonderful and terrible things, and loved every one. I have seen you sad and loved you. I have watched you grieve and loved you. And now I have the pleasure of watching you grow into this next phase of your life."

I paused because she was crying. But Rhiannon smiled through her tears, stroking my face with her soft fingers. "Don't stop, baby. Please."

"Will you please be my wife, Rhiannon? Will you marry me and spend the rest of eternity letting me care for you as you care for this broken world?"

Her answer was a kiss so sweet I never wanted it to end. But the kiss was a ruse, a wicked distraction as she pulled the velvet box from my fingers. "Ah-ah," I chided, tapping her nose. "You haven't answered. No peeks at the ring until you do."

Rhiannon smiled. "The answer is yes. Forever, yes."

She started to open the box, and then stopped, looking back up at me, her blue eyes searching. "You are, by far, the best man I have ever known. I don't have all the beautiful words you do, but I am so grateful to know you, and even more grateful that you love me as I love you."

"Those words are plenty beautiful," I said. "Now please open the box."

She did, gasping at the giant aquamarine ring within. It was the color of her eyes on a sunny day, and reminded me of the sea. Of this place where she had been born and died and been made queen. She seemed stunned, so I pulled it from the box and slid it onto her finger.

"It is so perfect," she finally whispered. "Thank you."

"Thank you for being my home," I breathed. "Thank you for letting me finally be myself."

Rhiannon's arms flew around my neck. "This is everything I thought I could never have," she whispered against my neck. "Can we get married in the garden? In the place where it happened?"

I knew what she meant, and a lump formed in my throat. It was a sad spot to marry, but I knew exactly why she wanted to do it there. "It would be a good way to close that chapter for the cottage," I said.

She laid back on the pillows, gazing up at me. "Yes, with all our friends and family. It would also be a fresh start for us."

"Then that is what we will do," I agreed, pulling her against me.

We stayed like that until the sun began to dip closer to the horizon. "Come on," she said, slipping out of bed. "You have dinner to make me, and I think the stars are going to be lovely tonight."

I got out of bed behind her. And because I would follow her anywhere, I became her shadow as we walked into the next phase of our lives together. With Rhiannon, I was exactly where I belonged.

Thank you for reading *The Swan*, the second book in *The World of the Orphium Maere*. If you would like to find out how the Board of Directors meeting at O-Tex went, please join my newsletter for your bonus epilogue.

ABOUT THE AUTHOR

Allison Carr Waechter is probably feeding a monster cat right now. She lives in Minnesota with two enormous felines and one very supportive Book Daddy. She is a former college writing instructor, has some degrees in in English Literature, and loves books with magic and romance.

LET'S CONNECT

Join Allison's newsletter at www.allisoncarrwaechter.com
for things like:

- Exclusive access to a library of bonus content for all of Allison's books
- Exclusive access to sneak peeks at character art, covers, etc.
- News about new books, special editions, and translations
- The latest news about works in progress
- Priority access to Allison's limited eARCs

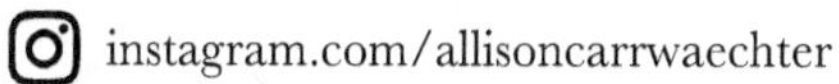 instagram.com/allisoncarrwaechter

ALSO BY
ALLISON CARR WAECHTER

THE TAPESTRY BOOKS

These series all exist in the same universe and timeline, and have some overlapping characters.

THE IMMORTAL ORDERS

Dark Night Golden Dawn

Beneath the Alabaster Spire

Awaken the Fifth Order

At the White Wolf (novella)

Behind the Iron Gate (standalone, sequel, FALL 2025)

THE AETHEREALS

The Hollow Plane

The Ravaged Dark

THE WORLD OF THE ORPHIUM MAERE

The Consulate

The Swan

The Angel (coming 2026)

BLACKBIRD HOLLOW

Co-written with Victoria Mier

Welcome to Blackbird Hollow (September 2025)

www.ingramcontent.com/pod-product-compliance
Lightning Source LLC
Chambersburg PA
CBHW070601300726
48975CB00006B/1673